Dearly DEPARTED

www.**totallyrandombooks**.co.uk

LIA HABEL was born into a time of unparalleled ugliness – it was called 'the Eighties'. It was horrible – but yet it brought Lia the video for *Thriller* by Michael Jackson, and a burning interest in zombies followed. A self-described 'zombie anthropologist', Lia has seen a *lot* of zombie movies. She lives in Jamestown, NY, with her three cats, Ebeneezer, ZZ and Bloody Mary. *Dearly, Departed* is her debut novel.

Dearly, DEPARTED

LIA HABEL

DOUBLEDAY

DEARLY, DEPARTED
A DOUBLEDAY BOOK 978 0 857 53000 4

Published in Great Britain by Doubleday,
an imprint of Random House Children's Books

A Random House Group Company
This edition published 2011

1 3 5 7 9 10 8 6 4 2

The Random House Group Limited supports the Forest Stewardship
Council (FSC®), the leading international forest-certification
organisation. Our books carrying the FSC label are printed on
FSC®-certified paper. FSC is the only forest-certification scheme
endorsed by the leading environmental organisations, including
Greenpeace. Our paper-procurement policy can be found at
www.randomhouse.co.uk/environment.

Set in Constantia

RANDOM HOUSE CHILDREN'S BOOKS
61–63 Uxbridge Road, London W5 5SA

www.**totallyrandombooks**.co.uk

Addresses for companies within The Random House Group Limited
can be found at: www.randomhouse.co.uk/offices.htm
THE RANDOM HOUSE GROUP Limited Reg. No. 954009

A CIP catalogue record for this book is available
from the British Library.

Printed and bound by CPI Group, (UK), Croydon, CR0 4YY

For my mother, who taught me early
on that real ladies can give orders,
real gentlemen can take them,
and real zombies don't eat brains.

'It is told that Buddha, going out to look on life, was greatly daunted by death. "They all eat one another!" he cried, and called it evil. This process I examined, changed the verb, said, "They all feed one another," and called it good.'

Charlotte Perkins Gilman,
The Living of Charlotte Perkins Gilman

'Not many young girls feel very happy about the past, and the past is very beautiful. Very beautiful.'

Barnabas Collins in Dark Shadows
episode 250, Dan Curtis, 1967

PROLOGUE

Bram

I was buried alive.

When the elevator groaned to a stop in the middle of the rocky shaft, I knew I was buried alive. Trapped thousands of feet below the earth's surface and hundreds above the bottom of the shaft, dangling in a dimly lit ten-by-ten-foot cage over the black bowels of the very mine I had been so relieved to get work in.

I pulled myself to my feet and pushed my best friend Jack aside, hitting the button that controlled the elevator. I hit it again and again, wailed my fist on it. Nothing. The glass-paned lantern dangling from the ceiling flickered wildly as the kerosene within dwindled, as if it were attempting to ward off its own death with bursts of exaggerated life.

Dread became a solid, burning thing within me, something twisting my own flesh to its will, speeding my heart and making my skin slick with sweat. Before I knew it was coming up, I doubled over and retched through the grated floor. Jack sat calmly beside me as I heaved, his bloody eye sockets and the gaping wound in his throat mocking me, mocking my attempt to rescue him. He looked like some kind of hellish fun-house clown.

The dam broke, and I finally started screaming. At Jack. At God. At everything. There was nothing left to do but scream. I hadn't screamed when the monsters had descended on us. I hadn't screamed when I'd had to run from them, or when I fought them, or when I'd dragged Jack to the elevator, blood bursting from the hole in his neck. Everything had happened so quickly, it'd seemed like there was no time to scream.

1

The monsters. Mad, animalistic, discolored, broken and battered from throwing themselves after their prey, each one thrashing like a person trapped beneath a frozen pond might struggle against the ice in desperate search of air . . . all teeth and hunger . . .

I slid down the wall of the elevator and buried my face in my sticky, itching hands. The coppery scent of the blood on them nauseated me, and I leaned back, my screams echoing back to me through the endless mineshaft. The elevator was covered in Jack's blood. *I* was covered in Jack's blood. I was wearing more of his blood on my ratty waistcoat than remained, still as a stagnant pond, in his own veins. My cheap old pocket watch was caked with it. Even the digital camera still feverishly clutched in Jack's hands was slashed with red. Stupid New Victorian piece of crap. I'd always ragged on him for being so attached to that camera. Couldn't even get the pictures off of it, not without a computer – and no one around *here* had a computer.

Still, Jack had been so proud of it, of the snapshots he took. And I'd dutifully posed every time he'd ordered me to.

Slowly, trembling, I pried it out of his rubbery fingers.

The lantern dimmed. I tried not to panic. I figured out how to turn the camera on, hoping futilely that the conspiracy theories were true – that the New Victorians could track every bit of tech their people used, every digital letter, practically every thought. Didn't they put chips in their citizens, tagging them like cattle? Maybe, if the smuggler who'd snuck it through the Border hadn't cracked and killed the ability, it'd work. Maybe.

If nothing else, I could record a message.

Just as I figured out how to shoot video, the lantern died, plunging me into perfect darkness. I swallowed back a sob and spoke aloud, my throat raw, my voice the voice of a ghost in its tomb.

'If this thing is working . . . my name is Bram Griswold. I'm sixteen. It's . . . July 4th, 2193. I live at the Griswold Farm, Long Road, West Gould, Plata Ombre, Punk-Controlled Brazil. I worked here to help support my mom and my sisters . . . in the Celestino mine. And these things, these, these people . . . they were eating . . . eating Jack . . .'

That did it. I started crying. I dug my nails into the wounds in my own arms, the places where the monsters had bitten me, seeking desperately to use pain to pin myself to reality, to coax my mind back from the edge.

It didn't work.

I said it.

'I'm pretty sure I'm going to . . . to die here. Emily, Addy . . . I'm sorry.' Tears ran into my mouth, a strange relief after the taste of vomit. 'I'm so sorry.'

CHAPTER ONE

Nora

I slipped a white hand between the heavy velvet drapes.

'Is it here, Nora?'

'No,' I murmured.

The girl standing behind me released a huff of air, and tugged impatiently at her cuffs. 'You're so lucky to have your own carriage. Public transport wears on my nerves. If it's late, you start to suspect that you missed it, and if it's early you *have* missed it . . .'

'Then why are you panicking? You're not *taking* public transport. You're coming home with me.'

'Because we've been here for almost an hour! You know me, I grow anxious whenever I have to wait, whatever I'm waiting *for*. Remember that time our final grades were delayed for a *day* due to a computer mishap? God, I thought I was going to die.'

I lent only half an ear to Pamela's nervous chattering, my gaze drifting back to the yard outside. The wrought-iron gates of St-Cyprian's School for Girls were flung wide, and a steady stream of electric carriages poured in through them – sleeker and curvier than those of the First Victorians, and designed with room for a driver within. Those belonging to the upper crust of the school were crafted of elegantly molded alloy metal, done up in inky purple or mahogany brown and shining like glass. A few of the richest girls had their own carriages, and these were pearly white, to indicate the – largely imagined – innocence and purity of their passengers.

The carriage that would come for me would not be white, and so I felt compelled to add, 'And it isn't mine, Pamma. It belongs to my aunt.'

'I know.'

Pamela Roe, my best friend since childhood, stepped in front of me and resumed sitting atop her steamer trunk. She was of Indian heritage and average looks, with black, sweet eyes and long hair the color of chocolate.

'We could carry the trunks down to the yard,' I offered.

It was the last day of the term, and the halls of the school were noisier than usual. Everyone was heading home for the holidays. A sea of trunks and swirling skirts churned just outside the alcove where Pam and I had squeezed ourselves and our things. The window there afforded a good view of the crowded courtyard below.

'We'd end up crushing ourselves.' Pamela cut her eyes to the hall. 'Being crushed is very unladylike. I'd rather wait for a porter.'

'We'll be here an age, then. Better get used to it.' Every hired porter I'd managed to track down that day had already been occupied, already dedicated to fulfilling the whims of one or more of the upper-class girls. St. Cyprian's was one of the most prestigious private schools in the Territories, a formidable building set on a few acres of manicured land. It was done in the mid-Victorian style, all real stone and wood and a city's population of statues and gargoyles – no plastic, no holographic projectors. During my years there I'd often had occasion to feel like I was forever fated to stand, alone and motionless, in the midst of the school's daily dance . . . and today the feeling was magnified. Pamela and I were left perched atop our belongings in our relatively plain frocks, as bright young things and servants rushed about us. Their belongings were more important than ours, their destinations more glamorous.

Pam fell silent, leaning against the hallway's dark wooden paneling. I occupied myself by drawing a pearly stylus over the screen of the digital diary in my lap. I was working on my final paper for history. My shoulders hunched up as I wrote, a habit my mother never could hammer out of me.

Nora Dearly, I jotted atop the page. *December 17th, 2195. Assignment Number 14. Early New Victorian History.*

'How does it feel to wear color again?' Pamela asked.

The sudden question echoed in my head like a gunshot. My shoulders dropped, and I let my pen go still. I glanced down at the high-necked dress of red taffeta I'd put on a few hours ago, at Pamela's insistence. She'd picked it out for me – indeed, she'd packed my trunk with all of my black mourning weeds, aired out my white handkerchiefs and hidden the black-edged ones, done everything in her power to make the transition easy for me. Pamela had the supernatural speed and invisibility of a born mother, when it came to arranging things and caring for people. Today was the year-and-a-day anniversary of my father's death, and I was no longer in mourning.

At least, outwardly.

I *could* wear color again, now. I could dance again, sit in the front row of church again, visit friends again, all with the approval of Those Who Supposedly Knew Better. But that didn't change the fact that I didn't really want to.

'Fine.' It didn't sound right. 'I mean . . . of course I'm glad to wear color again.'

Pamela didn't buy it. She saw through my every lie – she always could. I hated and respected and loved her for it. Her eyes fell to my diary. 'You've been ignoring your work again, haven't you? Isn't that due in two hours?'

I'd heard this before, and didn't really fancy hearing it again. 'Pamma, you have your own studies to fret about. Don't worry about me. Everything'll get done.'

'I just . . . do.' She sighed. 'I've been recopying my math and handing it in for you. It worries me, is all. You were doing well for so long, but the last few weeks I've been having to make excuses again . . .'

I reached out to lay my hand on her arm. She was wearing

7

a much-washed dress of blue lawn. 'Really, Pam. It's all right.'

Pam bit her inner cheek. 'You shouldn't hold on to your emotions, is all I'm saying. It isn't healthy. I know that your period of mourning is over, and that no one will make exceptions for you any longer. But just don't let that make you go . . . cold.'

This from the girl who'd served as my human hanky uncountable times since my father's death? *Ha.* I decided to let it slide, but I couldn't help adding, 'I'm not holding them in, Pam. I'm saving them up for Aunt Gene.'

She smelled another lie, and gave me a look of miserable condemnation. But she didn't press the issue. Instead, after a moment, she said, 'If you go off on her, you'd better record it, you know. Video, not just audio. Or it didn't happen as far as I'm concerned.'

I knew I was forgiven. 'If I do, you'll be the first to hear about it. I showed you her letter, didn't I?' Well, more accurately, I'd hurled her letter at Pam while raging about the audacity of my aunt going to a grand ball the very day we were out of mourning for my father.

Pam's eyes flicked away to the window, and she hopped to her feet, her high-button boots clopping on the floor. 'There it is!'

Beautiful. With a sigh of my own, I shut my leather-bound digidiary.

A quick scan of the hallways revealed that there were still no porters to be had. I helped Pamela carry her trunk through the hall, down the sweeping front staircase, and through the ornate wooden doors.

Aunt Gene's carriage was an unremarkable black Model V, plain next to its neighbors on the circular drive. By the time we'd set Pam's trunk down and adjusted our windblown bonnets, Aunt Gene's part-time chauffeur, Jorge Alencar, had found a place to park it and was striding across the lawn towards us.

'Miss Dearly, it's been a long few months,' he said, his voice warm. He was a tall man in his fifties with leathery skin and receding gray hair. 'Miss Roe, a pleasure to see you as well. I'll get the trunks up, if you young ladies want to settle in.'

'Thank you. Mine's in the alcove with that narrow window.'

Directions given, Pamela hooked her arm in mine and started to drag me towards the carriage. Her family didn't have a vehicle of any sort, and she always looked forward to a drive. Why, I had no idea. She usually fell sound asleep the moment we started moving.

'Let's try to focus on the holiday,' Pamela started.

'There isn't much to focus on,' I argued. 'Different day, same . . .'

Pam gave me an admonishing look, and continued as if I hadn't interrupted. 'What *I* think we should do is plan something fun, like a party. We could make crackers, and play games, and put a coin in a pudding, and all of that. We could invite my cousins . . .'

'Ah, Miss Dearly, always going out of her way to help those in need,' called a familiar voice from behind us.

Pam forgot the rest of her sentence. 'Nora,' she said warningly as I drew to a stop.

My fingers tightened on her wrist. I knew who it was without looking. 'Miss Mink.'

'Yes, me. How astute of you.'

I wasn't in the mood for her games, but I turned around. Yellow-haired Vespertine Mink, one of the school's most popular and powerful students, stood there regarding us as one might an interesting insect. 'What do you want?'

She crooked her sharp little smile at me, and bobbed her head in a shadow of a curtsey. 'I just wanted to tell you how wonderful it is to see one of our best and brightest literally lending a hand to the less fortunate.' She lifted her eyes to Pam, and her lips parted. 'Oh, forgive me, Miss Roe. I didn't see you standing there.'

Pamela held her head high, in spite of the slight. 'Miss Mink.'

'Is that all, Mink?' I asked. Vespertine's eyes darted back to mine. I wanted them on me. Pamela was a charity case, a scholarship student, and I did my best to take every blow for her that I could. We both lacked the ability to play politics that most of the high-bred girls at Cyprian's seemed to have been born with, but, unlike me, Pamela had to care what people thought of her.

'Not quite, Dearly.' Vespertine took a step closer. Like us, she hadn't wasted time in changing out of her teal- and gray-striped monstrosity of a uniform. She was dressed in a bustled gown of emerald faille with a fashionable ruffled hem that whispered upon the grass. 'I have a bit of good news to share with you.'

'Oh? Make it fast. We have somewhere to be . . . and I'm sorry to say that you're not up to your usual standard today.'

'Miss Mink?' Pamela asked, voice weak.

Vespertine flashed another smile. 'My mother will be joining the school board next month, are you aware?'

Open threats I could work with. I lifted my chin. 'Oh? How interesting. Tell me . . . is Lady Mink *less* or *more* catty than you generally are? I like to be prepared for my first meetings with people – especially people who pretend to be important.'

'Miss Mink?' Pam attempted a second time, her voice seemingly small and far away. Vespertine didn't acknowledge her, but stood there regarding me with a mixture of hatred and disgust. *Ten points for me.*

'Miss Roe is speaking to you.'

'Who cares?' she asked.

'Miss Mink?' Pamela edged closer to my side.

Vespertine's head whipped up, wavy blonde hair bouncing about her neck. 'What?'

For a moment Pamela seemed to be riveted by Vespertine's glare, and I feared that she'd forgotten her crumb of wisdom, or brilliant comeback, whatever it was. I'd never known Pam to be particularly handy with a cutting remark, but after a moment she smiled and asked, 'Is there some reason your family cares to commemorate the year 2178? Some special achievement, perhaps?'

Vespertine's eyes narrowed. 'Oh, shut up.'

Pamela's mouth rounded in a beautiful mockery of surprise. 'Have I offended? I was only curious, for that's nearly twenty years ago now.' She directed her attention down the drive, to the unfashionable, dull brown Mink carriage – which had the year 2178 molded right onto its doors. 'Your family has, what . . . fourteen horseless carriages? Heavens, that's a lot.'

Inwardly, I did a little dance. Nobody knew why the Mink family sent that ancient thing for Vespertine all the time, unless it was some twisted way of teaching her humility. In which case, I was fully on board and would tattoo the date on my forehead.

Mink tossed her head. 'Fine! Play your stupid, childish little games. I'm through talking to the likes of you. Dearly, you're out. You're so out. Roe, I'd watch my step if I were you, or it's back to the ghetto you came from.' She gave me one final, nasty look before stalking off towards the open yard, where her well-dressed clique stood watching us.

'Looking forward to it!' I called after her. Pamela caught the handle of the carriage door and pulled it open. 'I can't believe you said that!' I exclaimed, unable to contain a true grin.

'I can't believe you speak so to her in general,' Pam said as her expression grew somber. She urged me into the carriage and stepped up after. 'That was an incredibly stupid thing to do, but she was asking for it.'

'I couldn't care less what Mink thinks of me. She's a beastly little piece of work. But you . . .'

'I know. I need her favor. I need everyone's favor that I can get.' Pam glanced to the window. I was always quietly amazed that she already had slight wrinkles under her eyes. The good mood I'd enjoyed for all of two minutes faded away.

I tried to think of something to say to reassure her. 'Let me deal with her, Pamma. She's my enemy, not yours. She'll ignore this one episode if I keep her attention on me, so don't fret. I've been doing this for years . . . ever since she first tried to get me to be her lackey and carry her books. It's old hat with me.'

Pamela nodded mutely. I could tell that she was still upset.

Sensing passengers, the flat screen that was mounted inside the cab glowed to life. First the date shimmered into focus in scrolling golden letters. Then came the news. The screen took on the appearance of paper, and brown ink lettering began to spill headlines across the page. It was a silly affectation, really; aside from antique books and very official correspondence, everything was digital now.

'Here,' I said, settling back into the squeaky faux leather of the seat. 'News. Confirmation of exterior reality.' St Cyprian's was meant to create ladies who floated when they walked, played a little piano, and were otherwise charming and unobtrusive. To that end, it was a sheltered environment. Television was forbidden and access to the Aethernet was strictly filtered.

Pamela removed her bonnet and took up the screen, pulling it to her lap. 'Oh, wonderful!' She was suitably distracted.

'Enjoy,' I muttered, pulling my digidiary out again and borrowing the car's feathery stylus. I figured I could finish writing my paper in an hour or so, and didn't want to lose my train of thought. I felt the carriage rock slightly as Alencar loaded one of the trunks.

'Nora . . .'

'We'll be off in a few minutes.' I felt the carriage settle again. 'That's the other trunk going on.'

'No, Nora – look.' Pam's hand found the sleeve of my coat. I glanced at her face, and realized that she was staring at the cab's screen. I looked. The headlines were still up.

• *Construction of Elysian Fields Halted After*
Water Main Disaster
• *Government Identity Databases Possibly*
Compromised, Insiders Say

And one headline I found of real interest.

• *Punk Forces Massing on Southern Border*
Following Terrorist Attack

I only vaguely registered the fact that Alencar was in the driver's seat and that the embroidered barrier between the front and the back of the carriage was slowly rising. When the engine turned over an electrical current charged the windows, replacing my view of the outside world with my reflection in a mirrored, solid surface. I met my own eyes, startled by the change, and saw worry in them.

The world had apparently gone to hell since I'd been in school.

I was absolutely burning with the desire to learn about the latest Punk movements, but Pam was more interested in the headlines having to do with panic and plumbing. I let her push the buttons.

The in-cab NVIC channel was a limited form of service that offered only a handful of current events clips from the last hour or so, along with a selection of the previous night's shows. It took us an hour to watch it all.

The topic that was receiving the most coverage was the rumored security breach on the government databases. There was no evidence that identity theft had actually been committed, but that wasn't stopping any of the talking heads from ranting about it. Our people, as a rule, do enjoy a good moral panic.

The Prime Minister, Aloysius Ayles, had yet to comment upon the matter. I had always considered him fairly useless when compared to the former PM, his father, Lord Harvey Ayles. Therefore, I didn't read too deeply into his failure to speak out.

As for the water main explosion – there was little to learn, save that it was resulting in hundreds of city workers getting overtime. But, as usual, Pam had to get herself worked up over it.

'I'm not so sure you should go home, Nora,' Pam said, pressing the edge of a fingernail lightly, rhythmically, against the base of her thumb as she watched the screen.

I lived in the Elysian Fields. Generations ago, the New Victorian government had started a tradition of granting gifts of land to those who had made great contributions to the nation. But even with the advent of terraforming technologies, land was a limited resource. By the time my father had earned his plot the government had begun building underground sites, constructing housing plots in the vast pre-existing shelters from the war years. The Elysian Fields was the largest of these, housing perhaps three hundred families. It was soon to open its second level.

'That's silly,' I said. 'You know these yellow journalists, they grab onto any rumor and throttle it for ratings. The more controversies they can connect in a single sentence, the higher their score.'

'I don't like it, though.' Pam looked to her wrist, where, like everyone else, her ID chip had been injected at birth. 'And that bit about the identity theft is scary. I mean, you can't exactly go about life without your chip, can you? The idea that some-one could mess with that info gives me the creeps. Dad says they even keep a log of the readers you pass by, so they know where you are.'

I shrugged. 'I'll believe it when one of the Ayles gets on and says that it's true. Until then, I have other things to concentrate on.' I shifted my knees, drawing my diary closer to my chest.

Pamela nodded, and fixed her eyes on the show again. After a few moments she asked, 'Do you ever talk to Lord Ayles?'

I kept my eyes trained on my diary. 'No. Not since the funeral.'

Pam left it at that. I backed into my mind, forcing myself to write. By the time I looked up again, the rolling of the carriage wheels beneath us had lulled her to sleep.

I used the silence to my advantage, scrawling out my final paper in the shorthand that Salvez had taught me. For all my procrastination, the thing was done rather quickly – like a jab at the doctor's office. I gave my history teacher what I've given every teacher who's assigned the same topic since I started school. Truth be told, I've only had one or two who actually cared about what I had to say. Most have been more concerned about my penmanship.

'*We are the children of a new Golden Age,*' I began. '*The world has been assaulted by both fire and ice, and we are still here. We, as a people, have chosen to survive.*'

CHAPTER TWO

❧

Nora

A hundred and fifty years ago, the world was a terrifying place.

A long list of horrors had assaulted the human race by that time. The poles of the earth had disappeared once more beneath deadly mantles of ice, and winters had become long and hard for an increasing number of nations. Humanity had been forced to migrate in massive waves towards the new temperate zones along the Equator. Entire countries had been wiped off the face of the earth by catastrophic storms. Cuba, Indonesia, England, Japan. Gone.

The entire planet suffered, but the Americas, I think, faced more than their fair share of disaster. Refugees from Canada brought with them a new strain of influenza that killed one out of every four people it infected. Famine followed. And then the Second American Civil War, and its nuclear destruction.

No one won that war. The United States ceased to be. Survivors took shelter wherever they could, banding together in new tribes that were not based on race, or class, or nationality.

But the worst was still to come.

It was the eruption of the supervolcano under Yellowstone that finally emptied the US. In a last desperate bid for survival, several of the strongest tribes united and decided to strike southward. They were my ancestors.

The fathers of my tribe were a rag-tag lot. The remains of the American and Canadian military. Conservative religious sorts, their women dressed in long skirts and their children educated from books that most of mankind had long ago forgotten about. Mexican militia men. Survivalists, hardy men and women who still flew the flags of their dead countries. Basically, whoever had managed to *live*.

My forebears rode into Central America like the army of Genghis Khan. I don't think this is a bad thing – I'm here, after all. Khan is usually pegged as an evil man, but really, he was best motivator the world has ever seen. He united half the known world by permitting his vanquished enemies to sign up and share in the plunder. My ancestors did pretty much the same thing by inspiring the people they conquered to join in as they pushed further south. They gave everyone the same goal – expansion.

It worked well, for a while. In the ensuing Settlement Wars against the Latin American tribes pushing their way north from Bolivia and Brazil, my forefathers managed to carve out a nice swath of land from Mexico down to the northern hump of South America. But after a few years, they had gone as far as it was possible for them to go. By the time the Treaty of 2055 was signed, all of the armies involved were on their last legs. Survival had become more important than supremacy.

So, we got the lands that came to be known as the Territories, and the tribes to the south agreed to carve up what was left. My people watched the tribal infighting that followed, watched the smaller wars that erupted, and the message became clear: they had to work together.

And thus, the Territories found peace. My people settled down and began rebuilding. This they did *extremely* well. As the years passed they revived technologies thought forever lost, like the ability to produce and use biofuel and solar power. They established trade routes and sent expeditions to the north to search for resources and antiquities. But their society was still a primitive one, and their country was still not completely united. It was a tangle of villages and small towns populated by farmers and artisans, governed and protected by the military. After the first generation had put down its roots, the leaders of my people began to speak about the need to create a true government and a true nation.

And as they talked, life in the villages went on.

It didn't happen overnight. It wasn't a fad or a craze. But my people, being conservative as a general rule, had never forgotten the past. As the years wore on, it seemed like they remembered and rediscovered even more of it. While the tribes to the south envisioned shining, futuristic Utopias for themselves, or fell into disorganization and squalor, my people became more and more old-fashioned. Long dresses for ladies became the norm. Etiquette became a national pastime. Violence and crude behavior were frowned upon. Respect for one's superiors was expected, as well as an understanding of where you happened to fit into society.

Within another few decades my people had officially fastened onto the Victorian era as a model of civility, order, and prosperity. When it came time to ratify our Constitution and name our country, the people voted overwhelmingly for 'New Victoria'.

Why? Scholars have been kicking that one around for decades. Best theory I've run across is that, well . . . the Victorian age was so distant in time that none of our ancestors could really have an emotional attachment to it. After hundreds of years of plagues and storms and wars and starvation, how could they? And yet, most people knew what it was. Most people had some image of it in their mind, or had heard of some Victorian historical or family figure, or knew some Victorian story . . . *Dracula*, or *Moulin Rouge*. Of the buildings and books and old films that managed to survive, lots of them contained titbits of Victorianism. And figure, back then, that although the towns were becoming cities and the villages were becoming towns, most people still lived in the country. The fancy language of the Victorians seemed naturally intelligent and beautiful to them; their clothing like the garments royalty would wear; their manners and morals perfect, almost godlike.

People knew *just* enough to see it as a sort of Golden Age. They didn't see its ugly side. And that's what they *wanted* –

what they needed. A new Golden Age. History without a dark side. Even the First American Civil War seemed gentlemanly and refined in comparison to the Second.

Having been beating so hard and so hot for so long, the heart of my people wanted to be calm. It wanted to know tranquility and stability. It wanted to know beauty.

And so, my people chose to create it.

For a time, everything was peaceful. Trade flourished. Technology became plentiful and cheap. The culture grew in leaps and bounds. Traditions were established that continue to this day.

And then the Punks came along.

At first they had many voices and no name. In fact, they refused to name themselves, forcing their enemies to do it for them. Really, I think 'Punks' is fairly boring, but my forefathers thought it would do.

The Punk movement rejected the new aristocracy that was slowly arising from our strict social order. For them, no title could elevate one man above another. As the cities grew, they longed for political power to remain in the small farming towns and villages – in the hands of 'the people', as they saw them. They railed against our society's increasing use of computers, arguing that reliance upon 'thinking machines' would cause the nation to go intellectually soft. They spat upon the mass-produced goods our factories churned out, and praised the individual artisans who still made things with their hands.

But it was the rebirth of holographic technology that *really* set them off. The man who would become their leader, Jeremiah Reed, called it, 'The pretty lie that will steal the real bread out of the mouths of the stonemason and the bard alike.'

In their eyes, our society was repeating every mistake every society had ever made – creating an upper and an underclass, dominating the less privileged, chasing after shallow comfort and luxury.

The movement grew. They attacked factories, burned politicians' houses, took to the streets. It came to a head in the Reed Massacre, where a hundred Punk protestors stormed a shirt factory to destroy its computerized machinery, and were fired upon by the New Victorian military. Three days of violent civil unrest followed as the Punks were purged from our lands. They were driven south, to die or eke out their own civilization – whichever came first.

They didn't go quietly, though. Fighting continues along the Border Zone to this very day. The only reason we haven't annihilated them is because, deep down, they're still our brothers. Flesh of our flesh. That and, as my one teacher used to tell me, '*We outnumber them ten to one, and it's cheaper to kill them one at a time. Makes us look better to the other tribes, as well.*'

The end.

I rewrote my paper in longhand and sent it wirelessly to my teacher's school address. After I touched the send button, the minute hand on the little watch icon in the corner of the screen hit five. I'd just made the assignment deadline. Satisfied, I reached into the pocket of my black woolen coat and fished out a cookie from its wax paper wrapping, popping it into my mouth. Work, reward. Timeless values.

I then leaned forward and disconnected the cab's screen from its clip. I brought it into my lap and turned down the sound, before letting my fingertips flick through the stories. I'd behaved myself while Pam was awake, knowing she wasn't apt to like the footage they'd probably show. She got sick at the sight of blood. Some of the other networks aired special news programming for ladies, devoid of anything 'indelicate', but NVIC wasn't one of them.

How did I happen to know this?

My dark, secret, unladylike vice is watching war documentaries and news footage.

It was something I had shared with my father.

Military insiders reported this morning that Punk forces have been seen organizing along the border of Brazil and Bolivia. Despite a strong offensive by our troops, their number appears to be growing, causing analysts some concern. This follows the terrorist attack on the town of Shaftesbury on December 15th.

My shoulders started rising as I watched, confused. Shaftesbury was a rural Victorian hamlet in Ecuador that contained all of two hundred people. Why would they attack *it*, if they had gotten that far into our territory? Why not pick a bigger target?

The screen glowed before my eyes, showing a map of the skirmish and shaky home video of the fighting in the streets between the Punks and the town's citizen militia. No matter their politics, or the actual blood that spilled every day at the Border, part of me couldn't help but admire the way the Punks did battle. Their clothing was piecemeal and ratty, their machinery naked and primitive – but those strange rag-and-bone men of the desert went in with wild cries and obeyed no rules. They'd hide in the water, in the trees. They seemed capable of creating war machines out of absolutely *anything* – tanks that walked upon massive metal legs made from parts of rusted-out trains, bombs crafted of junk wrapped around anything that would explode.

It was fascinating. It was oddly thrilling. It was nothing a *girl* should be interested in.

It was my narcotic of choice.

As I watched, though, I began to realize that the Punks didn't seem to have a plan of attack. They were simply lashing out, aiming their weapons at anything that moved. They didn't act like men with a mission.

They were absolutely enraged.

I watched in shock as they engaged in direct hand-to-hand combat with the Victorian villagers. In fact, few of them seemed to *have* weapons. They just went right in, grabbing and punching. I even saw one man try to bite another. The villagers were shooting at them, a positive hailstorm of bullets, but only a few Punks fell down. The rest just kept running straight for the militia.

The broadcast switched to footage from the Border itself, where the Punks were launching similar attacks, throwing themselves and whatever they had at our forces. I'd never seen so many Punk soldiers in one fight. I could see their home-made bombs going off, sending burning shrapnel in wide, fatal arcs close to their own lines – stupid, to say the least. I thought they were wild *before*. I'd never seen them so intense.

'What has you guys so angry?' I whispered to myself.

The other news clips didn't provide much more to go on. The general opinion seemed to be that we just had to deliver them a firmer spanking than usual, and send them back to their lands to think about what they'd done. There was no discussion about why they were suddenly stepping up their attacks, or what they hoped to accomplish.

I leaned back again and slid my hand behind my neck. Weird. Just weird. The screen went black from lack of activity, and I found myself gazing at my own reflection in the low light of the electric lamp mounted on the ceiling of the cab.

I despise my face, and think I always will. My features are so little and childlike that I sometimes fear that I'll never look like a proper adult, even though I'm almost seventeen years of age. I have pale skin, brown almond-shaped eyes, and black hair the length of my hunched-up shoulders that likes to form itself into thick ringlets, even though I constantly try to teach it not to.

Mostly, I hate the fact that mine isn't the face of a girl who studies war and history instead of hem lengths. It's not the face of a girl who's top of her target shooting class. It isn't the face of a girl who can stand up for herself, who's lost almost all of her defenders and doesn't want any more – who just wants to be left alone to slog it out as best she can.

But it's all I have.

Aunt Gene was very fond of mirrors, and liked this feature of the Model V. Further proof that she was out of her mind.

Rather than dwell on her, I let my head roll onto Pamela's shoulder and did my best to join her in slumber.

I dreamed of him.

When I dream of my father, I always dream of that ugly, noisy day when his life ended – of that day when nothing stood between him and death but a few hundred more painful breaths. Odd, pronounced veins had spiderwebbed across his face by that point, and his lips were blue. He drew away whenever I came near.

And so I *stayed* near. I lay beside him as he slept, stubbornly held onto his hands when he spoke. I would have clutched him to myself, save that there were always colleagues of his or doctors in the sickroom, and my aunt insisted on some level of decorum. Horatio Salvez, the man who assisted my father in his research and served as my informal tutor, was the only constant presence that I did not detest.

My father and I had lost my mother when I was nine. He had seen me safely through that, my first encounter with real grief. I couldn't have made it without him. He had let me weep, let me storm; he had even permitted me my baby blasphemies, saying nothing as I cursed God and smashed my china dolls in an effort to force inanimate objects, representatives of the world outside myself, to share my pain.

I would see him through this. I would have walked the way for him, if the Grim Reaper had materialized in the room and given me a choice.

It was always quiet in the sickroom. It had once been his study, but a bed was moved in for him when he could no longer scale the stairs to his bedchamber. It was a dark, masculine space, everything carved and gilded and stained. People moved within it like monks about the silent grounds of a monastery.

That day I had tiptoed from the room to put on fresh clothes. On my return trip, Salvez found me and told me that he was dying. Of course, it hadn't been in so many words. Mr Salvez was a skinny, bearded man with a tender face and a weary voice – wearier now than ever.

'I think he will leave us in a few moments, Miss Dearly.'

I ran to my father's sickroom, my slippers slapping violently on the hallway floor. When I reached the door, his co-workers opened it. I hurried to my father's silk-draped bed and searched the shadows for his face. It was so dark, like a livid bruise. My love for him warred with common human horror at the sight of it.

'Papa?'

When he opened his jaundiced eyes, tears sprang to my own. I leaned down to kiss his cheek. He tried, limply, to push me back.

'Please don't,' I whispered, unable to keep myself from crying any longer. I had tried so *hard* not to trouble him with my tears. I had tried so hard to be strong, ever since he had returned from his last southern tour with some rare disease – but I no longer had the will to fight. '*Stop it*. Stop pulling away from me. You yourself said that it's not contagious – and if it were, I wouldn't *care*. I love you . . . I love you.'

I kissed him and kissed him and kissed him, and he let it happen. He wrapped me in his tube-studded arms afterwards, though I could feel how weak he was.

'I love you too, NoNo,' he said, his voice raspy.

I laughed without thinking about it, the sound distorted by my sobs. Only he called me NoNo. My first word as a child had been, '*No.*' My mother had thought that I was attempting to pronounce my name. Only my father had understood that I was starting out on a long career of stubbornness.

We were silent for a time, his hand heavy on my back, the buttons of his nightshirt pressing painfully into my cheek – a pain I welcomed, a pain which told me that he was still there, beneath me.

'Nora,' he said. 'I have to tell you something.'

'I have a thousand somethings to tell you.'

He urged me to sit up. 'No, child. You must understand . . . you are incredibly special.' His hand slid shakily up into my hair. 'My body . . .'

Before he could finish, it began. I watched it happen.

He died in pain, his body contorting and twisting, as if he were attempting to free himself from the encircling chains of death. His mouth opened wide as he tried to pant out his last words, but only senseless sounds escaped his lips, and I knew that it was useless to try to understand. I cried for him as I had never cried before, until I thought my lungs must be bruised like his skin.

His colleagues let me have only a moment with the body, until it was no longer my father, before trying to usher me out. When I realized that they wanted me to leave the room, I became a catamount. I twisted in their arms, screamed, fought to gain another minute with him, another *second*, but they wouldn't give it to me. For all of my struggling, they seemed to be gripped by an even fiercer sense of urgency. I was physically carried from the room by two of his doctors.

They took the body to the mortician that very night, to await the burial. When I tried to follow it out the front door, Salvez wrapped me in his arms from behind and held me back. By then I was too weak with grief to fight.

Aunt Gene, ever brusque, mourned my father's passing by dealing with the florist, the priest, and the mason who would chisel the date on the stone. I never saw her cry. I knew that it was her way of coping with the death of her brother, but it seemed so cold to me. I still haven't forgiven her for it.

As for me, I took to my bedroom. It was a large, cheerful

room decorated for a little girl, with cherubs molded into the pink ceiling and carvings of wings etched on the parquet floor. I hid in the enormous dollhouse that had been my altar as a child, nestled amongst my stuffed animals and other toys. I don't know how many hours I spent there. I remember sunlight peeking in through the little shuttered windows at times, moonlight streaming through them at others. I remained there until I could muster up a memory of my father other than the horrific spectacle of his death. I had to.

It was the memories of his stories that helped.

My father had been a skilled storyteller. The poems of the ancients had echoed so beautifully and with such vividness from his lips, the heavy tales of the First Victorians, the epics of the thousand-year gods. I had especially loved to hear stories of war and heroism – tales that had filled my playtime, tales I'd wanted to live out myself one day.

Over the following days, I ate with those memories. I dressed with them. I attended the funeral with them. I thought of the many times he had indulged my childish imagination, letting me be a fairy for a day, or a mermaid, or a soldier. I had convinced myself over the years that I would be a brilliant soldier – brave and true, self-sacrificing. Women were forbidden to join the army, of course, but my father had told me stories about girls shaving their hair, strapping down their breasts, and enlisting as a John or a James. He had joked that he would smuggle me in, when I would play war with my teddies. He had drilled me in the courtyard behind our first house and given me my first shooting lessons. Me, petite and un-soldierlike as ever a girl could be.

Not that it mattered now.

The funeral of Dr Victor Dearly was an affair of state. My father had been a hero, decorated and highly honored. He had started his career in the military as a surgeon and infectious disease expert long before I was born, but by the time I was nine, he had distinguished himself as a man of valor. I knew the story well. The Prime Minister then, Lord Harvey Ayles, had come to inspect the unit my father was traveling with as part of a morale-boosting tour, and the Punks had attacked. Ignoring the danger to his own life, my father had run directly through the fray to shield the PM with his body, taking five bullets in the process.

Both survived the incursion. He'd been offered a position in the Minister's cabinet, he'd been offered Surgeon General. He'd not taken either position, preferring to head up the Department of Military Health. My mother had *hated* him for that. The world had been ready to offer him a position amongst the elite, and he'd rejected it. Bless her.

Because she had passed away, it fell to me to pour the first handful of earth into my father's grave. Lord Ayles himself was beside me as I did it. He was once a handsome, vibrant man, but time and illness had turned him into a respected recluse. The fact that he had insisted on attending the funeral told me, and everyone else, that he still greatly esteemed my father. He sat in a wheelchair surrounded by bodyguards, swaddled in a shawl, tinted glasses and a floppy hat hiding his face.

Lord Ayles called me, 'Miss Nora'. He told me that my father was the best of men.

The mason had yet to carve the date of his death on the stone. For some reason I took comfort in that fact, even as the dirt struck his coffin.

'Miss Dearly?'

I jumped a bit as Alencar's voice rang out from the intercom, awakening me. He rapped on his side of the carriage's dividing window before lowering it. I pushed myself up. Pamela stirred beside me.

'There's a problem, Miss Dearly.'

I glanced to the window on my right as it became clear

glass once more. We were idling in a line of carriages in the empty, hilly area between the mansion district and the west end of the city of New London. Some distance ahead sat the entrance to the Elysian Fields, a marble gatehouse set into the side of a low hill. The road before it was crammed with vehicles.

'What's going on?' I asked.

'It must have something to do with the news,' Pam decided groggily.

'They're not letting vehicles in,' Alencar said, drumming his fingers rapidly upon his simple black mobile phone. 'Foot traffic only. They're trying to salvage all the equipment they can from the lower level. Apparently the second level has become our new public in-ground pool.'

I patted Pam's shoulder. 'See? No problem.' I leaned forward and poked my head into Alencar's half of the carriage. 'Let me out here, and take Miss Roe home. It's just a few minutes away. I'll be at the house by the time you get back.'

'Nora! Unescorted?' asked Pam.

I fought the desire to roll my eyes, but then Alencar had to go and back her up. 'No, Miss Dearly. I can't let you walk on your own!'

'Mr Alencar, darling Pamela . . . I will be walking *home*. In an *underground housing complex* filled with *city workers*. How much trouble could I possibly get into? Besides, Aunt Gene's expecting me. I'm late.'

Pam slowly opened her mouth. Noticing this in the rearview mirror, I withdrew my head and gestured with my index finger at Alencar. With my other hand, I punched the button that would raise the partition between us. 'Give us one moment, would you?'

'Nora, I don't want to have to worry about you. Let's just do this the other way around. We can visit with my family, and you can drive back here in a few hours.'

I took a breath once the divider was up. 'Pamela, you really need to stop worrying about me. You're not my mother. I don't have a mother, and I don't want one.'

She reached out to lay her hand over mine. 'Nora, you, of all people, know that telling me not to worry about something makes me worry all the more.'

I turned and wrapped my arms about her neck. She didn't waste a moment, but embraced me in turn. 'I can take care of myself, Pam. I want to. I don't want to burden you any longer . . . can't you see that? I'm fine, I promise you. It's been a year and a day.'

'Nora,' she protested.

'Go home and see your family. Say hello to your father for me. And I'll see you tomorrow, OK?' I gently extricated myself from the seat beside her and forced myself to look into her eyes. 'OK?'

It took her a moment, but I knew all was well when she let go of me long enough to capture one of my curls and gently tug it. It was an old salute of hers. 'OK.'

I knocked on the partition, letting Alencar know that I was leaving. His door opened shortly after mine. The air was filled with shrill horns and beeping. 'Are you sure this is a good idea, Miss?'

I pulled my gloves on. It took my eyes a moment to adjust to the flashing lights. 'Absolutely. I want to stretch my legs, anyway.' I turned and waved with both hands, as Pamela watched me, pensively, through the open door. 'Good night, Pamma!'

'Good night,' she said softly.

I turned around before Alencar could stop me, and set off, walking quickly across the small bridge that led to the tunnel entrance. A constable at the gate ran his scanner over my wrist. He nodded when the computer approved me as a resident, and I folded my glove back down.

'Welcome home, Miss Dearly,' he said, and tipped his hat.

CHAPTER THREE

Nora

The gate was unlocked, and I headed into the Elysian Fields.

I followed a concrete tunnel choked with vehicles for a few hundred yards, before exiting directly onto the main street of the first level. It took me a moment to get my bearings as the vast liquid-crystal sky screen came into view, providing me with an artificial version of the same fading evening I'd just left outside. Each of the EF's levels was to have the same luxury. The plan was to dig as deep as possible into the earth, level after level, in order to provide the city with more housing and improved emergency shelters.

I lived in the neighborhood of Violet Hill, on the western side of the Fields. I decided to follow the side streets rather than the main avenue to avoid the march of machinery and men in red hard hats. They were clustered about the new gate that led deeper underground, and were currently using thick chains to drag a drill-nosed mole machine up the ramp.

Aunt Gene dreamed of living in a mansion on the surface again, but I liked it down here. Two main streets formed a cross in the center of the level, and these held shops and businesses; the side streets spiraled out from there. The houses along these side streets were new, designed after Gothic revival architecture, with columns and yawning arched windows. Every four houses shared a courtyard garden with a small fountain in the middle, save for the houses on the edge, which were styled with more privacy in mind. Ours was one of these. It had a wide lawn out front and one in back, which met the wall – although, virtually, it was designed to look as if it ran out to the horizon. They even gave us holographic trees that moved in the nonexistent breeze.

After I got beyond the workers, I found that the streets were largely empty. I encountered a few servants out walking their mistress's yippy little dogs, and spared a nod for each. At one point I ran into a pair of constables who didn't bother to size me up before tipping their caps. But no one approached me or tried to speak to me. I found it refreshing. I felt like I had room to breathe, even if my thoughts were still rather morbid after the dream I'd had.

Once the constables passed by, I saw no one until I came upon the man in black.

Living in my head, as I was, I didn't even really comprehend that it *was* a man I was coming upon. I saw only a shadow lurking beneath the flickering gas lamp at the last turn before my house. As I drew nearer, I saw that it was a tall figure, obviously a man, draped in a full black hooded cloak. It was difficult to see his face in the murky light.

I steadied my shoulders and kept walking. Ours was a safe neighborhood, and it was only common sense that gave me any pause. I had never been accosted in my life, truth be told.

The hooded figure turned my way. 'Miss Dearly?'

I stopped.

Politeness and wariness warred in my head, but school-bred politeness found itself winning out. 'Yes?' I replied.

The man came closer, with a shuffling gait. If he was planning to jump me, he wasn't going to do very well at it. 'I apologize for my boldness, but if I could beg a moment of your time, I promise not to abuse it.' His voice was slow and dry, but something in it was surprisingly lovely. Calming. Like the autumn wind blowing through leaves.

I pressed my lips together and shook my head. 'I think perhaps you should call at my home and ask to speak with me. Our meeting would be improper any other way.' I began to walk again, faster this time.

'Please,' the man pleaded. He made no move to chase me. 'It's about your father.'

I jerked to a stop and turned around. 'My father? Who are you?' My voice came out harder than I had meant it to. I tried to shake off the ghost of my dream, an uneasy feeling wriggling in my chest.

The man gestured with a gloved hand. 'I . . . was in the army with him. He saved my life.'

I studied him for a moment before deciding to humor him. I dredged up a small smile. 'I am glad for that. He was a noble man.'

The man nodded with reverence, as if we were speaking about a saint. 'He . . . *was* . . . a noble man. A loving man.' He took a step forward. 'And I know he'd be happy to see that you're safe.'

And with that he was upon me.

He moved like lightning, grasping my wrist. I twisted my arm as my father had taught me, trying to yank my wrist out through the place where his hand had to close over his fingers, but to no avail. I kicked out at his shins, aiming for the area where the flesh was thinnest over the bone, but he evaded me.

'Let me go!' I screamed. I struck him with my free hand, and he grabbed that arm too.

'Miss Dearly, please understand! You're in danger! I'm here to help you . . . your father would want me to help you!'

This was such a ridiculous statement that I unthinkingly ceased my efforts to free myself, if only for a second. 'My father is *dead*! Unless you've come from the hereafter, I'm pretty sure you've no *idea* what he wants!'

The man also stopped struggling, and with what sounded like grim amusement said, 'Well, about that . . .'

'*Halt!*'

It was the two constables I'd passed before, their feet pounding against the concrete. They were already drawing their electrified billy clubs from their belts. One blew on his silver whistle, summoning his comrades and causing a beacon, in a station somewhere, to announce his location.

The cloaked man dropped my arms and hissed, 'You might think that this is some kind of sick joke, or that I'm crazy, but it's the truth! I swear to you, you're in danger – you have to come with me!'

I stared up into his hood, at the place where his face should be – and for an instant, as the flames flared in the street lamps, I saw his eyes.

They were opal white, cloudy, the eyes of the blind.

I fled to the constables, my heart hammering in my chest. Realizing that he would be leaving alone, the cloaked man ran in the opposite direction. One of the constables stayed with me as the second gave chase. I heard sirens coming from far off.

'Do you know that man, Miss?'

'No.' I caught my breath. 'He must be a veteran . . . he said he knew my father, Dr Victor Dearly. I don't think he wanted to hurt me, not really.' He acted like he was trying to save me from something. Poor man was probably driven mad by war – *departed*, as they called it.

The constable relayed my story into the speaker clipped to his lapel. He then escorted me to my house, which was only about a block away. I scanned the streets we passed, suddenly frightened of every shadow, every motion of the fake trees, the whoosh of the recycled air. In my anxiety, I wondered how I was going to explain this to Aunt Gene, showing up with the police in tow. She wasn't exactly a paragon of sympathy. She'd gut me for having been walking alone, to begin with, never mind speaking even one *syllable* to a strange man. Somehow, the whole affair would be my fault, instead of just the part where I, stupid git, decided to leave the carriage.

On top of that, Pamela was going to have my head. I was going to be divvied up like a hog slaughtered on Christmas Eve.

I knew the constable would want to ring the bell, and so I didn't even try to convince him that I could just enter the house. When I heard the familiar 'pa-ping!' I hid my hands in the sleeves of my coat and curled my toes in my squeaky new boots, trying to think of what I had on the butler, Matilda, that I could use to keep her from singing. I was coming up with a whole lot of nothing. I'd used her tryst with the valet next door *last* time.

Matilda, a stately ebony-skinned woman, answered the door – or at least, her head did. She kept her body out of sight, peering around the edge.

'Nora?' she asked, her jaw dropping when she saw the cop.

I made my move.

'Oh, Auntie! You won't believe what happened!' I cried. I rushed into the house and wrapped my arms about her slender waist. That's when I realized that she was wearing a poppy-colored ball gown, of all things.

God had intervened.

'I . . . what?' she stammered.

Thinking that she was speaking to him, the constable did the filling in for me. I trained my eyes on Matilda's, begging, wordlessly, for assistance. And, to make sure she got the point, I tugged on the bustle of her pretty dress. I had no idea why she was wearing it, but I had a feeling that it might just be my salvation.

Matilda was a star.

'Thank you *so much* for ensuring the safe return of our *darling* little girl.'

The copper was skeptical. 'You are the mistress of this household, then?'

Matilda peered at the man, all the while very carefully keeping her hands out of range of his scanner. 'Of course. Are you implying something, sir?'

The constable coughed. 'Not at all. It's simply odd for a lady to answer her own door around here.'

Matilda bristled. 'Honestly!' She pulled me against her side, a bit too tightly. 'I've been waiting for my niece to return from school for *hours* now. She's been gone since September. What kind of guardian would I be if I didn't fly to the door, wings on my feet, when I thought that she had finally alighted upon her own stoop?' She said this in the tone of voice she normally used when I was caught stealing freshly baked goodies. At that moment, I considered it a priceless gift.

'Ah, of course, my lady. I should have realized.'

'And now I learn that she faced mortal peril whilst making her way home!' To my amazement and quiet glee, Matilda squeezed out a real tear. 'This never would have happened when I was a child! Society is crumbling around us! Oh, it is too much to bear!'

After the constable had swallowed his embarrassment and jotted down my information in his digital notebook, and the door was shut, Matilda and I whirled on one another and spit out, 'What the devil?' in perfect synch.

Matilda caved first. 'All right! I'm sneaking out tonight to attend a masquerade. I was just waiting for you to show up before I left. I knew it'd be you when I opened the door – I didn't know you'd be bringing the cops!'

'Why should you have to sneak out? You can do what you like in your free time.'

'Well, the fact that your aunt is going to the same ball rather complicates matters.' Matilda held her head high, but I could see that she understood perfectly well that Aunt Gene would *never* consent to hobnobbing with the help.

My heart began to smolder with anger at mention of the party. I ignored it. For now. 'Aren't you worried that Aunt Gene will see you there?'

'Masquerade. Masks.'

'Ahh.'

'And you?'

'That weirdo on the street said that he knew my father, and tried to get me to go with him.'

'Wow.'

'Yeah.'

There was a moment of silent appraisal, her eyes on mine, before negotiations began.

'I won't tell my aunt if you don't.'

'Deal.'

Well, that was easy.

The doorbell rang, making us both jump a mile. It was Alencar with my trunk. He took one look at Matilda and immediately said, 'I see nothing.'

'Good man. Nora, you'd better go visit your aunt before she has to leave. I need to get back into hiding.'

'Why do you hate me?'

She held out a hand. '*Do it.*'

I slapped my gloves into her hand as a final retort, and made my way towards the stairs. She was right. But every step up the winding staircase brought me closer to accepting that I was very tired, I was very nervous, and I'd practically been kidnapped – or so I now told myself – by a strange, unstable man but a few yards from my front door.

I reached the threshold of my aunt's suite and knocked.

'Enter.'

I did so, with a curtsey and a stiff, 'Good evening, Aunt Gene.'

The former Mrs Genevieve Ortega was seated at her vanity, putting the finishing touches on. Her icy blue gown spilled out across the floor behind her, and her silvering hair was done up in an elaborate pouf. She was an attractive woman, but with a hardness about her mouth and eyes that her brother had not had. Like my father, she spoke with the round, prim accent of the far north.

'Ahh, Nora. How was your trip?'

'Long.'

'I am sorry to hear it.' She turned to look at me after applying one last swipe of rouge. 'You have not yet changed?'

'We only just arrived.'

'Well, rectify that immediately. You haven't even taken off your coat? Has Matilda lost her mind?'

Rather than argue, I took it off and folded it over my arm. I could feel Aunt Gene's eyes roving over me. 'Where on earth did you get that dress?' she asked.

I shrugged. 'It was in my closet at school.'

Aunt Gene took a cleansing breath, and informed me, slowly – as one might inform someone of limited intelligence – 'That's an autumnal dress, my dear. And it's obviously several seasons ago that it was made for you.'

I forced myself to smile, and tried to make it as nasty-looking as one of Vespertine's. 'Funny how that works, when you've been in mourning.'

Aunt Gene rose from her vanity and came near. Without her sitting there, the drawers of the vanity automatically shut and the electric candles that had provided her with light to work by retracted back towards the wall. 'On that note, I think it would be a nice gesture if you packed up your mourning weeds and gave them to your little friend, Miss Roe. Someone of her station can make more use of black . . . it *does* wear so well.'

So much for not fighting.

'Now, I am going to attend Bertha Cotney's ball tonight, as I told you in my last letter. I'm sure I shall be in quite late. Matilda will be here to help you, of course.'

'Of course.' I breathed once, and then asked, 'And you feel you *must* attend this party, for some reason?'

Aunt Gene eyed me. She, too, understood exactly where we were headed. 'We are no longer in mourning, niece, as you just pointed out.'

'By *hours*, Aunt. One could be forgiven for thinking that you counted the minutes.'

Aunt Gene's mouth set into a line. 'I shall not be spoken to so by a child. Your father would be ashamed.'

The anger kindling in my chest burst into a roaring fire, even as I did my best to keep my composure. 'Look, Aunt Gene. When I got your letter yesterday, I fully intended on coming home and making a scene in defense of his memory. But I'm tired, and I'm not in the best of moods, and, at the end of the day, you *are* my elder . . . and therefore I'm willing to shove my cards back up my sleeve and let you act just as shamefully as you want to. Is that what you want?'

She slapped me.

I glared at her and cut to the chase. 'He's only been dead a *year*.'

'And that is a year of *wasted* time,' Aunt Gene spat.

'You complete . . .'

'Silence, you little hussy. You have no conception – no understanding.' Her fingers curled into fists, and her voice was low and dangerous. 'Your uncle left me a year before your father died. I have been out of society for more than two, because of this. *Two years.* Good marriages have been made in that time, marriages that might have included me.'

'Is that really all you can think about?' I asked, my fingers coming to rest against my cheek.

'It is all that we should think about, Nora!' Aunt Gene said heatedly. 'It is through marriage that we can both improve our positions. I want to get out of this hole in the ground. I want to take my place within the best set again. Why do you not understand this?'

'Because we're perfectly comfortable down here!'

'Life is not about comfort, life is about *striving!*' she bellowed. 'You had best internalize this virtue now, before you find yourself in the gutter.'

I laughed at her exaggeration. 'We're far from living in the gutter.'

Aunt Gene looked daggers at me. 'Are we so far? Do you even know what has been sacrificed for you? Your father – by his own doing, I might add – was not a terribly rich man. It has been your former uncle's mercy payments that have been keeping us afloat. Your father bequeathed us only his good name and social status – his pension isn't even worth mentioning. We are drowning in debt, Nora.' And, as if she didn't think that I would believe this without proof, she walked over to her golden roll-top desk and began to pull out bundles of actual paper envelopes. 'Here, look!'

I didn't want to, but I couldn't help myself. My cheek still stinging, I stepped closer to my aunt, and looked at the papers in her hands. They were from creditors.

What had she done?

'The house is mortgaged,' she said, voice vibrating with anger as she flipped through the letters. I picked each one up as she discarded it, staring at the tiny, condemning print. 'We have accounts at every shop you can imagine. It will not go on forever. There will be enough for your schooling and your debut, and then . . .'

I stopped listening, at this point. My entire body felt cold. I knew exactly what she was suggesting.

I was to debut, immediately find a rich man – no matter temperament, personality, or level of hygiene – and marry him.

'I won't,' I croaked.

Aunt Gene lifted her head, and gestured to her dress. 'If you won't, then I will. But only to save myself. It is time for you to grow up, time for you to consider your family's future. I cannot be responsible for you forever.'

I could feel my face growing red. 'Wait a minute. You got us into this!' My mouth seemed reluctant to move, slow to give voice to the furious thoughts crowding my brain. It made me even angrier. 'Did you think you could get away with this? Continue to live as you had been? You'll get us *out* of this, or I'll bury you myself!'

My aunt's eyes went very dark. 'Are you threatening me, niece?'

Oh, how I longed to threaten her. I longed to beat her into a bloody pulp. But I held my tongue, though my hands, clutching the letters of debt, were shaking.

Satisfied with my silence, Aunt Gene swished away, picking up her faux fur stole and mask. 'I suggest you spend some time this evening thinking well and hard about this situation, and what part you must play in its solution.' She pulled the cord for the bell that would tell Alencar that she was ready. 'Now, good night, Nora.'

I said nothing. I didn't trust myself.

'Good *night*, Nora.'

'Good night,' I muttered hatefully.

She lifted her chin, and left.

My brain began to buzz again. Solution? I could go to the family lawyer, convince him that she had done this monstrous thing and that I had been ignorant of it. That, in being appointed my guardian, she had ruined me. I could beg a favor from the former Prime Minister, and publicly disgrace her.

But, as usual, there was no solution I could enact *myself*.

I didn't want to think about it anymore. I didn't want to think about anything. Instead, to distract myself, I dug out all of the letters of debt and took them to my room, where I hid them inside the little artist's desk in my dollhouse. I wrote Pam a quick note telling her that I had gotten in all right, and sent it to her phone. I took a bath, and changed into a long, billowy white nightgown trimmed with frothy lace.

I didn't feel like sleeping, though.

I made my way slowly through the quiet house, figuring I'd get something to eat in the kitchen. The help normally left around seven at night, and Matilda wasn't about, of course, and so I was well and truly alone. Only a few gas lamps had been left on. The house seemed just barely alive, one shade out of perfect darkness.

I loved this house. I loved the gilded, tooled leather mounted with black wainscoting along the back hallways; I loved the ethereal pastel hues of the rooms my mother had frequented, with sunburst-shaped flat screens filled with stars near the painted ceilings; I loved the murals of mythological figures mounted on the walls. Beneath its vaulted ceilings my mother had lectured, reproved, and loved me; my father had indulged and inspired me.

I decided that I couldn't let my aunt's folly and selfishness take it away.

I would burn the place down before I'd let anyone take it from me.

The kitchen had several windows that faced the street. I opened one of them, and pulled up a chair. A loaf of bread and a hunk of sausage provided me with a few sandwiches, and it was over these and a cup of tea that I brooded.

The street outside provided little entertainment. Occasionally an electric carriage would purr by, and once I saw two figures walking arm-in-arm. One was a man, the other a woman, her silhouette cut off by the parasol she carried above her head. Parasols with miniature electric gas lamps atop them were all the rage. Hers had a pink light in it, which meant that she belonged to a family that allowed its children to follow the quaint old practice of dating. White indicated that a girl's family would arrange a courtship for her, and blue identified a married woman. Green stood for a woman who wasn't keen on men at all, but whose head could be turned by the sight of a pretty skirt.

I imagined walking with a young man in the dark, and bit into my sandwich viciously. All of the boys I knew were fast turning into unimpressive adults. They had let me play soldier with them when I was a girl, but now expected that I would smile and nod brainlessly at whatever they said. Amazing, how quickly they had fallen in step with adult society's rules.

I cleaned up the kitchen myself, and resumed strolling the

first floor of the house. Behind the wide, lavish front parlor was the room that my father had died in. I hadn't been in it since his passing. The door wasn't locked. I let myself in.

Spirits appeared to have taken up residence in the room, all of his furniture and *objets d'art* shrouded in white sheets. I walked over to the bed and pulled the sheets off of it. Its velvet curtains had been taken down. It was on this bed, with its carved wooden posts, that my father had last enfolded me in his arms. I lay down upon it, wishing, desperately, to feel the buttons of his nightclothes against my cheek rather than the smooth surface of the naked mattress.

The thoughts I'd tried to bury started popping up again. I tried not to think of Aunt Gene at the ball, glittering and flirting. She was good enough at it that; in her youth, she had ensnared Mr Ortega, an investment banker. She had learned how to play the game early on, a smiling elitist that my mother had grumbled about whenever she was unhappy with her own social situation – only to lose that position due to her inability to have children. Lack of an heir was one of the few reasons that a divorce might be granted by the courts. It had been a cruel blow to Aunt Gene.

When my father died, she'd really had no choice but to become my guardian. She'd needed what little money there was to be had from it.

Indulging myself, lost in my own misery, it was a moment before I realized that I had heard a noise outside.

I sat up. The room was dark and still, and couldn't have done a better job of reminding me that I was alone in the house, and that a creepy man had targeted me not a few hours before. A little shiver gripped me.

Terribly conscious of my body's every noise, I swung my bare legs over the side of the bed, my nightgown falling down over them as I stood. Moving as slowly and quietly as I could, I approached the curtained windows. There, I hushed, and listened.

Nothing.

I could have sworn I had heard something snapping, rustling, like someone attempting to find their way through the boxwood bushes that grew beneath our windows on that side of the house.

Doing it quickly, before I could question myself – like ripping off a bandage – I opened the curtains.

There was nothing outside but artificial moonlight.

'Calm down, Nora,' I sighed. 'It was an animal or something. Time for bed.'

I left the sheets that had covered my father's bed puddled on the floor, shut the door behind me, and climbed the vast staircase. As I took the time to close and lock the windows in the upstairs hallway, I could hear the recorded shivering of the virtual leaves in the virtual trees outside. I comforted myself with the notion that I'd heard the same recording downstairs.

Not until I was bundled up in bed did it strike me that the recording was also eerily reminiscent of the hooded man's voice, dry and hushed.

CHAPTER FOUR

Nora

Pamela came over the very next morning, fresh and bright in a tidy new dress of lavender cotton sprinkled with violets. I was perched in my bedroom's bay window with a book, and I saw the ribbons streaming from the base of her bonnet and the front of her cape as she approached the front door. As I left my seat, the window's sheer organza curtains automatically swung shut behind me.

Matilda, once again innocent in her usual severe black dress, let Pam in. She was going to go through the motions of taking her calling card and announcing her to me, but I got to the bottom of the stairs just in time.

'Pamma! No uniform again today! You look normal!'

'I know!' Pamela grinned, skipping away from the butler. 'So do you!'

The moment the words escaped her lips, I saw her features soften in regret. I shook my head and took her by the arm to escort her to the parlor. True – I was no longer in mourning – but I was wearing a dark silver dress with a squared neckline and heavily trimmed sleeves. It wasn't like I was swaddled in candyfloss colors.

Aunt Gene watched us as we passed, seated at her writing desk in its alcove just beneath the main staircase. She had a tiny office there where she could keep an eye on both her e-mail account and the door.

I had adopted a policy, since the night before, of studious ignorance. *Oh, my aunt is sitting there? Oh, I have an aunt, at all? I had no idea.*

'Have you talked to your aunt, yet?' Pam asked, as she collapsed gracefully onto a settee in the parlor and took off her hat. Without waiting for my answer, she reached out to touch the thick glass top of the tea table. Digital buttons designed to look like cameos swam into view within it. She tapped one with her finger, causing the sun-shaped screens to alight all along the ceiling. They had been reflecting the same dirigible-studded sky that the big screen did outside; now, they showed the tail end of the usual morning children's programming. Miss Jess Novio, renowned TV governess, was hosting the same show that I had watched religiously as a child, still distracting tots the nation over so that their nannies could have a few more moments for their tea and mending.

'This is how we make our curtsey! Down we go! *Down we go!*'

'I'd already decided that I wouldn't breathe a word of what had transpired the previous evening – either on the streets, or in the house – and I wordlessly communicated this to Pamma with an even look. My adventures were a secret, and I wanted to keep it that way.

'Well, I won't pretend that I'm not slightly disappointed,' Pam said, flicking through the channels. She rarely got to watch television at home, and it was her habit to turn ours on for the noise whenever she came to call. She stopped flicking when the screen showed footage from the Territorial golf tournament currently taking place. 'Dad's addicted to this. It's *all* he wanted to talk about last night.'

'How is your family?' I asked, throwing myself onto the overstuffed sofa.

'Very well.' Pam turned to look at me. I knew that I was still going to be kept under close watch for a while, and so, to reassure her, I flashed her a slight smile. 'Oh, you'll come dine with us tomorrow night, won't you?'

'Love to,' I said, as golf scores floated by above us.

'Now, young ladies, is this really the best use of your time?' Pamela and I glanced to the door, where Aunt Gene was standing in a wrap of purple shantung silk. Pam rose and curtsied, respectfully. Aunt Gene nodded graciously at her.

'We've not yet decided what we'll be doing today,' I said shortly.

'Oh! I was thinking that perhaps we could visit the shops downtown,' Pam said as she took her seat. 'They're already starting to get spring fabrics in. Mother had this dress ordered for me – do you like it, by the by? – but she said I might have another.'

I seized upon the opportunity. 'I *do* like it, you know, it *really* suits you,' I began, hoping that a sudden whirlwind of girlish voices would be enough to drive my aunt off.

'I have a better idea,' Aunt Gene interrupted firmly. We were both forced to hush up and look at her. She rewarded us with a syrupy smile. 'Why don't you join me in paying a call on the Allisters? I was just about to get dressed for it.'

Oh, not the Allisters. Lord Allister liked nothing better than to show off his collection of stuffed birds, and Lady Allister barely ever said a word, leaving everyone around her feeling as if to sneeze was to impose upon her. And their son could be described as milquetoast at best. He made most of my teachers seem like raving degenerates.

'Oh, can we?'

I looked at Pam, whose face was alight with excitement.

Aunt Gene's smile widened. 'Of course. Wait for me here.'

The moment she was gone, I wormed across the fancy sofa cushions and gripped Pam's arm. 'What? Why in blazes would you want to visit with *them*?'

Pam yanked her arm away and rubbed it, reproachfully. 'If you haven't noticed – their son, Michael? Is *cute*.'

I gaped at her. 'I think the fumes are getting to you, living in the city. He is so *boring*.'

She waved a hand. 'Bah, but he's pretty to look at.' She lifted her eyes to the ceiling. 'Besides, do either of us have a choice as to where we're going right now?'

The question struck me as cryptic. I wondered if she was talking about today's trip, or something else.

Thirty minutes later we were in Aunt Gene's carriage, Pam compulsively adjusting her bonnet, me meditating upon all of the ways it might be possible to kill myself with the in-cab stylus.

The Allisters lived aboveground, about five minutes from the entrance to the Elysian Fields, twenty minutes from the city. Their manor, Vermil Park, was set far back from the road and surrounded by an ornate brass fence. Maybe it was electrified. I could fling myself against it . . .

'So, Miss Roe,' Aunt Gene said after many minutes had passed by in silence. 'How are your studies progressing?'

Pamela stopped fiddling with her hat, her hands sliding into her lap. 'Very well, ma'am. I'm maintaining my academic grades, and I think I'll be permitted to participate in archery competitions again this year . . . at least, for the first part of the year.'

'Why wouldn't you be?' I asked her, drawn from my daydreams by the weirdness of her statement. 'You're amazing. You could go to the nationals. You can shoot an *apple* off of a tree.'

Pam cleared her throat. 'Well, my mother is of the opinion that girls should stop focusing on things like that well before their debut. There are other things to focus on. Things that will be more important in the future.'

I could tell she'd been fed a line. 'Oh, come *on.*'

'Your mother is a wise woman,' Aunt Gene said. Her eyes slowly gravitated towards me as I sat there, staring at my friend. 'You're both of an age now where such considerations should be foremost in your minds.'

I ignored her, and kept my focus on Pam. 'How long ago did she tell you this?'

Pam looked to the mirrored window. 'A few weeks ago.'

Her voice stiffened very slightly. 'I thought I told you.'

I hadn't the faintest memory of this. Where had I been a few weeks ago?

Watching my father's war holo collection on endless repeat and burrowing my face into my pillow at night until my nose hurt.

'Pam, I . . .'

'Best behavior, girls,' Aunt Gene said, as the carriage made a sudden turn. Pam looked away from the window. She met my eyes for a few moments – in which I attempted to telepathically tell her how sorry I was – before she pretended to become distracted by her purse.

The carriage drew to a stop, and Alencar helped us out. The Allisters' butler was waiting for us and saw us in immediately, which told me that we were making a scheduled call. It was probably Lady Allister's visiting day. Relief washed over me like cool water. That meant that we were only going to stay for twenty minutes, at most. I could handle that. Half an hour, tops. After that, I'd be able to beg Pam to forgive me for the fact that I'd been so consumed with my own problems, I hadn't listened to hers.

'Welcome, Mrs Ortega.' Lady Allister stood to receive my aunt. She was a short, doughy woman with tightly curled brown hair. I couldn't help but notice that she was clad in a disgusting amount of pink.

Pam and I hung back, saying nothing. As neither of us had debuted, we were not 'officially' visiting. Aunt Gene didn't even need to introduce us if she didn't want to. But she did. 'May I present my niece, Miss Nora Dearly, and her friend, Miss Pamela Roe?'

We both dipped into curtsies. Lady Allister bestowed upon us a watery smile. 'Of course. How charming. Please, sit.'

We did.

And the silence proceeded to swallow us up.

It was up to Lady Allister to lead the conversation, if she

felt like any. As usual, she didn't. Previous visits had taught my aunt that it was futile to attempt to start one, and good manners prevented Pam and me from even trying.

To save our sanity, we studied everything in the parlor, in turn. All of the fabrics were dyed shades of raspberry. The fireplace was of white marble, and large enough to roast two people, lengthwise, on a spit. Specimens from Lord Allister's taxidermy collection were in evidence, all showy birds – swans, white peacocks. I knew that part of his fortune was invested in a large exotic animal preserve and gene bank in northern Nicaragua, but it was still a shock to see how he didn't let the dead ones go to waste.

Eventually, the door opened and Michael Allister walked in.

'Ahh, Michael,' Lady Allister said. Apparently she *was* awake. 'How are you, today, son?'

Michael Allister was a sandy-haired boy of about sixteen. He was built well, but I'd never liked his face. It was too weak in the chin, too lofty in the nose. His almost comical expression of surprise faded once his eyes landed upon me, and he offered me a broad smile before addressing Lady Allister. 'Very well, Mother. I apologize for barging in. I had forgotten that it was your day to take calls.'

'Oh, no, dear, no trouble at all. In fact, why don't you take the two young ladies for a walk? Young ladies should not be inside on a lovely day such as this – or young gentlemen, for that matter.'

Aunt Gene's look told me that I had better go, and that I had better enjoy it.

Michael obediently bowed, and waited for us. Pamela bounded to her feet, while I followed at a slower pace. We exited through a side door, Pamela and I lowering the veils attached to our bonnets to keep the sun from our skin.

The Allisters' lawn was large and flat, with carefully cloned peacocks making their gallant promenades under the trees, and ducks bobbing on placid artificial ponds. It was an impressive sight.

'So.' Michael folded his hands behind his back as he walked. 'How are you finding the holidays so far?' Out of earshot of his mother his voice seemed to deepen and become firmer.

'Very nice,' Pamela said.

'Very . . . interesting,' I decided.

Michael nodded slowly and looked at me. 'You won't be attending any of the holiday parties, I take it.'

'Ah, no, no,' Pam said, despite the fact that he had been addressing me. 'We're not out yet.'

Michael flashed Pam an odd look. 'I'll be kept from them, myself,' he said, nonetheless. 'I've been thinking of arranging something for the younger set. Holiday seems destined to be dreadfully dull, otherwise.' He glanced in my direction again, and Pamela took the opportunity to scoot nearer to him.

Her eyes shot over at me. 'Oh, I was speaking to Miss Dearly yesterday about doing that very thing! It would be *splendid*. Wouldn't it be *splendid*, Miss Dearly?'

'Hmm. *Splendid*.'

Pamela seemed gratified. Turning back to Michael, she went on. 'I'd be happy to help with the planning! My father makes the *best* Christmas cake.'

Pam's father was a baker – not the best thing to remind a rich boy of, if she liked him. Michael was going to think she was trying to ingratiate herself with his family for personal gain. But I watched his face, and he didn't seem put out. Rather, he appeared to be amused, and was nodding liberally.

I sent her a look that told her that she and Michael needed to be alone. I upped my pace a bit, elevating the hem of my skirt to make it easier to walk.

The direction I headed in took me off the manicured path and onto the lawn with the animals. For lack of anything better to do, I attempted to slowly shadow a peacock. It gave forth its haunting caw when it saw me approaching, and headed in the other direction, leaving behind a long gem-colored tail feather. I stooped to pick it up. It flashed, brilliant, in the real sunlight.

'And my cousin is headed to the front lines,' I heard Michael say. They were catching up to me.

'Oh, how awful,' Pam sympathized.

'Which company?' I asked, turning about.

Michael's eyes fell upon the feather in my hand, and I held it out to him. It was technically his, after all. He shook his head, and chuckled. 'Keep it, with my compliments. Ah, a new company: 145th.'

This struck me as odd. 'Another company? Where do they keep getting them? There're only so many of us.'

'There're always grunts willing to sign up. As for the commanders – good second and third sons.' Allister shrugged.

He was right, of course. *Poor* second and third sons. Only the firstborn could inherit property. Younger sons of the elite normally joined the armed forces or went into the clergy.

Pamela tangled her fingers together under the ribbons of her purse, and regarded Michael with a sincere, gentle expression. 'I'll pray that he will return safely.'

'I will, as well,' I said.

'Ah, my thanks. That'll free me up to pray that if he does suffer hardship, he shares it with at least a score of the Punks.' Michael started down the path again. 'As if they stand any chance with this latest offensive. Filthy pigs – no morals, no religion, no thought for the future of their people. Disgusting.'

I fell into step behind him and Pam, and, for once, managed to keep my opinions to myself. There were always the rumors – that Punk people took more than one husband or wife. That their regional delicacies included such things as bugs and interestingly shaped specimens of fungi. That they performed occult ceremonies where children were sacrificed to enormous, demon-possessed machines. Codswallop, all of it.

'So, Miss Dearly,' Michael said, turning to walk backwards. Pamela watched him over her shoulder. 'You will want to help us with this party, won't you?'

Pamela's eyes grew wide as my mouth opened.

'If Miss Roe will have me,' I replied. Pam's smile was worth the indignity of Michael's self-satisfied nod.

'Ladies!' Aunt Gene called from one of the mansion's many doorways. 'It's time to be on our way.'

'Ladies,' Michael echoed her, bowing.

We said our goodbyes, and headed across the lawn. I reached for Pam's hand and whispered, 'Finally, we can talk.'

'About what?' she asked giddily.

I sighed. I'd lost her.

'We must hurry, girls,' Aunt Gene said, ushering us in the direction of the drive.

'Why?' I asked, suddenly suspicious.

'We've many other calls to make.'

'*What?*'

'Surely, niece, you understand that we are not so socially pathetic as to have only *one* house to visit.' Gene's smile was cold.

As I climbed into the carriage, I once more contemplated my fate, and how the stylus would figure into it. Shoving it violently into my nose would probably be the best way to go. If I did it hard enough, I might be able to stab myself in the brain. A proper student's suicide.

'That's bad luck, you know,' had been Aunt Gene's comment on my peacock feather. We'd just dropped the ecstatic Pamela off in town. I hadn't had a chance to get her alone all day.

I considered that fairly bad luck.

That evening found me lounging upon my father's deathbed in my nightgown, drawing the feather under my nose. The lamps were lit and I was alone again, my aunt gone off to another party. Matilda had taken a legitimate night off, and was out with her current beau.

I shut my eyes. Aunt Gene wouldn't be home until late, and I was considering getting some blankets and sleeping in the study amongst my father's things, the books and objects that *he* had treasured. Perhaps I should just get up and do it, before I fell asleep. We'd been shuttled from one house to another all day long, forced to smile and coo over annoying dogs and babies and make nicey-nice, and I was exhausted. Never again would I let that foul woman trick me into a carriage.

Grumbling to myself, I rolled off the bed and stole into the hall, where I found bedclothes in one of the large cupboards. I re-entered my father's room and threw them in a pile on his desk, so I could have both hands free to untangle the blankets and lay them out.

As I worked, I thought of Pam. I was going to have to find some way to make it up to her. I didn't want to text or call her – I wanted to do it in person. Maybe a trip to the ice-cream parlor tomorrow, far away from Aunt Gene. I needed to get her to spill, and I needed to spill *to* her. I'd grovel. I'd put every-thing right. She'd left us a happy girl, but I still felt like I needed to correct something.

Grief was one thing. Selfishness was another.

When I removed the last blanket from the desk, my eyes fell upon my father's holo projector.

Setting the blanket aside, I took a seat on the edge of the desk. I smoothed dust off the lenses with my fingertips and wiped them on his stained green ink blotter. The projector was a large one, high definition, but otherwise shaped exactly like the little brass mini projector that currently sat in my un-packed trunk upstairs. Pamela hated that thing.

How many happy hours I had spent with my father, watch-ing documentaries and war holos – especially *A Definitive History of New Victoria*. How often I had begged for the

Definitive battle scenes! Almost as often as I had begged for a reading of *The Jungle Book*.

For old times' sake, I flicked the projector on and loaded it up.

'Hello, Miss Dearly,' it said, recognizing me from my chip. 'Resuming track. 1:1 scale.'

Logically, I knew that the men that shimmered into being around me weren't real. The lamplight even diluted them, making them appear more ephemeral than usual. The good manners that my mother had drilled into me as a child, however, kept me from stepping through them. *'Don't play with the hologram, dear. It annoys other people, and spoils the illusion.'*

So I stayed out of their way as Jeremiah Reed incited them to rebellion, keeping to the edge of the virtual crowd. I shut off the lights one by one, and their coloration became more vivid.

'They'd give your jobs to *machines*, gentlemen!' Reed cried.

'Fast forward,' I said. 'Three hundred seconds.'

'Confirmed,' the female voice told me.

The holograph sped up, a swarm of lights playing over the walls of the room. With a whoosh and a sudden screaming explosion, I found myself in the middle of a battle, the Punks fighting tooth and nail against the red-coated New Victorian army for a few miles of land. I'd watched this stretch of the holo many times, and it never failed to enchant me, as disturbing as that might sound.

I tried to get out of the way as the narrator droned on about tactics and geography, but the fighting was everywhere. My feet melted through the dying; bullets flew through my chest. Eventually, I decided just to stand there in the middle of it, in the midst of all the yelling and violence. I didn't find it frightening. I found it exciting.

Even if these men had gone on to die, they had truly lived.

'Play beginning!' I cried. 'Thirty-two times speed!'

I let the ice age bury me in white. I let the lava from Yellowstone come up to my knees, let the iridescent ash that would go on to blot out the sun rain down upon my face without ever touching it. The arrows describing humanity's movements towards the Equator skimmed my waist. I'd never done anything like this before. It was amazing.

It made me forget myself, for a few moments.

'Back to mark five!'

And then bombs were going off again, and New Victorian men were marching over me. I shut my eyes to take in the tramping of their feet, the calls for maneuvers, the gunfire. I recited the narration from memory.

It was a year and two days, and I honored my father by going where we had gone together, and smiling. A little.

Faintly, over the voice of the holo's narrator, I heard the sound of shouting.

It wasn't in the recording.

My eyes popped open. I couldn't see anything at first; the light from the holograph was still surging around me. 'Stop program,' I said. The figures around me melted away, the darkness of the room suddenly overwhelming. I listened.

There was definitely something outside. Talking, the crunch of gravel.

My heart pounding, I moved stealthily over to the window, like I had the night before. The noise stopped by the time I got there.

But I'd *definitely* heard something.

I held my breath, steeling myself. I had never thought of myself as a coward, and now I had to prove it. I would look out to assure myself, just as I had the night before. Nothing there then, nothing there now. Probably just some little boys playing in the dark.

I parted the curtains.

A skeletal face peered back at me, blackened eyes rolling in sockets seemingly unsupported by flesh.

It smiled.

Its fist came sailing through the window. I screamed and reeled back. Then the entire world seemed to be exploding in on my father's study, glass showering inward as even more . . . *corpses* . . . pulled, leaped, slithered their way inside.

That's the *only* way I could describe what I was seeing.

They were men. They *looked* like men, at least – *human* – but like people who had been dead for months, *years*, in all stages of decay – flesh hanging limply off limbs, bones exposed in some places, parts missing. A few of them were wearing faded gray uniforms with various insignia on them. Needless to say, I didn't stay long enough to check their identification.

I bolted from the room, and slammed the door shut behind me. Without the master key, I couldn't lock it. Behind the door I could hear more of the things entering, laughing, talking.

'It's all right, Miss Dearly. We're not here to hurt you,' said one, quite loudly. His voice had a ticking quality to it, as if he was forcing air out past flesh that wanted to cave in. The voices of the others were low and garbled. Some weren't speaking at all, but growling and moaning.

'Our commander would be very disappointed if we took his fun away.'

I ran.

If my heart had had feet, it would have been up the staircase before the rest of me. I paused at the top of the steps for a split second, my breathing short and hot, trying to decide where to go. *Dad's room*, my brain said. *Get a gun.*

Thank you, brain.

As I turned to head down the hall, I saw them already on the staircase below me. God, they were fast. And yet not well coordinated – the faster they ran, the more they seemed to stumble from side to side. One was bypassing the rest, though, scrambling hand-over-hand up the wooden banister like some kind of crazed, rabid monkey, his eyes boring into mine. The first one I had seen. Their leader?

Don't care. Gun.

I raced down the hall and into my father's bedchamber. I locked the door and fell to my knees, feeling about underneath the bed in the dust and the dark. He had kept the keys to his gun cabinet beneath, or . . . oh, God, had someone moved them?

I could hear the things throwing themselves at the door, screeching in anger when they found it locked.

Please, please . . .

My fingers encountered jingly metal, and I drew out the keys. I groped my way over to the gun cabinet and managed to get it open. I pulled out a shotgun, if only because I knew that the shells were stored in a metal box immediately underneath it. Fumbling, trembling, I tried to load it.

They were beating down the door. They'd set up a rhythm, and were starting to shake it in the jamb.

I got the shells into the gun, and snapped it shut. I stuffed the loose pockets of my nightgown with more shells. Then, forcing a breath, I looked around. My father's bathroom was accessible from here, but there was no exit from it. Wide glass doors looked out onto my father's balcony, but I'd have to jump to the ground from there . . .

. . . or climb the trellis to the roof.

Plan in place, I moved to the balcony doors and threw them open. My father's bedroom was immediately above the study, and I could see even more of the creatures on the ground below, storming in through the windows. How many were there? Going down was not an option.

I slipped the gun's strap over my head, and started to climb the white trellis that was mounted on the side of the house. It was rife with roses, and their thorns pierced my skin and snagged my nightgown. Drops of blood beaded on my fingers.

About midway up I heard the door break, and a howl of triumph from the monsters. It wasn't long before they were out on the balcony with me. One of them caught my nightgown in its bony fists. I gasped, losing a few inches of height and one of my slippers as it yanked me down. I dared to look back, and saw the thing baring its teeth at me, or what was left of them, as it tugged me closer. Another was latched on just beneath him, curling its grey tongue over a stain on one of the trellis crossbars.

It was drinking my blood.

Horrified, I kicked out at the head of the one holding me. Surprised, it let go, and I scuttered upwards. The moment the edge of the roof was within reach of my fingertips, I started pulling myself up. The monsters growled in rage.

Rooftop reached, I turned on my hip and got off two rounds right into the thing's stomach. It fell from the trellis and banged into the iron railing of the balcony, but caught itself, and remained standing. After a moment's pause, it lunged for the trellis again.

I stared, stupefied. It should have been dead.

'Nooooora!' their leader cried out.

I reloaded my weapon and then started kicking at the trellis, trying to dislodge it. I didn't dare use my arms. But despite my best efforts, two, then three, then four of the things started climbing up toward me.

'Come on!' I wailed. Their weight and my kicking should have knocked it down. Why wasn't it falling?

It was then that I realized that their leader was already on the roof, having pulled himself up via the decorative molding on the eaves. He grinned at me. 'Don't you want to come with us? You're bound to be the most popular girl at the party.'

I leaped to my feet and leveled the gun at him, leaning into the slant of the roof. The mob beneath us swelled with more corpses, a writhing mass of crawling things reaching for me, howling for me, almost at the hem of my nightgown again. The one who had tasted my blood was particularly manic, panting like a rabid dog.

The talking one had to go, though.

Somehow I found the purchase to pull the trigger, even though my fingers were slick with sweat and blood. One round sent him staggering back, and the second blew off a good chunk of his upper arm with a splatter of black ichor. He didn't fall down. He didn't even cry out in pain.

Instead, he laughed.

'*Why won't you die?*' I yelled. It was a cry from the gut, a terrified voice not my own.

'Oh,' he replied, taking a step closer, 'I think you can guess why.'

And then I felt someone grabbing me from behind, as my eyes were blinded by the light of electric lanterns. I cried out in panic and tried to wrench myself away. I was prevented from doing so, but in turning I saw soldiers clothed in black, with cloth masks over their faces and flashing red beacons pinned on their shoulders. I heard shooting all around me, below me. One of the soldiers whipped out a powerful automatic rifle and took out the talking monster with a single shot to the head. I saw the body tumble down off the roof, and heard it land with a splash in the fountain below.

Had the cavalry arrived?

The soldier holding me pulled off his mask, and I saw those milky, blank eyes again, set in the pale face of a young man. With ever mounting horror, I realized that the departed fellow had come back for me.

The soldier standing next to him took off his mask as well, and I saw exposed cheekbones and a hollow, bony eye socket.

Oh God, oh God . . .

The one with the blind eyes smiled thinly. 'Sorry about this. Maybe next time, you'll listen to me.'

A black bag fell over my head. I screamed, smell the rising vomit on my own breath, and passed out cold.

CHAPTER FIVE

Bram

'*Move, move, move!*'

With the girl slung over my shoulder, it wasn't as easy to get *down* the side of her house as it had been to climb up it. I did my best to tuck her securely against my neck, and then used two of the rappel lines to slide down. The other members of my team waited for me to hit the ground before they hooked in and fell after.

The battle was just picking up steam. We were already winning, of course, because we had guns. Around us, enemy soldiers dropped in mid-stride, gore starbursting from their skulls. The lights in the houses nearby were rapidly going out as everyone realized what was going on and – very wisely – hit the deck.

'We should have just gone in and grabbed her to begin with,' Tom griped, as he squeezed off a shot.

'C'mon,' I said, choosing to ignore his statement of the bloody obvious. It was over. We'd been trying so hard to hide, and here we were fighting, gangland style, in the middle of the royals' capital-freaking-city.

I was going to get reamed out mercilessly when I got home.

'Vulture has landed.'

I heard the squealing of brakes as a van pulled up in front of the house, and the wet crunching sound of it taking out a couple of enemy soldiers for us. The rear doors, which declared the van a *Municipal Vehicle of the City of New London*, swung open. Metal benches had been welded along the two longest sides of the van's interior, and I hauled myself up by one of them, taking my cargo to the back before returning to help my teammates up.

The moment Tom's last foot left the ground, the van took off. He and Coalhouse got the doors shut, swaying helplessly back and forth all the while. The van held extra ammo and equipment, and these things shifted beneath nets that had been bolted to the floor.

'That was intense,' Coalhouse said, as he fingered his empty eye socket.

'Don't pick at it,' Tom said, a remnant of annoyance still in his voice.

'Tom, do not *lecture* me like I am your girlfriend. You *have* a girlfriend.'

'If you think he can lecture me, you're sadly mistaken!' the girlfriend in question said over the intercom, filling the metal cavern with her voice. She was driving. 'Hey, Bram, did you see me take those two out in front? That was *wicked*. Totally un-planned, too. I am just that awesome.'

'Yeah, Chas,' I said, distracted. We were all safe and accounted for, and my emotions were starting to settle. I tried to keep in mind the possibility that we were being pursued, but somehow that didn't seem important.

I looked to the girl. I knew that Tom and Coalhouse were looking, too.

The smell of her blood was filling the cabin.

'Brace yourselves, gentlemen,' Chas's voice sing-songed.

I knew what was coming. While the others took their seats and strapped in, I stood up and quickly hauled myself hand-over-hand down the length of the van. As we crashed through the gates of the Elysian Fields guardhouse, I tumbled toward the girl and pulled her into my arms to absorb the impact.

She made a little sound, like a gasp. I froze.

Was she conscious?

The sound of the van's engine roaring in my ears, I lifted a hand from her side to the edge of the black bag Tom'd thrown over her head. I truly hadn't wanted to have to do it this way. Not that I'd really been convinced that invoking the name of her father and asking nicely would get her to come with me.

But part of me had hoped.

When I'd splashed my way back from the attempt at a non-invasive extraction, tired and terrified and very, very angry with myself, the others had teased me about not being able to pick up women. Well, I had her now. She was light in my arms, and so warm it almost burned.

I pulled off the hood, bracing myself for a scream.

She was still out.

I pushed her hair out of her face and wiped off her mouth with my sleeve.

'Wow, she's cute.'

I lifted my eyes and glared at Coalhouse. 'Inappropriate.'

She wasn't cute. She was beautiful.

Dearly's daughter was so pale and small, it was hard not to compare her to a muslin rag doll. Her cheeks were still flushed from the fight, her lips red. This was only the second time I'd seen her in color, her image familiar from silvery daguerreotypes and black and white monitors, where her hair might have been any shade of dark.

I stood and carried her to one of the benches, using the straps to secure her to it. We needed to get her cleaned up, before someone started calling dibs. 'You got the first aid kit, Coalhouse?' I asked. My voice was gruff with faked professionalism, I could hear it.

'Uh, yeah. Hold on.'

One puffy sleeve of her nightgown had slipped down, revealing a white shoulder. As Coalhouse retrieved the kit from beneath the netting and stumbled over to me, I tugged it up and smoothed it over her skin.

All the while I rattled off a long list of curses in the soundproofed room of my mind.

Twenty minutes later the van rocked to a stop. Tom shouldered his gun and slowly opened one of the van doors, viewing our surroundings through his sights. 'I don't see anyone.'

'I got nothing,' Chas said, her voice low on the intercom. 'Buzzard is thirty minutes on our tail. They'll get the next ship out.'

I freed the girl and picked her up again. This time I cradled her in my arms, bridal style. 'OK, we do this fast. Right, guys?' My teammates nodded.

Tom kicked the second van door open, and out we marched. We hustled past the docks and boat slips, past the metal-shingled guardhouses. We were at the New London port – which, even for this time of night, was strangely empty. The part of my brain still capable of processing irony told me that everyone was probably inside watching news reports of the 'kidnapping' that we were still performing, right beneath their noses.

One of the two ironclads we'd commandeered for this mission, the *N.V.S. Christine*, was waiting for us at the very end of the port, as far as possible from the lights of the city. We stomped up the gangplank, which was retracted immediately after us. I heard shouted orders and the sound of clanking machinery as the crew prepared to pull out. We wouldn't be on the water long – just a quick trip down to Colombia. We'd be on a truck to base in another hour, tops.

I carried the girl into the body of the ship, down to B Level, where the medical teams were already assembled. Coalhouse had injected her with a sedative in the van, as instructed. I wasn't afraid that she'd wake up, now, and so I gripped her a little more securely than I'd been willing to before.

Everything was rushing, the sound of feet on metal grating, computers booting up. The head of the meds in Dr

Dearly's absence, Dr Horatio Salvez, stood in the midst of it all, pointing here and there and occasionally pausing a moment to absorb a screen full of information proffered by a lackey. White-coated technicians, all of them living, scrambled to follow his directions. A few were still busy erecting the little screened rooms they'd use to start fixing us up.

'There they are!' I heard one of them shout. She sounded relieved.

'Oh, goody,' Chas whispered. 'I hate going to the doctor. I'd rather be back underground in the water playing Ophelia,'

'What about mold,' Tom reminded her. 'Fuzziness on a girl is never attractive.'

'Oh, now that's just *gross*.'

Squabbling as they went, Chas and the others were pulled off for their post-mission checkups. We'd been hiding in the waterlogged second level of the Elysian Fields for two days, which was a rather long time for people like us to go without medical care. Our handlers had probably been freaking out.

As for myself, I headed toward Salvez. The moment he saw what I was carrying, he shooed a petitioner away and came over. 'Oh, poor Miss Dearly,' he sighed. He reached out and lightly touched her cheek.

I was surprised by the growl that wanted to well up in my throat when he did this, and fought it down. I told myself that it was stress, that it was not my illness's way of saying, *'Get your own takeout.'*

'Here,' I said, miming the motion of handing her over. I needed to get away from her. 'Take her.'

Salvez stepped back, and pointed toward a gurney. 'Put her there, for now.'

I did. The warmth of her body lingered in my hands.

'Go with Dr Evola, he'll see to you.' He bent over the girl and pushed up one of her eyelids to check something. 'We should make landfall soon. I believe we are, as the old saying goes, hauling ass.'

Charles Evola must have heard Salvez say his name, because he was waiting for me. He waved and gestured for me to join him behind a nearby screen, pointing out a tangle of thick power cords on the floor before I could trip over them.

'Tough few days?' he asked me.

'Yeah,' I said. *Understatement.*

I unbuttoned my jacket, unhooked my holsters, unsnapped my bulletproof vest, and pulled my black T-shirt off. I knew the drill. I took a seat, and remained still as a stone as the tech hooked several sensors up to my scarred, stitched, stapled, superglued skin.

'Too bad it's not over yet.' Charles was a young, tan man with golden hair and a brass-rimmed monocle snuggled beneath his left brow. He peered at the screens arrayed around us as they flashed a series of gray and emerald green symbols. He then punched a sequence of characters into a chunky metal keyboard, and a chugging sound commenced. Thirty seconds later a holographic image of my internals sprang up from a screen on a nearby crash cart.

'No new wounds. Nice going, there. A little muscle tearing, but we'll knit that up at your next tightening . . . not about to cut you open *here*.' He studied the image for a few seconds more, and murmured, 'You know, of all our boys, I swear you have the best joints. You have the joints of a thirty-year-old. A *living* thirty-year-old.'

'Gee, thanks.'

'Never let it be said that I don't give compliments.' Charles shut the image off and opened the top drawer of the crash cart. Several prepared syringes, of the large and scary-looking variety, were arranged there. 'OK, then, time for drinks!'

I lifted my arm without having to be ordered to. I have a valve permanently installed in my forearm for the purpose of getting my meds, and another one on my inner thigh for drainage. Charles delivered the stuff with an equal lack of fanfare, and with the dexterity of someone who's performed the same operation thousands of times before.

My gaze drifted toward the equipment table as Charles worked. Everything there was crafted of shiny stainless steel, and I couldn't help but catch my own reflection several times over. I regarded it more morosely than usual. My skin is almost marble white, incredibly pale – not just sunless, but bloodless – and sits tight against the muscles of my face. My eyes *were* blue, but are clouded over now. I still have my hair, which is brown and unremarkable, but hey, some guys lose it when they die. I suppose I should count my blessings.

'Got the girl, then, huh?' Charles asked.

'What?'

He grinned. 'Dearly the younger.'

'Oh. Yeah.'

'Little advice? Let her hear you before you let her see you. Might help.'

'It's a little too late for that.'

'She saw you?'

'She was on the roof, shooting at the Grays.'

Charles whistled. 'Nice. Girl has spunk.' He pushed the plunger on the last syringe, and I watched its pale blue contents swell the veins in my arm. When he withdrew the syringe the tiny motor in my valve kicked on, pumping the stuff further into my body.

I pushed myself to my feet and flexed my wrist. 'Yeah.'

Dr Salvez's head poked through the curtain. 'Wolfe's already on the horn upstairs. I can tell him that you're still being tuned up . . . ?'

Time to face the music. 'No. I'm done.' Occasionally, being a surprisingly *healthy* dead guy can come back to bite you.

'And so it begins,' Charles said, with sympathy, as he handed me my shirt.

I put it back on and stretched my arms. Indeed.

It took me all of five minutes to walk to my own funeral. The briefing room was on A Level, a bare-bones area with a wall-sized screen on the starboard side. Company Commander James Wolfe's ruddy, bearded face was currently blown up upon it. For the last few days he'd been wearing the sort of expression a martial arts master does while plowing his fist through a few layers of brick.

I was the only one in the room. I paused just inside the doorway in salute. 'Captain.'

'Griswold, you will explain to me what just happened,' Wolfe demanded, without preamble. His heavy ginger brow and hooked nose appeared more menacing than usual – wherever he was broadcasting from, it was dimly lit. His voice boomed at me from the surrounding speakers, although, to be honest, he produced the same effect in person. As he hadn't told me to be at ease, I lowered my arm and maintained my stiff posture. 'Sir, with all due respect, the situation was not as simple as we were led to believe.'

On the screen, Captain Wolfe pinched the bridge of his nose. 'Did I ask for *excuses*? No, I did not.'

I made myself meet his eyes, and began. 'We met up with the municipal vans south of town two days ago, as arranged. No complications there. We arrived in the Elysian Fields around midnight that night, and were smuggled into the second level. Seeing as the living had left the area for the night, I ordered a few men to canvas it and make sure we were secure. And that's when we found that we *weren't*. The enemy was already there. They'd set up shop in one of the pre-fab mansions. At least a hundred of them. Let me remind you that I had fifty men.'

Wolfe's hand clenched. 'What did you do?'

'I ordered the scouts to return. The last thing I wanted was a *war* down there. We didn't even know if all the Grays were in that house, and we couldn't confirm whether or not they had weapons. Raiding or torching the place might have driven their scouts, maybe even another *company* of them somewhere, into immediate action. They might've gone after the girl. Or the living on the first level.'

'You *idiot*,' Wolfe growled.

'Your opinion is respectfully noted.' I continued. 'I did send one scout up to the first level to find Miss Dearly's house and keep an eye on it. He saw no sign that she was there. And so, we waited. The next day the second level flooded . . . I can't tell you whether the Grays did it, or whether it was just an accident. The living showed up to rescue their machinery, and we retreated as far as possible from the gatehouse. We couldn't exactly launch an attack with hundreds of city workers down there – it was tough enough staying ahead of them so that we weren't spotted. That night our guards did take out a few Grays in hand-to-hand . . . and so we learned that they were aware of our presence, too.'

'Why didn't you strike *back*?' Wolfe asked, enunciating each word loudly and slowly, like an obnoxious tourist.

'*Because*,' I repeated, 'the last thing we needed was a zombie battle playing out right where hundreds of living people could watch it. There're already outbreaks leaking onto the news! Thankfully someone in the military is spinning them as normal Punk attacks.' I looked at the scuffed black flooring. 'I went up myself that day to try and intercept her. Snuck out.'

'And how did that go?' Wolfe asked, voice dripping with sarcasm.

'She didn't buy it.'

'No, I wouldn't think so,' Wolfe spat out.

I dug my fingernails into my thigh, slowly, to keep myself from speaking faster than my brain could work. 'She spent the next day up top. We planned to go in and get her tonight. We were on our way there when the scout I'd left at her house radioed to tell us that the Grays had decided on the same thing. My team got the girl out of there; the others stayed behind for cleanup. So, in the end, you got your fight, Captain.'

'Griswold, shut up.'

I did so, and watched Wolfe sliding his hand up and down his face in an attempt to calm himself. Yeah, I'd screwed up in letting the fight get to the first level of the complex – but I'd been attempting to avoid one completely. Wolfe seemed to think that we should have gone in with guns blazing, which would have been a mind-bogglingly stupid thing to do.

A shaft of light slipped into the room, fading a corner of Wolfe's image. I glanced behind me. My teammates entered, each making his or her salute before wordlessly falling back. Chas sent me a small, encouraging smile.

'The girl is on the ship?' Wolfe asked, hand still over his eyes. He didn't acknowledge the arrival of the others.

'Of course, sir,' I said. 'We're en route to Z Beta Base. ETA about two hours.'

Wolfe nodded, and let his hand fall. 'From now on, you will follow my orders exactly. If I do not specifically *tell you* to do something, it will not occur to your rotting mind to do *anything*. Any mission I send you on will include detailed instructions. You will follow these, and if there is time left over you will retreat to a nearby wall and do your best broom impression, waiting for further orders from a *living* person, like the *tool* you are. Is that clear? This goes for *all of you!*'

I didn't look back at my friends. I was afraid I'd get too angry. 'Yes, sir.'

'Excellent. Now, take the girl to Z Beta, and barricade her in her father's quarters. *Only* the living are to speak to her, and they are to tell her *nothing* of importance until I arrive there. Keep her fed, safe, and as ignorant as she is now. Do you understand?'

'Understood, sir.'

'Good. You can expect me back in thirty-six hours. I'm going to be wasting *my* time combing the back of beyond, looking for her father. I will be in touch with Dr Elpinoy, Griswold.'

I saluted again, and the screen went dark. Lamps automatically lit around the rim of the riveted metal ceiling, filling the room with a gentle glow. I still didn't turn around, although I let my spine soften. I hated having to submit to Wolfe like that, especially with other people watching.

'You know he's full of crap, right?' Chas spoke up.

'Grade A, gourmet crap,' Coalhouse agreed.

I shook my head. 'I know. But we have to do what he says. At least until we find the doctor.'

'No.'

I turned around to look at Chas. She fixed me with her black eyes. Chas – no last name, or so she claims, seeing as 'Chastity' is bad enough – is tall for a girl, of Colombian heritage, with shaggy bleached blonde hair and skin that was once the color of caramel, but which now has a faint cast of blue to it. The front part of her jaw was beat up pretty bad in battle about a year ago, and the techs opted to cut out the damaged teeth and bone and replace them with a metal plate. Since then she's scratched various designs into it, including a winding, thorny rose. 'We can't do that to his daughter, Bram. This isn't her fault. She deserves to know what's happening.'

'As much as I agree with you, Chas,' I said, 'at this point, it'd be insubordination.'

Chas ran a finger teasingly along the neckline of her T-shirt. 'Ooh, long word. Say it again. I don't know what it means, but it sounds so *dirty*.' I couldn't help but laugh. I held it back as best I could, crossing my arms over my chest.

Tom rolled his neck. Tom's short – only about 5′4″ – but strong. He carried heavy personal cannon in the Punk army, and still has the arms to prove it. He's missing his nose, and the area over it's been grafted with skin from his thigh, so as not to leave a gaping, offensive hole. It makes him look kind of like a shark, especially with his dark eyes and bald head. 'Yeah. We gotta tell her. Otherwise, she's gonna lose her mind, and then we'll get in trouble for *that*.'

'And with Wolfe gone, you're the highest ranked on base,' Coalhouse said. He's of African descent, his thick body giving him a hardy appearance that makes his rotten face all the more disturbing to look at. The right side of his face, the side missing the eye, is bonier than the other, and his curly brown hair is patchy in places. 'You're the boss. I mean, screw what he said about following orders. Situations *change*. You know that, and you change with 'em. We've got your back.'

'For perhaps the first time in recorded history, Coalhouse and I agree on something,' Tom said. 'But if the sky starts crying fire, just for the record? I'm leaving you losers to get wasted.'

I couldn't help but smile a little. Tonight, their faith meant a lot. 'So, what do we do with her?' I asked. 'I'm open to ideas. I'm not saying I'm going to *use* them, but I'm open to them.'

'Your room,' Tom said, pointing at me.

On the list of ideas I'd expected to hear, that ranked pretty low. 'What? Why *mine*?'

'Because of your contingency plan.'

I immediately understood what Tom was getting at – and really, when I thought about it, it was a far better idea than Wolfe's. Far safer for the girl. *Oh, sweet, sweet justification.* 'OK. My room, then. We'll let her wake up, get her bearings. Let her feel a little bit in control.'

'Exactly,' Chas said, as she reached into the pockets of her cargo pants and came up with a cigarette and a match. 'That's what I'm talking about.'

I gestured to myself. 'And, in the meantime, what am I supposed to do – go camping?'

'You won't be out on the streets too long,' Tom said, with a slow grin. 'Man, I just keep seeing her up there, in that fancy dress, shooting at the bloody things. That . . . was beautiful. Truly, so beautiful that the existence of a loving, *awesome* god can be its only explanation. I have found religion, my friends.'

'She's still a royal,' I pointed out, in a half-hearted attempt to convince myself. 'You know how their girls are. No offense, Chas.'

'Why would I take offense at that? I *know* I'm not one of them,' she snorted as she struck the match on her chin plate.

'Mark my words,' Tom said, unswayed. 'In an hour she

71

wakes up, slams back a fifth of somethin', and asks for a uniform.'

'Huh. Maybe I should date *her*,' Chas said, with mocking thoughtfulness.

I sighed, and sought solace in my mind. OK. I'd completely disobey Captain Wolfe and court my own court martial. Why not? I'd already tasted humiliation and failure. Not like the week could get much worse. Besides, for thirty-five hours and forty-five minutes, he couldn't touch me.

That aside, I had two of those hours to myself. Two hours in which I could forget the trouble to come and ignore the uneasy feeling that I was making the wrong decision. Two hours in which I wouldn't have to touch her, wouldn't have to look at her.

Ten minutes later I was at Miss Dearly's side, staring down at her. They'd cleaned her up, and were keeping her behind a partition in the area where the living doctors and techs were working. Without having to ask, I knew that they had chosen this area for a reason.

No dead people on assignment.

Within my body, another battle raged. I ignored it – the sharpness of my senses, the prickling in my skin. I kept my hands to myself.

Silhouettes against the cloth partitions around me told me that I wasn't as alone with her as I felt. I remained silent by her side, listening to her measured breathing and the sounds of the meds at work within the hull of the ship.

I could think of a lot of things I'd have liked to say to her, though. I made plenty of dead man's promises to her in my mind, as the boys shoveled coal beneath us and the boat made like a ghost for friendlier shores.

CHAPTER SIX

Wolfe

I slowly pressed the button on the portable com unit that would terminate the call with Griswold, and did my level best to keep from leaping up, ripping the handlebars off my motorcycle, and using them as a sledgehammer on the nearest crushable object.

I would derive a deep, personal satisfaction from beheading that boy, someday.

I tucked the com unit away in my coat, shifting slightly in my seat. The bike was a skeletal construction of pipes and exposed gears, designed to be broken down for storage. It wasn't meant for someone of my size, and I'd be lucky to get back to my men before it collapsed beneath me. The last thing I felt like doing was taking a stroll in the dark with zombies on every side of me. I still had so much to do, and so little time to do it in.

I continued to sit there, though, surrounded by night-shrouded trees, the buzzing of insects and the distant croaking of frogs keeping me company. Clouds of mosquitoes drifted in and out of the bright yellow light of the electric lantern I'd strapped to the front of the bike back at camp. I found the sight simultaneously compelling and creepy. I could feel the mosquitoes in my beard, at the edges of my uniform – a hundred wriggling, hungry things. They wouldn't go after the dead. I was the only living human for miles.

This thought didn't exactly put me at ease.

Round one of the game was over. I was still angry. I was still confused – desperately confused. I was still praying without thinking about it, my body tensing and canting forward, as if it was instinctively attempting to bow to some icon that might grant me my every wish.

But the worst of it was over. For a second, I could breathe easily.

A rapid volley of explosions shook me out of my impromptu moment of peace.

I gunned the engine and took off toward the east.

After half a mile or so, the trees began to thin out. I swerved to a stop. This time our battlefield had been the site of an ancient town, likely abandoned during the Settlement Wars. No buildings remained; only the odd protrusion, here and there, of an old wall from the mossy ground, or the over-grown hump of a fallen house. Vines snaked over everything.

A few of the bombs that had just gone off had sparked small, smoldering fires in the undergrowth. By their light I could vaguely make out a phalanx of my troops, clad in black, red beacons flashing. They were systematically taking out the last of the enemy zombies we'd been sent to dispatch – the crawlers that always seem to spontaneously show up at the scene of a fight, like maggots on meat. Crawlers are the worst. Blind, worm-like zombies, rotten and often limbless creatures that writhe their way impatiently across the ground, waiting to bump into something edible.

As I swung myself off the motorcycle, I popped open the holster at my waist and drew out my pistol. I put a few of the crawlers out of their misery with headshots as I picked my way across the field toward my men.

One of the grunts, Private Franco, saw me first. He put his weapon away before approaching me. He was a dead man of unremarkable build, his face hidden by the regulation black mask. 'Sir, permission to speak, sir!'

'Talk.' I shot another crawler, black blood and semi-liquefied brain matter spraying the grass. 'What's going on?'

'I think this is definitely the group of enemy zombies we were sent to get, sir. Some of the healthier ones 'ave taken for the trees, and after we clean up 'ere, we'll go after 'em.' He ran a hand under his nose. I found myself idly wondering if zombies ever itched. 'They'll do a run with the flamethrowers in a few.'

'Any idea where this group came from?'

'Naw, but there's a *big* ol' walker in the clearing over yonder. Betcha five to one, these're Punks, these ones. Probably ambushed by a wild pack.'

Franco flicked open a pocket on his utility vest and drew out a small night vision telescope. I accepted it, removing the lens cap as he told me where to look. When I did, I saw the top of the walking tank he'd mentioned, two of its legs and part of its body rising above the tree line a few yards off. He was right – it was enormous. No wonder the zombies had attacked. That thing would have attracted attention for miles.

I handed him back the telescope. 'In the morning, have some men work on that thing and get it back to base. I'm heading back to camp. Do your job, and make sure I don't have to shout at you later. My list of people to shout at is long enough as it is.'

'Sir!'

I returned to my bike and took off again, this time headed slightly northwest. My men stepped back as I drove past, pointing their weapons at the sky and saluting. I didn't pay them much attention.

I did run over one of the dead zombies on the ground, though, for good measure.

Our camp wasn't meant to be anything more than a pit stop. Aside from the three equipment trucks and the communications van, there was my tent and a long, communal tent for the dead. Those zombies not currently assigned to the front lines were feigning sleep, waiting to relieve their fellow soldiers at sunrise. A few were hanging about outside, and stood to salute me as I walked past. If they'd been human soldiers I might've stopped to talk with them, but dead men have no morale to encourage, and dead men can't be loyal, and therefore there'd be no point to it.

'You're out after hours,' I growled, without looking at them. 'Get inside.'

'Sir,' one said, as he tapped out his pipe.

Waste of perfectly good tobacco, that. Waste of time, waste of effort, waste of resources, waste of words. The dead are such a waste.

I marched over to the communications van, wrenching aside the mosquito netting they'd draped over the opening for me. There were three zombies seated within, monitoring plastic-edged screens full of glowing symbols and words. They stood, and I waved them down before they could salute.

'Report,' I said, looking at Ben, the zombie I'd left in charge. He was a modestly built man with ashen black skin.

'Good news, sir,' he said, smiling widely. He was missing his upper lip, the teeth beneath exposed, which only made his smile more Cheshire-like and gruesome. 'Dr Dearly's plane did crash. We were able to get a hit on his coordinates.'

I released a short breath. *Finally.* I pulled my digidiary out of my belt and handed it to him. 'Good. Give 'em to me.'

Ben nodded, and grabbed a stylus. 'Orders, sir?' he asked as he wrote.

'What do you think? Let's pretend you can think for a minute.'

He shut my diary and returned it. 'Well, sir, I assume we're to continue monitoring the airwaves for more rogue transmissions from the leader of the Grays.'

I looked at the coordinates. I resisted the urge to punch the air, and instead focused on increasing the level of annoyance in my voice. 'No. No, no, no. This is why *I* do the thinking. This is why *I* had to come and take over *your* company, before someone else got seriously hurt.' I looked down at the dead man, who regarded me with that heavy, unintelligent look so many of them have. 'Our objective right now is to locate the doctor. After you guys clean up here, you're going after him. I'm traveling with you for another day. Then I'll return to base on my own.'

'Sir.' Ben saluted.

I stalked out of the van, diary in my hand. It felt like a passport to freedom. The moron couldn't have landed in a better spot.

I turned on the little lantern suspended from my belt and almost ran to my tent. Once there, I felt my way through the semi-darkness to the trunk that sat at the foot of my cot. Inside was a warped, battered suitcase filled with an ancient assortment of radio equipment.

My heart was hammering. I slapped at a mosquito that had managed to get inside my collar and unbuttoned my waistcoat, reaching into the long pocket sewn in there. I drew out another piece of paper. Written upon it was a long series of numbers. Anyone would have mistaken it for a list of betting odds, or perhaps merely dismissed it as ancient, out of hand, it being non-digital.

All in all, I'd come out ahead that night.

Onward.

Chapter Seven

Nora

I kept telling God that if He got me out of this I would never take His name in vain again, ever, and I would go to church every Sunday like the good, good girl I was.

And then I would find myself thinking, *Oh, God*, again, as I made my way over to the toilet to be sick. This time, it was because my brain had just registered the fact that my hands were carefully bandaged.

It had really happened.

And the dead people had patched me up after it happened. *Oh, God*.

They were dead. They were freaking dead. They were rotting and horrible and skulls and bare teeth and . . . dead. I kept closing my eyes and seeing their bones, their chalky flesh.

Moving.

I hauled myself back onto the narrow bed and folded my arms around my knees. I had woken up a few hours ago in a small, windowless room. There was a thin blue carpet on the floor, a desk with books neatly stacked on it, the bed, a tiny bathroom, and not much else. My nightgown was stained and torn, but still on me. They hadn't disrobed me, at least.

There was a teddy bear with wooden button eyes at my side, so worn that his stuffing was on the verge of falling out.

Were dead people afraid of the dark too?

I could hear them out in the hallway.

'Oh my gosh, guys. If she wasn't a pretty girl you would not all be hanging around out here.'

'Shut up, Chas.'

They'd been there for the past hour or so. Three of them – two males and a female. The female's voice was husky, and yet strangely perky. The two male voices were guttural baritones, though one sounded decidedly crankier than the other.

'Seriously, let me talk to her when she wakes up. Girl to girl.'

'No offense, Chas, but you'd scare the crap out of her.'

'Want to say that to my face, Coalhouse?'

'What's left of it.'

'This was not part of the agreement!' said a mature male voice I hadn't heard before. 'Outside! I mean it, or the deal is over!'

'Relax, Elpinoy. She's still out cold.'

'Or body temperature, as the case may be.'

'*Silence! Go! Out!*'

There were sighs and protests, but slowly the other voices faded away. 'Miss Dearly?' The older voice was at the door.

I didn't respond.

'Miss Dearly, if you are awake, I just wanted to let you know that you are safe here. We'd . . . prefer it if you didn't leave the room, but we will have breakfast for you in the morning.' There was a pause, and then the voice informed someone else, 'Er, better wrap up and go see if you can find some *actual* food for her. Really nice things, I mean. Try Alpha Base first, only go to town if you have to. Don't use credit, there should be money in the tin in my office.'

'Sir.'

'And clothes, we'll bring you some clothes. Dr Chase must have something. Ah, what else? I suppose that's it. At any rate, please do not be afraid.'

Yeah, right.

'I'm alive, by the way. My name is Dr Richard Elpinoy.'

My eyes opened. *Alive?*

I was across the room in half a second. The man gave a startled cry when I yanked the door open. He was a portly, dark-skinned fellow with white hair, his frame tightly wrapped in brown tweed. 'Miss Dearly!'

'Alive?' I rasped out. 'The others really are *dead*, then?'

He paused, and then timidly allowed, 'Well, the preferred term is "undead".'

I slammed the door shut with a whimper, and closed my eyes.

'But they mean you no harm!' he was quick to continue. 'I swear this to you. The ones who'd come for you, yes, but—'

'They're the bad guys.' It was the voice of the young man with the blind eyes.

My stomach went cold as I realized – although that hadn't been my first impression upon seeing him – that he was probably dead too.

And he'd *touched* me.

'Go away!' I found myself yelling. 'Dr Elpinoy, make him go away!'

'Um, you're in my room . . .'

'Bram, *please*. Oh, I knew this was a foolish idea . . .'

'Bram, if that's your name, *please go away*!' I didn't want to deal with anything that was not strictly alive and breathing, because I was pretty sure that I was departing my ever-loving mind.

'Look,' Bram said, exasperated. 'We put you in my room because of the door. Have you even looked at it?'

I opened my eyes. It was studded with a variety of locks.

'Ten,' he said, as if he could see what I was seeing. 'Fasten them all up, if you're scared. None of them extend out here, so it's not like we have the keys or anything.'

I quickly did so, thrusting bars and setting chains. I stepped away from the door, instinctively expecting him to try and test it. He didn't.

We were all quiet for a few moments, before I broke the silence by saying, in my best sweet upper-crust-girls'-school voice, 'I am sure that all of you are really just suffering from some horrible disease, and that I should feel nothing but pity for you. If you let me go, I will organize a charity function that you will not believe. It will be, as our ancestors used to say, *epic*.'

There was some furious whispering before Bram responded with, 'Ah, thank you, Miss, but we're already dead.'

I bit my lip. I was starting to crumble.

'And we can't just let you go. If we do, the others will come after you again. You don't understand . . .'

At that I tuned him out, returned to the bed, and allowed myself to fall to pieces.

'Little one, I was so gloomy,
Felt that life sure would undo me,
Till, one day, you happened to me,
My little one.

'Little one, no controversy,
You're my downfall, you're my Circe.
I'm a good guy, show me mercy,
My little one.'

The second time I awoke it was to the voice of Bing Crosby, an old singer I remembered from a holo in history class.

I wondered if there was a crazy person's license you had to apply for, some seminar you had to attend, or if you could just walk out of the house one day and get started.

I sat up and rubbed at my sore eyes. The room was the same. The only thing that was different was the music – and a piece of paper lying on the floor near the door.

Slipping from the bed, I padded over and picked up the note. Before unfolding it, I paused to listen. I could hear the scratchy sound of a pre-digital recording being played, but there was also someone singing along, voice quiet. It was Bram. He must have been appointed guard duty or something.

The note was from him.

Miss Dearly: I'll be outside, if you don't want to open the door. But when you're ready, I'd like to play a game with you. Ask me any question you like, and I'll answer truthfully. If the answer makes you feel a little safer, reward me by undoing one of the locks. I play to get my room back, you play for the confidence to be able to leave it.

Oh, by the way: could you wind my alarm clock?

– Captain Abraham Griswold

The music switched over to 'Pennies From Heaven'. Bram sang on without missing a beat. He was kind of good.

I really didn't want to think about the fact that the dead guy had a nice voice.

'You like this music?' I asked, hoping he would turn it off.

There was a pause, before he asked, 'Is that your first question?'

'Sure.' I was a little slap happy, at this point. I was cried out, I was tired, my hands hurt, and I was beginning to believe that this was all one big wicked hallucination.

'Yes. The world'll never have anyone like Bing Crosby again, or Fred Astaire, or Johnny Mathis. If anyone should have had life after death, it was them. But mostly I sing along to keep my vocal cords stretched out. It's the quiet sorts who end up grunting and groaning.'

He shut off the music, and the silence loomed large. I answered it by undoing one of the chain locks. He'd gotten that one for free; now, I supposed, I had leave to ask some meatier questions. I cut to the chase. 'If you're dead, how is it that we are having this conversation right now?'

I could hear his clothes rustling as he physically settled in for that answer. I slowly sat down on the floor, myself.

'It's caused by an illness. Your father called it the Lazarus

Syndrome, which is what most of us prefer. Little more dignified than some names I've heard. Some call it the Z.'

My brow knit in confusion. 'You mean . . . my father discovered it?'

'Named it, at least.' Bram sighed, and said, 'Give me a moment, this is complicated.'

I let him collect his thoughts, my stomach churning again at the idea that my father could have had anything to do with all of this.

He began.

'I guess the first case happened about eight years ago, now.' Bram's voice was slow and rough, the way it had been outside my house, under the gas lamps of the Fields. 'It started out normally enough. Punks got too close to the Border, royals . . . er, *Victorians* sent them packing. It was close fighting, hand-to-hand. I guess during debriefing the soldiers said that some of the Punks'd been particularly vicious, biting and clawing, but it's not like violence is considered out of the ordinary during a battle.

'One soldier'd been chewed up real good, though. He was rushed to the field hospital. By all accounts, he was cheerful through it all, a good trooper . . . but some sort of blazingly fast infection appeared to set in. Your dad was traveling with his unit at the time, so they called him in. He did all he could, but the soldier died in terrible pain just a few hours later.

'Five minutes after the official time of death, as your father was turning off the vitals monitor and preparing to draw the sheet over him, the soldier sat up. He was uncoordinated, convulsing, and obviously suffering from some sort of brain damage. How severe, permanent or not, Dr Dearly couldn't say. But hey, the guy was alive!

'As your father and all the staff gathered around to witness this miracle, relieved, amazed . . . he decided to make a meal out of your father's arm.'

I covered my mouth with my hand, willing myself not to

be sick. All I could think of was the monster hooked on the trellis below me, savoring my blood.

'He bit three different staff members as they tried to subdue him. He seemed to lose his mind, just go nuts – like a berserker. Do you know what a berserker is? A soldier who just goes completely blind with rage and power and adrenaline and lashes out at anything you put in front of him, heedless of his own safety? That's what it was like. They hit him, even got a tranq in him at one point, but he wouldn't go down. Eventually they got smart, and they shot him. Of course, it wasn't till they shot him in the head that *that* worked, either. Took out both his knees and one of his arms, and he was still crawling towards them, until they got the head.

'Within eight hours, the three staff members who'd been bitten were dead – and then, alive. Dr Dearly, thank goodness, is an observant man, and he shot them all the moment they started twitching again. Which varied. One sat right back up, one took a couple of minutes.'

'What about his bite?' I asked, wrapping my arms around my shoulders. I was suddenly cold. I pressed my lips together so hard that it hurt.

Bram ignored my question. 'The Victorians,' he continued, 'realized that this wasn't something that should be ignored. The Department of Military Health was assigned the task of finding out what was causing it, and your father demanded to be included on the team. Ten months later, he managed to identify and isolate the agent that he believed to be the cause. The Prime Minister came down to get a personal glimpse of this achievement . . .'

'And that's when the Punks attacked again, and Dad saved him?' My brain made the connection without telling me, the words flying out of my mouth.

'Right.'

I tried to force my rapid thoughts to slow down. I had a million questions, but I knew that if I got a million answers all at once, I'd go crazy. "OK. I get the Lazarus reference, but why "the Z"?'

'Well, because what we're enduring seems awfully similar to ancient descriptions of creatures known as zombies.' My silence was the equivalent of a blank look. Bram asked, 'You've heard of zombies, right?'

'No, but my father was big into mythology and stories.' I thought longingly of the figures carved into the ceilings of our house, the carefully chosen paintings.

'The living dead? Walking dead?'

I was quiet again for a moment, before trying, 'OK?'

Bram sighed. 'Moving on. Your dad convinced the PM, after being offered all those cushy positions, to make him head of the DoMH – we call it the Doom, around here – and let him research it. Said if he was Surgeon General, or something like that, he'd be under too much political scrutiny. PM agreed that the public did *not* need to know about it. With any luck they'd find a cure before the whole thing blew open.

'Meanwhile, even the *Punks* were starting to get freaked out. Whatever it was, it wasn't something they knew anything about. The public will never be told about this, either, but there are areas along the Border where the royals and Punks are now banded together in an effort to control the monsters. Little truces, all over the place.'

I stared at the door without seeing it. *What?* 'That's not true. I saw on the news that the Punks are . . .' I trailed off as I realized *what* they were. They weren't angry.

They were scared.

Or sick.

Oh, God.

'Well, most Punks think that the roy . . . *Victorians*, sorry, engineered the Lazarus to kill them off, and that's why they're suddenly fighting back so violently, yeah. But not all of them. Some are united in fighting the evil dead. Have been for about . . . five years, now. It's not a wide-ranging truce, and it's pretty uneasy at times, but . . . there's a bigger threat out there. One that has to be kept under wraps. Can you imagine how the people on both sides'd freak out if they knew? The panic?'

I didn't know whether to laugh or cry.

'Anyway, the sickness kick-starts the brain, reanimates the body after death. I could go into more detail, but you know, we have all these great visual aids out here, which would really help me out . . .'

'Nice try.'

I heard him chuckle. I willed myself not to like the sound. And I undid one of the locks.

I lowered my hand slowly to my lap, and leaned my head back against the wall. 'How can I be convinced that you're a "good guy", then? You're talking about corpses that apparently like to . . . eat people?' I hoped he wouldn't confirm that.

'Yeah, we seem to be naturally cannibalistic,' he said, so casually that it chilled me to the bone. 'But that's what I meant, when I told you that your father saved my life. In his research, he recognized that some of us were coming back more . . . intact, than others. Memories, personality. Some of the new undead his men encountered seemed to be wandering, lost, overwhelmed – not necessarily looking for their next meal or anything. And so his mission became . . . well, in the absence of a cure, helping us to deal with our illness.'

I felt as if someone had thonked a brick between my eyes. Suddenly, it made perfect sense. My father had seen monsters come true, an old tale sprung to life – moving, thirsting before his eyes. It would have been the same had it been a dragon he had discovered. He would have tried to tame it.

'It's like . . . look, as a living human being, you have things you need. You need food, water. If you don't have these things, no matter how civilized you might think you are, you'll regress. You'll go insane without them. You'll kill others, trick others for them. It's simple animal instinct. It's hard to remember how to be nice when you are in agonizing pain from hunger.

'Well, I have things I need too. I instinctively crave fluids, because I'm drying out. I crave protein because I'm damaging my body's tissues every time I move, even though I can't use that protein to rebuild them anymore. And the prions living in my brain crave new hosts and tell my synapses to make me a little nippy. In short, I'm newly rewired with a burning desire for a nice, warm body. You know, like every other teenage boy.'

I rocketed away from the door to the other side of the room. 'Shut up! *Shut up!*'

He must have heard my voice retreating, because he called out, 'Miss Dearly, you're still locked in! Geez, it's OK! Just listen, all right?'

A horrible thought occurred to me. 'Did the monsters get anyone else? In the city? My friend Pam is . . . oh, she is going to be sick with worry . . .'

'No, no. As far as I know, we got all of them. Trust me, that was my fear too. Will you calm down, please?' He sounded both annoyed and . . . desperate?

Screw his desperation. He didn't know the meaning of the word.

'Like I'm going to let some sick, rotting cannibal tell me to calm down!' I shrieked.

'I'm *not* a cannibal!' He was angry, now. 'I've *never* tasted human flesh, OK? Your father got to me before I could!'

I took a breath.

When he spoke next, I could tell that he was standing directly outside the door. 'The methods that Dr Dearly developed keep us going . . . our minds, as well as our bodies. It's hard to explain without being able to show you anything, but look – I eat *tofu*, OK? Nummy, nummy tofu. Hurrah, protein that I can't use. But it takes the edge off. I get topped off every day too . . . there's a small army of doctors in this facility who do nothing except tune us up, like carriages in a garage. So physically, we're as fine as dead people can be, and mentally, we have our bearings. We don't have to fend for ourselves. We're not lost and confused. We know exactly what we are.'

Bram stopped talking, then. He seemed to know that I would want to digest this – *ha, ha*. And so I crept nearer to the door, again, allowing the sensation of my bare feet on the hard floor to ground me as I let my mind turn over this information.

He was a monster. He appeared to have the ability to rationalize, to think, to experience emotions. Perfectly normal ones, like aggravation and amusement. He was quick-witted. And although he sounded impatient, I realized that he had to have some capacity for it in order to sit outside the room so long and talk to his ignorant captive.

But he was a monster.

And a teenage boy?

'How old are you?' I found myself asking.

'I died when I was sixteen. That was two years ago, though.'

I was surprised. 'You look good, for being dead for two years.'

He laughed, then, fully. 'I thank your father for that. But yeah, the others you saw tonight, they don't have the benefit of our technology. Your taxes at work.'

I hesitated in consideration for a moment, before undoing one of the locks.

'Thanks,' he said, at the sound of it.

'But no more questions.' My voice was growing hoarse again.

'Three was better than I expected to get in one session, any-how. Oh, did you wind the clock?'

I looked to the bedside table, where there was a brass alarm clock. 'It says three-fifteen. In the morning?'

'Bah, no, it's almost five a.m. now. If you could keep it going, I'd appreciate it. If it's left unwound for too long it doesn't seem to like to keep the tension afterwards, and I have to take it apart and mess with it.'

I walked to the table and picked it up, doing as he asked. And then it struck me that I was setting a so-called zombie's alarm clock for him, and I swear I heard something snap in my ears. I started laughing uproariously.

I heard the monster's bemused voice outside, asking me if I was all right, but that just made it funnier.

CHAPTER EIGHT

Bram

When Dick Elpinoy came by with a breakfast tray and a canvas satchel a few hours later, Nora spoke to me again.

'I give. "Topped off?"'

'Is this question going to count?' I asked.

'Just answer it.'

'Saline cocktail,' I responded. 'Plumps up the muscles, bathes the joints.'

Dick gave me an odd look as one of the locks clicked open. I was used to it.

'Doc Elpinoy's here with . . . whatever those are.' I pushed myself to my feet. I'd made a nest of blankets on the side of the hall opposite the door. I picked one of them up and tossed it over my old digital cathedral radio.

'Crum-pets,' Elpinoy said, in the tone of voice he often used to remind me that I was a filthy, uncivilized Punk boy from the outback.

'Right. Anyway, I'm going to go borrow a shower, since you have mine. There's nobody else in the hall but the doctor. I'll be back in a bit.'

There was a beat, before the girl said, 'OK.'

I picked up the brass lantern that I'd been using to light my section of the hallway, and headed down the hall, my combat boots making heavy sounds on the floor. I paused behind the next corner, out of curiosity. There was a minute's silence, then the sound of the locks being undone – four, five, six.

'Good morning, Miss Dearly. I—'

'Thank you.' The door slammed shut, and the six locks were done back up.

The doctor caught up with me in the hallway. 'You've been speaking to her? What did you say? You know this is a sensitive matter.'

'Yeah, it's not like she's the daughter of the man who's practically our lord and savior, or anything.' Dick Elpinoy and I didn't get along. He was too hoity-toity for my tastes; I didn't follow rules well enough for his. But now we were united in villainy. Or something.

'Look, Bram.' Elpinoy tugged on the hem of his jacket. His clothes were always too tight. 'I went along with your idea because I happen to be in agreement with you, for once. Locking her up and not telling her anything would simply lead to her either going mad or attempting to escape – and then we'd have no control over what she saw. Can you imagine the first zombie she met being someone like . . . like Dr Samedi, for example?'

'Hey, Doc Sam's a good guy,' I said defensively.

'In *your* book, perhaps.' We exited into another, busier hallway, and he lowered his voice. 'But what I'm saying is that we can't tell her *everything*. Wolfe will have our hides. Besides that, she's a fine young lady.'

'I'll be sure to remind her of that next time she starts yelling at us.'

Elpinoy stared at me for a moment, before recovering himself with a sniff. 'I can't say I blame her I just hope that you were respectful.'

'How is telling her the truth disrespectful? It's not like I enjoy introducing myself as a creature from beyond the grave.' I desperately wanted to roll my eyes, but we were discouraged from doing so. The muscles around the eyes are always some of the first to go.

'Did you tell her anything about her father?'

'No. I let her ask the questions. Predictably, the main questions she had were, "What?" and, "Am I going to be on the menu?" Oh, and, "What?"'

'*What* did you tell her?'

'Enough.'

We passed through the main hallway that led to the med bay, and I lost him in a crowd of recently returned soldiers. They'd arrived back about the same time Nora'd started talking, and the techs were still processing them. I cut through them without looking back, crossed the western courtyard, and continued on to the barracks on the other side. Rather than visit the communal showers, I decided to knock up Coalhouse.

'Coalhouse!' I shouted, as I banged on his door. 'Let me in!'

It took a few more bangs before he finally opened it. Coalhouse had joined the Punk army half deaf, a condition that hadn't improved with his appointment to the artillery. He had a hearing aid, but usually refused to wear it unless he was on a mission. He had the sharpest eye I'd ever encountered, though, and was one of the best snipers we had.

He popped his right eye in and wedged a thumbprint-sized piece of latex foam in with it for support. "Ey, Cap,' he said. 'What's up?'

'I need to use your shower.'

'What're you doing, going for The Holdover King of the World Award?'

A 'holdover' was anything that we found ourselves doing, or wanting to do, that didn't really serve any purpose now that we were dead. Eating was a holdover. Cutting our hair was a holdover. 'Showering is not a holdover, Coalhouse. No wonder you can't get a girlfriend.'

'We don't *sweat*, Bram. And they fill us up with that anti-bacterial stuff, so we don't smell.'

'We still get dirty. What're you, five?' I shouldered my way in.

'Is she still in your room?'

'Yeah.' Coalhouse shared his room with a handful of other soldiers, but his corner was a mess, clothes and comic books everywhere. I should, rightly, write him up for it.

He grinned. 'Ahh, the shower makes sense, now. I gotta say, I'm starting to see things from your point of view.'

'What do you mean?'

'Everyone knows you have a thing for black hair.'

I gave in, and rolled my eyes.

'Hey, she's hot. Literally. And circulation, I find that very, very attractive in a woman.'

I suddenly had an idea of what Dick had been getting at regarding Punk behavior – and I knew that it was my responsibility to nip it in the bud. 'Keep a civil tongue in your head, Coalhouse. She's Dearly's *daughter*. And she's already scared enough as it is. You address her as you would the Virgin-freaking-Mary, got it?'

I put a little bit of 'scary zombie' into my voice, a touch of death rattle, and it was enough for Coalhouse to take me seriously. He nodded, and sighed. 'Yeah, yeah.'

'Aren't you supposed to be with your boys?'

'Huh?'

I cupped my hands around my mouth. 'BOYS. SNIPER TRAINING?'

Coalhouse glanced at the clock, mouthed an expletive, and dashed out the door.

I showered in tepid water, resting my forehead against the plastic wall. I hadn't slept at all, between the girl wanting to talk and . . . well . . . wanting to talk to her, too. Not that we physically needed sleep, but it was necessary for our mental health.

I didn't need Elpinoy to tell me that I'd talked too much. *Nice stoic soldiering there, Bram. Well done.*

She made me nervous. When I get nervous, I talk.

Well, there was that and the fact that she was living, and therefore . . . *fascinating*. It happened every time new living people showed up to work with us. Part of our brains wanted to know everything about them, monitored the way that they moved, unconsciously focused in on the temperature of the air that surrounded them, relished the sound of their breathing.

Deep down, we all probably wondered what they might taste like.

I shook off the idea. I hadn't had breakfast. I finished up and threw on a pair of Coalhouse's cargo pants and one of his T-shirts before heading for the mess.

There were a few zombies chatting in the western courtyard, but the eastern one was empty. The air was warm and heavy. A small flock of parrots exploded from a clump of trees outside the compound wall as rifles went off on the range.

'Honestly, you and your guns.'

I turned to behold Father Jacob Isley, the chaplain, coming up beside me. I smiled and stopped walking. 'You act like they're especially unholy or something. Are you trying to tell me that in the final showdown between evil and good, the weapons of choice will be guns and . . . cats?'

The priest gave me one of his singular smirks – wobbly due to lack of muscle control, and thus somewhat goofy. He stooped down to scoop up one of the cats in question, selecting it from the four or five that were currently milling about outside the base's makeshift wooden chapel. The ginger tabby nuzzled its head at his cheek, which held a bullet hole that would never heal. He kissed its nose.

'As if even the forces of the Almighty could tell *them* what to do. Hmm, sweetie?' He set the cat down. 'How are you today, Abraham?'

I liked Isley. He was a bit more worn out than the rest of us, preferring not to be subjected to constant repair. His religion was gentle and accepting, never forceful. And, hey, sometimes it was nice to be able to borrow a furry little thing to cuddle. He had a soft spot for cats and owned about twenty of them, now, strays from villages attacked by the dead.

'I'm doing fine. Miss Dearly's being kept in my quarters. It's a little weird.'

'Understandable.'

I knelt down to stroke the head of a black kitten, and it reared up for the contact. 'The Cute is strong in this one.'

'I know,' he sighed, with paternal pride. 'Do you think the girl might be open to a visit at some point?'

'Probably. I don't know how religious she is. She's braver than I thought she would be, though.'

'Well, let's hope that bodes well.'

I nodded slowly. 'For all of us.'

'Some people say a man is made outta mud.
A poor man's made outta muscle and blood.
Muscle and blood and skin and bone,
A mind that's weak and a back that's strong.

'You load sixteen tons, what do you get?
Another day older and deeper in debt.
Saint Peter don't you call me, 'cause I can't go,
I owe my soul to the company store.'

A digital gramophone with a flimsy tin horn was set up in a corner of the mess hall, near the window where sundries could be purchased. My regulars were gathered near it. The tip of Chas' cigarette glowed like the red buttons on the front of the grammy as she inhaled. She swayed her hips a bit to the music as it picked up.

Tom chose that moment to reach over and smack her rear.

Before anyone could blink, Chas slapped him. Tom dropped the fork he'd been using to eat his rations, and lifted a hand to inspect his cheek.

'Geez, woman, you're gonna dislocate my jaw.'

'Well, don't do that in *public*, you brute!'

'Wow.' Renfield adjusted his glasses. He was sitting across

the table from them with a book. 'I feel so privileged, being an audience to this . . .'

'Shut up, Ren,' the other two said simultaneously.

Given this setup, how could I not contribute? I took the long way around the mess, so that I could sneak up behind Chas. Tom saw me, and hid his laughter behind his fork as I reached stealthily over her shoulder and plucked the cigarette from between her lips. Chas whirled around with a punch loaded, but I ducked and squashed the cigarette out on the concrete floor.

'Bram!' she said in surprise, as she backed up and gripped the edge of the table in her hands.

'Yes, me. You shouldn't smoke, Chas. Does bad things to you.'

She tossed her hair out of her face. 'I get paid the same as you do, Bram. And I can buy what I want with it.'

'Yeah, but I'm your captain. So you have to listen to what I say.'

'Bull.'

'Yeah,' Tom said, leaning back. 'I'm her boyfriend. She really only has to listen to what *I* say.'

She moved closer to him. 'I am gonna kill you today, Tom. I can smell it on the air.'

'Really?' he asked. 'I would've thought the cigs'd taken care of your sense of smell by now.'

Ren, meanwhile, had buried himself back in his book. Ren was a scarecrow, the bones in his hands and forearms close to the skin. He had regal, sharp features beneath his sallow complexion, and a mop of curly auburn hair. He'd gotten to the point where he could tolerate the rudeness and roughness of the army, but he still preferred to retreat when he could. I didn't really blame him.

'So,' Chas said, as she slid into Tom's lap. Tom offered me his barely-touched plate with a lift of his eyebrow, and I sat down and took it. 'How's the girl?'

'Talking.'

'Seriously? That's surprising.'

'Yeah, I hadn't expected her to. Basic questions. I think I might've squicked her out. Probably should have kept my fat mouth shut.' I was beginning to feel very embarrassed about how much I'd prattled on.

'Well, we are kind of squicky. No use holding back.' Chas glanced to Renfield. 'You know, like, putting a doily over it?'

Ren didn't lift his eyes from his book. 'Hush, you insufferable woman,' he drawled, in that posh northern accent that drove some girls nuts, but just made Chas snigger.

'I *love* it when he calls me that.'

I studied my breakfast for a moment before digging in. Mixed in with the food was an enzyme that broke it down in our bodies, since our stomachs didn't work anymore.

'I still think I should talk to her,' Chas sighed.

'You'll get your chance.'

'If anyone should talk to her,' Renfield piped up, 'it should be me. We're the most compatible, culture-wise. I'm sure that on top of feeling as if she's been thrust into one of the many levels of Hades, with all of its attendant demons, she feels like a lady wandering, lost, amongst the mannerless cads of the slums.'

We were all silent for a moment, before Tom asked, 'You do realize that we're sitting right here, right?'

'Oh, I am horribly aware of this fact.'

'Just checking.'

'Elpinoy wants us to handle her with kid gloves,' I said. 'The full princess treatment.'

Tom cackled and slapped the table. 'Oh, a *princess*. She *is*. I haven't heard that word in forever.'

I grinned, despite myself. 'You have no idea how many times I said "royal" when I was talking to her last night.'

Ren's brow crinkled. 'What's the matter with "royal"? I mean, it's obviously *slang*, and therefore should be punishable by at least the loss of a finger, but it doesn't sound out-rageously bad.'

'Nah, it's not,' Chas said. 'Just stands for "royal pain".'

'Darling, don't go giving away all our secrets, now,' Tom argued. 'Let them think we're calling them filthy things in our heathen worm-language.'

As I shook my head and moved to shovel another tasteless forkful of food into my mouth, Dick came rushing into the mess with a few of the older soldiers on guard duty. I stood when I saw them. Nobody had to tell me that something was up.

'Captain Griswold, you're needed immediately,' Dick stammered.

'What's wrong?' I asked, already walking. My friends watched me go, but knew not to follow. At least, not immediately.

'Miss Dearly is, ah . . . awake.'

'Awake? She was awake when I left her.'

'She's . . . very awake,' Dick said as we exited the mess and started across the courtyard. 'She asked for you by name, though! I think that's progress, all things considered.'

'Asked for me?' *Oh, happy day.* 'For what?'

'Well, the thing is—'

'*WHERE IS HE?!*'

The scream carried out of my quarters, shot down the hall, and boomed out a window. More birds took to the skies. Zombies everywhere stopped to look. *I* stopped to look.

'I think, perhaps,' Elpinoy said, his lips as pale and soft as an uncooked fish filet, 'you might . . . under certain circumstances . . . be permitted to tell her a little bit more about where she finds herself, and why.'

I couldn't hold back. 'Oh, really? Are you sure? Because I wouldn't want to frighten the little lady. Didn't we talk about this earlier?'

'Bram, just go up there and take care of it!'

'No, no, I definitely think she needs to talk to the living.' I stepped back and held up my hands. 'I'd just disgust and disrespect her – and besides, how much could her feeble little high-bred mind be expected to absorb, huh?' My crew gathered behind me as I spoke.

'What's going on?' Tom asked.

'I'm not sure why she's so upset, and she won't talk to me!' Elpinoy admitted.

'*I WANT HIM, NOW!*' Whatever it was, she was obviously growing impatient.

Chas's head sailed in the direction of the scream, her eyes widening. 'Wow, Bram. Tommy here totally needs to take lessons from you.'

I was gone before I could hear his retort, running full tilt across the yard.

CHAPTER NINE

Victor

The afternoon launched bright and dry, and I pushed myself out of bed.

This was a bit of a challenge with only one leg, but I managed.

The instant I moved, the Doberman posted at the door began barking. It didn't try to test the reach of the rusted chain – if anything, it backed away from me – but it put out the cry. I'd suspected it would. Hence, why I'd remained curled up upon the straw-filled mattress in my mysterious prison long after I had regained consciousness. I wasn't sure whom it was meant to alert.

'Hush, boy,' I attempted to say. My voice was strained. I leaned heavily against the wall, dry bark flaking off beneath my fingers. My head was swimming.

This was not good.

The dog shut its jaw with a whine. It turned several times, its chain rattling. The relative silence gave me leave to think, but one thought crowded out all others.

I am an idiot.

When Wolfe had come bursting into my office with news that we had *finally* managed to intercept a transmission from the Grays – after months of scouring the airwaves, the Aethernet networks, the telegraph wires – and that it had to do with a plan to kidnap my daughter, I hadn't asked questions. This was probably due to the fact that in that moment, I had ceased to be a civilized man. The idea that anyone would dare lay a hand on my girl had caused my head to pound and my vision to blur. I began producing snarls and other vile sounds with an astounding ferocity. I had been as much an animal as my canine jailer. My only thought had been that I had to get to Nora, *somehow*. The idea of sitting and waiting had made me eager to invite death – either mine or someone else's.

It should have occurred to me that it had been at least a decade since I had flown an aircraft. But I have a very bad habit of doing very impetuous things. I had no idea what went awry. The air currents must have steered me wrong, for I had ended up far off course, and by 'far off course' I mean 'headed in the opposite direction entirely'. Then the navigation system had jammed. By the time I'd been willing to cry uncle and contact Z Base, I was crashing. I'd crawled away from the wreck, alive but leaving my left leg behind.

That was the last thing I could remember. How long had I been out? A few hours? A few days?

Wherever I was, I had not gotten there under my own power.

With this realization in mind, I began a slow visual inventory of my surroundings. I appeared to be in a hut of some sort, crafted of bleached branches and twigs. The ceiling was not solidly constructed, and white daylight filtered through it. The only furniture was the filthy mattress. The door was made of thick branches lashed together with rope. The floor was made of . . . sand?

I slowly bent down, using the wall for support, and reached out with my right hand to rake up a handful of it. No, not sand.

Salt.

Just then the door flew open, and crouched figures filled the doorway. The Doberman began barking again, twisting on its chain, dancing away from them.

I pushed myself to my feet. 'What is the meaning of this?' I overstressed my vocal cords, and ended up choking on the words. The figures advanced. Once they slipped out of the sunlight and into the shadow of the hut, I recognized them, through my coughing, for what they were.

They were Grays. They were zombies. Some of the worst

I'd ever seen – monsters crafted of bone and bare muscle tenuously knit together by rotting skin and sinew.

I couldn't speak. They grabbed me by the arms and dragged me outside. My eyes were overpowered by the light, and I went blind. The world became disorienting, frightening, as I simultaneously tried to stop my diaphragm from convulsing, willed my eyes to adjust, and tried to support myself with my remaining leg – all the while fighting against the many arms that had taken hold of me.

Unfortunately, the world didn't make much more sense once I *could* see it.

I was in some sort of fort. That, I could accept. It was what lay without the fort that challenged my understanding of reality.

Time, climate change, and terraforming have fundamentally altered the Central and Southern American landscapes, but the land upon which the fort stood seemed untouched. Desert stretched out for miles in every direction around it, an endless expanse of white salt covered in places by a few inches of shallow water. The hazy gray sky above seemed merely an additional part of it, welded to it at the horizon. Its reflection in the water suggested the disconcerting idea that one was floating inside a mirror.

I recognized it, even as my brain struggled to remember which way was up. I knew it from my studies. I was in Bolivia. I was in the immense salt flat they call the Salar de Uyuni.

'Come,' one of the zombies holding me growled, pushing me forward.

The fort reminded me of etchings I had seen in my grandfather's history books as a boy. He'd had a small collection of First Victorian books, bound in leather, each one surprisingly heavy for something which seemed likely to crumble apart at any moment. The fort sat on a raised, flattened mound of salt. Nothing but the trunks of small trees formed the outer wall, wide gaps between each, their tops hewn to points. The buildings were made of wood, poorly and inexpertly constructed, as my hut had been. Sunlight and salt had bleached everything, giving it the appearance of a boneyard.

How apropos.

The Grays were everywhere – hundreds of them. I realized that their clothing had been similarly weathered by the elements, resulting in the appearance of them having matching uniforms. Several of them stopped to snarl at me as my escorts hauled me past. Fear and uncertainty aside, I couldn't help but feel a swelling of pity for them. They'd not asked for this fate.

Turning my eyes forward again, I saw where I was being taken – the main building of the fort. It was a longhouse with a flat roof, the door blocked by a flap of cracked leather. Crates and barrels were stacked up around it.

When we reached the building, the men holding me shoved me inside. Unable to support myself on one leg, I fell. Once more, my eyes were startled by the sudden shift from bright to dark. It took a few more moments for them to adjust, far longer than it would a living person, leaving me prone and helpless on the ground.

'Dr Dearly,' a rasping voice said. 'How nice to see you looking so well.'

Squinting, I pushed myself up. Undead soldiers, perhaps fifteen of them, stood at attention along the two longest walls. They were equipped with long pikes crafted of salvaged metal and wood. At the end of the building were two wooden desks and several upended crates, all littered with radio equipment and tattered paper maps. Behind one of the desks sat a figure clad in a mismatched assortment of salvaged military issue and a brown cloak, with a dirty linen shawl swaddled about his shoulders and the lower half of his face. His hair was dark.

I didn't try to speak. Instead I looked forlornly at the equipment. All I needed was five minutes alone with it, five minutes, and I could send a message back to base.

All right, so there was some hope that I'd make it out of this. *Shape up, Victor. Game on.*

'You know who I am. Who are you?' I finally said. My voice had grown a bit stronger.

'Major Dorian Averne, of the 42nd,' the man informed me.

'Major,' I said, with forced politeness. 'I'm not familiar with the 42nd.' I decided that my initial survival strategy would involve declaring my complete ignorance of what was going on. This would not, naturally, be terribly hard to do.

The man stood. His cloak obscured his figure, making it impossible to calculate exactly how tall he was, or guess how big or how strong. He walked with a quick, snappy gait, which was unusual for a zombie. If he was a zombie.

'I doubt you would know of the 42nd, Doctor, seeing as we're on opposite sides of the conflict.'

'You're an officer in the Punk army, then? Well, respectfully met.'

Averne stepped closer to me. The skin on his upper face was dry and cracked, heavy lines marring his forehead and the area around his eyes. I began to suspect that he was dead. 'I would sooner chew my own arm off than respectfully greet you, but I will admit that it's nice to speak with a man capable of producing more than a syllable at a time.'

I shifted back onto my hips. 'I'm sure it is. Now, may I inquire . . . am I a prisoner of war? If so, I ask to be put in contact with those who can negotiate for my release.'

Averne tilted his head to the side. 'Do you think that any-one would?'

I began to suspect that something was very, very wrong. 'Yes. They would.'

The man turned from me, and acted as if I hadn't spoken. 'I have a gift for you.'

Wonderful. 'Oh?'

He gestured to the back of the room. I turned my head, slowly, to behold more of the large wooden crates. Now that my vision was clearer, I could make out the markings on them.

What I saw made me wish to be blind.

They were New Victorian army supply crates.

One of the crates had been pried open, and a few of his soldiers – new recruits, I couldn't help but suspect, from the haunted looks on their faces – were working at unloading its contents. My heart sank as I saw vials, bottles, kerosene burners, all of the trappings of chemistry. 'I wish you would do me the favor of inventorying the contents of these boxes, and letting me know if I need to have my troops fetch anything else for you. I don't want to hold up your research.'

'Research?' I asked, no longer playing dumb. I was dumb. Completely adrift.

Averne nodded, a hypnotic bobbing motion. 'I've read your papers. I know how close you are to a vaccine.' He flicked his hand towards the boxes again. 'I want it. Now.'

I decided to drop all pretense. 'You're mad. First of all, there is absolutely no way I can do my work in an open-air laboratory in the middle of a salt flat. I don't care if those boxes contain supercomputers the likes of which we have never before seen, it will not happen.'

I saw his hands tightening within the folds of his cloak.

'And furthermore,' I said, suddenly feeling plucky, 'there's no cure, and there never can be. The nature of the disease prevents it.'

'I didn't say that I wanted a cure,' he hissed. 'I said that I wanted the *vaccine*. I know that *that's* possible – and if you lie to me, and tell me that it's not, I will take immense pleasure in cutting off your other leg.'

He snapped his fingers, and one of his guards stepped forth, sweeping his pike downwards. It slammed against my sternum, knocking me backwards. Averne leaned over me as I lay upon the salty earth, noisily sucking in air. 'Your precious *heroes* managed to get to your *brat* first, you'll be happy to know!' he bellowed.

My heart sang with gladness. Thank God.

'But my troops up north have their orders! If so much as *one* of my men has survived, then your people are as good as dead! They'll infect you, as you've infected us! If you want any of your people to survive, you'd better make the vaccine, and *quickly*!'

Dread filled me anew, as I realized what he meant. 'I can't. I truly *can't*. I don't have—'

'Her blood?' Averne's voice was filled with sick amusement. With his unnatural quickness, he launched himself at another nearby guard and dragged him, by the throat, before me. Before the rotting creature could fight back, Averne twisted his head back, rendering him alert, but paralyzed. I saw the zombie's eyes rolling wildly in his head as he fell to the earth, his brows and lips twitching spasmodically. I stared at him, uncomprehending.

'*He* does. She was wounded and he took a sip. *Find it*. The dead don't digest anything, so it's in there. It is somewhere inside him.'

The very idea was absurd. He was bluffing. My mind yelled math at me, told me that it was impossible that the creature before me had been hustled this far south that quickly. But . . . how long had I been unconscious? What if he *had*?

At the very idea that *anything* had tasted my daughter's flesh, I lost all control. With a cry I pushed myself up and grabbed Averne's cloak, pulling him down to my level. I got one punch in before his guards were on me. One of them kicked me, and I heard a rib crack.

'Take him to his cell!' Averne ordered. His voice was acidic with rage, as he stood up and straightened his scarf. 'Bring the equipment to him! If he does not begin tonight,' he pointed to my leg, 'start slicing.'

I spent the rest of the day sitting upon the mattress in my cell, watching Averne's maggot-men pile up boxes of medical and scientific supplies. By the time they brought in the refrigerated box filled with the familiar little vials of my daughter's blood, I knew I'd been set up.

I tried to piece it together. Had someone wanted Company Z distracted? How had they gotten their hands on my daughter's blood, or on my classified research? I refused to believe that someone within Company Z was involved. In fact, my fellow scientists would have known that I didn't need her blood to work from, or most of the lab supplies – all of my efforts lay in computer modeling. It had to have been someone who didn't understand what we were doing, or how we were doing it.

They couldn't have known I would hop on a plane, either – so how did Averne's men know where to find me? Did they have radar? Had a Punk infiltrated the Victorian army? Where had the crates come from?

I nursed a growing sense of sick, helpless dread – the sort of dread I had fought so long and so hard to keep any capable, moral zombie from feeling. What was going on?

'Dear . . . ly?'

I turned in the direction of the rough, barking voice. Its owner was a fresh zombie, a middle-aged man with dark skin and dreadlocked hair. He sported a massive bite on his neck, dried blood caked around it. He had a bewildered, lost look in his eyes, and the uncomfortable body language of someone completely unprepared for the sort of situation in which he now found himself. He was accompanied by two of the Grays from earlier.

'What is it?' I asked.

The zombies stepped through the doorway and looked around. The Doberman backed up and watched them warily. When the one who had spoken failed to do so again, the Grays grunted. One shoved him in the back.

'I'm . . . sorry,' the man said. He paused every few

syllables, his face screwing up as he attempted to get the words out. 'Av . . . erne . . . said to . . . come . . . watch you work. These two . . . don't speak.'

I sized the man up. 'You are his envoy, now?'

'N . . . no idea. My name . . . is . . . Henry Ma . . . Macumba, I . . . I was . . . brought here . . . yesterday. I just . . . happened to be . . . there and . . . and he told me . . . us . . . to . . . watch you.' Something in his voice sang to me of his imminent mental breakdown.

'Do me a favor.' I gestured to the walls. 'One of these branches must want to come out. I need a crutch if I'm to do anything.'

The man stood there a few moments longer, before wandering to the nearest wall and starting to grope about. I needed him to focus on doing something simple and concrete. Usually, I made fresh zombies concentrate on shoving shaped wooden blocks into little holes. The Grays watched him narrowly as he worked.

'You're . . . Victor Dearly?'

'Yes, I am,' I said.

'I . . . don't know how . . . you're here . . . or me . . . but it's an h . . . honor . . . sir.' He took a wheezy gulp of air in an in-stinctive attempt to steady his voice.

'That's good, there. You have to concentrate on *forcing* the air in and out. There's a muscle beneath your lungs, your diaphragm. Try to feel it and move it.' Some people talked very easily after death, others did not.

Henry took several breaths. 'OK.' The next branch he pulled on came out of the wall easily, leaving a gap. He held it for a few seconds before bringing it to me. 'How . . . is that?'

I used it to push myself to my foot, shakily. 'It will do. I thank you – but how do you know of me, may I inquire?'

'I'm from . . . Shelley Falls,' Henry said. He spoke with more control this time. 'Just a . . . little . . . Victorian village, the other side of . . .'

'I'm familiar with it.'

'The . . . monsters came . . . yesterday,' he went on, his eyes darkening. 'They k-killed everyone. They brought . . . two of us here, but the other one, Quinto, I think they . . . he wasn't there when I . . . woke up.'

'When did you wake up? Did you see the sky?'

'It was . . . dark still.'

So he wasn't but a few hours old. I felt a surge of hope. 'Have you eaten anything today, perchance?'

Henry shook his head vehemently, his features tightening in fear and disgust. 'N-no! I saw . . . I . . . I would . . . never . . .' He looked at the other guards, his eyes widening.

I had to get the Grays out of the hut before he realized that he was looking his ultimate fate dead in the eye. I had to keep him in the moment.

'Look,' I said, turning to face them. I tried to inject some authority into my voice. 'I will take this gentleman here to be my guard. If I'm to do any work for your leader, I'm going to need another pair of legs.'

The Grays snarled. I figured they'd gotten the gist of my statement, and weren't happy at the idea of being kicked out.

I stood my ground. 'What help can you offer me, hmm? Do you even understand what I am telling you now? I am sorry to insult your intelligence, but really, you're only going to get in the way. This isn't the largest laboratory I've ever had to work in. Mr Macumba has his orders. He'll watch over me.'

The shorter of the two gave me a skeptical look – a response that impressed me, honestly, as it told me that there were still gears grinding about in his head somewhere. He looked at his partner, and rolled his shoulders. He seemed to understand. After a moment of unintelligible deliberation, the Grays stepped through the door and began to shuffle away, in the direction of the longhouse.

When they were gone, I put a hand on Henry's shoulder. 'Mr Macumba, I shall do everything in my power to help you, if you will help me in turn. I do not plan on remaining here, a helpless prisoner. I am here by my own stupidity, and thus it falls to me to take responsibility for my own escape. My daughter, who lives still, is out there. It will take more than a ramshackle wall of wood and the engineerings of an undead madman to keep me from her.'

I could see that Henry's eyes burned with the realization of what must have happened. 'Can . . . can we . . . you . . . they said you died . . . I . . . I can't feel . . .'

'We are not destined to become monsters, Mr Macumba,' I said, gripping his shoulder more firmly. 'I have been dead for a year, now; I left behind others who have been dead far longer than that. And they retain their personalities, their minds. They are good people.'

The man licked his dry lips. 'Then I'm . . . dead. Like . . . the others.'

I nodded. This was always a make or break moment. The world seemed to go silent about us, the salt outside the open door glowing bright in the red light of sunset. Henry dropped his eyes, and searched his soul.

He found it, at least for the moment. 'I'm . . . yours.'

'Good man.' I looked to the boxes. 'Somewhere in this mess there must be some water. See if you can find any, and take it with you. Tell Averne that I'll begin tonight. Keep yourself hydrated. Stay out of the sun. Don't eat anything, no matter how hungry you might feel. You have no need for food any-more, and your body can do nothing with it. Come back to me once night has truly fallen.'

Henry nodded, and asked, 'And . . . A-Averne, what do I t-tell him . . . if he grows angry?'

I tightened my grip on my newfound crutch. 'Tell him what I told the others – that I'm happy to have you watch me, and serve as my assistant, but only on my terms. Or, if you're feeling lucky . . . you can tell him that Dearly said that he can go to hell.'

CHAPTER TEN

Nora

The bastards had cut me open.

Someone was going to *die.*

Die *for real.*

I hadn't noticed it until after breakfast. I suppose being chased and kidnapped by monsters had made me hungry, for I ate more than I planned to. My stomach was still a little wavery. Crumpets and tea were like mother's milk, exactly what I needed.

After eating, my attention had turned to the bag. It was an unremarkable canvas satchel, handmade. Inside, I found another note. I wondered at the literacy level of the undead. It appeared to be higher than one would expect.

Miss Dearly: We're so glad to have you here! I was so relieved to hear that the mission to rescue you was successful. My name is Dr Beryl Chase, and I'm still living, just so you know. Please let someone know if you have need of any other clothes or toiletries. I think my shoe size is probably larger than yours, so I threw in some slippers instead.

– B. Chase

I dumped the contents of the bag out on the bed. Dr Chase had provided me with two puff-sleeved dresses of muslin, one with blue stripes and the other covered with pink flowers, as well as a corset, bloomers, stockings, and the aforementioned slippers. In a separate cloth pouch I found little bottles of shampoo and soap and a toothbrush and the like, as well as a tiny brown glass vial of perfumed oil. It smelled of violets and chocolate.

Yeah, like I needed the zombies to find me any more delicious. Wrinkling my nose, I capped it again.

I looked at my torn nightgown. I should probably take a shower, if only to make myself feel better. I stood up, my hands drifting automatically to the top button. My fingers were clumsy, bandaged as they were, and the tiny button repeatedly slipped out of my grasp.

Annoyed, I sat on the edge of the bed and began to unwind the linen bandages. I examined my left palm, once it was unbound. Aside from a long, old scar, a memento from my china doll genocide eight years ago, it was pockmarked with new cuts from where the thorns had dug into my flesh. I curled my hand into a fist, and opened it. Nothing serious. Still hurt like the dickens, though.

It was harder to undo the right set of bandages, with my non-dominant hand, but I tugged and worried at them until they finally fell loose. I unwrapped my wrist last, and found, to my surprise, that there was a bit of cotton fluff taped over the side of it. I peeled the surgical tape back to find a short, deep cut – far too clean and deliberate to have come from a thorn. Several neat little stitches held it closed.

The world stopped for an instant, and I felt my recently-eaten breakfast pool in my stomach. What could have cut me there?

The answer slammed into me, and it was only through sheer resolve that I was not sick again.

They'd taken my ID chip out.

Now there was no way that anyone could trace my whereabouts.

'Bram!' I shouted, storming to the door. I started to bang on it, ignoring the searing pain that this caused. '*Bram!*'

It was five minutes of screaming, slamming and stamping my feet – and a minute of contemplating the cold, horrible idea that I might have to leave the room to find anyone, and maybe this had been their plan all along, and *Oh God, oh God* –

before I heard Dr Elpinoy's nervous voice. 'Miss Dearly?'

I threw myself against the door again. 'Bram! I want to talk to . . . to Captain Griswold, whatever you call him!'

'Surely, Miss, if I can be of any assistance—'

'I want to talk to Bram! I want to talk to him this instant!' I felt my throat tightening, my voice rising away from my control. The next sound that came out of my mouth amazed me. '*WHERE IS HE?!*'

'Yes, yes, if that's what you prefer.' Dr Elpinoy sounded downright scared. 'Right away. He'll be here right away.'

He disappeared, then, and I took to pacing – partially with relief that I wouldn't have to leave the room, after all. He was gone for a minute, five. Another voice appeared at the door, a younger female voice.

'Miss Dearly, is there anything—'

Like a child, I hugged my burning hands over my ears. 'I won't talk to anyone but Bram! Get away from me! *I WANT HIM, NOW!*'

The female voice didn't answer. I'd never really had the chance to experiment, before, but it seemed that irrational screaming was enough to make most people scram. *Who'dathunk?*

Soon I heard heavy footsteps thumping down the hallway. 'Miss Dearly?' Bram was at the door. He sounded worried.

I kicked the door as I let go of my head, ignoring the pain that blossomed in my foot. 'What'd you do with my ID chip, Bram?'

There was silence, before he said, 'I'm sorry. Does it hurt?'

'Screw the pain! Where is it?'

'Coalhouse cut it out while you were still unconscious, in the van.'

'*Bloody hell . . .*'

'And we . . . nuked it. To make sure.'

'Marked.' My face was on fire, my limbs shaking. 'All of you. I will take all of you out with my own bare hands!'

There was laughter building in Bram's voice as he responded. 'As cute as I'm sure that would be, your attempt . . . if we thought the people who might try to trace that chip could make you absolutely, one hundred percent safe, I would carry you to them and hand you over myself.'

I gingerly rested my fingertips against my forehead, breathing deeply, trying to calm myself down.

'There are some very bad men out to get you, Miss Dearly.'

'You have got to be kidding me.'

'By the way, you have *quite* the vocabulary, for a princess.' He still sounded amused.

This statement was random enough to get my attention. 'Princess?' I asked, confused.

'You know, a princess. A New Victorian girl.'

My lips parted to fire off another question, before it clicked. 'You're a Punk.'

'Born and bred.'

'Fantastic.'

'I won't hold the fact that you're not a Punk against you, though. We try to get along around here. Dr Samedi boxes our ears if he overhears inter-tribal bickering.'

I couldn't help it. I laughed.

I could hear Bram sitting down on the floor outside again. Something bumped against the door, making it shiver the slightest bit against the locks.

'Get your feet off the door, peasant,' I said, trying to make myself sound as haughty as possible.

I could almost hear his grin. 'Open the door and make me, princess.'

I huffed some of my hair out of my eyes, and lapsed into silence. That he was a Punk didn't really change things – the fact that he was a monster was of far more immediate concern.

'What are you doing?' I asked after a moment.

'If you're going to need me, even if it's just to yell at, I'm going to stay right here.'

'No. I want to take a shower. I'm not about to, if you stay out there.'

'Excuse me, but – huh? Then there will be two doors between you and me.'

Some of the blood stayed in my cheeks as I found myself spluttering, 'But you'll *know* I'm taking a shower!'

'. . . *you just told me you were going to!*'

I flumped onto the floor again, sitting cross-legged, my arms over my chest. 'If I ask you a question and give you a lock, will you go away? Look.' I undid one of the locks. 'That's for my summoning you here.'

He sighed, and said, 'Sure. Shoot.'

'Who are these "bad people"?'

Bram was quiet. What he said next seemed completely un-related to the question. 'I'm sorry for going on so long last night.'

'Going on?'

'I should have been more . . . I should have talked less. I didn't mean to tell you so much in one sitting. I wasn't kidding about the visual aids . . . I could do a much better job if you were out here. And geez, Captain Wolfe is going to have my backside for talking to you. But I didn't mean to scare you.'

He sounded so apologetic, I almost felt bad. I sat up taller. 'Generally, when I ask a question it is because I want inform-ation. So you don't need to feel sorry. You just need to talk.'

'OK, then.' I heard him shifting again. 'The bad people are mindless, ravenous killing machines that seem to come in three different varieties. There are the lone wolves, seeking prey where they can find it. There are the zombies that seem to have banded loosely together for the purpose of hunting. And then there are those who wear gray uniforms and serve an unknown leader, whose bases are located Who Knows Where, for reasons completely unknown.'

'Now that's scary,' I said, honestly, recalling the uniformed monsters.

'Exactly.'

I threw another one of the locks. 'And why did they want me?'

'We don't know.'

'Guess.'

'Well, I figure it has to be because you're immune to the Lazarus.'

I snorted, even as my heart started to hammer. 'How do you know that?'

'Your father figured it out. You asked me about his bite . . . well . . . he was a carrier. He infected you, at one point. And here you are.'

The world went dark on the edges of my vision. I lifted my head slowly, to look at the door. For a good ten minutes, I forgot how to speak.

CHAPTER ELEVEN

Bram

'Excuse me?'

I knew perfectly well that she had heard me, and so I didn't repeat myself.

There was the sound of a lock clacking open. 'Talk,' she demanded.

'I wasn't waiting for a lock. You don't need to give me one.' I was stalling, because I knew full well that I was overstepping my bounds in explaining everything to her. I'd written the note proposing the stupid game we were now playing in an unthinking moment, when my main concerns had been sparing her the shock of finding me outside and, eventually, getting her to move to her father's quarters.

'Just do it!'

I fought the sigh that wanted to rise in my chest. 'In biting him, the first host gave your father the Laz. Thing is, it didn't kill him. Dr Dearly always told me that he figured it would, given what he'd just witnessed. He put two and two together right away. Sat down and wrote final letters to you and your mother, kept his gun handy. He ended up using it to shoot the ones who did die and wake up.' I paused. I really, *really* wasn't sure how much I ought to tell her. Dr Dearly had become a great friend, since we met – he'd taken me into his confidence.

'I was what . . . nine, then, when that happened? Eight?'

'Sounds right, yeah. I don't know.'

'He wasn't home a lot, then. He was deployed.' Her voice had taken on a breathy quality. I wondered if she was watching her memories play out just behind her eyes, scouring them for things she hadn't noticed before.

Ineffectually licking my lips, I continued. 'At first he was ecstatic, figuring that they'd be able to formulate a vaccine or something from his blood. But, turned out he hadn't fought the sickness and won. It was just . . . it's hard to describe. Let's just say it was making itself at home in his flesh without killing him.' I steepled my fingers together and watched them, rather than the door. 'Unfortunately, he was still capable of passing it on. So Protocol D was born.'

'Protocol D?'

'Protocol D,' I began to quote. '"No living person *not* interested in becoming acquainted with the sensation of his or her own body shutting down shall come into contact with the bodily fluids of Dr Victor Dearly. This includes, but is not limited to: offering a hand should he cut himself, using his bathroom, or drinking from his 'I Love New London' coffee mug."'

Nora didn't respond at first, but then she said, a little stiffly, 'Professionally worded, that.'

'The ones who are well-adjusted 'round here are the smart-asses with an appreciation for gallows humor. Higher-ups not excluded.'

'Then . . . that's why. That's why we didn't see him for so long. It seemed like forever before he came home from that tour of duty . . . not until after he'd saved the PM.'

'Yeah, he had to go back after that. For his ticker tape parade, and all. It'd look odd if he didn't.'

'But, I don't get it. I don't remember . . . seeing any monsters, or . . . or being sick? Or him looking sick. How'd he give it to me? How would he know that he had, if I'm immune? It doesn't make any sense.'

Holdover King of the World that I am, I took a breath and held it, focusing on the feeling of my lungs expanding with air I couldn't use. I held off replying for five seconds, ten. I didn't want to tell her. Why had I started this? I should have just slept in the hall without writing her a word of warning. Let her open the door, see me, and scream. It'd been the scream I'd wanted to prevent, but now, looking back, it would have been pretty easy to tolerate. Could have nipped at her ankles, for good measure.

The lack of sound behind the door told me that she wasn't at all certain that she wanted to hear the rest of the story, either.

'Do you remember him being . . . jumpy, at all?'

Her continued silence told me I'd hit the nail on the head. It was a minute before she spoke. 'I remember . . . we went out to the park one day after he'd come back. He was looking around at everything so anxiously, as if afraid that something was out to get him. My mother had told me, you know, before-hand, "Your father hasn't been home in ever so long, he's been in the outback, he might have to get used to things again." I thought it was that.'

'Yeah, like that. Miss Dearly, do you remember . . .' Here goes. 'Do you remember when your mother died?'

'Yes. When I was nine . . . see, this explains a lot.'

I sat up a little straighter, alert, wondering if she'd gotten to the right conclusion by herself. She sounded so suddenly animated.

'I was sent to St Cyprian's when I was nine. I did *not* want to go, and he said it was because my mother said I had such a temper, and my family was moving up in the world and I needed to learn how to be a lady, whether I wanted to or not. It was so *unlike* him, because up until that point, and even afterwards, he encouraged me to be myself. But no, he . . . he was so adamant about it, and off I went the very same day. Like, literally . . . whoosh, out the door. I've always wondered about it. It was so weird. Probably the weirdest thing that's ever happened to me, 'til now. It wasn't until a few days later he told me my mother had taken ill with a fever.'

'It was to keep you safe,' I said, interrupting her. 'You have to believe me, it was to keep you safe. Because . . .'

It wasn't coming out easily. Nora urged me on with a whisper. 'What?'

'It wasn't a fever. Your mother had gotten the Laz.'

No reaction.

'It wasn't on purpose,' I quickly added. 'We didn't know as much about the disease then as we do now. He knew about it spreading via the bodily fluids, and he took precautions, but somehow . . . she got it. He did what he could for her, but she succumbed. And . . .'

This was the bad part.

'Tell me,' Nora said, her voice thick. Was she crying? My guts wrenched at the idea that she was crying again. It'd been hard enough to listen to the first time.

'He . . . kept her. For a few months. He wanted to see if he could come up with some kind of cure. She responded well to his methods, for a while. He thought that everything would be OK, that he could put it all back together, somehow. But sometimes, with the Laz, it just messes too much with the brain. After a while, she wasn't your mother anymore, she was just a host. Like the things that came after you. A little reasoning power, ability to follow orders, not much else.'

And then she was definitely crying, mewling sobs that tore at my insides. I almost tried the door to see if it was still locked. The only thing I wanted to do, the fiercest instinct that I had at that point, was to take her into my arms again and comfort her.

A dark, sulky part of my mind reminded me that even if I could have done that, it would have only terrorized her further.

'Miss Dearly . . . Nora?' I asked, scooting closer to the door.

'Please . . . don't . . . talk,' she pleaded in hiccups.

I nodded, not that she could see. For a good ten minutes, I listened to her cry. The sound – and not being able to stop it – made my muscles tense, my jaw clench.

'That's why no one would let me look in her casket . . . Oh, God,' she eventually panted out. 'He killed her.'

'No!' I didn't mean to shout, and made an effort to lower

my voice. 'He didn't kill her, Nora. Your father is not a murderer. Do you know how many years he's devoted to trying to *save* people's lives?'

'Years he devoted to . . . ? He made my mother sick! Are you saying . . . he never told her? Told her what had happened to him? He never told *me!*'

'It was an accident!' I hushed my voice further. 'He never would have hurt either of you, if he could help it. That's why he didn't tell you. He loved you both so much. For as long as I've known him, you're all he's talked about . . . he's missed you so much.'

Wait.

Crap, I'd just gone and told her.

'What do you mean, I'm all he's talked about?' she asked.

Crap, crap, crap.

'Nora . . .' I could fix this.

'What do you *mean*, for as long as you've known him? You're a Punk! You were never in the army with him! You said you were in the army with him when we met on the street, but you're a *Punk!*'

Her voice was starting to do that hysterical thing again. Before the entire base could hear her and descend upon my hallway, I fought out, 'He's one of us. He's one of us, Nora . . . Nora, listen to me. Listen to me, and I'll tell you the truth . . .'

'He's not one of you!' she screamed. 'He's dead! He's really *dead*! They buried him. *I* buried him! I put him in the freaking ground!'

She tried to compose herself, then, with several deep breaths. I gave her as long as she needed, all the while mentally designing my tombstone. *R.I.P., Capt. Abraham R. Griswold. He was completely useless and made girls cry.*

When she spoke again, she'd lost the battle with her lungs and was sobbing. 'They kicked me out of his room the minute he died. They wouldn't let me be with him . . .'

'Because they knew he was going to wake up,' I said.

'They carried the shrouded body from the house on a stretcher, and they wouldn't let me follow,' she wept. Her voice was shaking.

'He was awake under the sheet.'

'He said something about his body, just before he . . . oh my . . . no . . . no . . .'

I began to worry that she was going into shock. I touched the door. 'Nora, let me in. I swear, I won't hurt you. That's the last thing I'd do.'

'No, no, no . . .'

'At least open the door, Nora. Let me see you. OK? Open the door.'

'*No, no, no!*'

I took a breath, and summoned up the scary zombie voice. I didn't want to do it, but maybe it'd get her attention. 'Nora, *open the door!*'

Sudden silence.

'Nora, are you all right?'

Nothing.

'Nora?'

I kept talking, but she didn't respond for a good ten minutes or so. When she finally did, I was on my feet and pacing, wondering if I ought to fetch Evola or Isley – did she need a living doctor, or a priest?

'What about me?' Her voice sounded broken. It frightened me to hear it, out of nowhere, in the quiet of the hall.

'Huh?'

'What about *me*? My . . . immunity?'

I forced myself to sit again. 'What happened when you came home for your mother's funeral?'

'What? I . . .' It hit her. 'My hand. I broke a porcelain doll, and it cut my hand . . .'

'He subjected your blood to testing. By that point, he'd begun to think that there might be a slim chance he'd managed to pass the ability to carry the Lazarus on to you – and if he had, he couldn't send you back to your school. But you surpassed his wildest expectations. Test after test, your blood refused to "take" the Laz. I mean, the disease proteins themselves wouldn't even replicate. We believe there's a very small percentage that . . .'

'So, after her funeral . . .'

'Everything went back to normal.'

I heard her draw in air. 'He went back to the outback, after that – I only saw him at holidays. But at some point, I had to have been exposed.'

'Yep. Trust me, there are vials of your blood down in the lab . . . cloned for research. We could probably do a full body transfusion, with what we have. You're immune.' I couldn't help but smile. 'No matter what, you'll never become one of us. You might be one of the only people on earth guaranteed to die for good.'

'Why?' she choked out.

'Genetics. Sheer, stupid luck.'

She actually laughed a bit, bitterly. 'I suppose this makes me just as big a freak as you are, then.'

I bristled. 'I am *not* a freak.'

'Oh, you're not?' she shot back.

'No. A freak is something rare. There's an entire company at this base, over a hundred of us. There are more roaming the countryside, and still more under the command of General Whoever, out there. Now, feel free to call me what I am – call me a corpse, call me dead, call me a killer if you want. I've killed people in battle, I'll admit it. But don't call me what I'm not. I am not a freak, and I am not a cannibal, and . . .'

I would have added, 'I'm not a monster,' if it hadn't at that moment hit me that I was going all self-righteous on a girl whose world I had just turned upside down.

Smooth, Bram. When will I learn to shut up?

She was quiet for so long after this, that I honestly started to fear that she would never speak to me again. 'Miss Dearly?' I eventually asked.

'You can call me Nora.' Her voice was tearful again.

'I'm sorry for going off on you.' I felt like crawling off and finding a way to kick myself in the rear. One twist of the leg, might not be too hard. 'I'll leave you to your thoughts.'

'How did you know I was thinking?' She sounded wary, as if she now suspected me of mind reading.

'Your voice goes breathy when you are, I've noticed. My hearing's actually pretty sharp. Some of the doctors think we have slightly heightened senses, since the illness wants us to hunt.'

'I'm sure being blind helps with that too.'

'Huh?' I was confused. 'I'm not blind.'

'You're not?'

I realized what she meant. 'No, no. Almost everyone's eyes cloud over after death. Mine are just worse than usual. My vision is fine. Well, mostly. The world's a little foggy, but given the things I've seen, I figure that has to be called an improvement.'

'You're . . . very resilient, for someone who's dead.' Her voice was a little steadier.

'And I think you're far stronger than any of us were prepared to give you credit for.' I kept shooting my mouth off like an idiot, telling her things I'd been ordered not to, and she kept going with it. I was impressed, honestly.

I heard one of the locks moving back, and then another. The door opened slowly, as far as the single safety chain left connected would allow it. The room was dark beyond, and I couldn't make out anything aside from her tear-stained face as she leaned close to the gap from her position on the floor. Her dark eyes were red-rimmed, but also so serious, so stern.

'So my father is a zombie?'

'Yeah.'

She blinked hard, and swallowed. 'Then where is he?'

CHAPTER TWELVE

Pamela

'Come away from the window.'

I didn't move.

'*Pamela Roe*, you come here this instant.'

Two cub reporters had begun camping outside our house the evening prior, digital notebooks open wide in anticipation. One had a camera, and kept it almost obsessively pointed at our front door. I wondered how many reporters were hounding Nora's Aunt Gene.

I studied them with a mixture of apathy and burning defiance. A part of me wanted to march out there and give them a show they'd never forget – cry and beat my breast, tear my clothes, beg for the return of my best friend.

The other part was so numb that the world seemed to be drifting by, as in a dream. Everything seemed inconsequential; everything seemed destined to rot. We were all going to die, or have something horrific happen to us, so what difference did it make? What could possibly have kept those questing men outside from their warm beds, aside from hunger for a scoop? Fear of the Punks? Concern for Nora's well-being? Greed or ambition?

I was terribly, painfully present in the world, and so far removed from it.

'*Pamela!*'

'Yes, Mother.'

I took a slow step back, the hem of my skirt caressing the carpet. I hadn't opened the curtains, but had watched the reporters from a gap between them, through the inner drapes of threadbare gauze. Through a veil.

'You mustn't let them see you, Pamela,' my mother fretted.

'They'll get a picture of you, and what will it do to us to have your face on the news?'

She was right, of course. I would do well to listen to her. It was my fault that she was in the house to begin with, condemned to idleness. My mother, Malati, was a broad, strong woman, and was normally employed in helping my father in the bakery. Since Nora's disappearance, however, she had to act like a 'respectable' woman, and that meant being sequestered in the house with me.

We could not call on anyone. We could *take* calls, but they must be brief. We could not be seen working, in any capacity. The ideal female heart was to be so sensitive, so flooded by shock and sadness in a situation such as this that listless grief could be the only response. To be seen as carrying on with life would mark us as strange, cruel, masculine – and, for me, it would be social death.

We'd not had these rules before I started at St Cyprian's. My parents had sent a scholarship application to the school eight years ago in an attempt to get me to stop crying over the fact that Nora had been sent there, away from me. It cost them nothing to indulge me, and they never imagined anything would actually come of it. The desire not to be separated from my sister-by-choice had changed the course of our lives forever.

Nora and her mother (and Dr Dearly, I suppose, but he had always been away) used to live in a townhouse one street over from my father's bakery. I remembered her now, tiny as I had been, creeping in several times a day to sniff about the tarts and cookies. I had been jealous of her at first, because she had prettier dresses and the naturally curly hair that had been my ultimate worldly desire at that age. In fact, when our mothers initially introduced us, I had chosen to greet her by yanking on a fistful of her hair to see if it was real. Her response had been to deck me in the nose.

It had been love at first fight.

After that violent first meeting we had played together,

attended the public grammar school together, practically lived in one another's houses. Even once Dr Dearly had attained his share of status, and his family had moved to the mansion underground, we had found ways to see each other every day. A day spent apart had been incomprehensible. The longest we had ever been without one another had been the two months between the time when she was shipped off to school and my acceptance there. Charity cases took a while to process. Those had been the most tortuous two months of my short and uninteresting life.

And now here I was, alone, without her – with an interminable, Nora-less future a possibility, hanging there above me like the sword of Damocles, ready to drop. It wouldn't have been half as terrible if the messenger who had arrived at our house the previous morning, stiff of bearing and stony-faced, had simply told us that she had died. That would have been the end of it, book Z in the series, nothing left to do but mourn, or curse her into the afterlife.

But not *knowing*, and not being able to do *anything* about it, that was worse. Every time it hit me, the awful scrabbling sensation of not *knowing*, that feeling of helplessness, I wanted to pull my own hair and scream.

My mother sat down in her worn rocking chair and took up her embroidery. Her hands were dry and calloused from working; they were unused to the dainty pastimes of high-bred ladies. The handkerchief she was working on now was the same one that she had been working on for the past three years. 'I'm as worried as you are, but that's no cause to act like a person possessed. Let God give you strength.'

I slowly closed my eyes and concentrated on my breathing. My body had seemed beyond my control in recent hours, heaving and tearing, home to strange phantom pains – as if Nora had been a part of my flesh that had been severed off. I obeyed my mother. I prayed for God to look upon us with pity.

I prayed for God to bring Nora back.

That afternoon three uniformed army investigators came to speak to me. I sat next to my mother upon our overstuffed satin sofa, the newest bit of furniture in our parlor. Beside it stood our Christmas tree, its wax candles unlit. Only our kitchen and the bakery were electrified.

The investigators were tired-looking men with tobacco stains on their hands. They filmed me with a portable recorder as I answered their questions. They didn't accuse me of anything – they didn't even appear particularly interested in my responses. I probably held a fairly low position on the suspect list.

No, I hadn't heard anything from Nora after she and her aunt had dropped me off at home. Yes, I was accustomed to receiving calls and e-mails from her, and I hadn't gotten any. Yes, they could download the contents of my phone. No, she hadn't seemed troubled, outside of the usual. And even that hadn't been as bad as it normally was.

'She seemed a little better,' I said.

'Better?' one of the investigators asked.

'She lost her father last year, and she was still depressed. But that day, she looked better.' That did it. My shoulders began to jerk. My mother moved closer and wrapped me up in her arms. 'We went visiting. She said she didn't want me to worry about her any longer. I even felt mad at her for not paying attention to *my* worries. She wasn't a hundred percent, I know that. But I felt like I could be *mad* at her!'

'I'm afraid I must ask you gentlemen to leave,' my father said. He'd been roaming in and out of the bakery, keeping an eye on the proceedings. He was still wearing his apron, and his arms were covered with flour. 'As you can see, she's terribly troubled by all of this. She'll get ill.'

'Of course, Mr Roe. We'll be in touch if we learn anything, or if we need to inquire further.'

Once they were gone, I gave in to the tears. My mother stroked my hair. I couldn't even answer a series of simple questions. I wanted to go out there and *find* her – dredge every lake, comb every forest, interrogate every suspect. I wanted to help, I wanted to *do something*.

But I couldn't even answer a series of simple questions.

My father knelt beside me and took my hand in his. He was an active man with dusky, freckled skin and dense, curly white hair. He had the smoothest voice. 'Here, pet. Calm down. They're working as hard as they can. Everyone's worried. It's all right.'

'I want her back,' I sobbed.

'We all do,' my mother said. By that point, she was crying herself.

'Can't I please watch the news?'

'Pamela,' my father asked, 'do you think it would make you feel better or worse to watch the news?'

My mother had mandated that I not be allowed to watch or read the news, lest it upset me. I lifted my head, and saw her bite her lip. But she didn't argue.

'Better,' I said. 'I want to know what's going on.'

We only had one tiny screen, which normally hung on the wall of the bakery for customers to watch while they waited in line. My father left, and came back with it a few minutes later. There was a space for us to mount it on our own wall. He handed me the screen's archaic wood and brass remote device, the lettering on many of the buttons worn down from frequent use, and ran a cloth-covered cord to the kitchen for power.

The first channel I landed on was showing a 'daily visual novel', or DVN, as they were commonly called. So was the second. My blood ran hot at the idea that we'd apparently been attacked, that my friend had been taken hostage or *killed*, and some people were still following their *stories*. My tears dried on my cheeks.

On channel three a New London television personality, Madame Maureen Winters, was interviewing . . .

. . . was that Mink?

Yes, it was! I sat up, gaping at the screen.

'Here we have one of Miss Dearly's schoolmates, Miss Vespertine Mink. Her mother has been good enough to agree to this interview, in the interests of informing the public and aiding the ongoing investigation. Good morning, Miss Mink.'

Vespertine had tried to don an expression of mourning, but she just looked pouty. She was wearing an ivory satin Glengarry hat topped with an enormous black feather. 'Good morning, Madame Winters.'

'Tell us, how was Miss Dearly the last time you saw her?'

Vespertine pretended to think. 'Well, she was very agitated. She and her roommate were heading home for the holidays. Ah, her roommate is a scholarship girl . . . I doubt anyone would know her name, so I shan't mention it. Always so giving, Miss Dearly. Always going out of her way for the less fortunate.'

My fingers dug into the upholstery of the sofa.

'I'm not sure what was wrong beyond that, though. She was very short with me. I said that I hoped to see her well come January, and I took my leave.'

Madame Winters nodded seriously. 'Do you think that there's any chance she could have known about the upcoming attack?'

Vespertine folded her hands primly in her lap. 'Well, I can't remember ever seeing her so upset before. I'm afraid I couldn't say one way or the other.'

'Oh, it's amazing you remember how to dress yourself every morning, Mink,' I muttered. Mom flashed me a look of confusion.

'She was under stress?'

'Oh, yes, I think so. I'm sure she didn't know anything about the attack, though. Why, if she had, wouldn't she have reported it to somebody?' Vespertine's face was full of suggestion. Her lips then rounded, and she added, as if it had just occurred to her, 'She *does* have a habit of watching war holos, though . . . I wonder if, perhaps, she watched a particularly savage one that gave her nightmares? I don't think she sleeps well. She always looks like something out of a gothic play in the morning.'

'War holos?' Winters leaned forward in her seat.

'Yes . . . Punk history, I believe. I can hear them through the wall. I have the suite next to her room.'

One of my fingernails actually popped *through* the upholstery.

'Goodness,' Winters said, slowly. 'That's . . . different, for a young lady. And how strange that she should then be targeted by what was, most likely, a sleeper cell of Punks . . .'

'Please turn to channel four,' I said, as I stood up. I was afraid I was going to be sick.

Mom did so, even as she asked me, 'Pamela, is that true?'

'Yes,' I said, hugging myself with my own arms. 'She watched them all the time, she thought they were interesting! Her father got her into it. She always took after him, you *know* that . . . she wasn't in on this! She was writing a *paper*! She's out there, hurt, or . . . and Mink's trying to *ruin* her . . .' I couldn't breathe.

'Pam.' My mother stood up and took me by the waist, guiding me back to the sofa. 'Calm down. Calm down, or I'm turning the screen off and your father will—'

'No.' I took deep breaths, and tried to cool my cheeks with my hands. 'No, leave it on, please.'

NVIC was a riot of tickers and computer graphics. While I grieved for Nora, others grieved for the loss of their security. The incident was being interpreted by most as an attack by covert Punk troops against a symbol of New Victorian pride, the Elysian Fields. They figured now that the flooding had been the start of it. The Prime Minister had yet to make a statement, but other officials had. They claimed that there was no reason to suspect that another attack was imminent. Few mentioned Nora at all. To them, the Punk intrusion was what was important.

I tried the other news networks. Some anchormen were calling for the PM to go into hiding, for our troops to be immediately recalled from South America, for a curfew and additional security measures to be put into place. They wanted to know why the footage from the EF's security cameras hadn't been released.

Others spun stories of their own to make up for the lack of facts.

'I am forced to conclude,' the host of one show thundered, 'that Miss Nora Dearly, the child of a man of some legend within the army, has run off with some young buck and that the army has arranged this elaborate staging to hide the fact!'

Mom balked at that one. '*What?!*'

I leaned against her big, round shoulder, my eyes starting to sting again. I should have listened to her. She angrily flicked back to NVIC.

'In other news,' the anchorman said, 'the clinic which serves the Elysian Fields' populace has seen an increase of patients exhibiting odd symptoms. Spokesmen from the Ministry of Health have declined to comment on whether there might be any significant cause for concern, but do urge anyone suffering from the following to seek immediate medical attention.

'The symptoms include: sudden high fever followed by a plunge in body temperature, an exceedingly pale or bruised appearance of the skin, convulsions, lack of coordination, dementia, and pain in the extremities. There has been no evidence that the disease, if it is a disease, is commonly communicable.'

Apathy was beginning to sink in once more, and I paid the reporter no mind. If it wasn't about Nora, I couldn't care less.

My mother patted my shoulder. 'Do you want to go up-stairs and take a bath? I'll get dinner ready.'

I nodded miserably, and stood up. Mom left the screen on. As I climbed the stairs I heard my brother, Isambard, enter the house. He called out for my mother, who greeted him. These noises were so utterly ordinary that they now seemed strange, and I continued up the stairs in search of silence.

Once I was alone inside my room, I shut my eyes and tried to block out everything. I tried to shut up my chattering mind. I tried to internalize the feeling of being safe, secure, in my tiny, familiar room with its plain yellow walls and unvarnished floorboards and second-hand furniture. In my own home, with the people who loved me – that confidence, that acceptance. Face serene, mouth shut. The face I should present to the world.

I tried to tell myself that that's what Nora would do.

I knew that this was a lie.

Chapter Thirteen

Nora

Yesterday had been a hard day.

Although Bram seemed calmer now that he could see me, I didn't look at him in turn. I wasn't up to eye contact yet. 'A few days ago we received a transmission from the leader of the bad guys I told you about. We've been trying to intercept something like that for a while now. It's a long story. It told us that they were going after you.'

'For my immunity. Got it.'

'After we left the base, your father apparently took a plane from our hangar and tried to get to you himself. Needless to say, he didn't make it. We lost contact with the plane shortly after.'

'So you don't even know where he is.'

'No.'

'Why would he do something like that?'

'I wish I could answer that question. I've never seen him that angry.'

'But he . . .' I bunched the skirt of my nightgown up in my hands. 'If he was that worried about me, why did he just . . . die? Let me think he'd died, that is? You mean he's been here, walking around, talking, for a *year*? And he never tried to tell me that he was all right, that he was safe?'

Bram sighed. 'What would you have done if he did, Nora?' He drew a circle in the air around his face. 'We can't exactly live out in the open. I mean, this – all of this – is a big national freaking secret. The military's been keeping it under wraps for years. You think this is something the average person can handle? If people knew about us, there'd be chaos.'

My head felt hot. 'I'm not talking about him attending a

parent-teacher conference or taking me shopping, I'm talking about him sending me a note, leaving a short message, you know, to let me know that he *wasn't really dead*!'

'Nora, I don't know why he stayed quiet, but . . . whatever he did, he did because he thought it would be best for you. I mean, it's been years, and I haven't exactly written my mother.'

'And he never told my *mother*. He never told her, and he *infected* her!'

'I'm sorry.'

'I mean, what was he even *doing* here?'

'Working on a vaccine.'

'Oh, *now* he worries about that!'

'Nora . . .'

It took me a few moments to dredge up a simple, 'I'll be right back.'

'Nora?' Bram pushed himself onto his knees.

I bounced up and walked away from the door. I had to walk. I had to breathe. I was filled with so many conflicting emotions – hatred, anger, elation, fear – that I felt like there was no room for logical thought. I had to make some.

I'd need more than a few minutes for that.

'Nora?' Bram's voice was building up that worried note again.

I returned to the door. 'I need time. Please, can you just . . . go? Go, and don't come back until tomorrow morning.'

'Is that your final question?' he asked, lowering his eyes to the chain. 'Because, as much as I understand the weirdness of this situation – trust me, I am a believer – we don't have a lot of time. My superior's due back very soon, and my room's the last place he wants you to be.'

'Well, it's more of a request.' I was still stiff from sitting on the floor, and my head felt like it was stuffed with chewing gum – a mixture of information overload and fatigue. 'Just leave me alone for a while.'

He nodded. 'Fair enough.' He then asked, as if fearing he

would be refused, 'Can I give you something before I go away?'

'Yes, if you can slip it through the crack and if you promise it wasn't alive at any point in the last eight years.'

Bram laughed, and I almost felt safe for a moment.

The old envelope Bram had gone to fetch for me had been sealed. I hadn't known what it contained until I'd shut the door and torn it open with my chipped nails, slowly – as if I instinctively expected a zombie silverfish to lunge out at me. Once I had the paper within unfolded, I recognized my father's florid handwriting. Taped to the bottom of the parchment was a small silver tube about two inches long – an outdated video cylinder. New players didn't even have slots for them, anymore.

I wadded the letter up and threw it angrily onto Bram's desk. I couldn't read it, not at the moment. I was still dealing with the fact that my father was alive, in a strange sort of way, and had never taken it upon himself to *tell* me so.

Bram did as I asked, and stayed away. The only person I heard from that day was Dr Elpinoy. Every time he dropped off my food he tried to strike up a conversation, but I demurred. I spent the day alternately lying on Bram's bed and pacing over Bram's carpet, trying vainly to chase after my scattered thoughts. The hands of the alarm clock seemed to whirl past the numbers.

Confused, overwhelmed as I was, I had begun to consider leaving the room.

It was hard to concentrate. The room was seldom completely quiet. I could hear noises from the other rooms around me – the scuffling of boots and furniture, the low murmur of voices, radios. The undead really seemed to love music, for some reason.

It was Elpinoy, rather than Bram, who unknowingly offered me some reassurance. Quite simply, he kept coming back alive. He had spoken to the zombies outside my door with condescension, not fear. I would think that the last person you'd want to sass would be the one who might react by tearing you limb from limb.

So, despite the fact that my survival instinct was hollering like a drunk town crier, I started to accept that if I wanted to find out more about my father, I would have to go out and hobnob with the zombies. Once I acknowledged that my options were death and remaining in a windowless room for the rest of my life, I felt a sort of peace about my decision.

I slept deeply after achieving that, and woke up the next day ready to admit that . . . I was curious.

My father's letter only made me more so.

Nora,

By now, sweetheart, men in uniforms have come to tell you that I am dead. They have probably brought letters to confirm it, a flag, all the trappings. The Prime Minister himself might have paid a call – and surely, if I am dead, he would know about it?

Don't believe them for a second.

Watch.

I love you far too much to ever leave you.

Love,
Papa

Put perfectly, I had no bloody idea what the letter meant. Did he mean for it to be sent to me after he turned into a monster? After his sham death twelve short months ago? All the letter told me was that Bram had spoken the truth.

I needed to see what was on the cylinder.

But first, I needed to get ready.

The warm water felt good against my skin.

I poured out the last of the soap Dr Chase had sent me and scrubbed myself ritualistically for the third time. When I shut my eyes I could still see those decaying people, all naked eyeballs and snapping teeth. I was beginning to think less of trying to cleanse myself of these experiences, though, and more of trying to accept the fact that I would probably *never* feel clean again.

I was out of soap, either way.

I shut off the water and got out of the shower. There was no mirror in the bathroom. I towel-dried my hair and dressed in the clothes I'd been given, before packing up the canvas satchel. I included the letter and cylinder alongside the other things.

The clock said that it was almost six in the morning. I sat on the bed and watched as it ticked the seconds off. Bram would come at some point, but I didn't know when.

It nagged at me, I realized, not being able to see what I looked like. More than I thought it would. I tried to ignore it, spending further time drying my hair, coaxing my curls into proper ringlets with my fingers like usual. But after all the talk of disease and dead people, my subconscious had apparently decided that my continued sanity hinged on seeing my own face.

I stood up and went over to the desk. The top held nothing that looked like a mirror. In the interests of science, I slowly flipped through Bram's book collection. None of them were digital. He had a Bible, a grammar primer such as an elementary student might own, a few adventure novels (about explorers in the frozen Wastelands, apparently), and a large, illustrated biology textbook. I picked the last one up and opened it. It was worn, its pages dog-eared and scribbled upon.

It looked as if he had spent some time trying to identify the deep muscle groups of the body.

Should be right under these, he'd written in the margin. T*ry to feel with fingers?*

Ew.

I put the book back, and started opening the drawers. The top one held some pencils, a pair of scissors, and a sharpener shaped like a globe. The one beneath it held paperwork. I let my fingers walk through it, and pulled out whatever looked interesting. I found his papers of enlistment from two years ago. I found some clippings from Punk newspapers, and marveled at these for their odd textures and fonts, as well as the contents. They detailed such things as food shortages and rationing, weather predictions, church socials. '*Mrs Moreau's Kissing Cake was tremendously well received, as always.*'

As I was putting them back, I found another book in the drawer. A digidiary.

I seized it up and opened it. The screen sprang to life with a photograph in sepia. There was a young, compactly muscular man in it, standing outside a neat wooden house with two little girls in plain pinafores. The resolution wasn't great, but I wondered if it was Bram. I spent some time studying it – the hair looked similar – before giving up and fingering through.

'Password?' the thing inquired in a lilting female voice. I nearly jumped out of my skin.

'Uh . . .' I had no idea. Rather than just give up, I decided to have a go. 'Zombie?'

It beeped scoldingly at me. No.

'Undead? Bram. Abraham? Captain? Bing Crosby!'

I tried all of the words I now associated with the person known as Bram, but none of them worked. With a sigh, I shut the diary and put it back into the drawer, burying it beneath the papers. We'd play again later.

Finally, I opened his closet. Mounted on the other side of the door was a full-length mirror.

I looked a fright.

I spent ten minutes or so adjusting my corset, plucking at the blue dress – it was cut for someone with bigger breasts than I would ever have, and sagged in the front – and fluffing up my damp hair. I'd never worn makeup, but I bit my lips and pinched my cheeks to get some color in them. *Might as well try to look a bit more lively than the corpses.*

As I stood there, assessing my reflection, I had another idea.

I got the scissors from Bram's desk and went to work, cutting the bottom of the dress off at the calf. I then snipped away at the resulting strip of fabric, turning it into a ribbon I could use to tie back my hair. I trimmed the ends and tossed the scraps into the tin garbage can. *Tada.*

Feeling quite proud of myself, I lifted my eyes to the mirror. Upon actually *looking* at what I'd done, it occurred to me that no one but myself had seen so much of my legs in a year or more. Like all girls, I'd started wearing long skirts at the age of fifteen. I felt a flush of embarrassment, but tossed it off with a shake of my head. It was a necessary evil – a shorter dress was easier to move about in. Call it a tactical advantage.

Wardrobe quick-change completed, I went about exploring Bram's closet. Most of his clothes were regulation issue – fatigues in gray camouflage, black T-shirts, the black uniform I'd seen him in on the roof. Last in line was, I presumed, his dress uniform. It was of black wool, and included a jacket with a high Mandarin collar and trousers with a red stripe on the outside of each leg. I stood on my tiptoes to see the insignia. He had ordinary military bars for a captain, but the epaulettes were of red silk fringe instead of the usual gold. Each shoulder had a crest with a stylized *Z* beneath two interlocking rings embroidered on it.

The drawers held accessories and shoes. He was a size 14.

No handkerchiefs – made sense. He owned a battered pocket watch of cheap, light metal, with the same picture from the digidiary glued inside its cover, and an old camera that had definitely seen better days.

I opened one drawer only to find his underwear – black briefs.

I started to giggle madly. Zombies wore *underwear*?

'Nora?'

I shot away from the closet so fast you'd think the under-wear'd tried to bite me.

'Yes?' I squeaked.

'So you are awake.'

I put a hand on my chest and tried to calm my rapidly beat-ing heart.

'I . . . am.'

Neither of us made any further move to speak, until he said, 'So . . . will you be joining us today?'

I thought about it for a moment. Would I?

'Yes,' I said. There it was, my very own signature on my very own death certificate.

I approached the bed and picked up the satchel. As I slung it over my head, my eyes fell on the teddy bear. I picked it up too.

I could have sworn that the door walked to me, rather than the other way around, so suddenly panicked and dazed was I. It was a minute, two, before I could bring myself to unfasten the last lock. I paused, my hand on the jamb. He must have heard the chain falling loose, but he made no move to try the door. He seemed willing to go at my pace.

Taking a breath, I opened the door wide. With both hands, my eyes shut, I thrust the bear out into the hall. 'Keep this in mind, though: one false move, and the teddy gets it!'

I held this position for half a second, before opening my eyes.

Bram's mouth was twitching. 'Good morning to you too.'

His eyes fell from my head to my stockinged legs. 'Alice.'

I didn't know what to say to this at first. Then it hit me – white stockings, blue dress, hair ribbon. I slowly lowered the bear, my cheeks heating again. 'My face is up here, bunny boy. I'm just giving myself an edge, in case I have to run for my life.'

He laughed. I clammed up at the sound of it. I could almost hear the air being sucked out from the space around us as I saw just how *close* the undead boy was, just how *real* he was, just how *tall* he was. He was at least a head and a half taller than me, trim, but obviously strong. I thought of the huge shoes back in the closet, and my mouth went dry. He could tear me in two, if he wanted.

He probably *did* want to.

But instead of doing this, he bowed from the waist. 'Captain Abraham Griswold, at your service.'

I hugged the bear against my chest and watched him, feeling like a canny child. 'Good . . . morning.'

Bram made no move to come closer. He watched me with his silvery eyes, and I watched him right back. He wasn't all that bad-looking, strangely enough. He was dressed in one of his black T-shirts and camouflaged pants, his hair slicked back with water. His bare, ice-white arms were covered with wicked-looking scars, but aside from that, nothing was . . . broken. Or missing. Nothing about him seemed overtly weird. Whatever my dad had pioneered in the area of corpse preservation, it apparently worked really well. Or maybe Bram was just lucky. Blessed among zombies.

'Have you had breakfast?' he inquired.

I shook my head.

'Would you like to go get some?'

'Will I have to watch you eat?'

'No, not if you don't want to.'

I nodded.

He slowly offered his arm.

I squeezed his bear so hard I feared the head might pop off. *No way.*

'Right, then.' He seemed to accept the fact that I wasn't prepared to touch him. 'We'll walk right down this hall here. This way leads to the med facilities. That's where you'll always find most of the living people on base.'

'First, I want a gun.' I'd decided to make this demand during my second scrubbing.

Bram raised an eyebrow. 'Should I trust you with one?'

I stood up a bit straighter. 'My father taught me how to shoot. The first lesson was about *responsibility*. I don't want to hurt anyone, I just want to feel like I can defend myself.'

'Question two, then. Will you trade me the bear for a gun? At the risk of sounding like a wuss, I'd really rather not have him caught in the crossfire. He's not actually mine.'

'OK, deal,' I said, surprised that he was willing to go along with me. 'But you don't get the bear 'til I get my gun.'

It was plain that Bram wanted to smile again, but he fought it back. 'OK, we'll go down the other hallway, then. Ah, I have long legs, I walk fast even when I walk slow. I take it you want to walk behind me rather than in front of me?'

Beautiful, we were on the same page.

Bram did walk slowly – with a stiff, almost grandfatherly gait. He had a very slight limp, and favored his right leg. His arms barely swung at all. It was rather eerie. Even at my normal pace, though, it was easy to keep behind him.

There were doors all along the low, dark hallway. I saw a few of them crack open as we passed, and just as quickly close again. It made me nervous. By the time we emerged in a wider, better-lit corridor, my skin was covered in goosebumps. Luckily, it seemed that no one else was there to see them.

'Armory's that big door over there,' Bram said, lifting an arm to point. I nodded, and followed him. I watched as he entered a combination into a keypad near the door, and then stooped down a bit so that an eye scan could be performed.

'That must be inconvenient for the ones that lose eyes,' I commented.

'I have a friend who's clinging onto one of his until it rots. You might've seen him. He doesn't wear it on missions, it falls out too easily.'

I remembered the zombie with the empty eye socket, and shuddered.

The computer confirmed that Bram was really Bram, and the door slowly swung open. I leaned to the side, peeking around him.

Sweet Father of All.

I handed Bram his teddy bear as I walked into the armory. It was a weapon-lover's paradise. Rifles and shotguns and blunderbusses, arranged by caliber and model, were mounted in rows along the walls. Shelving held equipment of all sorts. Cabinets filled with drawers topped with bulletproof glass stored every kind of grenade and handgun that I'd heard about, ever. I pulled one of the drawers out and leaned down to look at the wares inside. I could see the New Victorian flag – a field of Wedgwood blue, sprinkled with white stars – engraved somewhere on each piece. Either the undead had a lot of cash to blow on black market New Victorian weapons, or they were legit.

At that point I realized that Bram was standing there in front of the only exit, teddy bear in arm, watching me. I turned around to face him.

'What sort of gun do you want?' he asked.

'Well, I've had the most experience with a .22 caliber. My father taught me to shoot with one, and I take marksmanship as a phys. ed. course in school.'

'A .22 doesn't usually have the force necessary to make an exit wound in the skull, though. You'll be aiming for the head – remember that, *always* aim for the head, any other shot's a wasted shot. I'd recommend a shotgun again, quite honestly. I know it's annoying to reload it, but given your size, I'd say the more power, the better. Or . . .' Bram set the bear down on one of the lower cabinets with, I noticed, quite a bit of respect and care, and opened one of the drawers. 'Maybe a .38 or .45 pistol.'

I dared to draw nearer to him, and looked down at the guns. 'I've not had much experience with pistols.'

Bram touched the glass, and clear red buttons swam into view. He entered another access code. 'No time like the present to learn, eh? Here, we'll get you a pistol *and* a shotgun. See, they say it's "survival of the fittest", but you and I really know that it's "survival of the most heavily armed".'

Ten minutes later I had a shotgun on my back and a pistol in a holster at my hip, and we were walking back through the hall that led to Bram's room. I felt a little more confident with some firepower strapped to my body, I had to admit, even if I only knew how to use fifty percent of it. Eh. I'd figure it out.

We stopped momentarily so that Bram could put the bear in his room. 'Why do you walk so slowly?' I found myself asking. 'I heard you running in the hall, before. Are you hurt? Is that why you're limping?'

He glanced back at me. 'No, the limp's an . . . old wound. I told you, our bodies don't heal. We try to keep from wearing them out when we can. If I don't need to run, I don't run.'

'But you sing. And you talk a lot. Won't that wear out your vocal cords over time?'

A shadow of a smile flitted across his lips. 'You've got to have some joy in your life. Else, what's the point?'

'Good answer, I suppose.' I paused. 'You have a nice voice.'

His smile was boyish, a little self-conscious. 'Thanks.'

We continued forward in silence, although he didn't take his eyes from me. He moved so slowly and knew the hall so well, it seemed that he didn't need to watch where he was going.

'You sure you're OK with this?' he asked.

I swallowed. 'As OK as I'm ever going to be.'

He turned his eyes forward. 'Right. Brace yourself.'

Alarm bells went off inside my head. 'For what?'

'A bunch of people fawning over you.'

Huh?

We stepped out into another wide, bright hallway, a mirror of the one that led to the armory. Windows along the walls looked in on what seemed to be laboratories and operating theaters. A set of stainless steel double doors marked each end of the hall, and through their high, reinforced windows, I could see sunlight.

Unlike the last hall, however, this one was filled with people. Standing about were nurses and doctors and techs, as well as several other zombies, who all stopped talking when I walked in. One of the techs turned on his heel and ran into one of the labs, and everyone in there stopped what they were doing and came to the window to peer out at me. Everything had come to a standstill. No one spoke.

Until the dead people started to whisper at one another, their eyes on me.

I found my hand drifting down my dress, towards the pistol.

'Miss Dearly!' It was Dr Elpinoy's voice. He was at the edge of the crowd, but quickly approaching as it parted to let him pass. 'Oh, it's so good to see you! You poor thing! Shall I find you some breakfast?' He turned to speak to a living man behind him. 'You! Go ready the kitchens. Here, we—'

I pulled out the pistol, just to prove that I could, holding it with both hands and aiming it at an angle towards the floor. I didn't take the safety off. Elpinoy jerked to a stop. I heard a few gasps.

'Nora . . .' Bram said, warningly. 'Remember that whole "responsibility" thing?'

I narrowed my eyes, and shook a few curls out of my face. 'That's close enough, Doctor.'

'You gave her guns?' Dr Elpinoy asked, turning on Bram.

He was livid. 'You gave the girl *guns*?' He made several fluttering, useless hand gestures, before producing a rather high-pitched, '*Why?!*'

'She asked for them,' Bram said, matter-of-factly.

'Bram has the right idea, doing what I want,' I said, trying to make my girlish voice a little deeper. I didn't do very well. 'Trust me, I don't want to harm any of you. I just want things to go at my speed, and I want information when I ask for it. Got it?'

One of the zombies, a girl, gave a little squeal of excitement. 'Yay, she's not a loser! We are so having a sleepover!' I recognized her voice from the hall.

'Can I watch?' quipped a boy zombie without a nose.

My eyes flicked in that direction. I started to wonder which of them I should shoot first, but now for reasons that had nothing to do with my safety.

'Nora, put it away.' Bram leaned a little closer to me. I instinctively stepped back, and turned to meet his eyes. He was serious. 'Just for now. No one's attacking you.'

I pressed my lips together and slowly holstered the pistol.

'All right,' Dr Elpinoy said, adjusting his houndstooth waistcoat nervously. 'All right. Look, your father's office is this way.'

'Is there a video player there?' I asked. 'One that'll take an old mini cylinder?'

'Yes, there should be.'

I looked at Bram again, who nodded. On this wordless advice, I took a risk and stepped in front of him, following Dr Elpinoy.

CHAPTER FOURTEEN

Bram

Tom was grinning like a fool when I passed him. It made him look even more like a fanged fish.

'I so totally, *totally* called it,' he gloated. 'I think I'm in love.'

'I'll fight you for her,' Chas countered.

Both of them fell into step behind me. I turned around, blocking their way, and shook my head. 'Not yet. Go get Coalhouse and Ren. Meet me in the mess in about an hour.' When their faces turned to disappointment, I assured them, 'I'll try to bring her with me.'

With only a little grumbling, they gave up and left.

In moving away from me, Nora'd informed me of her comfort zone. About three feet. I maintained this distance from her as we entered the office, and mandated, with a well-placed look, that Dick do the same. I watched her as she took in the room, eyes large and cautious, muscles taut. She was ready to flee at a moment's notice. She didn't need any more gawkers to worry about, so I shut the door. At the sound she turned sharply to look at me, lips parting in an unspoken question.

'Keeping everyone else out, not you in,' I said. I hadn't been in Dearly's office in several days. Everything was as he had left it. Protocol D had mandated his segregation from the other living workers on base, and thus he'd been appointed three connected rooms that he still used in death – his quarters, an office, and a small laboratory. They were crowded with machinery, books, and heavy pieces of furniture, the walls almost completely hidden by memos and small pieces of framed art. Dearly's taste for dark, highly decorated surroundings had not translated well to cramped military spaces.

'You can stay here from now on, Miss Dearly,' Elpinoy said, making his way through the clutter to one of the doors. 'These are your father's quarters.' He opened the door, glanced inside, and immediately shut it again. 'We'll get one of the soldiers to clean his room out properly, of course.'

Nora looked at me again. 'If my father has a room, why was I put in yours?'

'The locks,' I reminded her. 'These rooms don't have any locks. Dr Dearly wanted to be completely accessible at all times – especially if he needed to be put down. That was his contingency plan.'

Her eyes widened even further. I wouldn't have said that was possible. 'Put down? You mean . . . to kill him?'

I attempted to change the subject, and waved a hand towards the laboratory door. 'Your father didn't want to endanger anyone. As you can see, there are plenty of living workers here. They rotate them out from our alpha base, which is further north, to reduce their overall exposure time. No undead at that installation. But your father didn't want to stay there. He felt more comfortable here, with us, even before he died.'

Nora set the satchel she was carrying down on her father's desk, and paused for a moment to look at the photographs displayed there. She picked one up. It was of her, as a child, in black and white.

'How do you know all these things about my father?' she asked softly.

I looked at Elpinoy. I'd stand a better chance of having her believe it if *he* said it. Elpinoy studied me gravely for a moment, keeping me in suspense, before announcing, 'Well, your father and Captain Griswold are very close.'

Nora looked up. I had an odd suspicion that if I went on about how well her father and I got along, she'd take it as some sort of come-on, and that was the last thing I wanted to burden her with. But, as usual, the mouth moved anyway. 'He's been teaching me biology and chemistry. I asked him to, about a year ago . . . after he died. Figured it'd be good to get some medical training. And he talks about you all the time, I told you that. He's always been incredibly kind to me. Found me himself, when he accompanied some soldiers on a training exercise. I was . . . he talked me down.' I bit my tongue and fought the urge to hit myself on the head.

Nora smiled, very slightly, and suddenly the world was a happy place.

'He's been working in here,' I went on, a bit loudly, moving into the lab. Nora opened her satchel and dug around inside until she found something. Soon she and Elpinoy joined me in the next room.

The lab was tiny, but one of the most powerful on base. Multiple computers were set up within, each sporting a tall, segmented screen that could be adjusted for the task at hand. A row of counters, cabinets, fume hoods and sinks housed the usual tools of genetic and medical science, and a long, black, sharp-edged machine dominated the southeastern corner. I still didn't know much about it, but I knew that was used to synthesize medications.

Nora glanced into a nearby glass refrigeration unit. 'So that's all mine?' She was looking at the vials of blood held within.

'That's all yours.' I sat at one of the computers and pressed some buttons. The monitors around us glowed to life.

'You're going to use it to make a cure?'

'No, I'm studying it,' Elpinoy said. 'As intimate as that might sound. While a vaccine is what we're after right now, it's my personal belief that a more permanent solution lies in genetic therapy. Your DNA, and your father's, can help with that.'

Nora's face slowly turned in the direction of the computer screens. Her voice, when she spoke again, was stiff. 'But you don't have anything, yet?'

'No. As far as I know, they're getting closer to a vaccine by the day,' I said. 'Your dad was running the latest batch of computer models when he raced out of here.'

'We've been working from the information he left behind,' Elpinoy interjected. 'We have everything, just . . . nobody really *understands* it the way he does. The Lazarus has been his life for almost a decade. Chances are we can continue with his work, but it's going to go much more slowly. And now we're running out of time.'

Nora stood on her tiptoes to look up at the monitors. 'And so you need him back.'

I nodded. 'Well, for this, yes . . . and because he's the Zombie Party's national hero.'

For once, Dick was not a pompous jerk. 'We all love your father, Miss Dearly,' he said. 'This is not a question of politics.'

I didn't want to be presumptuous to the girl who had thought her father dead for over a year, but I added, 'I think I speak for the undead lobby here when I say that we'd crawl through hell to get him back, vaccine or no vaccine. And if you think about it, it's not like a vaccine's going to help *us* any.'

'This is all very touching,' Nora said, eyes still on the monitors. 'But right now, he's not my hero.' She opened her fist, revealing a mini recording cylinder, and offered it to me. 'Play this.'

'Not your . . . ?' Elpinoy's eyes widened, and he turned on me. 'Bram, what did you do?'

I took the cylinder and popped open a tray on one of the computers to insert it. 'She deserves to know what's going on, Dick.' I shoved the tray in with my elbow as I bent down to flick the button that'd lower the lights.

'Yes, but—'

Dr Dearly interrupted Elpinoy with a soft, 'Hello, NoNo.'

His face swam into focus on one of the large screens. We all fell silent. It was startling to see Victor looking so young. His round, but aristocratic face had fewer lines crossing it, his sleek hair was fully black instead of salt-and-pepper, and his hooded brown eyes were clear behind his half-moon spectacles.

Nora's arms went slack.

Dr Dearly, pale and trembling, was seated in front of a green tent wall smeared with blood. Someone had obviously tried to clean it off, and, for some reason, stopped halfway. 'I'm sorry to have to do it this way, sweetheart. I swear, I don't want to hurt you, only . . . I'm not sure how long I have. I have to do this before I become . . . inhuman.'

'It's really him,' Nora whispered.

'As you can tell, something very bad has happened here. And if you get this, I did not survive it. I'm not sure how much I should tell you, because chances are the government is going to clamp down on this . . . they won't let anyone know. You're an intelligent girl, Nora, so you destroy this when you're done watching it, all right? You destroy this cylinder. You beat it up with a hammer 'til it's dust, or you throw it in the fire, and you don't say a word to anyone about it.'

He took off his glasses, and wiped his forehead. He was sweating like a racehorse. My tongue felt heavy in my mouth. I remembered sweating like that. I also remembered getting really confused around the same time.

Suddenly, I felt like I shouldn't be watching. The message was meant for Nora. But I couldn't look away.

'You may have heard a priest, at some point in your Sunday school-goings, say that to grow too attached to mere things is dangerous. He would not like what I am about to tell you, but he is full of poppycock.

'Far more powerful than religion, far more powerful than money or land or even violence, are symbols. Symbols are stories. Symbols are pictures, or items, or ideas that represent something else. Human beings attach such meaning and importance to symbols that they can inspire hope, stand in for gods, or convince someone that he or she is dying.

'There are symbols of me everywhere around you. I am in

everything I have ever touched. I am in every memory you may have of me. I am in every utterance of my name. I am in every atom of your blood.'

He looked deeply into the camera. He was crying. 'I know I'm speaking in riddles, but they're the only things that make sense right now. Darling, find me there. Find me within you. Find me within you and know that I didn't mean to leave you. Be brave. But don't believe those who say I *am* gone. I am not. It is impossible for human beings to truly die. We leave too much behind.'

'Turn it off.' Nora was tearing up again.

'It's almost over,' I said, looking at the digital clock above the insertion slot. Mini cylinders only had five minutes of recording time.

'I love you, Nora,' Dr Dearly said. He continued to stare relentlessly into the camera. 'I'm sorry.'

The screen went black. I hurriedly brought up the lights. Tears were trailing down Nora's cheeks, and she was leaning against the counter.

'Miss Dearly,' Elpinoy began.

'Don't call me that,' she snapped. 'Don't call me that! I'm not related to that . . . that *liar*! He lied to me! He never told me any of this, and he always acted like we were against the world, him and me!'

I decided to go for it, scooting my chair a touch closer to her. 'Nora, he loves you. We'll find him.'

'I don't want to find him!' She stepped away, staring at me with wide, angry eyes. 'I never want to see him again! You want to run off and find him? Be my guest! He's dead to me, he's dead, he's *dead!*'

With that she stomped off into the office, and threw herself into her father's heavy leather chair. I looked at Elpinoy, figuring I'd see loathing in his eyes – but he just looked helplessly back at me.

'What do we do?' he asked.

I followed her to find out.

Nora was curled up in a tight little ball by the time I reached her side. I knelt down and asked, 'What do you need us to do?'

She didn't respond. It seemed like she drew into herself whenever she became overwhelmed. It left me feeling useless, but it was easier to deal with the silence when I could be near her. So I sat against the desk, listening to the ticking of Dearly's old wooden clock and the warm humming of the computers as I waited.

After twenty minutes or so of brooding, Nora turned to me. She set her chin forward in a stubborn little motion, though her voice was quiet. 'Seeing as a vaccine wouldn't help me, either, I guess that puts me in the undead lobby.'

'Yeah, I guess,' I agreed, not quite getting it.

'So it's my job to help you.'

'OK?'

Seeing that I was stymied, she sighed and pushed herself up. As she spoke, Elpinoy slowly entered, keeping his back to the wall. 'Look,' she said, 'I'm getting it. I might be a little slow on the uptake right now, but I'm getting it. And what I'm getting from it is that there's no way I can go back to being normal after all this. Whatever I feel about him at the moment, I'm kind of like my dad, now. I'm on your team. I've been bitten, in a way.'

I understood. 'OK.'

She tossed her hair out of her eyes. 'So, let's keep going. What's next?'

Elpinoy's mouth dropped open like a trap door. 'Miss Dearly, really . . . if you'll make yourself comfortable in this room, you can have more time to think . . .'

'If I take more time to think, I'm going to go insane,' she shot back at him. 'I took last night to think. Right now, I need to keep busy. Give me something to do.' She nodded, to no one. 'Give me something to do.'

'Captain Wolfe would not approve.'

I leaned my head back. 'Dick, where is Captain Wolfe?'

'He's still out with the troops on patrol. He's scheduled to return at any moment. In fact, I should radio him. He said not to use the radio, lest the Grays intercept, but I could tell him that . . .'

'Feel up to meeting another zombie real quick?' I asked Nora. 'I promise you, he's probably the least dangerous guy here. He can help us.'

Elpinoy trailed off, his face souring. 'What are you doing, Bram?'

'Sure,' said Nora. 'Why not?'

I stood up and flashed Dick a smile. 'I'm going to introduce her to Doc Sam and let him teach her Laz 101. Right this way, Nora.'

'Don't you *dare*, Bram! She is *not* ready to – hey, wait up!'

The hall was vacant this time around. I guessed that some-one, maybe Samedi himself, had told everyone to get back to work. When we got to the right door, I opened it for Nora. She looked me up and down, but stepped quickly inside. I followed, not bothering to hold it for Dick, who had to struggle to get the heavy thing open for himself.

'Now,' I said to Nora, keeping my voice low, 'prepare your-self for some real weirdness.'

'That will make the twentieth time today,' she whispered back.

The lab we had entered was built to the same plan as Dearly's quarters – three rooms connected by doors. Unlike Dearly's, however, the lab doors were heavily reinforced and fitted with electronic locks. About five or six people were currently at work on various projects, but they all stopped as they realized who had just joined them.

One of them came rushing over, pushing up her goggles as she did. Dr Beryl Chase was a curvy woman in her thirties, with strawberry blonde hair and eyes the color of green apples. She wore a black hobble skirt and high-necked blouse beneath her white lab coat. 'Oh, Miss Dearly, I'm so glad to see you!' She glanced down at Nora's dress, and laughed. 'Well, I doubt you'll grow into it, but it'll do. You've a . . . keen fashion sense.'

Nora realized who she was before I could even open my mouth to begin an introduction. 'You're Dr Chase. You sent me the bag of clothes and things.'

Beryl nodded. 'Yes, that's me.'

Nora dug up a little smile for her. 'Thank you.' She worked her mouth, and added, 'I recognize your voice from the hall yesterday – I didn't know who you were. I'm sorry for yelling. And I won't cut the other dress up. I'll pay you back.'

Beryl waved a hand. 'Don't worry about it. And sometimes a girl just needs a good scream.'

'Oh, such truth in so few words,' quoth the sonorous voice of Dr Samedi.

Nora looked in the direction of the voice.

I waited for it.

Nora leaped behind me. 'OhmyGodohmyGodohmyGod,' she chanted below her breath, her hands gripping into my lower back.

I stiffened. I hadn't expected *that*.

Dr Samedi approached – a professionally-attired body without a head. Around his neck, above his wing-tipped collar and blue cravat, was a thick ring of steel studded with dome-headed screws.

'It's all right, Miss Dearly.' Beryl glared in the direction of the body, which stopped in its tracks. 'Baldwin, put your *head* on. You're scaring her!'

'Nora,' I said softly, 'just watch this. It's freaky, but you'll appreciate it, I know it. And let go of me, before you leave a mark!'

Nora took a shaky breath, and slowly peeped out around me. Her fingers gradually uncurled from my back.

Samedi sighed. 'Fine, fine.' He returned to the workstation

from which he'd come, where his head was hung on a spidery brass armature, positioned so that he could look down at his current project. He lifted it carefully, and, with only a few alignment problems and eventually a few clicks, reattached it. He removed his goggles and blinked heavily several times. He'd been a man of young middle-age when he'd died, with wavy chestnut hair and expressive, almost feminine eyes. His complexion was gray, now, and he had several rows of stitches and staples along his forehead and left cheek, where he'd received a deep gash. His left ear was missing.

'There,' he said, twisting his neck a few times. 'Is that better, Beryl?'

'Much. There, Miss Dearly, all is well.'

Nora was staring at the doctor with round eyes. 'I want to go home,' she whispered to me. 'Forget that last speech, I want to go home.'

'Working on it,' I replied, before lifting my voice. 'Hey, Sam, how's it going?'

'I want to go home *now*.'

'As well as can be expected,' Samedi said, moving closer again. He smiled at Nora and bowed. 'Dr Baldwin Samedi. It is an honor to meet you, Miss Dearly.'

Nora didn't move to curtsey, and instead just blurted out, 'How can you *move* without your *head*?!'

Beryl laughed. 'As usual, you're a hit with the ladies.'

'Are you saying that I'm a hit with you, Dr Chase?' Samedi feigned shock, but then sobered his expression and addressed Nora. 'Well, young lady, I can move without my head essentially because my brain is here, now.' He tapped the metal collar. 'I have implanted wireless electrodes in my skull that communicate with the collar mounted on my neck, which then feeds the information to my spinal cord and permits move-ment of my body. Occasionally it does misfire, but that's why we keep Dr Chase about – she knows how to hit the reset button, as it were.'

Behind his back, Beryl mimed hitting Samedi with a crowbar or mallet.

I spoke up. 'Dr Samedi and Dr Chase are the best engineers we have working with us. They work on weapons systems, customize our equipment, and create the prostheses that some of us use.'

'Prostheses? Like . . . fake arms, and things?'

'Yeah.'

'Better after-living through cybernetics,' Beryl said, adjusting her nametag.

'Anyway, I wonder if you could walk us through the Laz, Sam. I've been trying to brief Nora as we go, but it might be good to hear it from a doctor.'

Samedi cocked his head. 'Doctor? I'm an engineer, not an epidemiologist. With Dearly gone, that's Elpinoy's purview.'

Elpinoy tugged his jacket closer about his body, as if it could offer him protection. 'No. I won't do it. We're already way out of line. *Wolfe is going to be furious.*'

'I see your point,' Samedi said.

'Oops,' I mouthed to Dick.

Samedi stepped over to a computer and typed in a command, bringing up a few rows of folders on the nearest monitor. He tapped through them until he found an image of the Lazarus prion. He hit a button, causing a hologram of it to rez over a nearby horizontal screen. Nora moved to get a better look.

'Prion Zr-068,' he began. Samedi was the perfect man for the job. He sounded like a documentary narrator, tone clipped and humorless.

'What's a prion?' Nora asked.

'It's a protein. That's all. It is neither alive, nor dead. Just a chunk of biological building material. In fact, the great majority of us have this same protein within our bodies from the moment of conception, and it does us no harm.' He changed the image. 'The difference is that a Lazarus prion folds in a different way – literally, it's crumpled up, it's a different shape. Once introduced to the body, this diseased protein starts replicating by telling our normal proteins to re-fold themselves. A sort of deadly origami. The syndrome begins to manifest. It is an *incredibly* fast disease – its incubation period averages six hours.'

Nora gaped at him. 'You're dead in six *hours*?'

'Dead,' Samedi confirmed, 'and then, not dead. The body reanimates anywhere from one second to six minutes after death. Now, the faster you "awaken," the healthier you are. The brain does not begin to die until after the heart and lungs do . . . it's the lack of oxygen that kills it. So, how intact you are upon reanimation depends on how long your brain has been without oxygen. It is entirely possible to reanimate completely brain-dead.' He pursed his lips. 'Those are unfortunate creatures.'

'How can a protein be so harmful?' Nora rubbed her wrists together.

'Prions are also responsible for such things as mad cow disease. They damage the tissues of the body – brain tissue, especially. This one just happens to be incredibly virulent. Not even now do we fully understand how, or why, it works the way it does. As best we can figure, it reanimates and controls the body so that it can transmit itself to another host via the bodily fluids. You can also get it by eating the flesh of the in-fected, which is probably how it got started, perhaps in animals. Although in this form, it doesn't seem to infect our fuzzy friends.'

Samedi brought up a picture of Nora on the screen, which made her twitch a bit. 'Now, the reason *you* are immune – con-gratulations, by the way – is because you are blessed with a gene variation that is incredibly resistant to diseased Zr-068. Probably the easiest way to explain it is to simply say that your proteins refuse to bend.'

'My mother was right,' Nora said. 'Even my genes are stubborn.'

'Your father has a slightly different, but no less startling genetic variation, that resulted in so few of his proteins being destroyed at any one time that he was able to live many happy, symptom-free years, before he grew weak from an unrelated illness.'

'OK,' she said. 'So, why's it taking so long to make a vaccine?'

'Well, Dr Elpinoy will never admit it, but he suffers from performance anxiety—'

'Oh, shut up, you old cad,' Elpinoy said, finally uncrossing his arms. 'Miss Dearly, it's difficult. The human immune system won't attack prions, because it doesn't see them as foreign. It thinks they're normal proteins. That's why I'm here. What your father and I are trying to do is to attach a Lazarus prion to a genetically-altered bacterium, which the immune system will then attack. With luck, we can teach the immune system to respond to something it would otherwise ignore. But it's tricky, and potentially dangerous. If not very carefully constructed . . .'

'You might infect people by vaccinating them,' she finished. She was a fast learner.

Samedi stared at her for a moment, before mimicking the wiping away of a tear. 'Never did I think I would be so impressed by the youth of today. Between you and Bram, I'm starting to feel like we're not all doomed, after all.'

Elpinoy sighed. 'Yes, quite. In addition, there's the risk that the immune system will end up attacking *all* forms of the protein, good and bad. They're technically made of the same stuff, after all.'

Nora continued to regard Samedi with interest slightly muted by suspicion. 'But what about the already dead?'

'Oh, we keep the infected going,' Beryl chimed in. 'We treat them with compounds that kill off microorganisms and slow decomposition . . . and for some reason we've yet to figure out, insects like flies and beetles won't go near the infected, anyway. Maybe something tells them that zombies are no good to eat. Anyway, it's things like bugs and bacteria that are responsible for what we term "wet" decomposition.'

'Squishiness,' Samedi clarified, with a wiggle of his fingers.

Beryl shook her head at this, before continuing. 'They're basically embalmed. So, Baldwin there isn't going to balloon up with gasses, or ooze slime, or what have you. Victims are subject to more of a "dry" decomposition . . . they're almost like mummies.' She was getting excited now, science geek that she was. 'And bacteria are responsible for most of our body odors, so they don't smell like death or anything. They do wear out, but we can help them with that. It's just the prions eating the brain that we can't stop. We can slow it down a lot, but not stop it.'

'So, could there be a cure?' Nora looked at me out of the corner of her eye. I found myself looking at the floor. I knew the answer to that one.

'No,' Beryl said. 'Prions essentially cannot be destroyed. We've tried antibiotics, antiretrovirals, *acid* . . .'

'Freezing flesh, burning it . . .' Samedi ticked off.

'Autoclaving works some of the time, but not enough to be thoroughly trusted. Um . . . industrial cleansers of all kinds . . .'

'Your mother's cooking . . .'

'*Radiation* doesn't do it . . .'

'They've found prions on human bones in graves that are thousands of years old.' Samedi threw his arms wide. 'You can't kill them, for they're not alive! I, for one, welcome our prion overlords. They made me who I am today.'

'Besides,' I heard myself adding, 'The "cure" would really just . . . kill us for good.'

I lifted my eyes. Nora was still watching me. I couldn't read her expression, at first, but then her eyes slowly closed and she lifted her hands to her temples. I noticed that she was looking a little pale. 'OK, enough science class, now.'

'How about that breakfast? I told my friends we might join them, if you feel up to it.'

Nora was still for a second, before nodding. 'OK.'

Dick rushed out of the room behind me – probably headed for the mess, to bark orders at anyone who would listen. I moved to the door to open it for Nora.

'Thank you, Dr Chase, Dr Samedi,' she said.

'Don't mention it,' Beryl said, with a motherly smile.

'We'll be here all week,' Samedi informed her.

Nora didn't look up at me when she walked past. I followed her out into the hall, and walked at my normal pace for a few strides to get in front of her.

'All right, straight on, and then we'll cross the courtyard, outside . . .'

CHAPTER FIFTEEN

Pamela

The knock upon the door was prim and precise, and so I knew immediately whose it was.

'Come in, Isambard.'

I watched in the mirror mounted above my little vanity as my brother entered. He was a lean young man, fourteen years of age, with straight brown hair, hazel eyes, and a rather large mole on his cheek. He shut the door and bowed, a fussy movement. I bobbed my head, if only so that he wouldn't whine at me about not performing my 'reverence,' and focused again on my reflection. Normally such formality was forgotten around siblings, but Isambard always insisted upon it. 'What is it?'

I was getting ready for the much-anticipated Prime Minister's address, which we'd been invited to attend. One of his officials had come to the house yesterday evening to present my father with a thick white envelope sealed with pearly blue wax. No one but the PM could use wax of that color, and so we'd known immediately that it was of importance.

'The Prime Minister is sorry for the pain you must be experiencing, as acquaintances of Miss Dearly's,' the official had said, with a bow. 'He wishes you to know that his father has always thought fondly of the young lady. He would be honored if you would attend as his guests.'

When I'd thus learned that the envelope didn't contain bad news about Nora, I'd nearly passed out from relief. Isambard, on the other hand, had nearly had to resort to breathing into a paper bag in his excitement. I suspected that the invitation was all his peers had heard about during his morning lessons.

He still attended the same public school that I had until I'd started at St Cyprian's.

Isambard held out two cravats – one black with gray pinstripes, the other black with small red dots. 'I haven't a plain black cravat,' he said. 'Which is more proper?'

I stared at the cravats. 'I can't imagine that it matters, Issy.'

'But it *does*!'

'The one with the stripes, then.'

'But stripes fell out of fashion last season, everything's dots, now . . .'

'Give me strength.' I stood up and moved away from the vanity. I was wearing the lavender dress again. The material was thin and cool, and, accompanied by the memory of wearing it for the first time in front of Nora, it felt like ice against my skin –but I had none better. I approached Isambard and took the dotted cravat from his open hand. 'Put on the striped one.'

Isambard scowled and said several very quiet, possibly unkind things, but slung the striped cravat around his neck.

'It *sickens* me,' I said quietly as I folded up the dotted cravat, trying my best not to start crying again, 'that here we are, thinking about what to wear, when my best friend might be dead in a ditch somewhere.'

'Maybe,' Isambard said, as he knotted his cravat, 'you don't realize that a good showing on our part could convince the rich to help us.'

A slight breeze stirred the crocheted curtains hung over my room's single, open window, and played with the archery ribbons I'd arranged on the far wall. 'I know, logically, that everyone's already doing all they can to find Nora.'

He smoothed his cravat down within his black waistcoat. 'Who said I was talking about her?'

I actually heard the blood rushing in my ears. 'What?'

Isambard set his mouth in a line. 'I'm serious, Pamela. This could be a big chance for us, if you'd stop being so selfish.'

A million years went by, in my head, before I managed to ask, '*Selfish?*' The word didn't come out half as forcefully as I wanted it to.

My brother stepped closer, speaking rapidly, like a petitioner for a cause who'd managed to corner a member of Parliament on the public stage. 'Yes! You never seem to take advantage of the chances that you're given! Boom, you just happened to befriend a girl who became the daughter of a national hero! Like that, you sent off an application, and you were in the top school in the Territories! That's not luck – that's God's will, Pam. For *all* of us! All you have to do is make a good marriage from it, and we're golden!'

'*What?*' I tried again, disbelieving. It still didn't come out right.

'If you do it fast enough, I'll get into St Arcadian's before my schooling is up, for sure! Mom and dad will have less to worry about—'

'St Arcadian's?' St Arcadian's was the best boy's school in the Territories. I stepped closer to Isambard, forcing him back. 'Are you telling me that you think I should use this . . . this . . . spotlight, opportunity, whatever you might call it, to . . . to call attention to myself?'

'Of course!' he said, as if it were the most natural thing in the world. 'I mean, no one's going to ever care about our family, otherwise. Why not try to stand out while we can?'

'St Arcadian's,' I said, mostly to myself, as I continued to boggle at my brother. And then, the words came out. 'This is because you were too *stupid* to get in on your own, isn't it? *Who's* selfish, here?' He'd applied, I knew, and been rejected – twice.

My brother's face contorted in fury. 'Shut up!'

'No, *you* shut up! Don't try and foist your brown-nosing, ladder-scrambling ways on *me*! I've been lucky, yes, and I'll do what I please with what that luck has given me! Besides, this isn't about us – this is about Nora!'

'So you'd let the rest of us suffer?' he seethed. 'You think I'm going to be some no-name *baker*? Never! I don't belong here. I'm too *smart* to be here.'

'Then serve yourself, brother, but don't you dare try to tell me that Mother and Father have some stake in it. What would you do, have my future husband support them? They're proud people, they'd never accept that.'

'Why don't you ask Mom why she's willing to sit there embroidering, huh? If she were so proud, she'd be bucking tradition and working in the bakery as we *speak*.'

'She's doing it to protect me from embarrassment! I never asked her to!' My face felt hot, and I couldn't tell how loud my voice had become.

'And why do *you* need to be protected from embarrassment, then, if you don't care what the elite think of you?' he countered, nose lifted.

'Get out.' I ran to the door and opened it wide. 'Get out, and never set foot in this room again, do you hear me? You're insane.'

'What is all this?' My mother was just coming to the top of the stairs. 'What's going on?'

'Nothing,' I said.

'Nothing,' Issy agreed, voice surly.

My mother sized us both up, before telling Issy to go to his room. Isambard yanked his folded cravat from my hand and marched out, fixing me with the fire of his eyes as he passed. I glared right back, and tried to shut my door.

'Pamela, don't you dare shut your door on your mother.' I stopped and looked at her. She bent her head down. 'I do not want to hear you raise your voice ever again. Is that understood?'

'Isambard told me—'

'I don't care what he told you. I don't care what anyone tells you. We are going out into good society this morning. I know you are upset – we are *all* upset. But you must keep your head and act like a lady. Ladies never raise their voices.'

I stared at her in horror. Isambard was right. 'I'm not a lady,' I reminded her, voice breaking. 'My father bakes bread.'

'You can *become* a lady. You can have a better life,' my mother said, taking my chin in her hands. 'You are a smart girl. *Think*.'

It was hard for me to swallow, the way she held my head up. I tried desperately to keep the tears back. I thought of what I might say, how I might argue my way out of this. But in the end, all I said was, 'All right.'

Mom nodded and kissed my forehead. 'Breakfast will be ready in a few moments,' she called, for Isambard's benefit, as she headed back downstairs.

After I shut the door, I knelt down and tried to pray for strength and patience.

I ended up beating the floor with my palms until I could no longer feel any pain.

After a cheerless and awkward breakfast, we walked to the town square. It was perhaps a mile away from our house, but pretty much a straight shot up George Street.

The buildings of New London were a mixture of re-furbished pre-war structures and new edifices designed to suit. What was now the Cathedral of Our Mother, for example, was actually a centuries-old bank outfitted with marble columns and a granite statue of the Mother of All, her head bent solemnly over the proceedings in the streets below. Depending on cost and circumstance, some people chose to erect blank concrete shells of buildings and throw up holographic exteriors. Whenever the power grid went down they would flicker and die, though, and the city would look as if it had had been subjected to a silent bombing or the pillaging of a swift and ghostly army.

The street was crowded. It was eleven on a Tuesday, which meant that we had to contend with the usual shoppers and workers and schoolchildren returning for their afternoon lessons. Boys in low tweed caps bearing packages rushed right through the foot and vehicle traffic, the small screens chained to their wrists barking orders at them and providing them with maps. Street vendors hawked their wares from their carts by screaming about them.

'Apples by the pound!'

'Have you been reading *Barney the Vampyre*? The latest chapbook in this phenomenal series is out! Download it to your digidiary now!'

'Wind-up toys! Perfect for the holidays! Dogs, ponies, ballerinas!'

Screens glowed within houses and businesses alike, all showing the same thing – correspondents waiting outside City Hall for the arrival of those invited to hear the PM speak. Digital clackboards twirled bright advertisements at us as we walked past, reading the chips in our wrists and customizing the content to our publicly available data. As a teenage girl, it was supposed that I was interested in face cream and the up-coming spring fabrics and trims. Isambard's head turned to take these particular ads in. The skies above us were filled with silver zeppelins, most of them military, but a few flashing animated advertisements for new plays and television shows.

Young women in worn, but clean clothing sold vegetables and flowers from baskets beneath the shop and theater awnings. One had a small guitar and was singing 'Greensleeves'. I watched the flower girls with deep emotion. I kept expecting one of them to be Nora.

We were some of the first to arrive at City Hall. They'd set up a barricade against the press, so although they shouted at us, we were able to slip on by. Father, in his best clothes, the flour brushed out of his hair, provided the guardsman with our invitation. The guard nodded smartly, and turned to lead us in.

City Hall was a palatial building of iron and granite. The floors within were marble, the walls carved with relief forms of our former Prime Ministers, the ceiling painted with images of the Flood from Genesis. This was a recurring theme in New Victorian design, as our forefathers had considered themselves the survivors of a flood of ash, ice, and snow.

'Goodness me,' I heard my mother say, voice full of respectful awe.

We were escorted to the second floor, which contained a velvet-and-gilding amphitheater designed to seat five hundred people or more. Workers were bustling about the stage, and reporters were setting up their recording equipment in the back. Above the stage, on a long piece of blond marble, were engraved the words, 'Industry, Honor, Civility, Faith'.

'The Prime Minister would be honored if you would sit here, in the first row,' the guard told us. I swear my brother almost had a heart attack. As we took our seats, my mother slipped between him and myself, for which I was grateful.

I recognized some of the people who came to sit near us. In a rare turn of events, it ended up being myself, and my fellow classmates, who had to introduce our families. I took great pleasure in introducing my brother last, each time. They told us that they were praying for Nora's safe return, and we thanked them. As the room filled the introductions stopped, however, and soon we were simply one more family in the babbling crowd.

'Familiar with so many of them, aren't you?' Isambard breathed, tone smug. I ignored him. Truth was, I had spent more time with my classmates over the last eight years than I had with my own family.

And yet, I knew in my heart that they would never accept me fully. Issy would never understand that. He thought everything was so easy.

Ten minutes later the Deputy Prime Minister made his way onto the stage, and the gas lamps along the walls were dimmed. Final coughs were indulged in, and ladies fanned themselves in the artificial twilight, an endless whooshing of disembodied wings.

'Ladies and gentlemen of New London,' he began. He was my father's age, his chiseled features handsome, his skin the color of sun-baked earth. 'I am very pleased to welcome you here today, and so very, very glad to see all of you. In these try-ing times our people *will* remain strong. It is the ability to carry on with life that will see us triumphant in the end. Your very presence here is a blow to the enemy.'

There was thunderous applause at this.

'As ever, it is my honor to introduce the Prime Minister of New Victoria, Mr Aloysius Ayles.'

We all stood to welcome the Prime Minister as he stepped onto the stage. Mr Ayles was no older than his late forties, although lines already chased the corners of his eyes and mouth. He had molasses-colored skin, black hair, and a match-ing mustache and goatee. He looked much like his father, who'd retired from public life many years ago.

He gestured for us to sit down. 'I regret,' he began, in his usual forthright tone, 'that I have no news to share with you regarding either the attacks or the whereabouts of Miss Nora Dearly. Of course, all our prayers are with her.'

I fought back another rain of tears.

'I invited you here today on rather short notice, and I am sorry for that. I should have spoken sooner. All my attention has been focused on assigning our best and most capable men to the task of tracking down the villains who did this and bringing them to justice.

'On the practical front, I can inform you that we are recall-ing three companies of soldiers to keep closer to home. We are simultaneously reorganizing our troops so that we can step up our efforts on every front that is seeing active combat with the enemy. And we are growing a task force devoted solely to the mission of locating Miss Dearly, and bringing her home.'

The tension in his voice grew with every word. 'Why would anyone do something like this, really? Was their plan to murder, to rape and pillage? We've had no reports of confirmed deaths, no evidence of other homes targeted besides that of the late Dr Dearly. They were obviously on a tightly focused mission. What was its purpose, then?

'I believe it was to terrorize us. To frighten us. To make us alter our way of life. This is nothing new. Things like this will continue to happen so long as human beings have the capacity for fear.'

My shoulders were tight, and I tried to relax them. I glanced at my family. Dad was listening intently; Mom was crying a little. Isambard was looking around without trying to look as if he was looking around. His posture practically screamed, '*Adopt me! Someone notice me and adopt me!*'

Ayles lowered his eyes to the podium, and picked up a stack of papers. He showed them to the room at large. 'My notes here say that I should tell you that, "Our ancestors were not running *from* something, they were running *to* something." And then, that I should go on to explain exactly what it is about that "something" that the Punks find so objectionable. But earlier this morning, I decided that I shouldn't patronize you. You all know our history. You all know what makes us the strongest tribe on the continent.

'We chose, after a long period of blood and tears, to fix our eyes on a star and return to a time of civility, order, and beauty. We chose to honor those who died to earn us our place in history by making that place worthy of attention. We embraced such things as military power, high standards of conduct and morality, and technological progress.

'What makes us the strongest tribe on the continent is the fact that a group which opposes these values – a group which would have mankind remain in the new *dark ages* – is permitted to express its opinions, permitted to grow, permitted to *exist* . . . and, after it becomes a violent terrorist organization, is allowed to live on its own lands, *taken out of the lands of those it has attacked and continues to attack!*' He had to stop speaking, then – the applause was louder than even his amplified voice.

'They expect that fear will drive us to become like them . . . closed-minded, blind, angry. Our society will remain open and free so long as I am standing upright,' he continued, once the applause died down. 'We will never surrender to the desires of our sick, inhuman attackers. And I thank each and every one of you who came here today, who woke up this morning and dined and dressed and stepped out into the streets at the request of your leadership. It might not have seemed it at the time, but it was a noble, self-sacrificing thing to do. So long as our society is strong, *we* are strong.'

I stood with the crowd, though I didn't clap. Standing amid that final crescendo of applause, I wondered at the point of it all. The Punks wanted us to live like them? I would have been more than happy to be a village farm maiden with a wooden plow, if Nora were with me. I'd give in, if the Punks'd return her. Progress didn't matter *that* much to me.

At the same time, I couldn't help but feel that if they had really taken her, if they had done anything to her – I'd hate every last one of them until the day I died.

A few more families approached us as we made our way out, but not many. Isambard kept looking about like a lost puppy dog, eager for attention.

'That was wonderful,' Mom commented, cooling herself with her painted paper fan. 'I think that's just what a lot of people needed to hear. See, Pamela? You don't need to worry. Everything will be all right.'

'Yes,' Dad said. 'I just find it odd, though, that he didn't say more about *how* we're going to go after the Punks for this. We can't just let it go unpunished. I mean, if a group of them were living here, waiting to strike, why didn't the government know about it?'

'The Punks *want* us to punish them,' Isambard muttered. 'So they can point and go, "See? They're attacking *us*!" Better just to thumb our noses at them.'

I knew – as much as I hated to admit it – that what Issy was saying made sense. But my thoughts were still far away with Nora.

A second later, they were focused on someone else.

It was Vespertine Mink's fluffy hair that caught my attention. She was standing with her mother, Lady Elsinore Mink, and her mother's bosom companion, the much gossiped-about Miss Prescilla Perez. Both women were slender, fashionable brunettes.

Vespertine saw me, and regarded me with her customary coldness. She was, if not exactly pretty, arresting, with a smoothly sculpted nose, high cheekbones, and big gray eyes – but there was a morbid, calculating air about her.

Never mind that she had maligned Nora on a national broadcast.

I felt myself take a step towards her.

'Miss Roe?'

I felt my mother's hand on my shoulder and turned around. Michael Allister was standing before us with his family.

'Oh, hello, Mr Allister,' I said. If it had been any other day, my heart would have swelled in my chest – but right now, I wasn't the least bit interested. No matter how adorable he looked.

He pushed some his hair out of his face, and smiled slightly. He then took a step to the side, and said, 'May I present my father, Lord Leslie Allister, and my mother, Lady Allister.'

I mimicked him, introducing, 'My father, Mr Geoffrey Roe, and my mother, Mrs Roe, and my brother, Isambard Roe.'

There were reverences all around. Lord and Lady Allister, however, looked uncomfortable.

'Did you enjoy the speech, Lady Allister?' my mother asked, all politeness.

'Yes,' Lady Allister responded. 'Thank you. But if you'll excuse us . . .'

Lord Allister gave her his arm. With that, they walked away, leaving my parents to wallow in the wake of their blatant disinterest.

My father's jaw clenched. My mother's eyes widened, if only a touch. I wanted to run to her and hug the embarrassment away.

'Ah,' Michael said, obviously embarrassed himself, 'I just wanted to express my deepest sympathy, Mr Roe Mrs. Roe, Miss Roe.'

My father nodded, stiffly. 'Thank you, young Mr Allister. That's very kind of you.'

I could see Michael's Adam's apple bobbing through the collar of his shirt. Continuing to address my father, he said, 'I would like to beg leave to pay a call upon your house, perhaps sometime tomorrow.

Dad looked at mom, who looked at me. Michael was introducing himself as a friend, not as a potential suitor, else he would have asked to see me instead of the "house." But as if to stress his interest, he continued, 'Miss Roe and I met previously, at my parents' home.'

'We would be pleased to see you, Mr Allister,' my mother said.

Michael smiled, and bowed. 'Thank you. Until then.' He flashed me a smaller smile, before turning on his heel and hurrying off to find his parents. I watched him go, confused. Half of me *was* thrilled at the idea that he'd singled us out and asked to come over.

The other half felt guilty as sin.

I lifted my eyes to my mother. Mom looked as pleased as I might have admitted I felt, had it been a different time and place. The little bit of joy that this development had granted me evaporated. I remembered Isambard's words, and wondered. Was my mother viewing this as a chance to ascend the gleaming tower of the elite? Was she relieved that a rich boy might be interested in me?

And what am I doing?

I looked back at the crowd. The Minks were gone. What had I planned to do? Beat Vespertine up? Yell at her? She would never have received a better Christmas gift than my public humiliation.

Armies played the same games young girls and their families had to play.

CHAPTER SIXTEEN

Nora

'OK,' I said, bracing myself. 'What is his deal?'

'Doc Sam?' Bram asked, as he pushed the big steel door open and held it for me.

I stopped and looked outside. Fresh, moist air hit me. It smelled so green that my first impulse was to run out into the sunlight and just inhale. But first, I checked for zombies. There didn't seem to be any.

'Yeah, him,' I resumed, looking up at Bram as I stood on the threshold. 'How'd he . . . do that whole head thing? I mean, not the mechanics of it, but . . .'

'He cut it off.'

I felt my brow pucker. '*What?*'

Bram gestured for me to continue outside, and I allowed him to follow behind me once we were beyond the big steel door. After my encounter with the headless zombie, Bram seemed downright normal.

I wasn't sure if that was a good thing or a bad thing.

'Circular saw.' Bram fell in beside me and made a throat-slicing motion with his hand. 'He had been planning it for six months beforehand. Was pretty experimental, but hey, it worked.'

'But why in blazes would he do something like that?'

Bram pulled his mouth, as if debating whether or not to tell me. 'Because he tried to bite Dr Chase.'

I halted again, and so did Bram. 'But she acts so comfortable around him!'

'Mostly because she knows that if he tries it again, one good punch will render him harmless. Whenever he works with her, he takes his head off. He did it to reassure her, so she wouldn't leave. They're a brilliant team, we need them.'

I suddenly felt a chill, despite the sunlight tickling my skin, and wrapped my arms across my chest. 'Why'd he try to bite her?'

Bram ran a finger behind his right ear. 'He likes her.'

My throat started doing that funny tightening thing again. *'He tried to give her some kind of love bite?!* Is that what you're saying?'

Bram grimaced and lifted a hand to shush me. 'No, no! It was an accident! He . . . got brave one night, told her how he felt. She didn't return his feelings, I guess, and he got angry at himself. She tried to calm him with a hug, and . . . it happened. At least, that's how he tells it. He doesn't get angry often, so the hug and the emotions must have just fueled the Laz and made him lose control. I mean, he stopped after the first try. He didn't run after her, or anything.'

I allowed two fingers to rest against my lips for an instant, before asking, 'Is that a normal thing? Losing control?' I could hear the sick anxiety in my own voice.

'Not when we're healthy and mentally focused, no. And honestly . . .' He trailed off, and then relented with a sigh. 'We're the stable ones, Nora. The unstable ones destroy themselves out there, or go mad once they're in here. And we . . . take care of that.'

'What, you put them down?' I asked sharply. 'They use that phrase for *animals.*'

'Would you rather we keep them around, and let someone get hurt?'

I couldn't argue with that, but still . . .

'That man can have his head knocked off, my father thought someone might have to kill him someday . . . why? Are you all destined to go insane? Will you all become like those monsters back at the house?' My voice was softer than I wanted it to be. I'd tried so hard all morning to sound tough.

Bram trained his eyes on the ground. 'Do you really want to know?'

I took my new surroundings in again, restively. 'Just *tell* me things, OK? Tell me the truth when I ask, like I said before. I can handle it.'

'Yes. With medication and care, we have maybe five years to be ourselves.'

And he'd used up two already.

'We all know we're going to go at some point. Facing up to that is part of dealing with what we are. When I eventually lose it, I plan to lock myself in my room and keep myself there, if I can, until I've forgotten how to undo all the locks. My first choice would be to be shot, but, as I've gathered from experience now, you never know when you're going to go. Better to have too many contingency plans than too few.'

I looked at his face. It was so open, so calm. His dark eyebrows curved outward slightly over the blank canvases of his eyes; the masculine contours of his face betrayed no hint of fear. Here he was, telling me how he planned to face madness and death by imprisoning himself, and to him it was as if he was talking about the weather.

'It's all so awful,' I said. 'How do you stand it?'

He shrugged. 'I figure, looking back, who's to say how much time I ever had? I could have died permanently that day. Instead, I was given a few more years. And I plan to do something with them.'

I suddenly felt like a pathetic heel.

'C'mon,' he said. 'Let's go get you some food.'

He took me across an open courtyard studded with doors that led into squat buildings set around the perimeter. None of the buildings had more than two floors, and all were crafted of pressed metal and plastic painted with camouflage. A tall gateway separated our courtyard from another one exactly like it. I recognized the style from my father's war stories and holos – this was a hastily erected, temporary base. The parts were interchangeable, and could be snapped together in many configurations, but they offered no real protection against an attack.

We stopped outside the mess. I could hear voices within, and I flexed my fingers in unconscious preparation.

Bram opened the door. The mess hall was *filled* with zombies.

Squaring his chest, Bram marched forward. I scurried after him, unwilling to let him get far away from me. I realized, in that second, that I had ceased to fear him.

The undead sitting at the long, wooden cafeteria tables were another story.

There were more men than women, all of them older than Bram and clothed in black. There was no sudden silence as we passed, no flash flood of attention turned my way. Rather I was given furtive, stolen glances, which were then dissected in whispers. It was as if someone had warned them all not to stare. They were all dining on the same colorless, unappetizing meal – must be the tofu he'd spoken of. Through the low hum of voices I could hear the strains of Handel's 'Messiah'.

'What's with all the music I've been hearing?' I asked Bram.

'Life should be a jazz funeral,' he replied. 'I don't know. It's familiar, I guess.'

'Ren, you're insane,' a voice cried out.

Bram stopped, and I drew up behind him. A few feet away sat a table that had been taken over by four zombies that looked to be in their late teens. For some reason, it surprised me to see a group of zombies our own age. Two were eating, one was absorbed in a book, and the final one, the only girl, was peering into a pocket mirror and scraping a knife against her metal jaw. I recognized her from the med wing.

'We'll ask the young lady when she gets here,' the boy with the book said.

'Seriously, why do you *read* that crap?' asked the girl.

Book Boy snapped his volume shut, and removed his

glasses from his nose. 'I speak the truth! In all of these books the girls are *throwing* themselves at the romantic heroes – romantic heroes who are *dead*, who drink human *blood*. Be of good cheer, my brothers, for I tell you, there is *hope!*'

One of the other guys, a large black boy, rolled his lone eye. 'OK, you're cut off. Someone get him a cook book or something?'

'Or, you know, some fair damsel to seduce,' the girl said, looking up from her reflection. When she saw us, her mouth split into a grin. 'Hey, speak of the devil!'

The one with the book whirled around and held up his hands. 'Before we do this formally – you.' He looked at me, and I took a step back. 'Have you ever heard of vampires?'

I nodded. *Who* hasn't?

'Had you heard of zombies before you came here?'

I shook my head.

'*See?*' He thumped his book for emphasis. 'Vampires are just zombies with good PR! That could be *us* in a few years!'

The bald, noseless zombie sitting behind him rolled his fingers over his nonexistent eyebrows. I realized that I recognized him, too. 'You forget one important thing, Ren. Vampires *don't exist.*'

'Every myth is based on truth. And the ice hides many things.'

'Save it.' The girl stood up and brushed her hands off on her pants. She came over, stopping an arm's length away from me. Her gait was energetic, her smile cheerful, even though the lower half of it was metallic. I could see several designs scraped onto the metal, including a word – '*insufurabelle*'.

'Hi, I'm Chas.'

'Pleased to meet you,' I managed.

Bram took over from there. 'Chas is our Jill-of-all-trades,' he explained with a smile. 'And that's Tom Todd, grenadier.'

The noseless one nodded at me. 'Hey.'

'This is Coalhouse Gates, sniper,' Bram said, motioning toward the black teen.

'Welcome to the land of the dead, doll,' he said with a wink – or was it a blink? I couldn't tell.

'And this gent here is Renfield Merriweather the Third, engineering and logistics.'

Renfield donned his glasses again and stood up, bowing from the waist. 'My lady.' I bobbed in return, dependent on sheer muscle memory.

Bram indicated that I should take a seat. Every step I took in the direction of the table was a struggle, as the last thing my body wanted to do was move *towards* the undead. When my knees hit the bench, I knew that I had conquered my flight response, and I clumsily sat down. Bram sat right next to me.

Everyone was silent for a few moments, before Tom offered, 'That was some nice shooting on the roof.'

'Thanks,' I said, sliding my fingers over the fake leather of my pistol holster.

'Yeah, you made that easy on us,' Bram said. 'Not getting caught by the Grays, I mean.'

'Is that what you call them?'

'Mmm-hmm. They're our new toy. First ones showed up about a year ago.' Chas returned to her seat and took up her knife again. 'We only just managed to snoop in on a transmission from them.'

'That's what got us after you,' Coalhouse added. 'Seeing as it was about their plan to kidnap you. No idea why we didn't get a transmission before. Haven't gotten one since.'

'Yeah, I told her all this,' Bram said. 'But we were lucky, that the one we *did* catch was that one. They're a sneaky bunch. Wolfe has taken us out against 'em on several missions, but we've never quite managed to get the drop on them.'

My eyes swept along the table as they spoke. They were dead. *Dead.* They should be lying in boxes, wilted lilies sagging against their chests, worms crawling in and out of their flesh.

Instead, they were discussing fictional monsters and inter-cepted military transmissions.

The weird thing was, it was beginning to seem . . . maybe . . . just a little bit normal.

Dr Elpinoy made it seem even more normal when he suddenly appeared at our table cradling a tray in his arms like an infant. He hurried over and set it before me with just the slightest of fanfare. It was covered in baked breakfast goods and cups of tea – different kinds, judging by the varied colors. There was no meat, though, nothing savory. The cups and plates were made of paper, the utensils plastic.

Chas slowly lowered her knife. 'So. Jealous.'

'I hope this will be satisfactory, Miss Dearly?' Elpinoy asked, worrying his hands together.

'Yes, absolutely,' I said, feeling a bit overwhelmed. 'Thank you. You're very kind.'

Elpinoy smiled as if I had just complimented his entire lineage. Then his expression darkened, and he said, 'Ah, just . . . eat quickly.' Before I could ask why, he'd bustled off again.

I had to admit, as I looked at the tray, that I was starving. As I tucked in, the others made up for the fact that my mouth was busy.

'So,' Bram said, 'who wants to go first?'

'No,' Renfield said, flashing Bram a dirty look. 'Not while she's *eating*.'

'Not while I'm eating,' I affirmed, my voice muffled by pastry. 'Whatever it is.'

'Tell her about Z Comp,' Chas said.

'Sure.' Bram gestured around the caf. 'You're looking at about half of Company Z. Approximately a hundred and thirty dead, maybe twenty living at any one time, including our living captain, James Wolfe. Mix of New Vic and Punk folks, though we're technically on NV land.'

I swallowed and asked, 'Where's the other half?'

'Out on patrol,' Chas said. 'They got a call after our half

headed north to get you, and Wolfe went with them. Usual deal, just some bad zoms to take care of.'

'We're all one squad, here,' Bram went on. 'We're the youngest, so they sort of group us together for most things.'

'The children of the golden glitch,' Tom said, fluttering his fingers towards the ceiling.

I stared at him, lips halfway to a cup of tea. Without moving my head, I looked at Bram, who laughed. 'Talk about myths.'

'Hey, I think there might be something to it.'

'What?' I asked Bram.

'*Some* of the soldiers have this theory that if they had an evil, undead twin somewhere in the world, and both people were weighed, the good one would come out twenty-one grams heavier than the bad one.'

'I don't understand.'

'The soul,' Tom said. 'There's an old yarn says the soul weighs twenty-one grams. The golden glitch, the happy accident that makes it safe for you to sit here and eat cinnamon rolls without thinking that maybe you're stuffing yourself like a turkey for us to carve up. If we didn't have souls, you'd be toast. Literally, you'd be our breakfast.'

I dropped the Danish I was holding and forced myself to finish swallowing the suddenly hard, thick lump of food I'd been working on. I half thought it'd kill me.

'Tom, not cool,' Bram said, narrowing his eyes.

Tom grinned toothily. 'I thought it was clever.'

'You suck,' Chas said, 'so bad. My God.'

'OK, OK, I'm sorry.'

But I'd lost my appetite. I pushed the tray away. 'I would like to know how do *I* fit in?' Fueled by sugar and a little caffeine, I was relieved to find that whatever ability I'd ever had to make my voice sound grown-up had returned.

Bram asked, 'Fit in?'

'To all this. To the army. To . . . Company Z.'

Tom and Coalhouse shared a look. 'Uh,' Coalhouse said, confused, 'you don't.'

I shook more hair out of my eyes. 'You need to find my father. I figure I do too. Sounds to me like I'd better be included somewhere.'

'Nora, we'd be very grateful for your help,' Bram said. 'But you're not a member of Z Comp.'

'Yeah, you're alive,' Chas pointed out. 'Clearly, you're overqualified.'

I sat on my hip to look at Bram directly. Time to dial the stubbornness up to eleven. 'I want to join. I want to help. I've shot zombies. And given everything I've dealt with so far, why shouldn't I be able to help? You owe me.'

'Nora, you can't enlist in Company Z,' he said.

'Why? Because I'm a girl?'

Chas waved her hand. 'Nope! Ovaries are welcome here, so long as they're useless!'

'Why, then?' I bumped my fists lightly on the table. 'Look. I am furious about my father right now. I want to get him back. I want him to explain a few things to me, before I beat the prion-whatevers out of him. So, how do I join up and get out there?'

Bram cracked his neck and glanced at Tom. Tom lifted an eyebrow, silently asking whether he had permission to go on, before saying, 'You can't join because we're meant to be expendable.'

'Huh?'

'Any other unit, they'd have a policy that told your fellow soldiers to go after your pretty little rump and bring you back, dead or alive, if you got in any kind of trouble.' Tom pointed at me. 'Here, somebody drops or goes missing, we're officially ordered to leave them behind.'

Bram picked up the ball. 'You enlist, somehow get them to assign you to this company – let's ignore the ten billion reasons that neither of these things will *ever* happen – and that policy applies to you too.'

It took a moment for this to sink in. I'd never heard of such a thing before. I'd never seen anything like it in any of my holos. I'd heard plenty of stories about the heroic efforts made to retrieve fallen comrades. They didn't have that here?

As if they needed any more reasons to be depressed.

'That's . . . heartless,' I whispered.

Chas quirked her upper lip. 'Well, figure it their way. They send a living guy against a zombie, there's always a chance that he'll get the Laz, die, and turn on them. It's like sending soldiers to the enemy side. They send a zombie against a zombie, though, it's just a question of who wins.'

'But my father would never—'

'No, the Doc wouldn't ever think of us that way,' Coalhouse chipped in. 'But he had to justify saving us and keeping us around somehow.'

Tom nodded. 'A couple years ago, the NV higher-ups got tired of working with the Punks. They figured they should undertake one last big joint project and just exterminate us all. Stop playing footsie. Set the earth on fire, or something – kill all the zombies, and get back to their old dispute. Your dad convinced 'em to try using us first. He figured living soldiers wouldn't even have to know about the undead – an infestation'd pop up on the radar, we'd ninja in and take care of it. Surgical zombie-versus-zombie warfare. Thought we could continue to keep the whole zombie thing quiet that way.'

Coalhouse put a period on it. 'We've been doing our best, ever since. Building up our numbers.'

'We're weapons, Nora,' Bram said. 'Very expensive, fussed-over weapons, but to the larger government we're nothing more. And like weapons, they figure in the budget that they'll lose a few of us.'

'Nobody in the army spends a great deal of time trying to fish a gun out of a river,' Ren said, cracking open his book again. 'Far easier to buy a new one.'

It wasn't just Bram's face that was impassive during this

exchange. All of them appeared used to the idea, comfortable with it, even as it horrified me. They were either incredibly downtrodden, or incredibly strong.

The sensation of mild envy I was feeling told me that I had already decided it was the latter.

I rolled my shoulders. 'Well, I guess it's up to me not to require rescuing, then.'

The others looked at me incredulously. Bram took a breath, just as the door to the mess thundered open.

'Griswold!' a voice bellowed.

'We'll talk about this later,' he said, before climbing to his feet and standing at attention. 'Sir!'

I turned around, only to be confronted with the largest man I had ever seen in my life.

Chapter Seventeen

Bram

The end was nigh.

Nora stood up beside me. I hoped that she wouldn't notice how stiff I was, or how my hand itched to salute. I didn't need her to question me right now – everything had been going so well.

Wolfe was the *real* captain here, though, and we were all fully aware of it.

The sound of fifty soldiers standing and saluting echoed in the mess. Wolfe passed them all with nary a sideways glance. His eyes were on me. He was a gigantic man, easily seven feet tall and built like a bull. His uniform was like a wall of night approaching us.

'Griswold,' he said, stopping on a dime before our table. I nodded. He turned his attention to Nora, who lifted her chin and set her face in an expression of determination. 'Miss Dearly. How . . . surprising . . . to see you up and about.' His eyes swept over her guns. 'And . . . armed.'

'Thank you, Captain,' she said, with a little dip of her head. 'Is there any news of my father?'

'Not only armed, but aware.' Wolfe shot me a look that could melt steel. 'Actually, there is. We managed to track down his coordinates. Somehow he ended up going south, and we are extending our search in that direction.'

I looked at Nora and smiled. 'See? It's going to be all right.'

Wolfe shushed me with a twitch of his brow. 'I wish to speak with you at some point, Miss Dearly, regarding your father. But first, I must conference with Griswold here. If you'll excuse us.'

Nora sucked a breath in through her teeth and looked up

at me, the hard expression in her eyes melting away. 'Bram . . .'

Wolfe's nostrils flared, as though he could smell weakness. 'Is something the matter?'

'No, sir.' I thought fast, and asked, 'Miss Dearly, if I take you back to the med facilities, would you feel better waiting there?'

Nora nodded so fast I was surprised her head didn't fall off.

'Miss Dearly has proven remarkably adaptable,' I said, turning my attention back to Wolfe. 'But surely, it would be far better to let her remain where she's comfortable.'

The captain rolled a hand and said, 'Make it fast. I'll await you in my office.' He turned and stalked off. Walking through the crowd of soldiers, he looked like a Titan going for a stroll in the woods, head far above the trees.

'Thank you,' Nora whispered.

'Don't mention it.' I raised my voice and waved to my friends. 'Be back in a bit.'

'Nice meeting you, Nora,' Chas said.

'Yes, it was lovely,' Ren added.

Nora flashed them a nervous little smile and stepped closer to me. I allowed myself to bask in her unspoken trust, before leading her outside again.

'What do you think he wants to talk to you about?' she asked, once we were alone.

'Oh, a lot of things. I'm pretty much a goner.' I put my hands in my pockets.

Nora's brows drew together. 'Goner? What have you done wrong?'

'He told me, right after we got you in hand, to keep you in your dad's office and not tell you anything. So basically I'm in trouble for everything that happened from the moment you woke up onward.'

'Why didn't you do what he said?'

'Because we knew you'd freak out, and I didn't want to have to deal with that,' I said. 'And it wouldn't have been fair to you. You deserve better.'

'Thank you,' she said, her tone serious.

'You're welcome.' I chuckled. 'He just wanted us to march into the Fields, blow stuff up, and march out again. I wanted to see if you'd opt to come with me first, but then those coppers showed up. I figured it'd be less dramatic than, you know, an army descending upon the suburbs. Didn't work out so well, though.'

Nora actually giggled. 'Coppers aren't always fast. You probably could have just scooped me up and run for the hills.'

I paused at the big steel doors, and ignored the memories that her innocent words conjured up for me. 'Nah. That would have led them right to us. Besides,' I added, trying to joke again, 'you were putting up quite a fight.'

For an instant, Nora looked up at me from her tiny height – before she uttered an awkward little laugh and shoved me in the chest. 'Yeah, and after all this? I'd like to see you ever catch me again!' And with that she was gone, the doors bumping together behind her.

I stared at the doors until they stopped moving. I stood there until I was fairly sure I was composed. She *really* needed to not do things like that, because the Laz was *thrilled* at the idea of chasing her, and priming my muscles for the task.

Finally, I made my way to Wolfe's office.

Wolfe kept his quarters on the second storey of the barracks across from mine. The base's main office was housed beneath, staffed by unlucky and unhappy soldiers on an alternating basis. The woman there today, with a purplish complexion and a web of scars across her cheek, watched disinterestedly as I entered and ascended the stairs. I rapped on the door.

'Come in.'

This time, I saluted in his presence. 'Sir.'

'Sit, Griswold.' Wolfe was puffing on a cigar, and acrid smoke filled the room. He finished tapping out a few commands on his stainless steel, round-buttoned keyboard as I took a seat. I noticed that scraps of vegetation still clung to his uniform, and that the blood vessels of his hands were mapped out by insect bites.

'You have ten seconds to tell me why I shouldn't have you marched against the fence and shot for directly disobeying my orders again,' he said.

'I'll admit that I did disobey orders, and I apologize,' I said. 'But if we'd done it your way, sir, the girl wouldn't be comfortable enough to sit in the mess hall with fifty-odd undead people. She'd be too scared. She's . . .' *Amazing.* 'Coping.'

Wolfe finally looked at me. His eyes were bloodshot. 'Did Elpinoy know about this?'

I said nothing. I wasn't about to sell anybody down the river. Not even Dick.

Wolfe tapped his ash out. His movements were slow and tense, and I expected he wanted to rip me a new one. 'Griswold, you're fairly fresh. Your brain isn't too much like Swiss cheese, yet. You don't even look that dead. Why do you have such a tough time following directions?'

'I have a tough time following directions that don't make sense. That'll end in someone getting hurt.'

'Why? You're already dead. What d'you care?'

I didn't say anything. I didn't trust myself.

Wolfe puffed on his cigar and sat there like an idling dragon, milky smoke escaping his nostrils. 'The girl's latched onto you, has she?' he eventually asked.

'I doubt you could say that, sir. I'm just the one she's had the most contact with.'

'Hmm.' He eyed me narrowly. 'Just don't get too comfortable with it. You're not her little pal, Griswold. You're a monster. Remember that.'

My jaw clenched. 'Sir.'

'Now, I need to discuss something with you that will not leave this room.'

'Understood.'

He turned his computer screen around and hit a button, starting a video feed.

At first, I wasn't sure what I was looking at. The video was a jumble of disconnected scenes – ten-second slices of video, pooled from a variety of sources. There were street shots, shots from the interiors of buildings. Slowly, I recognized landmarks from the site of the extraction. Nothing seemed off; the video appeared to show people in the Elysian Fields going about their business.

Then came a man shuffling, aimlessly, down a street. A young woman collapsing behind a baby carriage, coughing so furiously that her body rattled.

Comprehension crashed through me, and I gripped the arms of my chair.

The Lazarus had been unleashed in the Elysian Fields.

At first, I didn't want to believe it. I forced myself to think logically. As the scenes clicked by, I watched for signs of rioting and violence. I didn't see any. I saw children playing in a park. Women exiting a market. Street-sweepers at work.

Then the video cut to a shot, taken from a camera mounted in an alleyway, of a well-heeled, velvet-clad woman nestling her head almost lovingly into the intestines of a doorman, his cap sitting in a pool of his own blood.

Jesus.

'Your men didn't get them all, Griswold,' Wolfe said in a low, dangerous tone.

'I wasn't there!' I fought out. 'We accompanied Miss Dearly onto The *Christine*! The others were to clean up and come on The *Erika*!'

'Are you trying to pass the blame off, Griswold?'

'No,' I whispered. 'No.' I watched the screen for a few more long, horrifying seconds, before standing up. 'We'll get on it. Now. We'll—'

'Sit down!' Wolfe said, lifting his voice. He twirled the

screen so that it faced away from me. 'Put your bones back in that chair, soldier.'

'But the longer we wait, the more civilians they'll kill!' I shouted.

Wolfe drew on his cigar, held it, and let the smoke waft out with his words. 'They're putting the Elysian Fields on complete lockdown. Going to spin it as biological warfare – which I suppose it is. Some of our living forces are returning from the Border, and should be arriving within the hour. They're gonna clean that place up.'

My jaw dropped, and I wouldn't have been too terribly shocked if it had actually fallen on the floor. 'They're sending the living against the dead? That's *suicide*! That's what *we're* here for!'

'You were never meant to go within twenty miles of significant settlements or living troops,' Wolfe said, stony-faced. 'Not yet, anyway. I send you in one time – *one time* – and look what happens. All because you don't listen to me. All because you think you know better than me!'

I punched my fists together and tried to think.

'I've been told to expect orders to split you up, send you out to the new infestations. Damn zombies are crawling farther and farther north . . . this whole thing's gonna blow wide open, soon enough. Damn Dearly and his *humanitarianism* – you ain't even human! And now I have to worry about *finding* the idiot!'

My fingers curled and uncurled as I began to pace around the office. 'We have to tell Miss Dearly.'

Wolfe's cigar exploded on the desk with the full force of his fist pounding against it. 'You say *nothing* to that girl, you got it?'

I turned on him. I could feel the anger causiing my dead heart muscles to throb out of sync with each other. It stung. 'That's her home town! She has friends there, family! You can't tell me you're not going to let her *know*!'

The captain made his way around his desk and stopped with his face very close to mine. I forced myself to maintain my position and meet the embers of his eyes. I didn't care if he was pissed off – I'd show him pissed off.

'Our mission, until I receive orders to relocate you, is to keep her safe and find her father. *Nothing else.* You tell that girl a word of this, I will send you south so fast your teeth will spin. Or, if I'm feeling my oats, I may just shoot you. You want that? You want to leave her here alone? Say a word, that's what happens. You get the back of a truck or a blind date with a bullet.'

I could bite his face off. My brain kept throwing that option out at me as I stood there, toe to toe with him. I could turn him into one of the things he hated most.

But I didn't.

'You're working on the rigs today,' Wolfe said, his glare never abating. ''Til nightfall. I don't want you anywhere near that girl 'til then, got it? Take the time to get your head right. Dearly ain't here to protect you now, so you better start doing what I say.'

'Yes, sir.' I was glad to hear that it came out as threatening as I'd meant it to.

'By the way – Elpinoy's not going to play your little games any longer. I've already spoken to him. That girl comes within five feet of a phone or a computer, I'll cut that much flesh off of you.'

Wolfe dismissed me with a flick of his head, and I beat it.

When I exited the gates that led outside the compound and stepped from the road to the flat, barren area where our vehicles were stored, the others on the rigs watched me closely. They could tell that something was wrong. *Good for them.*

I might've failed more spectacularly than I'd ever imagined, and the idea almost made me sick. I thought of the living trapped, dying there in the EF, and prayed that it wasn't my fault. I trusted my fellow soldiers; I knew they'd followed my orders and done all they could. But what if my refusal to do what Wolfe wanted had resulted in the Grays attacking the living, starting the whole mess, while we sat in the water and twiddled our thumbs?

Even as I envisioned the carnage going on, even as I swore myself up and down, I entertained a selfish, terrifying thought: what if the living figured out what they were facing? What if they figured out that there were more of us? They'd come after us. They'd pile us like logs and burn us. Destroy us.

Please, please, don't let me be responsible for that.

I had to focus, before I went mad or made another mistake. Before someone started trying to figure out what the matter was.

It only took me a minute to find Renfield. He was in his denim grungies, working on a monowheeled automaton in the middle of the yard. Another 'bot, with insectoid arms, sat motionless beside him. Whenever Renfield could manage it, he was out in the yard working on one thing or another. He was, to put it simply, a genius – of literature, history, mechanics. He wasn't much of a fighter, but when it came to machinery he was a real champion.

'Show me something that needs banging on,' I said.

He cocked his head owlishly at me. 'You speak of banging with a big hammer banging?'

'You got it.'

He rubbed his wrench against his jaw, and shrugged, pointing over my shoulder. 'We just got her in last night. Antique, practically. Her engine is good, but some parts just need to come out entirely.'

I looked. He was pointing to an airship – a real Punk airship, its wooden body worn and battered, its deflated balloon draped over a couple of nearby trees.

My body went slack with disbelief. 'You have got to be kidding. Where'd they find it?'

'I like to think that it was Santa finally coming through on years of passionate, but ignored childhood letters.' Ren shook his head. 'I don't ask. I usually don't like the answer.'

'How do they expect us to use *that*?'

'Well, first they'll pick out ten of us who still have good lungs, then . . .'

'Har de har har.'

Ren chuckled. 'I've no idea, my man. Perhaps as an aerial base from which to drop Things What Go Boom?'

'Maybe,' I allowed. 'But those things can't maneuver worth—'

'Manners,' he said, interrupting me before I could get to the dirty word. He started over toward it, and I trailed behind.

The ship was called the *Black Alice*, going by the words carved into its prow. The figurehead was a little girl in a pinafore and hair bow. I thought of Nora's shortened dress and bit my tongue.

We climbed the plank onto the ship. I gripped the railing, the black wood hard and polished beneath my hands, and my throat tightened. To any normal Punk these aircraft were as common a sight as sand, practically a symbol for the entire culture, and yet I hadn't seen one in a year or more. I wasn't so sure how I felt about the reunion.

'She might not be able to maneuver well,' Ren was saying, as he opened the doors that led below deck. 'But come and see.'

It was dark below. Ren grabbed a lantern suspended from the spare rigging and turned it on. It cast a cold, electric glow on our surroundings, one that my eyes instinctively interpreted as wrong. Electronics did not belong on a proper airship. Nothing *digital* belonged on a proper airship. The equipment I saw bolted to the floor and tied to the walls was all that any good Punk crew needed – heavy brass astrolabes, open-work globes with rows of peg holes for the recording of measurements, leather-bound books full of figures, shovels and tools.

Ren aimed the lantern away from the wall, towards the middle of the ship's belly.

Holy . . .

The thing had a major engine in it.

'Once we fix it up, this thing will be a rocket,' Ren was saying. 'We'll practically be able to fly to the moon. We shall be capable of some *major* buzzing of the living bases. Imagine the roar! They'll vomit up their own livers in fear.'

I shot Ren a bemused look. He cleared his throat. 'What? I can't be immature occasionally?'

Lifting my arms up, I gripped a beam and half-hung there. 'OK, then, Mr Immaturity. Tell me what I'm banging on.'

We'd made major progress on the *Black Alice* by the time the sun was setting behind the limp canvas of her air bag. As far as we could see, even now, she'd fly. It was just a matter of making her pretty and efficient again.

All that manual labor had helped to ease my mind, but after I returned to my room to take a shower, I found myself spending a little more time on my reflection than usual – rubbing my skin to see if I could bring any more life into it, combing my hair. After fifteen minutes or so, I came to the sad realization that there was very little I could do to change the guy staring back at me in the mirror.

I gave up, and headed to the med unit.

It was time for a staff change-off, and some of the doctors and technicians were busy donning their coats and locking up their cabinets. Things had quieted down a lot, but I could hear voices coming from Samedi's lab.

Nora was perched on a spinning chair, arms and ankles

crossed, expression dark. When I entered the lab she hopped off of the chair and came running over. The fact that she made this bee-line for me both warmed my soul and made me want to turn around, walk out the door, and find a cliff to fling myself off of.

Her city was facing a freaking plague, and I couldn't tell her.

I'd managed to forget this fact through physical labor, but now I had nothing to do but look at her, my mind burning with my betrayal. She wanted me to be honest with her. I wanted to be honest with her. But if I was, she'd be left alone in this place that she was only just coming to accept. Hell, she'd probably blame me for leading that plague to her home in the first place.

And I might never see her again.

'Bram, I need to call home!'

'Thank goodness you're here, Bram,' Samedi said. His head was on a nearby counter, but his body was animated, hands gesturing wildly as he talked. '*You* explain it to her.'

'Elpinoy was in, eh?'

'Yes!' Nora shook her head like an angry horse. 'No one will let me look at the news, or call my friend Pamela, or my aunt. You don't know Pam, she's probably close to *spontaneously combusting* over this! I did my part, I came out of your room! Now no one will tell me anything!'

'Phones and computers are on password protection, now,' Sam pointed out.

Great. How to tell her this? 'Nora, it's Wolfe's decision. Far as we know, any bit of intel the Grays get, they'll act on. Best to be cautious. That's why you can't call out.' There, that sounded OK.

'Then why won't anyone tell me if they've told my aunt where I am? Why can't I watch the news?' she demanded.

Samedi looked at me with a shrug. I wasn't coming up with anything, either. 'That's Wolfe again.' Might as well give blame where blame was due. 'He probably wants you to just . . . calm down. Let us handle it.'

Nora looked into my eyes. 'That's the stupidest thing I've ever heard.'

'Look, Miss Dearly.' Sam turned to face his head, so that he could see the front pocket of his lab coat to put his stylus away. 'When either one of us gets an order from Wolfe that *isn't* mind-bleedingly stupid? There will be no way that you will miss it, as we will both be leaping up and down and screaming uncontrollably, like adolescent monkeys on too much sugar.'

I decided to be as honest with her as I could. 'Remember what I told you earlier, about being a goner? I'm still here talking to you. And that means we have to obey the rules – at least for a little while. Something tells me that you know how that works.'

Nora sighed deeply. 'I'm too tired to argue with you people, anymore. I'll just guess the password on my own, how's that sound?'

'Good luck,' Samedi said. 'It's something danged complicated. I doubt I can even remember it.'

'Whatever happened to using the name of one's pet?' Beryl stepped out of the next room over, drawing her coat on.

Samedi turned around again, holding his head so that he could look at her. 'You're not rotating out yet, are you?'

'Only for one night,' she informed him. 'Some of the girls and I are going to go into town.'

'Oh,' he said. He seemed to shut down with that syllable. 'Well, enjoy yourself,' he offered weakly.

'I will.' Beryl moved to shake Nora's hand. 'Stay strong, OK? Good night, Bram.'

'Good night,' I said, as she parted from Nora and headed out the door.

'I'm starving,' Nora said, when she was gone.

'Why don't you go rest in your father's quarters, and I'll get your dinner? Won't subject you to the mess twice in one day.' Nora nodded, and walked out of the lab.

The doc watched her go, and then said, very softly, 'Don't let it happen.'

'Sorry?'

Samedi yanked his head back on, and once it was in place, looked at me very seriously. 'Just . . . don't let it happen.'

He shuffled off into the other lab, then, leaving me to stew in his words.

I ate with Nora in her father's office. She gorged on salad and bread and jam; I pushed my mush around my plate.

Eventually she slowed, and started moving her fork in a similar way. 'Bram?' she asked after a few minutes.

'Yeah?'

She looked up at me. 'I just wanted to say . . . thank you. Again. For all you've done for me today.'

Uh-huh. 'It's been my pleasure.'

Nora looked back to her uneaten tomatoes. 'What's Wolfe's story?'

'He was sent to oversee our base a while ago – before then he worked with the Punks, fighting the undead along the Border. For some reason, he came out of the woodwork to support your dad's idea of a zombie company, and asked to head it up. Before then, this was mostly a research facility, and there were only a few zombies on board. Only a very small percentage of the undead keep their minds. That's why our numbers are low, even now.'

Nora put down her fork. 'So there's a living captain, now, and a dead captain.'

'Nah, I'm captain in name only. Wolfe was here before I was. I took the battlefield commission test on a whim and passed, and your dad made angry phone calls 'til someone gave me my bars. He thought it'd be good for undead morale. Wolfe's the captain. I have no input. I'm just his eyes and mouth on the ground, mostly.' I smiled at the humor of it. 'Spare parts.'

'Sounds to me like he's not doing that great a job. Or that you guys like him much. Maybe you'll get a new one.'

I wiped my mouth. 'I hope not, honestly. Our existence is a crap shoot on a good day. The army could wipe us out at any moment. Especially with Dr. Dearly gone.' I hated to admit it, but, 'We need him. Better the devil you know. But it's weird, 'cause I guess everyone was happy to have him at first . . . back then every living person who chose to side with the dead on this project was greeted like a hero. Samedi was here when he came. He says everyone thought Wolfe was really enthusiastic about the dead contributing to the national defense. I don't know what changed.'

She didn't respond to this. When she did speak next, it was to ask a question. 'Can I ask you a favor?'

'What is it?'

'Can I sleep in your room tonight?'

I almost choked.

Her eyes got big again, and then she laughed, nervously. '*No!* I mean . . . there aren't any locks on the doors, here, and I don't feel as safe as I did in your room. Can I stay there, just one more night? Trade you?'

I cleared my throat, and wheezed out, 'Sure, sure, no problem!'

After cleaning our plates up, I took her there. She put her bag back on the bed and slowly removed her guns. I got a satchel of my own out of my closet and started packing up a few things. I was conscious that she was watching me, although nothing was said.

When I opened my desk drawer to get out my digital diary, she asked, 'Who's the picture of?'

I turned to look at her, the muscles in my neck tightening in anger. 'You went through my things?'

She at least looked abashed. 'Yes, I'm sorry. I just wanted to see.' She pouted. 'And anyway, if you woke up in a strange room, wouldn't you look through everything to see if there was a clue, or something?'

I would. I calmed myself down. I opened the diary, looking at the photo that sprang up on the screen. 'Me, and my little sisters. My friend Jack took it.'

Nora sat down on the bed, drawing her knees up to her chest. She wrapped her arms around her legs. 'Is that before you died?' she asked softly.

So she wanted my story, now. Great. I didn't want to talk. I was afraid of giving too much away. As I looked at her, though, I recalled how much I had been told about *her*, and I knew it was only fair.

I slowly sat down in my desk chair. 'I'm from a little town called West Gould. It's just a strip of road with a few businesses, really, to serve the farmers around. We're farmers too . . . well, *were*. The funny thing about the soil there is, after you clear the trees off it, it's gorgeous and you can grow almost anything – but it's thin. Few years later it's useless, and you have to let the forest take it again.'

'What'd you grow?'

'Lots of stuff. Corn. Pomegranates.' They seemed like such useless details, now. 'After we decided to let the forest back in, I went to work in the coal mines in East Gould. There's still a lot of coal there, deep down. Good work, if kind of dangerous. Mom took in sewing, washing, but there're so few people around West Gould. She did all she could. She could have had work elsewhere, but she had to stay with my sisters . . .' I ran my thumb over the screen. 'Adelaide and Emily.'

'How old were you?' Nora asked, resting her chin on her knees. 'If you joined the army when you were sixteen . . .'

'I didn't join the army when I was alive.'

Nora went quiet.

'They came for us in the mines. Whole bunch of 'em.' I tried to speak quickly, both for her sake and my own. 'They got Jack. Ripped his throat out. I managed to get us into one of the big elevators and close the door, but I'd already been bit . . . and it was too late for him. They chased us, they watched me as I locked us in. Watched while he died. They kept trying to get us, beating themselves at the door.'

I looked at Nora. Her expression was sorrowful. I couldn't take it, and glanced down again.

'I took the elevator to the surface. The elevator wasn't even supposed to *work*. If I'd known it would work, I could have saved someone else, maybe, but . . .' I shut my eyes. 'The elevator stopped twice. I figured it was going to be my coffin, but both times, it started going again. The mine was chaos. There were monsters up there too. I heard later that the army went in and caved the whole thing in, but there were no soldiers around when I reached the surface.

'So I ran. It was cowardly, but I was hurt, and Jack was dead, and I didn't know what to do, so . . . I ran. And then I walked. All the way to West Gould. Ten miles. I don't know how I did it . . . just determined, I guess. I hadn't seen myself, yet. I didn't know that being bitten would do anything to you. I thought I'd made it out alive, that I'd escaped.'

'Oh my God.'

Settling back, I continued. 'At one point I remember stumbling, and then coming to and just continuing on. I mean, I was in pain anyway, I was scared and lost, and . . . I didn't realize that I'd died while I was walking. Sam always tells me he bets I was awake again before I hit the ground. It just didn't register.

'When I got home, it was past nightfall. I knocked on the door, *so* relieved to be home. And my mother answered it, and . . . screamed . . . I'll never forget that sound, like everything she loved had died. I tried to hug her, tried to get inside . . . I was covered in Jack's blood . . . anyway, she got the rifle, and she shot me in the leg.'

I patted my hip. Nora made a little 'oh' of recognition.

'It didn't hurt – just kind of pinched. And that's when I realized what must have happened. I got away from the house, limped off, hid in the tree line. That's when it all hit me, and I saw how I might've hurt my family, and I was so sick. So sick. I stayed there for a day or so. I just wanted to die. I would have killed myself, but I was too sick and scared to even move, to go find something to *do* it with.

'No one came out. They must've known I was still there. At one point, though, my little Emily ran out with that teddy bear, her bear, and put it on the porch. Anyway, Mom yanked her back in and screamed at her not to go anywhere near the door, to leave it alone. After dark I crawled up to the porch and got it.

'I knew . . . it was her goodbye gift. And so . . . I left.'

I lifted my eyes from the photo. Nora was looking at me, through me, her eyes intensely bright. I hadn't meant to make her feel even worse. 'I'm sorry.'

'No, no . . . it's not your fault,' she whispered. 'I'm the one who's sorry.'

I snapped my diary shut and stood up. 'That's enough about me for tonight.' I laughed, a bit darkly. 'It'll give you nightmares. I'll come for you about eight tomorrow, Nora.'

She nodded wordlessly. When I got to the door and glanced back, she was still sitting there.

'Don't forget to wind the clock,' I reminded her, as I shut the door.

Chapter Eighteen

Victor

Henry came after nightfall, as I requested.

Averne was with him.

Averne shoved Henry violently into the hut. I rose quickly from my bed, and thankfully was able to catch his arm in time to help him maintain his balance.

'I want you to know,' my captor said, 'that I'm watching you. No tricks.'

'None,' I lied, looking squarely at him. 'But surely you must see the value in leaving a fresh man to guard and assist me.'

'I do. But I also know that fresh men are tricky.' He glared at Henry, who shrank away from him. 'I expect a report. An honest report. You have plenty of parts that can be harmlessly disconnected now – while you watch.'

'O-of course.'

With that, Averne turned and tramped off. We both remained silent, listening to his footsteps retreat.

Henry turned to me. 'I would n-never do that to you.'

'I'd hoped so,' I said, as I sat on my bed. Maneuvering around the crates with my crutch was proving difficult. 'You're just in time.'

I reached beneath the bed, and pulled a small baggie from between the slats. I'd long ago started a habit of carrying a week's supply of the medication designed to prolong our brain tissue at all times, as my brain was my most treasured possession. I'd have to split the shots with my new friend, now, but they'd help.

'What's that?'

'Medicine, Mr Macumba. I haven't time to tell you every-thing right now, although I know you're dying for an explanation. Sorry, terrible joke, there.' I unwrapped a pre-loaded syringe, tapped it, balanced it. I pulled my cuff back to access my valve, and gave myself half. Henry watched, transfixed.

'Once we get you back to base, I'll install one of these in you,' I told him. I indicated that he should sit down on the bed and give me his arm, and he did so. 'Until then, we'll try to get a bit into your body. Might not help, but it can't hurt.'

'All right.'

I injected him. I was always amused when the recently re-vitalized winced at a shot. True, their nerves were generally more sensitive than those of the older stiffs, but most of it was just learned behavior.

'Hold your arm up,' I said, pushing on it. Henry did so.

'You're so c-comfortable with all this,' he remarked. I noticed that his speech had greatly improved. The dog growled and circled at the length of its chain.

I nodded. 'It's my life, now.'

'Who is that m-man? Averne?'

'I was hoping you could tell me.' I glanced to the boxes. 'I know nothing about him.'

'He's crazy,' Henry said, rubbing his other hand over the elbow of his uplifted arm. 'You sh-should hear him in the long building, rant . . . ranting.' He stood. 'Are you going to m-make the vaccine?'

'I would sooner carve my own guts out,' I said, as I struggled to my feet. I propped my crutch against a crate and reached into it, drawing out a tissue-wrapped glass vial. 'Besides, as you so eloquently put it, he's crazy. I can't perform genetic engineering with a bunch of chemistry supplies. Even if I could, without computer models to check my work, the vaccine would likely kill everyone we'd inject it into.'

Henry uttered a foul word, then, and I couldn't help but smile. 'Oh, *that* you don't stutter on.'

He gestured impatiently. 'Well, what are you going to d-do, then?'

'Something that chemistry supplies are very good for.' When he gave me an odd look, I unwrapped a Bunsen burner and twirled it in the light. 'Making bombs.'

Henry proved to be a good assistant, so long as I remembered to fully describe what I wanted him to do. As we worked together into the night, he told me of his family in Shelley Falls – all gone, now – with the attitude of a man who had always been very aware of the treasures he possessed, but had not yet realized what he had lost.

I remembered that feeling all too well.

By the time that dawn was starting to stain the sky pink, we had several sealed vials of nitro ranged in a row. I looked upon them fondly.

'Mr Macumba,' I said, 'unchain the dog, just in case.'

By now the dog had grown used to us, and it sniffed at Henry cautiously when he approached. Henry loosened the chain from the metal tie thrust into the ground, rather than put his fingers too near the dog's maw. The dog didn't run away, but sat down and waited, expectantly. It seemed to be unsure whether or not it was supposed to take advantage of its sudden freedom.

'The name of the game is not escape,' I told Henry, as I pulled on my torn jacket. 'The goal is to create a distraction, and get to the broadcasting equipment in the main shelter. If we can get a signal to my base, we can wait it out here.'

'W-what about the . . . the vehicles?'

This caught me off guard. 'I'm sorry, the what?'

'You ha-haven't seen all of the base?'

I shook my head.

Henry offered me his arm to lean upon, and nodded at the door. I obliged him. He guided me outside, into the cool night air. Torches had been lit around the perimeter of the fort, and bonfires were blazing within it. Hopping along on one leg was tiring, even with his help, but thankfully he only took me past a few huts before drawing to a stop and pointing into the distance.

'Can you . . . see?'

I looked. It was hard to see, at first, for my eyes were still adjusting and the darkness, in spite of the fires, seemed unrelenting. Eventually my brain managed to piece together what I was looking at, calling shapes out of the shadows.

Averne's little army had about twenty rusted tanks at its disposal. They were of a variety of makes and models, some of them refurbished with parts from old trains and plows and other heavy machinery. I was amazed.

I was not, however, terribly hopeful.

'The only problem with that is if we take one, there are plenty left to chase us with. And they will chase us. There's no way we can just sneak one of those out.' I steadied myself. 'I still think we should try for the radio first. But if we need to . . . you are right. We can run for these.'

'W-what about the others?' he asked shakily as I urged him to turn around and head back to our hut.

'If you have to kill anyone, kill Averne. As far as I've seen, he has no living men left – only the dead.' Once we reentered the hut, I sat down heavily on the bed. 'And unless they have their wits about them, the dead are not the most loyal of soldiers. They'll be too busy with the fire, anyway.'

Henry fixed his eyes upon the vials, which lay flat upon one of the crates on a piece of toweling – I had been unable to find a stand amongst the equipment. I took two of the vials and wrapped them in cotton wool, tucking them into my jacket's interior pocket. I took the syringes from beneath the bed, and put them into the pocket on the opposite side.

'I've n-never killed anyone b-before,' Henry breathed. Desperation had entered his voice.

Oh God, not now.

'I just . . . l-let me . . . t-think it out. I . . . I n-never . . .' He moved slowly towards the crate, seeking support.

I reached out and tried to catch his elbow. 'Henry, calm yourself.'

He wrenched his arm away from me, his eyes shooting downwards to mine. His face blossomed into an expression of pure horror as he saw me for what I was, and realized fully what he had become.

In my research, I have found that beyond mere acceptance of the fact that one has died ('I'm dead? This would explain why my heart isn't beating. This makes sense,') there is a second crisis that must be overcome. This moment surrounds you, like a shattering crystal, with a thousand questions and sensations. You realize that you can no longer truly feel your body. You realize that your own flesh is dead, decaying, something you should regard as diseased and disgusting. The hunger truly strikes you, then, and the fear of that hunger. Your life, to be trite, flashes before your eyes.

Henry couldn't have picked a worse time to have his existential meltdown.

'Henry, listen to me.'

'No! No, I'm fine!' He grasped at nothing, his hands flopping about in the air, before, to my horror, he grabbed the nitro. I could hear the vials tinkling against one another in his trembling grip. 'I'm fine, I just need a moment to th-think about this . . .'

'Henry . . . no. Henry, no. Put them back down.'

He obeyed me, but not in the manner I'd intended. He decided, for whatever reason, to move the nitro to the edge of the bed. I hurriedly stood up and struggled away. Even as he rattled the vials together in his sudden fit, he looked like he was trying to keep himself together.

I knew that wasn't a good sign.

'I'll put these . . . put these here. Away. So I can sit down. I just need to think, to think . . .'

I turned around just in time to see one little vial starting to roll away from the pack.

Rather than try to catch it, I caught Henry's collar and yanked him towards me.

The explosion was massive. The dog went tumbling out the door with a yelp and tore off running, chain dragging along the salt. Henry and I were both thrown to the ground; the contents of the crates became projectiles. Only by pulling Henry to myself and scrambling beneath the fallen debris was I able to save us from serious injury.

Henry was screaming, clawing, acting out of terror and instinct and pain. I patted my chest, relieved to find that the vials I had hidden there were still intact. I then turned my attention to the man writhing against me.

'SARA! SARAAAA!'

'It's all right. Henry, calm down. It's all right. You're here, you're here – look at me, *now*, and be strong. You must get through this. You *must*!' If we were to have any hope of trying again, he had to. But my heart was already sinking fast. 'Come on. Pull yourself together. We have to move!'

Before we could do that, our coverings were pulled back, and the angry light of the fires raging around us suddenly intruded. I felt a boot against my head, and then, nothing at all.

Chapter Nineteen

Pamela

Just a few hours after the Prime Minister's address, a new phrase started scrolling by on the news tickers and booming from the mouths of the talking heads: 'biological warfare'.

There was still no video of the Elysian Fields on offer – only the excited faces of the reporters as they described how the complex was going into complete lockdown, with no one permitted in or out. Eventually, footage appeared of red-coated soldiers entering the Fields and securing the ruined gates. Displaced residents formed massive lines outside City Hall, begging for aid and information. They were the lucky ones. Horrific tales circulated about those trapped inside, condemned by virtue of where they had been standing at the time the order went out and the soldiers marched in.

Most people were outraged over this turn of events, but it didn't matter. Those in power had their plan, and they were sticking to it. General Giles Patmore himself went on the air that evening to explain that during the attack the Punks had apparently released some sort of virus or bacteria that was making people terribly ill – killing them. The goal was to keep the disease, whatever it was, from spreading aboveground. He said that they were going to implement quarantine and keep troops down there until everyone who *would* die *had*.

The city was electric. People thronged the streets, pubs, and tea parlors to gossip, and as the gossip trickled down to the younger set, Isambard and his pay-as-you-go phone faithfully reported on what was being said. Some of the stories making the rounds were pretty wild – especially those told by refugees from the EF. Someone, somewhere, had started a rumor that the infected were attacking people and *eating their flesh*. Mother wouldn't let him finish reading that series of texts aloud, thank goodness.

My father, who got his gossip through the bakery, thought that stories like this were caused by mass hysteria – meaning everyone was going a wee bit crazy, all at the same time. That might explain it. But something told me to keep my ears open.

The next morning I was allowed to leave the house to pick up our daily groceries, as Isambard claimed that he had a sour stomach. I figured he'd really stayed up half the night texting under the covers, but I didn't argue – I was desperate to get some fresh air.

My mother made me wear her long black mantilla, a veil of lace and netting, to keep up appearances. The sky was gray, and I thought that I smelled snow on the air. Snow was very rare in New London, and when it did appear, it made everyone nervous.

The streets were thick with refugees. Some were looking for work, others for a place to stay. Some just walked, having no idea where else to go. Their eyes were haunted, to a man. It was spooky, making my way through a crowd full of ghost-shackled people who barely noticed me.

I purchased what I'd been sent to get from the little open-air market about a block from our house. The stall workers eyed the refugees with distrust. I wondered how overblown the rumors were becoming, how much damage they might be doing.

As I tucked the last paper-wrapped parcel into my basket, coffee-skinned Ebenezer Coughlin set up shop on the corner. Mr Coughlin was a busker, and a very talented one. He played a flat instrument with strings crisscrossed down the length of it, a Mink creation. As much as I couldn't stand the sight of Vespertine, her family was known for the stringed instruments they created, and it was impossible to deny the quality of their sound.

He drew the bow in a serpentine pattern over the strings, stirring the sounds together into one sweet chord. I stopped to curtsey on my way past. 'Good morning, Mr Coughlin.'

He let the bow lie on the instrument and tipped his hat to me. 'G'morning, Miss Roe.'

I glanced around. Refugees were resting under the awnings of the market stalls that had not yet opened. 'Going to play today?'

He shrugged, and set his hat down on the ground. 'Seems like the best thing to do. World needs a little more music than usual today, by my reckoning. Might help calm people down.'

I couldn't help but smile a little. 'Wise of you, sir.'

'Eh, I didn't get this gray hair for nothing.' With that, he took his seat and began to play. I put the last of the money I'd been given for groceries into his upturned hat and continued home.

Isambard had left for school by the time I got back. Mom accepted the basket from me and put it aside, and then took me by the arm. The mantilla slipped off my left shoulder.

'Let's get you fixed up.'

'Fixed up?'

'Yes, for young Mr Allister's visit.'

A thousand words bounced about in my brain. I let only one of them out. 'Oh.'

Twenty minutes later I was standing in my room, in the lavender dress again, as my mother adjusted the fall of the fabric and primped my hair and stroked my eyebrows into place. I closed my eyes and tried to concentrate on how nice it felt to be touched by my mother's familiar hands. But I couldn't shut my mind off.

Quietly, I asked, 'Are you excited that he asked to come over?'

I opened my eyes. Mom had paused, her hands in my hair.

Her expression was unreadable. 'Why do you ask that?'

'Because . . . I want to know what's expected of me. You told me before that I should concentrate on things like this, but it's all so confusing.'

She sighed and let go of me. She walked over to the vanity and picked up a blue ribbon. 'We truly thought about whether we ought to send you to that school.'

I was confused. 'St Cyprian's? Why on earth wouldn't you?'

'Because, Pamela, it's resulted in this. You're too low-class by birth to ascend far, and now too well-educated to be happy here.'

'Mother, I'm happy here. I love all of you.'

She shook her head and moved before me, sliding the ribbon around my neck. 'Trust me, Pamela. You know that your grandfather was a ditch-digger. I married up. I've played this game before, though never on the level that you will have to. And you have no choice – you have to play. If you do not try to rise above your station, you will be *kicked down*. You can either make some sort of gain, or have much taken from you. That's what you must realize . . . that's what I try to call your attention to.'

As she tied the ribbon in a bow, my eyes fell upon my archery trophies, and I understood exactly what she was talking about. I had a lady's education to live up to, now. Even if I actively chose to remain in the gutter, the stars would always be watching me.

'As for Mr Allister's calling . . . I *am* excited. I would be excited if any young man asked to come and see us, Pamela. You're entering that period of your life now.' She looked to the window. 'I won't lie. I pray every night that you will make a good marriage. But I don't want you to think that I would have you make *any* marriage.'

I bit my inner cheek. 'Isambard said . . .'

'Isambard needs to learn when to keep his mouth shut,' my mother said, firmly. 'Even when he speaks truth, he does not speak it in wisdom. And this is *not* the time to be thinking of such things, regardless. All of our thoughts are with Nora, and those in the streets . . . as they should be.'

I looked to my hands. 'But Mr Allister's still coming over.'

Mom kissed my forehead. 'Exactly.' She drew back and looked me over, before announcing, 'I have a surprise for you. I was going to give it to you for Christmas, but I think you need it now.'

She left me, and went to her room. While she was gone, I thought about what she'd said. For some reason, at that moment, I felt more annoyed than resigned. Despite my mother's reassurances, I felt like my crush on Michael had been soured by manners. Was I not permitted to have a single thing of my own? Could I not enjoy even an innocent crush without it becoming a serious affair?

At the same time, I felt sick with shame for wanting to enjoy it. I remembered the sound of Nora's voice mingling with Michael's, how happy we had all seemed that day in the garden of rare birds.

At that moment, for just a moment – I wanted to be free of everything. Every burden, every fear. Just for a *moment*.

I knew that this was unlikely to ever happen.

When Mom came back, it was with a long, irregular package wrapped in thin paper and tied with a ribbon.

'What is it?'

'Open it and see.'

I did, untying the ribbon carefully, so that I could add it to my collection. I ripped the paper away, revealing a gas lamp parasol, lacy white.

'When Nora comes back,' she told me, 'you shall be the prettiest pair out walking. What boy, rich or poor, could resist?'

I desperately hoped that this would come to pass, my fingers trailing along the buttons on the parasol's handle.

Isambard returned for breakfast, and I made a show of asking after his health and serving him at the table. His expression told me that he didn't know what to make of my show of kindness.

'What are you doing?' he whispered, when Mom had her back turned.

'Showing you what two-faced behavior looks like,' I whispered back. 'For when you get to Arcadian's.'

His scowl made my breakfast taste *so* good.

A little before ten he got ready to depart for school again. My mother waited at the open door to see him off. The street outside was still filled with people.

'My stars,' she commented.

'Dirty vagabonds,' Isambard sniffed.

I couldn't help but gawp at him. Perhaps he hadn't gotten the point. 'Isambard, some of those people are richer than our family ten times over.'

He looked at me. 'Well, now they're dirty vagabonds,' he said, tone dry and hateful. I realized that fighting with him was useless. It would be far better to focus my energies elsewhere.

As Mom was closing the door, we saw it. Making its way slowly up the street, through the crowd, was an electric carriage in enameled blue and silver. I stepped closer to the doorway to watch with her, to see if it really was him. Sure enough, I saw a hint of gold hair through the tinted window. 'It's Mr Allister.'

Mom shut the door and practically dragged me to the parlor. She did a once-over on me, patting things into place, before grabbing a book from the cabinet and throwing it at my chest.

'Oof! Mom!'

'Sit. Read.' She then hastened back to the door.

I did as I was told, and counted to ten.

The knock came perhaps five minutes interminable later. Mother straightened her own plain dress, waited for an agonizing fifteen seconds more, and opened the door. 'Ah, young Mr Allister! How pleasant to see you.'

I heard him respond with, 'Good morning, Mrs Roe. I hope I'm not intruding.'

'Not at all. Please, come in.' When I heard his feet on the floorboards I thought again of how, at any other time, I might have been positively giddy at the notion that Michael Allister was in *my* house. Today, I looked at the book on my lap and tried to muster up enough energy to smile.

Our parlor is a little shabby, but clean. The walls are painted a faded blue, and the cluttered fireplace and shelves are built directly in. When they entered, I stood up and curtsied. 'Mr Allister, how do you do?' Despite my melancholy mood, I felt my cheeks flush at the idea that Michael Allister was standing there.

He bowed. His gray suit was perfectly cut, and his cravat matched the green of his eyes. 'Very well, Miss Roe, how are you?'

'Doing as well as can be expected.' I sat, and so did my mother, which gave him permission to as well. He chose to sit opposite me, on the other end of the sofa. My skirt was currently hiding the little hole I'd put in it when I was younger.

'I hope you encountered no problems on the road,' my mother said.

'I think there's nothing *but* problems to be had on the road,' he said, looking to the window. 'Has this been going on since the arrival of our forces?'

'Yes, it started yesterday.' My mother adjusted her apron over her dress. 'We're the part of the city closest to the Elysian Fields, likely we'll see everyone move through here.'

'Ah,' he said, in understanding. There was nothing but the ticking of our old grandfather clock for a minute or more, before he offered, 'It's a good thing Miss Dearly isn't here to see this, really.'

'No, it's not,' I said. Michael and my mother looked at me oddly. I explained, 'I mean . . . she'd be in the thick of it, if she were.'

'Ah,' Michael said again. His tone of voice told me that he didn't quite accept this.

I swallowed and added, 'We all hope to have her back with us soon.' Michael reached into the pocket of his velvet frock coat, drawing out a handkerchief. It was embroidered with his initials in navy blue.

I shook my head and took a deep breath, even as I felt my cheeks burning.

'It would be a great honor to me if you would have it,' he said, offering it forth.

I slowly reached out to take it. 'Thank you.'

He smiled stiffly. 'I must admit, your family has been much on my mind. Miss Dearly's aunt, Mrs Ortega, is staying with us, you know.'

I shook my head. 'No, I didn't know that. Is she well?'

His brow furrowed. 'Yes, she's well.'

'And her staff?' I thought of Matilda and Alencar, and found myself suddenly worried about them.

'She would have to tell you – I'm afraid I don't know. They are not with us. Honestly, I think it's rather low of her not to have been in touch with you.'

My mother's posture straightened. 'Well, Mr Allister, you move in circles that are not likely to *be* in touch with us, aside from a few necessary words. Your parents demonstrated that yesterday.'

Michael coughed. 'I cannot apologize for my parents, but I am sorry that you were made to endure that slight. It was not my intention to subject you to that. I must have my parents' permission to speak with you, to come here, but . . .' He looked at me again. 'I do not care how grudgingly it's given, so long as I have it. I hope to count you as a friend.'

I admitted, 'I hope to count you as a friend, as well.'

My mother said nothing, but went about her handkerchief embroidery with more patience than usual, which told me she was repressing the urge to dance.

The rest of the visit passed in the usual way – talk of the weather, of school. Michael attended St Arcadian's. Chuckling, he said, 'I hope to have longer to spend with you, some day – the stories I could tell you about school. It might distract us both.'

'I half think I could outdo you,' I said. 'Keep in mind, I bring an outsider's perspective.'

Michael tugged on the lapels of his waistcoat. 'You think so, hmm? It's on, then. Verbal pistols at dawn.'

I actually smiled.

And then I heard screaming.

We all leaped up at once, like marionettes attached to the same string. Michael and I ran to the parlor window, while my mother went to the door. Pushing the curtains back, I could see a crowd fleeing towards the outskirts of the city. One man trailed behind them with a bloody arm lifted in the air.

A bow was clutched in his hand.

God in heaven.

'Miss Roe!' Michael shouted, as I ran away.

Without even thinking about it, I grabbed the first thing my hand landed upon from the umbrella stand near the door – which just happened to be my new parasol. My mother was standing in the open doorway, her fist to her mouth, and I had to physically shove her back to get out of the house. She grabbed me by my skirt and attempted to pull me back inside.

'Pamela, what are you doing?!'

'Let me go!' I yelled. 'Let me go! It's Mr Coughlin – it's Ebenezer Coughlin! Someone has to help him!'

'Someone will! Get back inside, it's not for you to handle!'

I wanted this to be true. I watched the crowd anxiously,

waiting for someone to go to Mr Coughlin's aid. But they just kept running. No one stopped.

I took my skirt in my hands and tore it away from my mother. I ran into the street, into the massive current of humanity, the only person going in the opposite direction. I used the parasol to shove people off if they wouldn't move, to fight my way through. All I could think of was getting to the poor man and helping him.

The ribbon around my neck came loose and fluttered away on the cold breeze as I finally got to the back of the crowd. I raced over to Ebenezer. 'Mr Coughlin! Oh, Mr Coughlin, let's get you inside . . .'

'She bit me! She *bit* me!'

'Come to the side of the street.' People were watching us from the surrounding doorways. I caught the empty sleeve of Ebenezer's coat and started to lead him in the direction of a nearby hat shop. I heard doors slamming, more screaming. 'Help us! Someone, help us! He's been hurt!'

'She *bit* me!' he warbled, voice tight with fear, 'And she *ate* it!'

I stopped in my tracks, every muscle freezing, including my heart. I slowly looked to Ebenezer's arm. He continued to sob about how someone had eaten it, just gnashed it up and swallowed it whole . . .

There was blood. A lot of blood. And a chunk missing out of his forearm.

My parasol clattered to the ground. I dropped his coat and put my hands over my mouth.

That's when I saw her.

She was stumbling up the street, a young woman with copper hair, skin the color of molding trash, eyes jaundiced yellow. A low, endless moan escaped her throat. She was walking on a broken foot, her ankle twisted to the side, useless. It might have been funny if it didn't look so painful, if it didn't tell me that something was dreadfully wrong.

Ebenezer saw her too, and started shrieking. He ran, blood splattering the asphalt behind him. I heard more people shouting, my own mother among them, but I was rooted to the spot.

This is what the illness did. The stories were true.

The shouting attracted the sick girl, and suddenly she was moving with lightning speed, honing in on me. She hit me before I could even think of running, forcing me to the ground, her teeth snapping at my head. She was like a mad dog.

Now screaming myself, I tried to push her off by the shoulders, to keep her mouth away from me. Fueled by some mysterious rage, she was impossibly strong. I struggled blindly, adrenaline surging through my limbs, my mind a wasteland of terrified emotions and jumbled ideas.

Then my eyes fell on my parasol, and I took a chance.

I let go of her with one hand, grabbed it, and started hitting. Whether it hurt her or not, I couldn't tell, but she was distracted enough to flail at the parasol instead of me. I was able to fight her back just far enough to squirm out from under her and struggle to my feet. Panting, I clutched my parasol like a baseball bat.

She came at me. I hit her, hard. It kept her at bay. But no matter how hard I tried to swing it, the parasol wasn't heavy enough to seriously injure her. I tried running, but she was so fast that she was able to catch me by my gown, just as my mother had done, and I had no choice but to turn around and face her again. Soon she had me backed up against the wall of a building, helpless prey. As I watched her approaching me, crouched low and hissing, I realized that I was going to die.

I'll never know what possessed me in that instant – what part of my brain was calling the shots. Perhaps Nora was dead, and her spirit was screaming instructions at me. But in a final, pathetic attempt to save myself, I turned the umbrella out like a javelin and thrust my weight behind it in time with her next animalistic lunge.

Whether guided by luck, or by the will of the universe, or

by Nora's phantom hand – when the woman ran at it, the spiked metal gas lamp on top went right through her eye. I screamed like a warrior of old, like the rampaging Punks in Nora's stupid holos, and bore down on my improvised weapon.

I heard a sickening crack.

She went down, twitching, at my feet.

I dropped everything and staggered to the side, trembling. My limbs felt like blancmange. I looked up. People were staring at me from windows and doorways. I heard pounding footsteps and then Michael was there, not ten feet away, looking at me as if he didn't know me.

I'd just killed someone.

I'd just killed someone.

I'd just killed someone.

The last thing I heard as I sagged to the ground, the pavement scraping my palms, was the wail of a siren.

CHAPTER TWENTY

Nora

I awoke the next morning a little . . . happy.

It was a bit surprising, given everything that was going on. And I wasn't sure who Happy Nora was, anymore – it'd been so long since I'd seen her last. But I was willing to become re-acquainted with her. I let her do her thing.

Happy Nora got out of bed and stretched her arms towards the ceiling, rolling upwards onto her tiptoes. Happy Nora suddenly felt there was something to look forward to out there, something large and bright and currently invisible but descending, fast, like a ray of sunshine from between the clouds. No matter how complicated my current situation, the simple fact was that I'd been in danger, and I'd been saved. I'd been torn back from the edge of disaster. And what's more, there was the chance, the *chance*, that I would see my father again, feel his arms around me, hear his voice.

I was angry at him, yes, but at least he was still out there to be angry at.

Things were going to be OK. More than OK. Yeah, there was a *lot* wrong with the universe just now – but in the end, it was going to be OK.

And Happy Nora viewed Bram's room, I found, not as a curiosity, but as a place where an incredibly brave, honest young man lived. In fact, the thought of Bram made Happy Nora bounce a little on her toes, and that's when I grabbed her by the shoulders and stopped her, a little embarrassed for both of us.

Don't get too carried away, there.

I didn't rifle through Bram's things again. I made his bed tight as a drum. I got dressed and brushed my hair and then sat, waiting, barely feeling the chair beneath me. I could have just left the room, but I didn't want Bram to have to come looking for me.

Happy Nora suggested that that might be *fun*, hiding somewhere just to see what he would do. Would he panic, or would he very calmly search every inch of the place, like a hunter? Which would we rather he did?

Thoroughly irritated, I told Happy Nora to scram for the day. We'd not found my father yet, after all – and he had a *lot* of explaining to do. I still hadn't gotten to call Pam, either. And the story Bram'd told me last night . . . the last thing he needed was someone making trouble for him.

He knocked twenty minutes later. I opened the door.

'Good morning, Br—'

He was standing in the hall, a silvery weapon supported against his shoulder. It had two crescent-shaped blades, one on either end, with a rod between them.

'What on earth are you going to do with *that* thing?' I yelped.

I took a step back, my heart rate picking up, wondering if this was it – if he'd come for me, like the Reaper, after all. Oh, how foolish I'd been . . .

Bram smiled with half of his mouth. 'Teach you how to use it.'

My fear and confusion immediately dissolved. 'Oh, *keen*.'

'Yes, they are, so be careful.' He turned his wrist as he handed it over, making the thing twirl. It caught the light, like a pinwheel. I took it in two hands. 'This is a modified double-loaded spring action scythe.

'Awesome.'

Bram leaned against the door frame, watching me as I examined the weapon. 'I figure that you're about the tiniest thing I've ever seen.' I gave him what must have been a murderous look, and he laughed. 'My sisters have to be taller than you by now. How old are you?'

'Almost seventeen,' I grumbled. 'Yeah, I'm short. How observant of you.'

'Nothing wrong with being short,' he said. 'I think it's cute. But it's not so good for fighting. Guns are the best weapon for you, truly, so long as you can keep the undead at a distance. But you're going to need something like this if you get caught up in ground fighting.'

I momentarily brushed aside the idea that he thought something about me was cute. 'Ground fighting? You mean . . .'

He held up a hand. 'No. No army for you. But hey, it's dangerous out there, and the more you know about defending yourself the better off you'll be. I think that's true for anyone, but especially girls.' He grinned. 'Tiny, tiny little girls.'

I squeezed my fists around the weapon as I glowered at him – and ended up on my rear end as the rod shot out an extension on either side. What had been a construct about two feet long was now as tall as me. Bram laughed like a maniac as I struggled to my feet. 'How do I make them go back in?!' I asked, my cheeks burning.

He came around behind me and put his arms on either side of mine, still laughing. 'There're two little levers. You slide 'em both at the same time.'

I did nothing of the sort. I was still. He was behind me, his chest almost touching my back. It hit me again how easily he could tear my neck out, how easily he could crush me, how he could . . .

He let go of me, and cleared his throat. 'Are you listening?' He wasn't laughing anymore. I cursed myself. I'm sure he was angry at me for hesitating, for freezing like a hunted deer when he'd never shown me the slightest indication of violence.

Contrite, I worked the levers. The rods snapped back in with a whoosh. I looked up at him, cheeks still pink, I'm sure. 'Yes, I am listening.'

There was no anger in his eyes. Instead, he looked

frustrated. 'We'll work in the yard together after breakfast. But first, we're going to visit Chas.'

'Why?'

He sized me up. 'You think you can fight with that thing in a ball gown, be my guest.'

I glanced down. I was wearing the second dress Beryl'd sent, and I hadn't cut it down. 'Ball gown? This isn't a ball – hey!'

He was already walking away. With a sigh, I followed, before I lost sight of him.

'Love's like a cigarette . . .
You know you had my heart aglow
Between your fingertips.
And, just like a cigarette
I never knew the thrill of life
Until you touched my lips.
Then, just like a cigarette,
Love seemed to fade away and
Leave behind ashes of regret . . .
And, with a flick of your fingertips,
It was easy for you to forget . . .'

Chas's tiny single room was in a barracks off the other courtyard. The other women I'd seen seemed to be housed in the same area, in long, multi-bunk chambers. Their radios and Victrolas warred for supremacy, and in the mix I could hear popular Victorian music, ancient symphonies, and strange beats that I couldn't identify.

Bram knocked, and Chas opened the door, her music growing louder. She had strips of tin foil in her hair, and a cigarette dangling from her lips – which she immediately hid behind her back when she saw Bram.

'Hiiii!'

Both of Bram's brows flitted upwards. 'Hi.' He looked at the foil. 'I'm not even gonna ask.'

'Martians are trying to control my thoughts, stupid.' She noticed me, then, and smiled. 'Hi, Nora! Ooh . . .' Her eyes fell to the weapon. 'Shiny.'

'Nora needs some more appropriate clothes if she's to use the shiny,' Bram said.

Chas clapped her hands together. '*Makeover!*'

Oh, God, no.

Chas reached out and took my wrist, pulling me within her room. I looked at Bram as I was hauled past, but couldn't even get a word out before he waved and shut the door.

I stared at the back of it. I was going to have to kill him. It was a crying shame, but I was going to have to. It was a matter of principle.

Chas had a window in her room, and she smushed her cigarette out in a glass dish before opening the shutters to let some sunlight in. Her room was a disaster area – clothes every-where, posters and prints rolling off of the walls due to the humidity, the floor practically carpeted with nameless bits of plastic. Some of these she kicked aside, clearing a path. 'Sorry about all this,' she laughed. 'I'm a slob.' She pulled the sheets over the bed, and gestured for me to sit down.

I did so, taking the modified-whatever with me. I propped it up against the wall, near a picture of a sharp-featured boy in a jabot and pearls. Or was it a girl? I couldn't tell. Chas caught me looking and said, 'Oh, that's Tory Angel – or Victoria Angel, sometimes. He's an underground singer, he *rocks*. Ever heard of him?'

'No. Is he a Punk artist?'

'Oh, no, he's New Vic. I was too, before I died.'

I looked at her in disbelief. 'You were?'

She nodded happily. 'Um-hmm! From Buffalora.'

Recognition dawned. Buffalora was on the border between

Panama and Colombia. 'I know that place! It was hit by a massive storm . . .' I looked into her eyes, and realized, 'The dead, a few years ago.'

'Ten points! Buffalora is my personal favorite government cover-up to date.' Chas pointed to her hair and added, 'Just let me get these out before we get started . . . but yeah, anyway. Gosh. Seems so long ago. I was pretty much *the* princess, let me tell you. Only child, spoiled rotten.'

'So you weren't in the army, either?'

She started unfolding her hair from the foil, revealing that she'd dyed in stripes of purple and pink. 'Oh, hell no. My parents would have cut off my arms and legs first. I was actually betrothed to the owner of a big vineyard. I was excited about it. Not over *him* – he weighed like, five hundred pounds – but I figured on free booze for life. I was gonna be like Marie Antoinette, you know? Partyparty. Then the dead invited themselves to the rehearsal dinner.'

Her voice was bubbly, but I couldn't help feeling pity for her. 'I'm so sorry.'

'Yeah, was an awful day. But . . .' She shrugged, and started working water from a ceramic pitcher through her hair. 'It's happened to better people than me. Mom and I were the only survivors. And by "survivors" I mean "awake again and not totally insane, like Uncle Marcos".'

'Where is she?'

'Next room over.'

I looked to the wall. Chas shook her head. 'The other one. But yeah, she's here. She works for Wolfe, and takes in mending and stuff. Camp follower. I actually think,' she said, as she draped a towel over her head, 'that death kinda saved our relationship? It was sorta strained for a while, there, but now we're best friends. You'll have to meet her, sometime.'

The idea of being introduced to another zombie didn't exactly fill me with joy, so I kept quiet. Still, I found myself somewhat cheered by the idea of a family continuing after death. Maybe I'd be able to say the same thing about my dad and me, someday.

Chas shook her hair. 'That'll do. Now!' She threw the towel aside and trained her eyes on me. 'Huh, I'm not sure where to take this. I got everything – I collect stuff from vacant houses when we go out on missions. I figure it's not stealing, not if the stuff's not gonna be put to use anymore.'

'Oh,' was all I could think of to say.

'How do you feel about short skirts?'

'Um, I haven't worn short skirts since I was a little girl, but I'm not completely opposed. I mean, you saw what I did with the dress yesterday. Calf-length is fine.'

Chas made a derisive sound and opened her closet door. I half thought the clothes in there, as tightly packed together as they were, would shoot out at her en masse. 'Live a little, girl! You're in the middle of nowhere! S'why I smoke, now, and do my hair like this, and all that.' She pulled out a skirtand held it to her waist. 'I figure, what's it gonna do, kill me?'

'I can't go outside like this!'

Chas leaned on my shoulder, both hands layered beneath her chin, and joined me in looking in the mirror. It'd taken her a while to settle on this combination, but now she would not be swayed.

I looked like a slut.

'I think it's adorable, you big dummy.'

I was wearing a swirly black knee-length skirt with a short crinoline beneath it, black stockings, and black knee-high boots. I had a white blouse with elbow-length sleeves tucked into the skirt. She'd tied my hair back with a white ribbon, just to get it out of the way.

'You can't even *see* your legs! And look, when you get

a thigh holster for your pistol . . . oh my gosh, that will be *so* cute.'

'It's completely immodest!'

'Well, I was gonna knock on the door, but now I wonder if I should or not,' said Bram from the hall. He was back, hidden behind the closed door.

I looked at Chas. 'Don't you dare.'

She backed up, with a giggle, towards the door. I glared at her, before looking to my weapon. Sensing my intentions, she held her position. It was like an Old West showdown.

We both sprang into motion in the same second – she running for the door, me for my blades. She got to her target first, and wrenched the door open. Just as I was picking up my weapon Bram was standing there, watching me.

I tossed the blades down on the bed and screwed up my face. Let him say a word. 'Well?' I spread my arms out. 'This was *your* big idea.'

He was looking at me as if he had never seen me before. I felt the heat rising in my cheeks again. I *could* move more easily, I wanted to move more easily – but that was beside the point. I felt practically naked.

Bram cleared his throat, and said, 'What is it with you guys and your rooms? You know, we *do* have the odd inspection.' He turned his head very decidedly from me, taking in the surroundings.

Chas smirked. 'Are you gonna write me up?'

'No.' He held out a hand for me. 'Come on, Nora. I want to start practicing sometime before midnight.'

I was left feeling very . . . lost. I wasn't sure if he approved or disapproved. And why did I *care* what he thought, either way?

I picked up the blades again and approached him, although I didn't take his hand. Chas smiled at me. 'You look really cute. Trust me. Just keep doing like you're doing, and you'll be fine. Nobody's gonna think you're a slut.'

'Doing like I'm doing? What am I doing?'

Chas fluffed up her damp hair. 'Spending time with a zombie, letting her touch you and talk to you and stuff, without screaming your head off? Anyway, see you later!' She waved as the door shut.

I walked with Bram out into the courtyard again. After a while he said, 'She's right, you know.'

'About what? The touching thing?'

'Yeah.' Bram glanced to me out of the corner of his eye. 'What we want most is just to be treated the same as anyone else . . . and . . . well . . .' He sped up a bit, and I had to trot after. 'She's right about the clothes being nice too.'

The last bit he said so quickly that I had to slice apart his words in my mind. Once I understood what he'd said, I stopped in the middle of the courtyard and laughed. It was too silly.

'Miss Dearly?'

It wasn't Bram speaking. I didn't move at first, because I almost thought I'd imagined it.

'*I think he will leave us in a few moments, Miss Dearly.*'

The sound of that voice was forever burned into my memory.

I turned around, slowly. Standing there, not five feet away from me, was my tutor Horatio Salvez.

I dropped the weapon and rushed to him, throwing my arms about his neck. He hugged me back fiercely. 'Oh, Miss Dearly, I'm so glad to see you here, you've no idea. I was there the night you were taken.'

I felt tears pricking my eyes. I pulled back so that I could look up into his thin, kind face. 'You were there? Do you work for the Doom, now? Or are you still working for my father?'

'Both. We're all here now.' He pulled me close again, and I didn't fight it. 'You've no idea how good it is to see that you're safe.'

'You knew about him, then,' I whispered against his collar. 'You knew he was still alive.'

His arms sagged. 'Yes. I'm so sorry that we couldn't tell you.' He pushed me back gently. 'I truly am. It was what he wanted to do . . . but you have no idea how many times I've wished I could make up for it.'

Horatio's eyes were filled with such remorse that I decided to let the issue go. Instead, I said, 'You can. It's apparently been decided that I'm not to contact anyone – or see what's going on outside the base. I feel like they're hiding something from me.'

Horatio glanced past me, to Bram, and then back again. 'Ah . . . actually, I've been tasked with bringing you to Wolfe. You can ask him about it.'

Finally. 'Perfect.'

Horatio nodded. 'I'll have her back in a bit, Captain Griswold.'

Bram picked up the scythe. For some reason, he was frowning. 'Head to the mess afterwards. I'll meet up with you after you eat, how's that sound?'

'Yeah, OK.'

Without further ado, Salvez escorted me across the eastern courtyard and through the central gate. There were zombies at drill in the western courtyard, and we had to keep close to the wall and take the long way around. Distracted by the sight of the dead soldiers, I didn't immediately pick up on the location of Wolfe's office – although it should have been incredibly easy to do so, seeing as a crowd of people was gathered outside of it. I recognized a few other Doom scientists, and heard Samedi's sardonic voice as I was ushered quickly inside the building.

'*Let's stay south of the Panama Canal*, he said. It's a natural firebreak, he said. *What can go wrong*, he said.' Samedi sounded upset.

'What's going on?' I asked Horatio. The woman at the front desk studied us as we walked past. She was a zombie, the lower half of her facial skin completely gone, her muscles withered and her teeth stained.

'Ah, usual rotation chatter,' he said, without looking at me. 'Our unit just got in. That's when Wolfe told me you were here.'

My bull-sense started tingling.

Wolfe was waiting for us upstairs. He stood when I arrived, and bowed. 'Miss Dearly.'

I curtsied. 'Captain Wolfe.'

As he sat again, his eyes lingered on my short skirt. I pressed my knees together, trying hard not to feel ashamed.

'How . . . lovely to finally speak with you. Please, won't you take a seat?'

I did so, arranging the skirt down over my legs. Horatio sat at my side.

'You've found clothing to your liking, then?'

'These clothes are for practice.' *You pervert*, I wanted to add.

'Practice? Should I ask?'

'Captain Griswold is teaching me self-defense.'

Wolfe's brows drew together, and he tapped his beefy fingers on the desk. 'He is, is he?'

'Well,' I said, a bit shortly, 'I am surrounded by the walking dead.'

Wolfe seemed to relax a bit at this statement, and even chortled. 'Good point, good point. I'm glad that you can keep that in mind, Miss Dearly – that they are not to be completely trusted.' He eyed me narrowly again. '*Never* to be completely trusted.'

I tried valiantly to keep my mouth shut.

'I'm sorry for not speaking with you sooner. You must be terribly confused. I have plenty of materials here to show you, though, explaining the nature of the soldiers at this base and your father's role . . .'

I tuned him out and turned inward. Bram'd already told

me what I needed to know – including the fact that he wasn't *supposed* to tell me. Interrupting Wolfe's little documentary session by informing him that I already knew everything might just dig Bram's grave a little deeper. That was the last thing I wanted to do. But neither did I want to waste any time.

'I apologize for interrupting, Captain Wolfe, but there is one thing which I *do* find terribly confusing.'

His head turned a fraction of a degree towards me. 'What's that?'

I decided to speak his language. 'Why am I subject to an information blackout?'

Wolfe was silent for a moment. When he spoke again, it wasn't to me. 'Dr. Salvez, would you do me the favor of letting me speak with Miss Dearly in private?'

'Ah, of course.' Horatio stood, and gave me an apologetic look. 'I'll wait outside for you, Miss.'

I looked at Horatio. 'It's Doctor Salvez, now?'

'Yes, it is, actually,' he said, unable to contain a proud smile. He bowed, and saw himself out.

The moment the door shut, Wolfe leaned across his desk. 'Miss Dearly, I'm taking time out of *my* day to talk to you. I'm keeping no secrets. I would hope that would earn your trust. There are some protocols that simply have to be followed.'

'Like Protocol D?'

Wolfe sat back, his eyes slitting. 'Yes. Where did you hear that term, may I ask?'

Brilliant. Attempting to retreat, I changed the subject. 'Even prisoners get a phone call. Last I knew, I wasn't being held captive. I've not even been told if my family knows that I'm safe.'

'No, you're not a prisoner.' He reached into the humidor on his desk and drew out a cigar. 'I *thought* you were an intelligent girl. As that is now up for debate, I will make myself perfectly clear. You are being kept here as a last resort. It is *not* the safest location, but it'll do. The soldiers here are, at heart, creatures who would sooner eat you than look at you.'

He wasn't telling me anything I hadn't already told myself a thousand times. I knew perfectly well that there was a certain level of danger associated with everyone here, and that I shouldn't trust them.

But . . . I was starting to like them. More than this blowhard, anyway.

'Chatting with your friends and watching DVNs should be the furthest things from your mind. You've got survival to worry about.' He pointed to himself. 'I'm worried about your safety. That's *all* I'm worried about.'

'I'm not talking about watching television,' I argued. 'Nothing stupid like that. I want to at least tell my friend, Pamela Roe, that I'm all ri—'

'If you're smart, you won't interact with the undead unless you must, and then you will take *everything* they tell you with a grain of salt.' Interrupting me was, for Captain Wolfe, merely a manner of opening his mouth. His voice completely over-powered mine. 'Do you understand me?'

I reminded myself that Wolfe was a captain in the army, and ground out a dull, 'Sir,' rather than what I truly wanted to say. It was clear he didn't take me seriously, and he wasn't going to give me what I wanted.

Wolfe set his cigar down on the ink blotter. 'And it sounds to me as if you ought to spend a little less time gallivanting around with Griswold. I don't think your father would approve.'

My head shot up. The way Wolfe was looking at me, I could tell precisely what he thought that 'gallivanting' might entail. I suddenly felt sick to my stomach.

I stood up. 'Captain, do you have a daughter?'

'I do,' he said. 'Two.'

'Grand. Then kindly save the lectures for *them*, and spare me.'

I might've insulted his mother, the way he looked at me. 'You watch your mouth, young lady.'

I didn't. 'Captain Griswold has done nothing but treat me like a lady – and like one with a brain in her head, to boot.'

The captain's enormous chest rose and fell like a bellows with his breathing. 'Miss Dearly, you might've gotten away with talking to your father in that fashion, but you won't with me. You're not a prisoner, no – but I have the authority to keep you in a *hole* until your father is found, and if need be, I'll do so. I want an apology, *now*.'

I wanted to storm out without another word, to show him just what I thought of his threats. If I didn't think it would get Bram and the others in trouble, I would have. Much as I hated to admit it, he *was* in power, and he did have the authority to make life very unhappy for all of us.

I forced myself to stand tall, so as to look down on the man as much as I could. 'I'm sorry, *sir*.' If the God of Sarcasm needed an avatar here on earth, I was up for it.

Wolfe reached into a box near his elbow and pulled out a little brass cigar cutter. 'Good. Now, just keep in the back of your *brain*, Miss Dearly, that if Griswold could, *he'd eat it*.'

My eyes widened in horror at this idea. When I realized that they had, I despised the bully for catching me off guard, for making me show weakness in front of him.

'Now, you're dismissed. You obviously don't want to listen to me, so I'm not going to waste my breath. Let's see how far you get on your own.'

Before my mouth could run off again, I turned on my heel and marched out. I leaped down the stairs two at a time and angrily punched my way out the swinging doors. Horatio, who had been standing outside, hurried to catch up.

'Are you all right, Miss Dearly?'

'Fine,' I said, through gritted teeth.

The crowd outside had dispersed, much like the one in the med hall the previous day. It was obvious that they were keeping something from me. I glanced around the busy courtyard, surveyed the dead people still at drill, but Bram was nowhere in sight. Horatio halted beside me, expression concerned.

'I'm going to go eat breakfast,' I said slowly, after counting to three. 'I'll see you sometime afterwards, all right?'

'All right, Miss Dearly. I'll be working in the med wing. Whatever you prefer.'

I would have preferred to see Bram.

Chapter Twenty-one

Pamela

Oh, how I longed for prison.

Upon my arrest, I thought that I'd be taken to New London's prison, known as Drike's Island. I had *murdered* a woman. Instead, they told me that I was going to be held at a local police station until law enforcement officials could 'sort things out'. I'd been in shock, still, and could only nod weakly in response when one of the constables explained it to me.

They'd taken me to the West Herbert Avenue station house. It was a claustrophobic brick building that, given current events, greatly resembled a panicked bee hive. Between the constables rushing about and the people coming in to petition for missing loved ones and beg for information, the screens mounted in the waiting area and behind the front desk were inaudible. Their constant flashing only compounded the overall aura of alarm.

The majority of the women in the dank communal cell into which I'd been placed were drunks and loiterers, repeat offenders who either slept their stupor through or curled up and waited to be released. To them, it was all routine. I'd not spoken to them. I wanted nothing to do with them. A few of the women were like me – individuals caught up in the rioting. They'd been eager to talk about their stories. I hadn't been eager to listen. I didn't *want* to be part of a world where things like this could happen – I didn't want to be reminded that I was. I didn't want to have to think about people fighting for their lives out there on the streets, or how fast the illness might be spreading.

I was terrified of the infected, though no more terrified than I was of myself.

Hours passed, and still no one told me what I was being charged with, or when. There was no mention of a bail hearing, or anything like that. I wondered if bail would even be required. I knew that it would take my parents a while to scrape together the money.

So, I tried to be patient. I tried to block everything out. I couldn't tell how many different policemen there were. I couldn't tell how many times a guard came to the door and passed around wooden bowls full of mushy boiled vegetables and tin cups full of water. I didn't eat. I barely drank. Every time a new prisoner was pushed inside I clamped my arms around my head and squeezed myself into a corner of the dark cell, as far away from them and the maddening flashing lights and the angry crowd outside the barred door as I could get.

Before I knew it a full day had gone by, and I was beginning to fear that my parents would simply disown me and leave me at the station. It was a real, hot, physical fear, and it grew worse as the hours wore on. The numb haze I had managed to enter into abruptly ended. I did things I never imagined I would do, stupid things like drumming my feet in infantile frustration over the lack of a barrier between myself and the people who continued to come and go, always coming and going – it was driving me mad, having nothing to put between them and me. I felt exposed, vulnerable, utterly alone. I wished they would take me to Drike's, give me my own cell in a *mile* of cells, and leave me to rot.

By the time the guard shoved the girl with the dishwater hair inside the cell I was swiftly turning into a wreck.

The girl was about my age, with a broken nose and no curves to speak of. Her skin was mottled with strange spots of black. She curled up in the fetal position on a bench, coughing.

I knew she had the sickness.

'Officer . . . officer?' I asked, pressing myself against the rusted bars of the cell. My own voice sounded strange to me. It took a while, but in time one approached me – a freckled young man with dirt-colored curls and a port wine birthmark on his chin.

'Is there a problem?' He spoke loudly, but he couldn't disguise his own timidity.

'Please, officer . . .' I looked at the girl. I kept staring at her until I was sure he was looking with me. 'I think she's sick. I think she has the illness.' When I returned my eyes to him, he was already walking away. I gripped the bars even more tightly. 'Officer, please!'

'Sit down and remain calm!' he barked back at me. His freckles were like stones scattered on a sugar sand beach, he was so pale. I fought back the sob that wanted to rise in my throat.

'*Please!*' I pleaded, as I never thought I could or would have to. When I realized that he wasn't going to turn around, I slumped back onto the thin, hard wooden bench and let myself cry. Most of my cellmates paid me not a bit of attention. They were probably used to it.

I didn't want to have to hurt another person. That's what I kept repeating, in my mind, over and over – they were people, they weren't monsters or anything silly like that, they were sick people and oh my God, I had killed that woman, I'd killed her, I'd killed her. Then the world went away again, and I clutched my own body, and prayed.

By noon or so, I wasn't the only one who was worried. My fellow prisoners slowly gravitated over to sit by me, and together we watched the girl as her condition grew worse. Everyone seemed to instinctively realize what was happening, and no one tried to aid her. A few slid their shawls over their mouths.

'What do we do if she goes ballistic?' a pimpled woman with a deep voice asked. No one replied.

Please, no. Not again.

Eventually one of the loiterers, an old woman wrapped in ratty blankets, stood up and started banging on the bars with a rag-bundled fist. Her voice creaked as she tried to yell over the din of the civilians gathered outside.

'We got a sick girl in here, real sick!'

I watched the girl's chest rise and fall.

'Why'd you put a sick girl in here, you idjits? She needs t'be in a hospital!'

I watched her chest fall.

'You hear me? Ramirez, I'm talking at'cha! You want us all ta get it? Is that it?'

It didn't rise.

She was dead.

Thank God. Thank God. I never thought I'd lift thanks to heaven over the fact that someone had died – but the dead couldn't attack the living. Far better that she was dead, and not by anyone's hand. Horrible to say it, but far better.

The old woman got into her stride, and bellowed, '*Sick girl in here!*'

'She's dead,' I said. The woman didn't hear me, and continued to yell.

The crowd of people gathered in the station took up her cry. Most of them headed for the street, newly reborn as a screaming, stampeding mob. Those of us in the cell, on the other hand, remained calm. Perhaps it was because we knew we had nowhere to run.

'Morons,' a woman sighed. 'They act like girls shy of their pimp's hand.' The woman sitting beside her laughed nervously.

I slowly slipped off of the bench and took a shaky step towards the girl's corpse. I had been knotting and worrying my handkerchief in my hands for the last few hours or so; now, I placed the wet and grimy thing slowly over her face, as a mark of respect. I suppose it was my way of apologizing for mentally celebrating her passing.

As if by magic, at that moment a gurney sailed through the exodus outside the cell, accompanied by two paramedics and the copper with the birthmark.

I turned around as they opened the squealing door. 'I thought you'd left us!'

The cop shook his head, sweat flying from it. 'No! The hospitals are swamped.'

'She's dead. It's too late.' I looked back at the poor girl, over my shoulder.

The handkerchief caved in over her mouth as she sucked in a noisy breath.

I screamed and fell backwards onto the bench again, my hands reaching out to catch hold of the bars behind me.

'She's got it!' I heard one of the paramedics shout. 'Get her on there, *now*!'

The paramedics lifted the girl by the arms and pulled her none too gently up onto the stretcher. My handkerchief slid from her face and landed on the floor. They managed to strap her down by her wrists and ankles before she came to.

She wasn't dead – far from it. She was snarling, snapping, fighting her bonds as the women about me wailed and uttered prayers.

'Sweet suffering,' the cop whispered.

I stared at the thrashing girl, her frenzied movements tearing her own skin beneath the restraints, rubbing it raw. She'd stopped breathing. I'd been sure of it. I'd seen dead, still bodies at family funerals before – she'd been *dead*.

'Pamela!'

I looked to the door. My mother and father were standing there.

The horror before me ceased to have meaning. I fell down

on the dirty cement floor as the gurney was pushed past, my chest heaving, my relief so profound that it almost hurt.

After I was processed out my parents wordlessly ushered me from the station to a waiting rented carriage. The streets were mad with people. Not one word had been said to me, not one touch given me other than those necessary to guide me. Their faces were stern and drawn.

The carriage didn't move after we climbed into it. I sat on one side, and my parents sat on the other. They looked at me as one might look at a statue, or a specimen in a museum – some dead thing of interest. Nothing alive.

'I'm sorry,' I offered, my voice thick.

I saw my mother's eyes shimmer, and I knew that there was some feeling there, something. But my father's expression remained stony, unreachable. It was so unlike him.

I started to get *truly* scared.

'Mr Culham, your city-appointed counsel down at the courthouse, said that they're not going to charge you with anything. That it was self-defense,' my father said.

I nodded, and took a sloppy breath.

'After Christmas, we'll send you to stay with your aunt and uncle in the country for a while. Her baby is due soon, and she could use the help. You can live with them until the end of your schooling.'

Tears pooled in my eyes again. 'What?'

My mother started crying, and dug a handkerchief out of her reticule. 'Oh, God above, Pamela, why? Why did you run out into the street?'

'Mr Coughlin was hurt!'

'He's dead, now.' My father stretched his fingers out along the knees of his trousers, and looked to the window. 'Dead. So what good did it do you to disobey your mother, hmm?' He laughed, then, in a funny way I didn't like. 'I tried to raise good children.'

'Darling, she's . . .'

'I tried to raise good children, religious children!' He was shouting, now.

'I didn't mean to kill anybody!' I cried. 'She was attacking me!'

'And so you *stabbed her in the head with a parasol?!*' He banged on the roof of the cab. 'You could have just laid her out, knocked her out! Run away! You're already the talk of the street!'

'I'm *sorry!*'

'I just . . . never imagined this. Never.' He slid his hand over his face, and I felt a tear travel down my cheek. Isambard was right. They'd wanted me to do something great, *be* someone great, rise in the world. Every inch I'd ever been given had been given to me because I was a good, obedient girl; because they knew that I would demure and take only a half inch instead, of my own volition.

I wasn't a good girl anymore.

I gathered every scrap of air into my lungs that I could, and hiccupped out, 'We need to go. All of us.'

My father hit the button that told the driver to start out, and shook his head. 'We've not been told to evacuate.'

I looked outside. There were people running. Shops were shut down, a light snow drifting past their darkened windows. 'Do you need to be told?' I asked. Dad gave me a warning look, and I shut my mouth.

'They'd tell us to go if they needed us to,' my mother said. She didn't sound like herself; she sounded wispy, like her vocal cords had been replaced by a dry reed. 'They've actually warned us against leaving the city, because medical care can be so scarce out in the country.'

We rolled along for a few moments, before I realized, aloud, 'They don't want us to spread it.'

'Hush up, Pamela,' my father said. 'Not one more *word* about it. We get home, you go straight up to your room, and you stay there. You don't *move* until one of us tells you to. The fewer people who know you're home, the better.'

I bowed my head. We rode in silence.

The street outside our house was desolate. As I stepped down from the carriage, snowflakes dancing about my face, I realized that the next day was Christmas Eve. The street should have been filled with busy, jolly people, even without the addition of the refugees. Instead, it was as empty and forbidding as a graveyard. The windows in the buildings around us were dark, giving them the appearance of having rows of black, grinning teeth. The clackboards were still.

'Where is everyone?' I asked.

'The power went off along the street before we came to get you,' my mother said, taking my hand and guiding me up the stairs to the door. She unlocked it, and pushed me unceremoniously inside.

The house was shadowy, the only light coming from the lamps in the kitchen. My mother urged me to head that way. My father disappeared down the hall and through the door to the bakery, probably to prepare Christmas orders, if those were even still standing.

Isambard was seated at the kitchen table. He glanced up when we entered, and fixed me with a look of such hatred that I almost withered again. He probably thought I'd ruined his chances, too. St Arcadian's was now permanently out of his reach.

For the first time, I felt truly sorry for him.

Neither of them spoke to me. My mother prepared me a simple lunch. I ate it slowly, half afraid I wouldn't be able to keep it down. At some point Isambard thumped up to his room, making a show of leaving me alone at the table. I followed not long after.

The climb to my room was familiar as ever, but I felt somehow alien. I set the oil lamp I'd taken to guide my way on my vanity so that the light would be reflected into the room, and moved to open the window. Cold, clean air drifted against my face. I shut my eyes and relished it.

I should take a bath, dress, and sleep. I'd had only snatches of sleep in the cell, moments where I'd opened my eyes and been unable to account for the last few minutes. Fatigue was making the whole thing worse – making me unable to contain my emotions, turning every word and glance from my family into a triple insult.

For in my heart, I knew that my parents didn't hate me. They had loved me enough to take me back in, even if only to offer me shelter. They didn't hate me.

They were afraid of me.

For a moment, the good girl within me screamed and raged. We would try harder than ever. We would be obedient, quiet, shame-faced. Perhaps we could escape exile to the country if we *tried*.

Trying, trying, always trying. Trying was my life. I was guaranteed nothing.

I opened my eyes.

In the stone courtyard below, where our building and the three others about it allowed enough space for a single tree and a few benches to live, I saw movement. I paused, my hand on the frozen sash, to see what was going on.

The back door to the building on the street behind ours opened wide, and a man came out. I recognized him as one of our neighbors, Emanuel Delgado. He was a good man, a fishmonger. He was very pale, though, and moving in what I could only describe as a 'top heavy' fashion. It seemed as if his legs were struggling to keep the rest of him up and in the proper position, and his torso was leaning forward, his shoulders strangely curved. In one hand he clutched a coal scuttle.

He headed for the drain in the middle of the courtyard where we all deposited the ashes from our fires. He did this, himself, very slowly and with great care, as if he was afraid he was going to drop the scuttle. He then turned and with a rolling, unsteady gait, walked back to his house.

I curled my fingers around the sash, my other hand sliding up to my throat from my chest. He looked ill.

He has it too.

But then again, I started to doubt myself. I was so tired. Was I going to be seeing these things everywhere, these indications of sickness? We weren't close to the Delgados. Maybe he had always had that pallor, maybe he always walked in that weird fashion. I'd only ever seen him standing behind his market stall. I didn't know.

His wife welcomed him back into the house. Did her expression seem unsure? Was she nervous? She was too far away. I couldn't tell.

I hurriedly shut my window and rested my forehead on the icy glass. I needed to stop thinking about the illness. I needed to stop thinking at all.

My second crime, in as many days, was stealing the keys to my father's liquor cabinet. I helped myself to a bottle of wine, and practically flew upstairs with it. A few sips, I knew from past holiday experiences, and I would be out like a light. I didn't even need to get drunk.

Although, for a second, I thought about it.

Chapter Twenty-two

Bram

'How often do you have to mention the eating thing?' Nora demanded.

'Once an hour, every hour, until the day I finally decay,' Tom answered, with a sweep of his machete.

'We need to find you a new hobby.'

I chuckled. It was late morning, and we were wading through a field of high, dry grass. Nora kept close to me. She'd insisted on coming along, after Wolfe had given the order and left. It wasn't really all that important a mission, but I figured she needed a distraction.

Tom, of course, had taken every opportunity he could to joke about 'the boxed lunch', and 'big game safaris', and it was starting to wear on her.

'Leave off, Tom,' I said. Nora flashed me a forbidding look, one that told me that she wanted to handle it herself. I rolled my shoulders. 'Or not.'

'Ignore him,' Chas said, adjusting her floppy hat. 'He just thinks he's the big man on campus 'cause—'

I shot Chas a look of my own. She shut her trap.

'Because what?' Nora asked.

'Nothing.' I stopped, and pointed with my blade to a long, low building about a hundred yards off. 'There it is. That's number three, I think.'

We'd been assigned the bold, reckless task of . . . turning one of the power stations back on. The base got power from three biodiesel stations, where algae and some other genetically engineered little buggers turned biological waste into fuel. There was a living staff that worked them all, but it wasn't large, and at the moment we just happened to be closer to tank three than they were.

'Here we are,' I said to Nora. 'Now, it's up to us to dodge through the gunfire of our enemies on our way to—'

'I know, I know, flick a circuit breaker.' She was almost hidden by the grass. 'I just . . . didn't want to be left alone back there, OK?'

'Got it.'

Nora held her position as my friends continued toward the tank, their bodies rustling in the grass. Once they were a little ahead of us, she murmured, 'I know the others are hiding something from me. If I'd had to sit around back at base while they all played mum, I'd have started throwing things. I hate being kept in the dark.'

'Hiding something?' I tried, keeping my tone light.

She nodded, and turned her face to the sun. 'I heard some of the scientists talking about the position of this base, like it was important. And everywhere I go, the last day or so, *everybody* goes quiet, or up and runs. I go to a girls' school, I know what that means.'

I was nervous, but I took a gamble. 'What do you think it could be?'

She picked at the knotted ribbon of her hat. 'I'm afraid they've found my father, and he's dead, or something. Or they're going to give up searching.'

Guilt knocked on the back of my skull as I found myself rejoicing in the fact that she was completely off base. Guilt – it was guilt, I swear – made me reach out and take her hand as she lowered it from her chin.

She stiffened at first, turning her brown eyes on me. After a second, she relaxed. She let me keep her hand. It was so *warm*. I couldn't get over how warm she was. I couldn't remember ever being like that.

'Nora, if they stop looking, I'll start.'

She rewarded me with a smile.

'Are you two done making out?' Coalhouse called. Nora

gripped my fingers reflexively, her mouth going slack. She dropped my hand and started fighting through the grass, pushing it out of her way. 'Can I borrow your machete, Bram?' Her tone was nonchalant, as if she were asking me where I kept the butter.

Really, my only option at this point was to blow my own brains out.

I followed in her shadow, beating the handle of the machete against my other hand. 'Now, you remember what I taught you during our lesson yesterday, Miss Dearly,' I said, mimicking Doc Sam's professorial voice.

'Yes, professor,' she sang back, making her girly voice even girlier. 'Aim for the cranium and slice it clean off, revealing and destroying the brain – for severing the head alone will do no good.'

'Excellent, young lady. That will be a merit.'

'Oh, a merit! My life is complete!'

'Oh, shut up,' Coalhouse shouted back.

'You get merits and demerits in Punk schools too?' she asked, giggling. She emerged from the high grass into a mowed area, and turned around.

'No. Never went to school, actually. Mom taught us at home. But I read a lot.'

'I saw. What's with the adventure books?'

I laughed. 'I want to visit the glaciers, someday. Some people still live out there, you know. Survivalists. I think it'd be interesting to try.' I held out my hand, but she didn't take it again. 'Besides, you think I'm cold now. Don't you want to see how cold I get living like Nanook of the North?'

'Seriously, I am going to hurl. And I don't even think I'm capable of that, anymore.' Coalhouse had his arms crossed, and was drumming his fingers on his biceps. 'I will bend the laws of biology and physics and spew if you two don't stop it.'

Nora rolled her eyes so largely I thought it must hurt, and turned on him. 'Stop *what*? We're *talking*. Like normal, nice people. You should try it, sometime.'

'He's just jealous,' Chas said, with an evil little grin.

Coalhouse let it drop, but by the look he gave me, I realized that, yeah – he probably was.

Even though there's nothing for him to be jealous about, no siree.

'If you'll excuse me,' Renfield said, as he started for the biodiesel tank. 'Since no one else seems to be interested in actually completing our mission, I guess it's up to me.'

'Don't wear yourself out, there,' Tom said.

Renfield made an angry motion to the heavens without looking back, and entered the building through a side door.

Nora released a breath of air and sat down on the ground, hugging her knees to her chest, her usual position. Chas flopped onto her back as if she intended to make a grass angel. Nora looked pointedly at Coalhouse. 'So! What's your story, then?'

Coalhouse sat and fingered his useless eye to make sure it was still in there. 'Well,' he began. Then he stopped. For some reason he looked at me, and then at her.

'What?' I asked him.

Coalhouse shook his head, and didn't respond. 'Right, then. I'm Punk. I joined the army when I turned sixteen. My parents own a dry goods store in the town of Tesla Lake, but I don't suppose you'd know where that is. Was always good at shooting game, so I went for the artillery. Saw some active combat with the Vics.' He looked down. 'They came eight months after I enlisted. Didn't get many of us, but I was one of the few they did. We fought 'em at night – brilliant, right? I didn't even see him, just felt it when he bit me.'

He pulled up his shirt, showing off the scar on his waist. The bite marks were black along the edges, clearly defined. I saw Nora's lips thin as she clamped her jaw.

'Sorry.' He rolled his shirt back down. 'Anyway, I managed to climb up into a tree – one of them big ones with the leaves that look like they've been polished. I died up there, tucked in amongst the branches, just as day came. Worst sunrise I've ever seen. I mean, it looked *ugly* and sick, like yellow alcohol. I figure it knew. Woke up a few seconds later. And the first thing I saw was him, still *waiting* for me.'

Coalhouse glared at Tom.

Tom pointed at Coalhouse and said, 'I have *told* you before, it wasn't *personal*. I had you treed! I knew if I just waited long enough, you'd come down! I didn't know you'd be past your expiration date. I was not there mentally.'

Nora jumped to her feet and backed towards me. Situation aside – I loved, *loved* it when she did that. It made me feel protective, like I was good for something. 'You bit him?!'

Coalhouse made a sound of annoyance and turned away from Tom. 'Same company,' he grumbled. 'He went missing, what, two months before?'

'Month and a half, maybe. Not that it matters. Geez, how many times do I have to apologize?'

'*You killed me*, you loser!'

'It was an *accident*.'

It'd been a while since Tom and Coalhouse had had an argument about The Topic, and Chas and I knew what was coming. Chas stood up and put her arm around Nora. 'Hey, Ren'll be done in a trice. Let us walk . . . er . . . *this* way . . .'

Nora didn't move. She was staring at the two zombie boys as they got into it, both rising to their feet.

'You *killed* me! That's not something you can ever apologize for!'

'Well, then, I'm not sorry.'

'You son of a—'

'Hey, you leave her out of this.'

'You've tasted human flesh.'

Both boys stopped and looked at Nora, who had spoken. Her eyes were round, her cheeks pale. She was looking at Tom.

Tom threw his arms down in frustration. 'Yeah, I have,' he muttered.

'*Mine*,' Coalhouse shot out.

'And others.' Tom looked at him and lifted a finger. 'You know what? You need to man up. You need to stop acting like a little girl – wah-wah, I was bitten, my life sucks so bad. *All* of our lives suck right now, OK? You might think yours is an extra-special sparkly rainbow *unicorn fart* type of suck, but it's not. Just get *on* with it! Throw that stupid useless eyeball away and get *on with it!*'

And it was on. Coalhouse pressed forward. There's something in our brains, with the Laz, that makes us prone to acting like posturing animals when interacting with our own. You see it a lot in the wild packs. 'Then you admit that you're a monster. Huh? You show us all what you'd *really* like to do to us. To the girl!'

Tom shoved Coalhouse's shoulder. 'Oh, come off of it. I haven't hurt a fly since I've been here.' He looked at Nora, and she backed up further, out of the reach of Chas's arm, to bump against me. I put my hand on her shoulder.

'It's OK,' I told her.

'He's eaten people.' She sounded honestly scared.

'Yeah, I have!' Coalhouse pushed Tom back, and he retaliated with a shoulder, sending Coalhouse sprawling to the ground. Tom's lack of height gave him an advantage, sometimes. He looked back at Nora, then, and took a few steps towards us. 'And I'll tell you what . . . to the things that made me this way? Those people tasted *damned* good.'

Nora started to reach for her gun, and I put my arm fully around her. I lowered my head slightly at Tom and let a bit of a snarl into my voice. 'Back off.'

He stopped mid-stride, and put up his hands, submitting. His eyes were intensely focused on Nora, though, and I couldn't tell what they contained – anger? Regret? After a moment he looked back at Coalhouse, still on his hands and knees on the ground. 'But the fact that I am a *man*, and not a little *boy*, means that I can accept it, and get over it, and not do it again.'

Coalhouse chose that moment to go for Tom's legs and drag him down into a kicking, scrabbling fight.

'Stop it!' Chas shrieked, stomping her foot. 'I will not have my boyfriend fighting if it's not over me! *Stop it!*'

'Let's say it's over you!' Tom grunted out, as he and Coalhouse wrestled with one another. 'If he thinks he's gonna finally get a girl, he might grow balls enough to beat me!'

'Screw you, man!'

Renfield came running from the direction of the tank. 'What in blazes is going on?'

I let go of Nora and marched over to the pair, kicking out at whatever of them I could reach. I didn't want to hurt them, but they were already doing enough damage to their bodies, carrying on as they were. 'Stop this, *right now*! You're *both* acting like children!'

A shot rang out, and everyone ducked.

As the bang faded, I turned my head. Nora'd let off a round, her shotgun pointed to the sky. Her hands were white where she gripped the gun. 'Listen to Bram,' she said, with unnatural calmness.

I realized that I had to get her out of there. I was just about to stand and start the 'let's head back to base' speech when she added, 'It's Christmas Eve, guys. You can save your fight for *Boxing Day*, at least.'

Wait. Her objection to the fight was that it was . . . Christmas Eve?

All was still for a few moments, before Tom got to his feet. 'OK. OK. Boxing Day, whatever that is, it's on.' He stretched his arms over his head and swaggered a bit, as if everything was perfectly fine. 'Not like we won't be here.'

'Sure,' Coalhouse said, a little uncertain. 'Boxing Day.'

'Can we go back now?' Nora asked, lowering the gun and looking at me beseechingly. I nodded, and climbed to my feet.

The journey back to base was largely silent. Coalhouse and Tom drifted back behind the group, towards opposite ends of the horizon, as far from one another as possible. Nora, who'd been keeping her eye on Tom, looked more at ease the further away he got.

'Tom really isn't a bad guy,' Chas said, noticing Nora's wariness.

'But he—'

'That was a while ago. I mean, it's a freaking miracle if you think about it . . . he did eat people, he was on his own for over a month. It's amazing that he kept his sanity at all. I really admire him for that.'

'Is that why you . . . date him?' Nora sounded a bit incredulous.

Chas laughed. 'Well, as far as only options go, he's a pretty good one, yeah. He can be a misogynistic nitwit at times, but I don't mind that so much. It's just words. I don't buy his bull.'

'Only option? There's a whole *base* of zombie guys here.'

'Only so many my age. I never got the whole older man thing. And Coalhouse, well . . . he *is* immature. It's not like he walks around with his blankie, but there're little signs there that tell you that don't wanna get involved with him that way. Like this argument he has to have *constantly* . . . and he's desperate for a girlfriend, desperation is never cute . . . and, well, he doesn't take a healthy view of the whole thing. He *survives* well enough, but he doesn't have a good attitude. It's only gonna get worse as he nears his final death.'

'What about Mr Merriweather?'

Renfield lifted his eyes from the ground long enough to deliver a dry, 'No.'

'Yeah, no way,' Chas agreed. 'The only things that get Renny hot are chess, books, and machinery. Girls just don't cut it.'

'A literate girl who could *play* chess would.'

'I told you, I just can't figure out how it works,' Chas said to Ren. 'I mean, you won't even tell me what a rook *is*. I still say it's some kinda animal, so I don't get why it looks like a castle.'

I felt Nora's eyes on me and turned to look at her, questioningly. She slid a fingernail over her lips. 'And Bram?'

Panic punched me in the chest. So far today she'd been willing to touch me, laugh with me, confide in me, and now she was wondering if *Chas* shouldn't go out with me? Had I misread something, somewhere?

Chas shook her head, and grinned. 'Nah. Bram's too busy waiting.'

'Waiting?' Nora didn't take her eyes from me. Maybe she wanted me to answer.

'For the right girl,' I said, curtly.

'And he has *very* specific physical preferences,' Chas said. I grabbed her wrist and squeezed. She'd better not.

She did. 'For some reason, he is terribly attracted to black hair. Tom's a leg man, himself . . . attached, unattached, doesn't really matter. But Bram likes the hair.'

With all the various methods of Chastity Disposal flying through my imagination – should I just shoot her, or should I open her skull and puree her brains with a motorized mixer, or perhaps set her on fire? – it took me a minute to notice that Nora was giving me a very shy smile.

I dropped Chas's wrist. I almost dropped my machete.

Nora looked away, then, and moved a few steps in front of us, leaping into the grass to flatten it for herself as she went.

'I win,' Chas whispered.

'Smoke all you want,' I whispered back.

I felt surprisingly light for the rest of the day. Normally, I felt heavy and lumbering whenever I moved. I felt like dead weight. But today was different.

After we returned to base, Nora went off with Renfield to clean up her father's quarters – and, I suspect, spend the remaining time yelling at anyone who refused to help her call out or order info in, Ren included. I truly admired that man.

As for myself, I worked with the remaining troops in the western courtyard, discussing strategies and going over formations, in case we needed to head out into the wilderness and help look for Dr. Dearly. A few times I caught Wolfe standing on the edge of the group, watching me with cold, dark eyes. I stared right back at him, daring him to try something. I was doing what he wanted, even if I was growing to hate myself for it.

An hour or so before dinner I went looking for Nora, blades on my back. I found her sitting on a bench in the med wing, dressed in the clothes Chas had picked out for her. She was holding the edge of the skirt down over her knees with her fingertips, and Renfield was staring carefully at the ceiling.

When I got near, Nora looked at me and pouted. Coincidentally, I stumbled over my own feet at that exact moment. I finished the walk over, trying to play it off. 'What's wrong?'

She continued to frown. 'I got a demerit, professor.' There was a kind of naughty amusement in her eyes that I found myself really liking.

I smiled slowly. 'What did you do, Miss Dearly?'

'She henpecked Elpinoy in a most spectacular fashion,' Renfield offered. 'I think at one point she was actually hanging on his back.' Nora made a sound of annoyance. 'Alas, I was looking at a computer screen with Dr Samedi at the time, and thus I'm afraid that neither of us can vouch for this with certainty.'

The laughter bubbled out of me before I could hold it back. 'Were you?' I asked her.

'I don't know if I was actually *hanging*.'

'Bram.' Elpinoy appeared in one of the lab doorways. He gestured to the exterior doors. 'Take her out. Now. Never in my life have I encountered such a little—'

'Lady?' I asked, trying to keep a straight face.

'*Out.*'

'*Phone call.*' Nora said, affecting his tone of voice and looking right at him. '*Let-ter.*'

'Not until Wolfe orders it!' Elpinoy marched into his lab again and slammed the door behind him.

Nora stood up, her skirt bouncing a bit atop its puffy petticoat. 'That man is an infuriating ponce.'

'And you're an excellent judge of character,' I said, as I pointed to the weapon on my back. Seeing it, she turned to follow me. 'Want to come along, Ren?'

'Perhaps later,' Renfield said, bowing to us both. 'I've many things to do, and miles to go before I sleep.'

'Fair enough. C'mon, Nora.'

'OK. Bye, Mr Merriweather.'

We made our way to the eastern courtyard in a comfortable silence. The sun was starting to sink, painting every surface with transparent orange light. I idly wondered if it made me look any healthier.

When we found an open, empty area, I stopped and unslung the blades. 'OK, from the top. Show me some different ways you might come at me. Just don't, you know, hit me.'

She laughed as she took the weapon. 'Why don't we work with a dowel or something, first?'

'Because we need to build up your arms. C'mon, I'm attacking. Grr!'

She laughed again. I loved the sound of it – it was tiny and breathy. And then she came at me. She'd obviously retained what I'd taught her yesterday, which was good. She swept the scythe up, vertically, showing me that she could go through my face. She lifted it high and twirled it, slowly, to show that she could hit the top of my head with one of the blades held horizontally. And then she paused, considering her next move.

'Idea?' I asked her.

'Yeah,' she said. She moved low, pretending to slice me off at the knees. I went with it, and fell down on my back. She stepped closer and put a foot on my chest, aiming the blade at my head. She grinned. 'I could use this thing to make zombies my size.'

'Good,' I commended her. 'That's very smart.' My eyes drifted to her legs, and I added, 'At least they'll die happy.'

'Hey!' She danced away, pushing her skirt against her legs and scowling at me.

I sat up and argued, 'Hey, I only saw stockings and bloomers!'

'That'd be enough to get me run out of town, where I'm from,' she said, even as she released her skirt. She planted the scythe in the dusty earth and leaned on it, looking at me. I couldn't tell if she was blushing, or if it was the rosy light of sunset playing over her skin. 'I guess Punk girls are looser.'

This phrase struck me as curious. 'You guess? Don't you know? You said you'd seen stuff on the Punks. I mean, half the time you talk like one.'

'Oh, yeah, lots of stuff.' She grinned. 'What, you mean the swearing?'

I stood up and dusted my trousers off. 'But you don't know what Punk girls wear?'

'Well, I've never seen a girl fight in a battle.'

'So you've only seen battles?' She nodded. I could tell, from her honest expression, that this was all she thought there *was*. 'So they don't teach you guys anything about, you know . . . the rest of us?'

'Rest of you?'

'Yeah, you know, the rest of us. You do know that the Punks at the Border are extremists, right?'

Nora didn't say anything. She picked up the scythe and started walking, and without thinking too much about it, I started after her. 'I'd never heard that,' she admitted. 'I mean, it's just the Border fights that get on the news. And we learn about Reed and all.'

'Everyone knows about Reed, and the Massacre, yeah.' How to explain this? 'The extremists at the Border either want to try and push back into our ancestral land – which is just stupid – or just want to make sure the Victorians never forget 'em. Some are mercenaries. But most Punk people don't go anywhere near the Border. They don't want anything to do with you guys. We have our own territory, now. We take care of ourselves, we trade with the other tribes around us.'

Nora looked shocked. 'So . . . they might not even believe in what they're fighting for?'

'No. Maybe. It's complicated.'

'What about the Punk army?'

'Any army men you see on the Border are usually there to keep the casualties on our side down, just like the Vic army's there to make sure we stay on our land. The army is always ready to take over if they have to, but only if the extremists get out of hand – or if the Vic army gets clever and tries to move across the border.'

Nora balanced the blades on her shoulders. 'Wow. What do you learn about us?'

'That you're a bunch of social-climbing, shallow, egotistical, cold-hearted neo-aristocrats that've completely forgotten the lessons of history.' Well, she asked.

Nora considered this. 'I'll give you about sixty percent of that, actually.'

I was heartened by this response. 'What else?'

Nora shrugged. 'I don't know. I mean . . .' She swept her hand over her skirt. 'I've always kind of liked the Punks. Don't tell *anyone*. I like to watch the Punks fight, in holos. It's so wild . . . and honest, in a way. I thought they were fighting for their beliefs, with all their hearts and souls. What could be more honest than *that*? But if a soldier went home? No, I don't know. I know some geography, we get that in school. And there are rumors, that you're all cannibals and murderers . . . well, in Tom's case, I guess that's true.'

I glanced at my dry, cracked hands and tried not to think of all the trouble I'd caused. 'Yeah.'

'What is it like, though?' Nora moved the weapon to her opposite shoulder, arranging it so that it wouldn't hit me, and stepped a little closer. 'It must be hard. Not having modern technology, and all.'

'We have technology,' I said. 'Just good, honest tech that requires *humans*. We don't let our machines think for us or dictate to us. The human brain is the greatest computer ever. Nothing you guys have will ever be better. I mean, take your father, for example – they have all these fancy computers here, and they still need *him* to make the vaccine.' I looked up. 'So, you guys think we're all dirt farmers?'

'Pretty much.'

I shook my head. 'Someday, if you want to, we'll cross the Border. It's doable . . . Doc Sam used to do it all the time. We'll go to Faraday, or Menlo Park. Those're nice towns. Pretty parks. I remember going there with my dad, the few times he showed up. Or I'll take you to the upscale rag clubs in Wardenclyffe, or to the automaton shows, or something. I mean, I've never been, but they talk about 'em everywhere. I've always wanted to go. The rich make their showing there.'

Nora stared at me. 'There are rich Punks?'

I was starting to enjoy this. 'There're *plenty* of rich Punks. They're mostly engineers and scientists and artists. Any great discovery or creation is awarded by the government with gold, you see, to encourage those who actually produce something of worth. They have these big competitions every year.'

Nora thought about this for a moment. 'Our rich tend to be the children of the rich. People who've built up their wealth over generations. Or people who invest in the stock market.'

I made a harsh sound. 'That's one thing we don't have. Stocks. What's a stock, a piece of paper and a promise? Same reason we don't have paper money – we don't play with things that don't exist. Anyone wants to invest, he invests in some guy's building in his garage. We learned our lesson last time. But yeah, we've got our dynasties, as we call them.'

Nora's expression darkened a tad. 'What must you think of me, then? The only reason I'm near the upper class is because of what my father did.'

I shook my head. 'Trust me, Nora, if I thought you were that type of girl, I wouldn't be in half the trouble I'm in. Besides, I don't care about that.'

She seemed to ignore my words. Instead, she faced forward and said forcefully, 'Because I'm not a princess. I have a temper and I'm impetuous and I have serious issues when it comes to keeping my mouth shut.'

'And you're self-aware too, obviously.'

She made a little 'hmph', as if to emphasize her point. She then lifted her eyes again. 'Trouble you're in?'

I didn't answer. 'So . . . we're more normal than you thought, maybe.'

'Yeah.' Nora played with the hem of her skirt, and added, 'And you're right. I haven't done anything to distinguish myself. But it's hard to do something when people won't listen to you, won't give you a *chance*, or just outright tell you, "No, sit down, shut your mouth, be a lady."'

'I can believe it.' I had to ask. '*Were* you hanging on Dick's back?'

'No! He turned his back on me and I shoved him.'

'Well done, you.'

Nora laughed until her shoulders shook. She got herself under control, and took a breath, brushing a hand past her cheek. 'You really need to stop talking to me.'

'Why?' I asked, tensing a bit. Was she finally going to tell me to get lost?

'Because I feel better when you do. And I forget to be angry. I need to stay angry if I'm going to get anywhere.'

I had to smile. 'Can I take you to supper? You can be angry afterwards.'

'Sure.' She smiled at me slightly in return. 'So, what do Punk girls wear?'

'Kinda like what you're wearing. Some go longer.'

'Then why do you act like it's such a big deal that you can see my legs?'

''Cause, where I'm from, there aren't that many girls.'

'Hmm.' Whatever her thoughts were on this, she kept them to herself.

As I escorted her back to the med unit, I had an idea. I took her into her father's quarters, and looked at the heavily ornamented brass computer on his desk.

'Nora?'

'Yes?' She was putting the scythe away in the corner.

'I know you cleaned up your dad's room and stuff today. Did anyone talk to you about taking this out? Or the phone?'

She looked to the equipment, and shook her head. 'No, Elpinoy never said that. So I'll be sleeping here, now? I'm really not sure if I want to.'

'Wolfe told me not to let you anywhere near a computer. But he also told me to keep you in here.' I walked over and tapped a few keys, bringing up the password screen. I turned the screen to show her. 'Gee, how'd that happen?'

Nora studied the screen. 'Do you know the password?'

'No,' I said.

She nodded, and then favored me with a slow, but full smile. 'Well, then, I guess I *do* feel safe enough to sleep down here alone.'

'Good to hear. It'll be nice to have my room back. On that note, I'll go get your grub.'

I heard the sound of air escaping the padded leather cushions of Dearly's desk chair as I walked away, and Nora's fingers flying across the keys. If she was given the chance, and could come by it honestly, she deserved it. That was the Punk way.

Timeless values.

Chapter Twenty-three

Victor

'I asked one thing of you.'

Elizabeth's eyes passed from me, as cold and distant as the digital echo of the stars above. Lovely Elizabeth, raven-haired and queenly, the woman whose face had haunted me from the first moment I saw it.

I fingered my cufflinks, tugging my sleeves down over my wrists.

'I asked you to make a better life for me and our child. For *us*. What are you *thinking*?'

'*I asked one thing of you.*'

I opened my eyes.

Averne's scarf-shielded face filled my vision.

He kicked me. I turned, blocking out whatever pain this might have otherwise caused. Unless we're terribly excited or attuned to it, little physically hurts us. Else, certainly, our entire unlives would be nothing *but* pain.

To my side, I caught sight of Henry. He was still out. His clothing was torn, his skin blackened and crisp in areas. Discolored blood was pooling in his lower extremities. His left arm was gone. I wondered if he had lost it in the explosion, or if they had taken it from him. I wondered what time of day it was, and how long I had been unconscious. Again.

Averne stalked away from me. I rocked back to my previous position, prone, on the salt floor of the longhouse. I took a quick physical inventory. My clothes were scorched, but I appeared to be in one piece. With effort, I pushed myself up. A few broken ribs shifted about inside my chest cavity, and I dropped down to my elbows.

'I asked for something which should be easy for you to

provide, given time and the proper tools. What's more, you should *want* to provide it, seeing as the city of New London will soon be *burning*, the world's biggest crematorium.' He swept his cloak aside and sat down in a chair constructed from a jumble of driftwood and wire. I would have laughed, if I could have found it in me. What was that thing, his throne? His cheese had well and truly left his cracker, as my dear grandmother used to say.

'You still assume that I can make the vaccine. If I *could*, I assure you, Major, the last thing I would do would be to hand it over to you.'

Averne stroked his fingertips along the arms of his chair. 'You would condemn your own people?'

'If what you say is true, they're condemned no matter what I do,' I said, my tongue leaden with the truth of my own words. 'I'd prevent you from compounding their misery by using the vaccine as a bargaining chip.'

He was at my side before I could even lie back down, kicking me again. 'How dare you insult me?' he cried.

I bit back the growl that wanted to come out. 'That's it, isn't it?' I rolled up again despite the jostling of my internal organs, gripping futilely at handfuls of salt. 'If you have the vaccine, you can dominate whoever needs it – and, with your dead soldiers, you can make anyone you *wish* to dominate need it. Look, *look* at your pathetic assortment of biological weapons out there, just waiting for their launch orders.'

'What else would you have them be?' he hissed. 'Your people made them for that exact purpose!'

I trained my eyes on Averne. 'If you think that the Victorians developed the Lazarus, you are sadly mistaken.'

'Liar!' He turned his back on me again, and took to pacing about the longhouse like a territorial wolf. The guards, I noticed, were gone. 'Your tribe created the illness as a last ditch effort against the "savages" – savages, it's worth noting, who have been giving your people a good fight for years!'

'That may be . . . but as far as I can tell, Major, the disease is an accident of nature. That, or the creation of a God who has had it up to His neck with all of us. Man had no hand in it. We're all victims.'

But he wasn't listening to me. He was muttering as he travelled, his hands scraping along the walls, his boots kicking up waves of white grit. I watched him for a moment longer, before reaching out to lay my hand upon Henry. He coughed and shifted. He was not well. I inched closer to him, pulling myself over with my arms. Averne provided me with a rather odd soundtrack to work by, as I began inspecting Henry's wounds and making him bandages from my own clothing.

Eventually I heard Averne say, 'There was no God involved in it. It pleases me, though, to think that *you* were.'

'What do you mean?' I folded my coat and placed it beneath Henry's head – making sure there was plenty of padding between his skull and the explosives. I had a limited number of hiding places from which to choose at the moment.

Averne smacked his fist into his palm. 'You know what I mean. The creation of the illness. Your name is all over it. I'm forced to believe that you had a hand in making it.' He drew to a stop. 'It pleases me to think that perhaps I will truly, finally have a chance to kill the man who killed my family . . . the man who turned my countrymen into monsters. And once your daughter is delivered to me, my revenge will be complete.'

'Revenge?' I asked, going still.

What Averne said next should have made absolutely no sense to me. 'He had to send his men after mine. It would have looked very strange if he hadn't. I thought my men would get to her first, but . . . oh, well. I can wait.'

Get to her? What on earth did he mean? Men? What men?

'*I'm with you, my man,*' Commander Wolfe had said, as our soldiers followed his orders and fueled up the plane for me. '*If it were one of my girls, I'd do the exact same thing. Trust me, better to take the plane; it's much faster to travel by air than by sea. With any luck, you'll get there before the boys do.'*

With horror, I realized that Nora had not, in fact, been saved.

'Wolfe,' was all I could get out. My rotten old heart was trying to hammer away, and I grabbed my chest as it lurched terrifyingly back and forth. 'My God, you're working with Wolfe. He must have sabotaged my plane, he . . .'

Averne nodded. 'You are a very intelligent man. Even now, when you are a man no longer.'

I felt pain then. I felt it in my heart, in my bones, in my skin, as if my sudden fury was incinerating my own flesh. 'If you harm her, Averne, I will crawl my way over continents to kill you.' I reached out for the wall, my arm shaking, and attempted to stand up. 'I don't know how you met Wolfe, or what sick game he's trying to play, but I will *not* give you what you want. All I can tell you is that I've been trying my best to *help* people!'

Averne swooped over and punched me in the chest. I felt my bones move anew, and sank to the ground. 'Is that what you call it? Is that *what you call it*, when the thing you've given birth to causes children to attack their own fathers?'

'I didn't create the Lazarus!' I yelled.

'Stop lying!' Averne screamed, his face inches from my own. 'Wolfe and I met on the field of battle! He sought me out! He told me that everything I had long suspected was *true*! I know that you made the illness – and you will understand me if I have to carve my story into your sorry flesh!'

I laughed. The sound gurgled out of my chest. 'Understand? Understand *you*? You want to torment my daughter! *She's an innocent girl!* She doesn't even know that I'm still alive!'

Averne drifted away from me again. His movements were bizarre – fluid, but almost disjointed. I'd never seen a fellow zombie move the way he moved. 'Innocent?' He kicked a piece of wood out of the way, and it cracked in two against the wall. 'My children were innocent!'

'You're a monster!' I cried.

Averne's eyes, in the lowering light, had ceased to shine, leaving me with the sensation of interacting with a sort of golem. 'Monster?' he asked, with a sudden clarity of voice. 'I'm the monster? I have proof that you created the disease.' Averne nodded, as if his own statement might have been something he'd not considered before. 'I must say, I've learned much, studying the files that Wolfe provided me. You have a much better understanding of the disease than anyone. How could you not be its creator? I engaged in experimentation myself, you see, but . . .' He waved an arm. 'You see what I have to work with.'

My soul screamed at me not to ask. 'Experimentation?'

He nodded, absently, as if he'd already forgotten what he was going to say. 'Yes. My men helped, me, of course. They sparred with the undead at my bidding, so that I could see how they fought. They were bit at my bidding, so I could see how the disease progressed.' He shrugged. 'Nothing out of the ordinary. Nothing a patriot wouldn't do to protect his tribe.'

Out of the ordinary? 'You sacrificed your own men?'

He advanced on me again. 'They were mine to sacrifice!' He tossed his hands skyward. 'I joined the Punk army when I was but a boy. I thought I was doing my country a service. Instead, what do I see? Brave men, dying at the hands of their own countrymen. Proud men, reduced to fighting for a few yards of dirt – only to have *your* people take them back again. And then, *then*, when your monsters started attacking us and the *idiots* in command started allowing for temporary truces? That was it. I took my loyal men, and I left.'

He got what he wished for most, then – I understood. I could see, in my mind's eye, the disgraced Major and his own private army, a one-man secession, constantly on the move. I saw his army decimated, destroyed by his madness and his interaction with the dead, until he was king of a heap of charnel-house bones. Who knows how much of it was true, and how much of it was my imagination? Did it matter?

Understanding did not equal acceptance.

I looked to the communications equipment on the table again. 'Wolfe's been equipping you, then?'

'Yes.' He twisted his fingers together. 'My men and I built this base. Think of it. All around us, people are fighting, living, *moving* . . . but who would brave a desert of salt? Wolfe even arranged for my troops to be smuggled into New London in city vehicles. I do so love hiding things right out in the open.'

'So, you're still in contact with your troops in New London?'

Averne glanced at me. 'No. It would be suicide to have them transmit to me from the center of your city. Too easily traced. But that doesn't matter. You see, Doctor, a virtue that my people possess, that I don't think your people do, is the ability to participate in the grandest schemes imaginable with only a handful of nuts and bolts and a little ingenuity.'

I was silent for a minute, before simply asking a very logical question. 'How do you know they're doing what you want, then?'

When I was a wee lad in school, I used to get my jollies by confronting my professors with facts that ran completely contrary to what they were trying to hammer into our thick skulls. Their expressions of bafflement and anger had never failed to amuse me. As comprehension sank in, and Averne started to rail and to beat me, I was laughing, wishing more than anything that I could see his face.

'*They've done it!*' he was shouting. 'Oh, believe me, they've done it! Everyone you ever knew, ever loved, ever passed on the streets will be dead within a week!'

'And then they'll move on to your people!' I retaliated, hugging my arms around my chest. 'They'll devour your people! And then they'll find a way – I know this sounds insane, but trust me – they'll find a way to travel to *Africa*, and they'll start the whole thing over again there! I don't believe –

I really can't believe, sir, that you have thought your cunning plan all the way through!'

He left off, striding over to the other end of the longhouse with a roar. My body was still shaking with laughter. I fought in several gulps of air and tried to move my ribs back into position.

Oh, I'd needed that. It put the entire thing into perspective. He didn't have Nora, not yet. He had no control over his own troops. I could work with this.

Henry stirred beside me, and slowly opened his eyes. 'Wh . . .'

'Lie still,' I whispered. 'Don't move your head. The bombs are there.'

His eyes widened. 'Not . . . m-more . . .'

'Just don't move your head.'

If fortune was on my side, paranoia would drive Averne to try and make contact with Wolfe. It would be exactly the distraction that I needed.

Averne left us alone, rambling to himself, ticking back and forth across the floor like a clock's pendulum. A few hours later, when the door opened, I could see the night sky outside. I thought of Elizabeth again, and closed my eyes. When I made it to heaven – *if* I made it to heaven – I had so much to apologize for.

The smell of cooked meat brought me back to the present.

One of the guards entered, his pike on his back. He was bearing a tin plate with several cuts of charred meat on it. He placed it on the table and grunted something to Averne.

'Get out,' Averne spit.

I didn't need to question whether or not the meat was human. I knew that it couldn't be. The earth around me stilled as my brain kicked into overdrive. The way he moved, *cooked* meat – how had I not realized it before?

Averne, whatever his story was, was still alive.

Chapter Twenty-four

Pamela

The power came on a few times during the night, but we were in the dark again come Christmas Eve.

The current tragedy in Isambard's universe was that I was being permitted to go to Midnight Mass with the rest of the family, and that my murderous presence would result in our sitting in the back of the church underneath the wooden balcony that held the seats of the aristocracy. Quite literally, beneath them. I wanted to tell him that he needn't worry about God not seeing him there in the shadows, but I knew that he, like many Victorians, went to church mostly *to* be seen.

I, myself, had been praying since I'd awoken from my self-induced slumber. I had prayed in the bathtub, in my closet. My shoulders were fast on their way to becoming permanently bowed.

I prayed because I couldn't get the Delgados out of my mind, and I needed to replace them with something else.

There'd been no further appearances of Mr Delgado, the potentially sick fishmonger. I'd kept vigil at my window, waiting to see if he would come out again. I had nothing else to do, no task to set my sights on, and hours of empty time only fueled my obsession. I began to think that if I stepped away from the window for an *instant* to get a cup of water or a shawl, he'd appear and be gone before I could return to see him. Never mind the fact that if the ill could really move *that* fast, we'd all be goners by now.

When it came time to get ready for church, I dressed in my next best gown, the blue lawn. My mother had burned my new one. She hadn't even tried to get the bloodstains out. I put no further thought into how I looked, and let my face remain unwashed and my straight hair unbraided. It was all starting to weigh down on me – the blade was dropping. The city was panicked. There'd been no news of Nora. Common sense told me that if I allowed myself to think that she was dead, I'd probably be doing my heart a favor – but I couldn't bring myself to do it. It felt like the ultimate betrayal.

I prayed as I waited for my father to call me downstairs.

We hailed a cab for the ride to the Cathedral of Our Mother. We sat in silence, neither of my parents looking at me. I watched the city through the windows. Although there were people on the streets, now, the crush was not as bad as it had been. That worried me.

The power was still on in the church district. The cathedral was opulent, everything on its exterior white and lovely. As my father helped my mother out of the carriage, I turned my attention to the statue above, which was high-lighted by rows of electric bulbs at night. The Mother looked pensive. I understood how she felt.

I knew I was not to speak, or look at anyone. I trailed behind my parents, obeying the first order, but not the last. I swept my eyes over the massive crowd, looking for signs of sickness. I noticed that the altar boys and ushers were doing the same thing, a fact that offered me some comfort. I hoped that everyone was all right – not only for our sakes, but for theirs. I truly, *truly* prayed that no one would suffer on this night, of all nights.

No one approached my family. No one even paid us much attention, although I caught one or two curious gazes. We found our seats, and the ceremony soon began. I knew it by heart; Mass was always the same. There were the prayers, the readings, the candles, the passing of the wine and bread. My attention drifted.

The hyper-present twinkling of the flexible flat screen tapestries captivated me for a while. The longest one was hung behind the altar, and appeared to have been programmed with an embroidered manger scene. Altar boys occasionally disappeared behind it, into the bank vault that it obscured, a leftover from the Cathedral's previous life as a bank. It was used as a storage room, now. The altar was set up where the teller counter used to be, centuries ago.

The priest droned on, and my thoughts floated back towards my family. They were seated next to me; I could reach out and touch them. Yet, some nagging, tickling thing in my head told me that all was not well, that we were in danger. Something had to be done, but I wasn't sure what. Where would I even begin? My family seemed willing to buy what the news told them, even if my father played at tearing it apart, calling the government foolish, the reporters no better than ghouls. They probably wouldn't even listen to anything I'd say, anymore, they . . .

'Pamela?'

My mother was looking at me, her eyes dim with worry. Everyone around me had already stood up, and there was a crush at the back to exit the church. Mass was over. I hadn't even noticed.

I rose to follow her. The same crowd that had sat sedately for the last hour, perhaps even derived comfort from doing so, was now frantic to get away. The rich were escorted to their carriages as if under gunfire, and people thronged the street to hail cabs. My father joined them, but after fifteen minutes of failed attempts, it became clear that he wasn't going to get one.

'We'll have to walk,' he said, tugging at his cravat.

Mom held onto Issy's shoulder. 'Are you certain it's safe?'

'When we came through, the streets were fairly empty. If nothing else, we can start walking and look for a cab along the way.'

'Mother, Father . . .' I began. I wanted to tell them that what we *should* do was figure out what was going on, where we were going to go, what we were going to do – but the words stuck in my throat.

My father took my hand, and started leading me down the street.

The trip seemed to last several lifetimes, when in reality it took only twenty minutes. Every shadow was an infected person waiting to leap out at me, to steal my flesh from me, my very breath. I almost ran after my parents, doing my best to keep myself physically close to them. An *inch* of space between them and me was not acceptable.

We passed a few people in the street, but no empty cabs. The people we did see we regarded with suspicion as one herd mind – I could see our heads turning at the same time. My mother clutched both Issy and me about the shoulders, after a time, and I half felt forgiven. At least, I felt included.

Soon we were standing on our own stoop, my father sliding the house key off his watch chain, my mother's arms relaxing. We'd made it. We were going to be fine.

That's when I saw the girl.

Her diminutive shape caught my attention as I waited for my father to unlock the door, and I turned, my heart heavy with dread, to watch her as she crept closer to us. She was only about five years of age, her movements halting and clumsy. Her skin was sickly, her eyes speckled with white. Patches of her breadcrust-colored hair were missing. She wore a long, plain dress with a sagging patch pocket on the front of it.

Bile rose in my throat, and I backed up the stoop. I missed the next step up, and ended up falling on my backside, knocking into Isambard. He caught himself on my mother's jacket.

'Pam, what are . . . *oh, God!*' Issy started screaming, and practically climbed over my mother to get closer to the door. My parents whirled around and cried out.

The little girl stopped in the street, fixing us with a look of almost palatable hurt. She started crying, little sobs that jerked her body in every direction.

I recognized her when I heard that cry. I'd heard it before, in the market, in the summer when the windows were open.

'Jenny Delgado?' I whispered.

'*Open the door, open the door!*' Isambard screamed.

'I can't find my family!' Jenny wailed.

She spoke.

I hadn't heard an ill person speak before.

I remained sitting, my joints locked, as I assessed the situation. The girl was obviously sick, but she could talk. She wasn't attacking us.

'Are you Jenny Delgado?' I asked a bit more loudly. She nodded, crying still.

She also recognized her name. Maybe there was hope for her. I had to get her to her family, to the hospital. She needed to see a doctor.

Why I decided all this, I'll never know. Perhaps, on this most holy of days, God was shining His mercy through me. Perhaps the alcohol I'd been using to get to sleep had killed some brain cells. I don't know.

I slowly stood up. 'Go inside and lock the door. I'm going to take her home.'

'Pamela, you'll do no such thing,' my mother said. She was on the verge of tears herself. 'Not again. Get inside.'

'No, I'm taking her home.'

'*She's ill!*'

'I can *see* that, Mother. And that's why she needs to go *home.*'

'Pam, are you that stupid?' my brother asked, in awe.

'She's a little girl!' I turned my back on Jenny and looked up at my family. 'She's a little girl, and she's lost, and she's scared! Just like the rest of us!' In the theatre of my mind I could see her father, a day ago, and her mother waiting for him at the door. I recognized now what I didn't then – the lack of panic, the lack of violence.

Maybe they were OK, after all. Maybe they were still sane.

Before I could protest further, Dad opened the door and moved down the stairs so quickly, it seemed he was trying to recover from tripping. He took my hand and pulled me towards him. His eyes were cold. 'Do as your mother says.'

'Father . . .'

He waggled my arm back and forth. 'Don't make me tell you again! Look what happened the last time you didn't do as you were told! Do you want to end up back in jail?'

My face flushed at the memory. I couldn't argue with that – I knew I couldn't. Reluctantly, I nodded my head and sidestepped him, following my mother and brother in their chaotic haste to get inside the house.

Glancing back at Jenny one last time, I saw that she was still standing there, watching me as she shook, her tearless eyes dim. They reminded me of the eyes of a homeless animal that had learned through harsh experience not to trust anyone, but still instinctively held out hope. 'I can't find my family,' she tried again, voice small.

I couldn't argue, but I could act.

Once we were inside, I fiddled about in the hall closet, waiting until my parents had retreated to the parlor, and Issy to his room, before popping right back out the front door. Jenny was still there, and upon my reappearance, uttered a chirp of joy.

I hurried down the steps towards her, making shushing motions, which she seemed to both understand and obey. I didn't dare offer her my hand, but I waved down one of the side streets. 'Come on, Jenny. You live over here.'

She sniffled. 'Really?'

'Yes, come along.' I was taking a stupid risk, and I might as well be quick about it.

We'd gone all of two yards when I felt a hand on my shoulder. I jumped and released a short, terrified scream, before I realized that the hand belonged to my father. He'd followed me. Cringing, I paused and waited for the scolding to begin.

My father, however, didn't say a word. He didn't even make

eye contact with me. Instead he pushed me forward, indicating that I should continue. Gratitude almost overwhelmed me, and I had to blink to chase back tears.

We walked together in an uncomfortable silence. 'Jenny,' I asked, after a moment, 'how did you get outside?'

She gestured feebly with her pudgy, bruised little fingers. 'Mama and Papa were in the kitchen, and Tata wasn't there. I wanted to go. I went out the bad door, not the good door.'

I tried to process this. 'Bad door? The front door?'

She nodded seriously. 'Bad door.'

Made sense. She was probably allowed to go in the courtyard. 'Do you know where . . . Tata went? Is that your grandfather?'

She nodded. 'Tata! Tata went down.' She looked to the ground.

My father's hand gripped my shoulder. 'He's . . . down?'

'Uh-huh.' She seemed unconcerned. Perhaps 'down' meant something other than 'dead', which is what my brain wanted to put in place of it.

Their street, Halperin Street, was just as deserted as ours was. We led Jenny to the right building and up the front steps, where I glanced at my father. 'We'd better ring, I guess.'

He pushed the button, wordlessly agreeing with me, though I was pretty sure I was going to have finger-shaped bruises on my shoulder come morning.

No one came to the door, at first. We rang several more times, with no success. It was only once I banged on the door and called out, 'We have Jenny, Mr Delgado! Mrs Delgado?' that I heard footsteps approaching. I took a step back.

The door opened slowly, just a crack. I saw Mr Delgado's white face looking out at me. I gasped. His eyes were streaked with blood.

He looked down, and upon seeing his daughter, opened the door and picked her up, holding her to his chest. 'Oh, my Jenny-girl!'

'Papa!' Jenny squealed with delight, throwing her little arms about him.

'Thank you,' Emanuel said again, before looking to us. '*Thank you*. She got out, and . . .' He fell silent, his eyes on mine. I filled in the blanks. He hadn't been able to go searching for her, not the way he looked. He would have started a riot.

I took another step down the stairs, even as I asked, 'Is Mrs. Delgado all right? And . . . Tata?'

He worked his blackened lips for a moment, before saying, 'Mrs Delgado is . . . fine.' I interpreted that as 'ill'. 'Her grandpa is . . .' He gripped his daughter all the more tightly, and I understood that her grandfather was dead. 'She's used to him being drunk,' he said, with the air of one who was going to use this explanation until she would no longer accept it, and maybe for a little while afterwards.

Never in my life had I felt such pity for a group of people. They weren't mad. They were trying to carry on as best they could. But still, the very sight of them was enough to force me back yet another step, and my father with me. I wanted to help, I wanted to reach out to them, but my instincts were guiding me the other way. I felt caught in the middle.

Mr Delgado watched us go. There was no anger in his face, only resignation. 'If you hear any news . . . would . . . if you could, would you let us know? We don't have power, and . . .'

'Yes, sir,' I said, without reservation. That I could do.

'Thank you,' he said again, as he shut the door.

My father took my arm and pulled me home, for the second time in a single evening. He was shaking. 'You *ever* do something like that again, you are on your own. Do you understand?'

'Yes, sir,' I answered again. As we climbed our own stoop, I looked up at him. 'Thank you.'

My father didn't smile, or even nod. He did, however, meet my eyes – and within his I thought I caught a glimpse of the real him, my real father, the one who had loved me and called me 'pet', the one that I'd killed by killing.

He was still in there, somewhere.

That night, after everyone else had gone to bed, I lit a candle and sat in the middle of my bedroom floor, staring into its flame and trying to sort out my thoughts. I was still slightly shaken from our walk back through the city, and from my visit to Halperin Street. My arms felt cold, and I rubbed my hands along them, trying to warm myself up. I never wanted to do anything like that again, especially not at night. I'd felt exposed, out in the open, easy pickings.

Even now, I didn't feel safe in my own bed. I couldn't sleep. I felt like I wanted to hide from the world outside my front door.

Hide.

We could hide.

I skipped back from this idea quickly, before I became too attached to it, and examined it for flaws. We'd have to take supplies with us. We'd have no way of knowing when it was safe to come out. But if we chose a good location, the infected might not be able to find us. If we stayed hidden for a few days, a week, it would give the world time to settle down. We wouldn't have to flee through the streets, or the countryside. After all, we had no transportation, and if more and more people left the city there was no guarantee we'd find even a handcart to help us.

The reporters were chanting, constantly, that our troops were on top of the quarantine. What if they were right? We'd just have to wait it out.

But how could I get my family to go with me? How would I explain it to them?

The answers to these questions would not come immediately.

Before returning to bed, I made my nightly trip downstairs for a few slugs from one of dad's wine bottles. As I leaned against the liquor cabinet and willed the foul taste of the alcohol to leave my mouth, I hugged my own body. I allowed myself to indulge in the numbing, paralyzing fear that wanted to take me over, just for a moment. I did so because I knew that the time was swiftly approaching when I was going to have to ignore it.

I was going to have to get my family into hiding, before we went the way of the Delgados.

CHAPTER TWENTY-FIVE

Bram

I hadn't even thought about Christmas, not until Nora mentioned it. After that, it was all I *could* think about. I had nothing to give her. I couldn't exactly arrange for a skating party or a trip into the city, or anything. I really sucked at this whole 'I am very attracted to you and would like to demonstrate this to you via attention and creative uses of my disposable income' thing.

I finally had to fully acknowledge it. I liked her. I liked her a *lot*. She was smart and courageous and pretty and she had gotten to the point where she didn't look at me like I was some sort of demon wearing a man suit.

Dearly was going to have my throat, if Wolfe didn't beat him to it.

When I went to bed that night, the Ghost of Christmas Past visited me. Since my death, my dreams have changed. I've never asked anyone if they experienced the same thing. I used to dream in color; now my dreams are black and white. They play like hastily spliced-together movie reels, the occasional image whizzing by that has nothing to do with anything else, like a subliminal advertisement. *Wooden shoes. Aunt Edna's floury apron. Men dying everywhere – help yourself to the buffet. No?*

We'd never had a lot of money, but Mom liked to get little things for the girls at Christmas when she could. Usually it was a new pair of hand-knitted stockings stuffed with chips of molasses candy and fruit and perhaps a copper or silver coin, if it'd been a good year.

The size of the gifts didn't matter to them. The fact that there were to be gifts at all excited the girls, made them as tight as little spools of thread all through December. By Christmas morning they'd usually had it, and they would unwind themselves all over my bed – bouncing on me until I was awake, whispering so that Mom in the next room over wouldn't hear.

'Wake up! Wake up, Bram! Santa came! Santa came in his big steam sleigh with all his automaton reindeer!'

'I heard it last night!'

'You did *not*!'

'Did *too*!'

'Did too,' I remember mumbling, hiding my eyes with my arm. 'I heard it. Emily's right.'

'See, I told you!'

'Why don't you go *draw* the steam sleigh?' I'd suggested, in order to buy myself a few more minutes of sleep. That had resulted in them tackling me anew, dissatisfied with my answer. The correct thing to say had been, '*We will go open presents, now.*'

My brain shorted, my dream footage flickering, and the presence above my body became Nora, her nose and cheek nudging at my arm. I moved it, opened my eyes, and took her in. She was smiling.

I awoke with a start, a split second before my alarm clock went off. The jangling bell only added to my sense of panic. I quickly filed that one under 'things to never, *ever* dream again if it is humanly possible'. Not only did I feel guilty, it's not as if my body could *do* anything about it. You kind of need a heartbeat for that.

I showered quickly, before the whole thing could depress me too much, and returned my attention to the problem of Christmas. I still wanted to do something for her. Maybe not anything grand – she was still surrounded by trouble on every side, after all – but something nice, maybe something to remind her of home.

Midway through brushing my teeth, I opened my closet.

My dress uniform caught my attention.

I swallowed my toothpaste, threw some clothes on, and attacked the door and ran out into the hall, idea suddenly in hand. I made my way to the med facility, chewing on my toothbrush and exploring my idea from all angles. Yes. It was traditional, involved dress-up, and had meaning. It was perfect. Genius, even.

I was so absorbed in my planning that I almost didn't notice that Dearly's office door was slightly ajar. Thankfully, the part of my brain that's always on high alert, the hunter, set off a little siren.

Nora wouldn't leave the door open.

My training kicked in, and I slunk against the wall. I slowly pocketed my toothbrush, and found that I was all thumbs. I forbade myself to think about the fact that I might be afraid. It was probably nothing – somebody most likely ducked in for something after she went to bed and forgot to close the door all the way. No big deal.

I edged closer to the door, slowly, listening for signs of life. There weren't any. The med bay was empty, the lights dim. A lozenge-shaped cleaning automaton slid back and forth on its predetermined track along the tile, the only movement I picked up on.

Although I don't like to do it often, as it makes me feel distinctly less than human, I took a sniff. At once, I relaxed. I could smell her – that unique combination of clean skin and hair that was Nora. No blood. I got to the door and pushed it open a bit further.

Nora was asleep at her father's desk, breathing easily. I opened the door fully and let myself in, keeping my steps quiet. She'd drifted off where she'd been working. A fountain pen was still clutched in her ink-stained hand, and her cheek was resting against a pile of parchment. I leaned over her body to look. The top sheet contained a list of names and numbers, completely random to my eye. She must have been dredging her mind for anything that might've been included in the system password. The computer screen on the desk flashed patiently, waiting for that password to be entered.

I tucked my hands into my pockets and watched her for a while. I found it funny, really, how much pleasure I could get out of simply resting my eyes on her. She didn't even have to do anything. After a few minutes, though, I made my way quietly into her father's chambers and got a blanket, which I tucked around her. I shut the door fully on my way out, and continued to Chas's room.

There, I could be as loud as I wanted. 'Chas, wake up,' I said, as I gave the door a few good pounds.

I heard a lot of crashing, and Tom's voice cursing, before the door opened a crack and Chas peeked out. 'Whuzzat?'

I sighed. 'Chas, it's seven a.m. Why aren't you up yet?'

She stared at me as if I'd just spoken Swahili.

'Right. Anyway, I need a dress for Nora.'

'She out of clothes?'

'I need a *pretty* dress. Like a . . . a . . .' I gestured to my shoulders, trying to convey the level of fanciness I wanted. I'm a farm boy, what do I know?

Chas squinted blearily at me, but eventually seemed to understand. She opened the door and let me in. In addition to the usual mess, there was a person-shaped lump under the blanket on her bed – Tom. I chose to ignore it. Cohabitation was against the rules, but the only thing they could sleep together *for* was companionship, and I wasn't about to deny them that.

'Like a ball gown?' she asked, as she made her way to her closet and opened it.

'No, not for a ball. Like a . . . church dress?'

'Huh?' Chas was lost.

'Don't question it, just do it.'

She pulled out several things, eyed them herself, and pushed them back. Five minutes later she held up two dresses for me – one bright red with chiffon flowers on the shoulders, the other light pink satin with black stripes.

'The pink one, I think, but . . . do you have any dresses that are tight on you?'

Chas was losing her patience. *'Tight?'*

'Yeah, you know . . .' I rolled my eyes, but pointed to my chest. 'Up here. She's way smaller than you. Not that I've been looking, or anything.'

'Are you complimenting my girl's boobs?' Tom muttered beneath the blanket.

I looked at the lump, and deadpanned, 'Yes, I am.'

The lump shifted in a self-satisfied way. 'Thank you, you're very kind.'

Chas tightened her fingers on the hangers and cut her eyes at me. 'As if he *grew* them.'

'I'll take the pink one. And . . . what goes with it?'

Chas let out a little, 'Raaaargh,' but dug everything out for me. She kicked me in the calf on the way out. It was worth it.

I snuck back into Dearly's quarters and laid everything out on his bed for her. I then tiptoed around Nora and returned to my room, where I put on the works. Beneath the uniform proper there's a black dress shirt and a red waistcoat, and there are cufflinks with the enameled Z-and-loops on them, and a chain for the waistcoat, and five thousand other parts that simultaneously make you feel pretty badass and like a girl for putting them all on so carefully.

I didn't put the hat on, seeing as I was inside, but I carried it tucked beneath my arm as I made my way back to the med hall an hour later. By that time engineers and doctors were appearing to work, coffee in hand, and their eyes followed me. I rapped smartly on Dearly's door.

Nora opened it, wrapped up in the blanket. She took one look at me, and her mouth opened to release a little, 'Oh.'

I bowed like a clockwork soldier, straight from the waist. 'Miss Dearly. May I enter?'

She nodded mutely, and stepped back to let me in. I shut the door behind me and grinned at her. 'Did you find the dress?'

'Uh-huh.' She was still looking at me as if she wasn't sure if I was really there or not.

'Well, put it on! It's Christmas, and we're going to church.'

She rested both of her hands on the edge of the desk as she backed up a little. 'We are? Where?'

'There's a chaplain on base. I thought we might as well do something. I know your father isn't here, and everything's crazy, but . . . I still hope you have a happy Christmas, Nora.'

She didn't say anything in response to this, but slowly made up the distance she'd put between us, keeping one hand on the desk. She reached out with her other hand, and stroked a finger along the edge of my captain's bars. Then, in a sudden fit of propriety, she yanked her hand back as if out of an open flame and hid it beneath her blanket. 'Wow.'

I vowed that I was never taking the uniform off, *ever*.

I bent my head, all proper-like. 'I'll wait for you in the courtyard.'

'OK.'

Samedi eyed me on the way out. 'Oh, you scoundrel. That's dirty pool.'

I jutted a finger at him. 'You just wish you had one.'

'I don't need one!' he shot back. 'I have maturity, and strength of personality! And . . . and the ability to hide my own head in glove compartments and lockers to see if she's cheating on me!'

Beryl handed him a file on her way past. 'You ever try that again, I'm going to drop-kick you into the next country.'

Once outside, I put on my hat. I shined the brim of it with my thumb, and waited, not daring to move – I was afraid I'd wrinkle the uniform. I'd only worn it once before, when I'd first gotten it. Who knew it held such power? And all this time, it'd been languishing in my closet.

Nora came out half an hour later. The pink dress actually fit her very well, and it rustled invitingly when she walked. Her hands were gloved, and a ribbon held her curls up atop her head. She stopped when she saw me, and flashed that same shy smile she'd first shown me in the field of grass. But then she set her shoulders, and came closer. 'You do look very nice, Captain.'

'You are lovely as always, Miss Dearly.' I offered her my arm.

This time, she took it.

I escorted her to Isley's little wooden chapel, which she eyed with interest. The cats soon had all of her attention, though. She giggled, picking up the same kitten I'd patted the other day. 'Aw!'

Jacob emerged from the doorway, and smiled. His face was drooping a bit more than usual. 'Miss Dearly, welcome.'

She turned to look at him. 'Hello.'

'This is Father Isley. Father, say – would you mind doing a Christmas service sort of thing?'

'Ah . . . well, certainly! I suppose I should!'

Jacob saw us inside, and we sat on a pew together. His cats followed after him, although the kitten opted to stay with Nora. She spoiled it with petting. I felt slightly jealous.

'You must forgive me,' Jacob said, as he tried to find everything. There were wooden boxes stored beneath the makeshift altar. 'Our Masses are so rare, I normally put everything away, or it gets filled with shed fur.'

Nora stroked her fingers along the kitten's ears. 'Are all these cats yours? Aren't you afraid someone will eat them?'

He lifted his head. 'No. True, in hunger, the undead may turn on any animal – but if anyone here did decide to eat one of my pets, I would hunt them down and make their final transition into the afterlife one of pain and fear. With God's blessing, I daresay. I think this is common enough knowledge to keep them safe.'

Nora laughed. 'I think I like your religion.' Her eyes took in the chapel, the rough carvings of religious icons, the rainbow painted on the wall over the altar. 'You don't normally hold Mass, then?'

'No.' He found the monstrance, and heaved it up onto the table. 'Religion is a difficult topic, here. Those who come from the lands where the Son is worshipped think that their resurrection is similar to His, and that they must be here to fulfill some divine destiny – but they've no idea what it could be. It leaves them feeling directionless. And after accepting that they've come back to life, some lose their faith entirely . . . after all, they've not ended up with the afterlife that they were promised, but here they are, dead as the proverbial doornail.'

Nora thought this over. 'But you still believe that God exists.'

'Me? Yes. How can I not? My proof is right here.' Jacob picked two cats off the altar – a black and white Hemingway cat, and a muscular black one. 'These little creatures. Animals can sense things we cannot, you know . . . earthquakes, on-coming storms, even illness. And yet I can sit here, nights, with my hand upon one as it sleeps, feeling its stomach fall and rise . . . it *knows* I am there, and still it slumbers on. So trusting! If I were a monster, surely, it would flee from my touch. It's the most profound example of divine mercy that I can think of, the unconditional love shown by these animals for someone . . . some*thing* like me.' He set the cats down on the ground. 'So, how can there *not* be a God, and how can I not try to be a good man so long as there is one?'

She smiled at his explanation, and looked to me again. 'What about you?'

'I think we're all here for a reason, some of us longer than others,' I told her.

She nodded, and played with the kitten's paddy paws. 'I'm with you.'

I had been raised to have faith in the good forces of the universe, although my family wasn't terribly religious. I was glad of that. It let me admire the way the wine glistened on

Nora's lips, the way her throat moved as she swallowed the bread, the sound of her voice as she echoed back the usual prayers, without feeling too guilty.

I had plenty to feel guilty about, on my own. I didn't need any help from God.

Nora and I parted ways after our impromptu Mass. She smiled and thanked me, and that was all I needed to make the holiday a legendary one.

That is, until I got my usual clothes back on, and went out into the courtyard to see about drills, and heard the roar of the trucks driving up outside the main gate. The others were back.

I ran through the gate and grabbed the first zombie I saw, a simple, but trustworthy man named Amed. 'Is he here? Did you find him?'

He shook his head. 'No. Found the plane. But no sign of him. Nothing.'

My arm fell slowly from his shoulder.

I told Nora myself. She was in her father's office, working on the password. The count on the screen said she'd made 141 attempts to guess it. Her face went white when I delivered the news that he hadn't been found, but she nodded stoically.

'I'm going to keep hoping,' she said. 'Father Isley is right. As long as there's hope, you keep going. And this is the closest I've been to hope in a long time. Even if we never find him, there was the chance that we *could*, and it . . . even though I'm still angry at him, it made me happy. I was happy again, when I didn't think that was possible.'

'They'll muster the other half, most likely tomorrow, and do another sweep,' I told her. That seemed to cheer her up a little. I still left the room feeling like I'd personally let her down, though.

I ended up distracting myself by spending the day with

Renfield again. He was still working on the *Black Alice*. I was so absorbed in my own thoughts that I didn't question him as he ordered me about, or even notice what he was having me do half the time. He was keen on getting parts out of the ship – to clean or restore, I figured. I did all the heavy lifting.

'How's the self-defense thing going?' Renfield asked, as he used a spot welder to fix a part on the engine.

'It's going. I've only had time for a few sessions with her. She's not going to become a martial arts master in a couple of days. And her hands are still healing.' But she was swiftly learning how to move with the scythe, and that was promising.

Ren nodded. 'Well, it's a distraction, at least.'

'For both of us.'

Ren chuckled, and moved down to sit beside me, lifting up the windowed portion of his helmet. 'You know, I think you're handling it very well.'

'Huh? Handling what well?'

He snorted. 'It's clear you like her.'

For some reason, I was embarrassed that he had noticed. 'No offense, Ren, but what do you know about girls?'

He held up three bony fingers. 'You forget – three sisters in addition to the two brothers. I know enough. I'm fairly observant.'

'Sorry.' I slowly turned over the wrench I'd been using, and thought of my own family. 'I know Wolfe was worried you'd contact them. I've always wondered – did you?'

'No.' Renfield watched the wrench twirl. 'Did you ever contact your family?'

'No. When my mom saw me and screamed, it was a horrible kind of . . . acceptance. I know, 'cause I've screamed the same exact scream. I know she needs money, I know that she loves me . . . the old me . . . but ultimately, it's better that she thinks that I'm dead and gone. Clean break.'

'Understandable.'

'But that doesn't stop me from . . . well. Do you ever . . . I don't even want to say "think". *Fantasize* about seeing your family again?'

'Every day.' His expression was wistful. 'I will, one day, before I'm gone. If they're horrified by my appearance . . . well . . . at least I'll know that they were. They'll know what I became. There won't be any questions, anymore. That's what I can't stand about this whole affair – the not knowing.'

I understood exactly what he meant.

I had to tell Nora what was going on back at her home.

I started my search for Nora after dinner. Christmas was a hard day for most of the men, and the failure of the troops to find Dearly had been a blow to morale, so I'd chosen to eat with them as a sign of solidarity. The living, Wolfe excluded, had done the same, and so the mess had been filled with twice as many people, their chatter quiet and dispirited.

She wasn't in Dearly's office. I forced myself not to think too heavily about it, and continued on. She wasn't in Sam's lab, or my room. In fact, the halls were largely empty. Where was everyone? I'd been one of the first to leave the mess, but I knew I'd seen people leaving behind me.

Roughly twenty minutes later, just as I was starting to panic, I heard music. I shut my eyes and listened. It was coming from the mess hall.

I exited the western barracks and ran across the courtyard. There were still lights on inside the mess, and I could hear whooping cheers and laughter in addition to the tune being played. There was a female zombie waiting outside, her dress trailing on the muddy ground.

'What's going on?' I asked, as I drew to a stop.

The girl turned around, revealing herself to be Chas. She gave me an exasperated look. She was wearing the red dress she'd shown me earlier, and an assortment of mismatched plastic jewelry. 'No, no. This won't do.'

'Chas, what're you doing?'

She pointed at me. 'Go get sexy again, and you can come inside and see.'

I coughed. '*Excuse* me?'

'Talk is, you put your dress uniform on before to impress Nora, and it worked really well. And then, like an idiot, you took it off.' She glared at me. 'Go put it back on.'

'Why? Seriously, Chas, what are you—'

She interrupted me by stomping her foot. 'Because this is stupid! Everyone's all depressed, and it's Christmas, and it's . . . *stupid*! So, I waited for you to leave so I could fix it and make it *un*stupid. Now, go!' She shoved me in the shoulder, forcing me to take a few steps backwards.

I only stared at her for a few seconds before going and doing as she asked. I returned to my room and put the whole uniform back on, all the while questioning the very fact that I was doing so. When I was done, I hurried back to the mess. This time, there was no one outside, and I pushed the doors open.

I groaned at the sight that greeted me. Chas had *not*.

The digital Victrola was turned up very loudly, and was playing desert rag – a venerable form of Punk music, descended from something called 'Gangstagrass', that combines folksy fiddles and banjos with ancient rap beats.

'It's goin' down
Like the Titanic in its last hours,
A dirty game for money and power.
It's goin' down
Like a hooker on a slow hustle . . .'

Soldiers were pushing the tables against the walls. Chas waited for the group nearest her to finish, before climbing atop one of them. 'OK, in fifteen minutes I'm calling a reel, so you'd better find yourself a partner! We'll make two lines. And guys can dance with guys, that's totally fine, we're not going to gossip about you. Much.' Nora was standing beside her on the floor, an expression of amusement on her face.

I made my way over. 'Chas, what are you doing?'

She regarded me with a grin. 'Hosting a dance.'

'And where did you get permission to host a dance?' I asked, using the same tone of voice I'd have used if one of my little sisters had tried the same stunt. Nora, back in the pink gown, gathered her laughter in her gloved hands.

'From the voices in my head,' Chas replied, chipper. 'They're always so nice to me.'

'You do realize that the meds are going to have your *head* on a pike for contributing to the soldiers' wear and tear.'

She stooped down and whapped me lightly on the nose, like I was a bad dog. 'You're only undead once. And if we're gonna wear out, it might as well be doing something *fun*. Nora doesn't mind.'

Nora shook her head. 'No, I don't.' She looked at me, and smiled softly. 'I told you, hope and joy, good things by me. It's Christmas. And everyone's worked so hard.'

Her smile only reminded me of the reason I'd gone in search of her in the first place. God, I didn't want to hurt her.

Not right now.

So, we danced. We did reels and walks and other English country dances, in two lines with graceful and prescribed movements – well, Nora was the only graceful one. She was the brightest light in the room, a dazzling laughing living girl, hooking arms and hands and twirling with the dead, completely unafraid. We waltzed, somewhat poorly. A few of the guys threw down in a dance battle, popping and shimmying in ways living men couldn't, seeing as dislocating *their* joints would be painful, and not just another trick in their dance arsenals. I'd had no idea they'd ever tried doing such things, much less put in the practice that some of them obviously had.

About an hour into the party, Samedi and Charles pushed a wooden keg through the doors. They got a hero's welcome.

'About time!' Chas called, spinning away from her current partner and running to meet them.

'OK, no. *No*, right here,' I shouted, following her.

'No *no*,' Chas said. 'Negative on no. Yes.' She caught the edge of the keg and laughed, slipping behind Sam as if to hide from me.

'It's not as if you guys can even get all that buzzed, you know,' Charles reminded me. He was grinning. He opened the suitcase he was carrying, revealing the syringes he'd use to pump the beer into any dead man who wanted it. 'Just a taste. Who's it going to harm?'

I was being outvoted on something stupid. I didn't like being outvoted on something stupid.

Nora caught up to me, and laughed when she saw the keg. 'Sam! So what, you're Company Z's dealer, now?'

Samedi pulled a length of tubing out of the pocket of his lab coat and said, 'Darling girl – the real question is, when have I *not* been a dealer?'

'OK, Sam, that statement requires explanation.'

Samedi ignored her. Charles snapped on his latex gloves.

I decided to talk. It was the only way to get back at him for this. 'Doc Sam is a wanted man. At least where I'm from. He's got an official pardon from the Victorian side . . . condition of his working here.'

Sam glowered at me. Nora tugged on my sleeve. 'Spill!'

'You forget, my young buck,' Sam said warningly, as he busied himself with tapping the keg. 'Whenever a young lady hears my story, she falls passionately in love with me.'

'What, like Doc Chase? That's a risk I'm willing to take.'

'Yeah, where'd you meet her?' Nora asked, stepping out of the way of the line that was forming as news of the open bar spread.

Samedi thunked the keg and sighed, stepping back. 'I long ago made a promise to Dr Chase never to tell her side of the story for her.' He looked sourly at me. 'You two should go dance.'

I suddenly felt bad. 'Look, I'm sorry, Sam.' But he was already walking away.

'Why's he upset?' Nora asked.

'I don't know. He's usually pretty cool, but sometimes he gets a little emotional.'

Nora looked to the dancing crowd. 'You know, I keep forgetting about that. Some of you guys are Punks and some are Victorian, and you're joined together, and . . . do you guys ever fight, or anything?'

'Not really,' I said. 'In death, stuff like that really doesn't matter, anymore. I mean, sometimes it comes up, some petty thing, but . . . when you know you only have so much time? Where your roommate was born ceases to matter. We only have a few years left. Why would we want to fill them with hatred and pain?'

Nora turned her face up to me. Her mouth remained neutral, but for some reason, I liked the way she was looking at me. Like she was inspired by me. Like I'd said something that had really resonated with her.

I offered her my hand. 'Let's dance.'

She smiled.

For a few hours longer we touched one another, swept close to one another, with no fear or regrets. At the end Nora swayed in my arms to something slow and very old, after being convinced that yes, this is how we slow-dance behind Punk lines, and no, I'm not telling you that just so I can hold you.

Something was off, though. I found myself sniffing at her for the second time that day, leaning in close to her ear. She stiffened a little bit. 'What is it?'

'You smell like . . . chocolate,' I realized.

She dipped her head. 'Dr Chase lent me some perfume.'

I started to laugh. I knew she was going to hate me for it, but I did. 'Chocolate-coated living flesh.'

She flushed. 'Shut up!'

'I'm not making fun of you!' I protested – a little unconvincingly, seeing as I was still guffawing. 'I think it's sweet! Wait, wait, I didn't mean it that way . . .'

She glowered at me, and hid her face against my chest. 'Stop it.'

I obeyed, instantly.

It was the best moment of my life.

Wolfe chose that moment to crash the party.

'Everyone. Out,' he said. His voice thundered over the crowd. Revelers stopped abruptly where they were, and Coalhouse shut off the Victrola with a zipping sound. A few zombies scrambled to hide the keg amongst their bodies. 'Everyone to barracks, *now*. Except for Griswold.'

Nora slowly pulled herself from my arms. I looked into her worried eyes. 'I didn't mean to get you in trouble,' she whispered.

'You didn't. Go.' Her eyes lingered on mine a moment longer, but she did as I asked, her shoes making little clipping sounds on the hard floor as she left the mess. My friends gave me apologetic looks, but raced to catch up with her.

Wolfe and I stood, buoys on the water, as the others flowed around us and out the doors. Once the last zombie had shuffled out he asked me, voice ringing off of every hard surface, 'What the hell has gotten into you?'

I wasn't about to rat Chas out. 'My apologies, Captain. It seemed like a little Christmas party was in order. Miss Dearly had no objections.'

'Oh, obviously.' He was looking at me as if he'd just found me on the bottom of his shoe. 'No objection to dancing with you, either, I saw.'

I didn't dignify this with a response.

'D'you get some kind of thrill out of pretending to be human, Griswold?'

The phantom sensation of Nora's head against my chest answered for me. 'I am human.'

'Reality begs to differ.' He laughed mirthlessly. 'You're a disease vector, Griswold. You're a very big rat. A very big *flea.*'

'No.' Suddenly, it didn't matter. He could call me every name in the book, slice me to ribbons, send me wherever he wanted on whatever sick quest he could come up with. He could march me to my final death, and I would go, whistling a tune. 'We're all human. We're dead, but we're human. We feel, and we see, and we have just as small a chance as anybody drawing breath of living a good life, of being loved. *We're human.*' I smiled. 'I'm pretty successful at it too, you know. I look great, and I had a girl in my arms, and I haven't degraded another person or stolen their fun away.'

'Shut up, Griswold.'

I didn't listen to him. 'Yeah, tonight, I'm not your equal – I'm your superior. So get the hell back to your office.' He took a step closer to me, and I held up my hand. 'If you don't, I *will* bite you.'

He stopped, and worked his fists. His hair had bristled up, like an animal trying to magnify its size. Hey, he was humongous and strong and living, but one taste, and I could take him down. And he knew it.

'Tomorrow, you're going south,' he said, voice throaty. 'All of you. You're being reassigned. The Punks got *miles* on us today. They're scared, and they're driving northward.'

I stiffened. 'No way in *hell* am I fighting my own living people.'

'You'll do it,' he said, his anger barely held in check. 'Or I'll shoot you myself. I've been patient. I've been nice. I even let you stay here with Dearly's girl because she wasn't afraid of you – she's just as sick in the head as he is. But you are my toy, Griswold. You do what I say.'

'Well then, little Jimmy, let me tell you what you should be doing with your *toys*. You should be sending us to the Elysian Fields.'

He turned his back on me. 'Our men have lost the EF.'

'*What?*'

He didn't answer me.

'You said you were taking care of it!' I yelled. He didn't respond, and pushed his way angrily out of the doors. I watched him go, my body suddenly tight with terror and powerlessness. They'd lost it? Nora's home was gone?

All she loved, gone.

I *had* to tell her. *Now*. No more secrets.

I ran out of the mess, and ended up pulling up short. Nora was standing there in the moonlit courtyard. She turned to look at me, full of expectation – so full of life.

How *could* I tell her?

CHAPTER TWENTY-SIX

Nora

'Are you in trouble?' I asked.

'Yeah,' he responded. He took my hand, and started to pull me in the direction of the big gate. 'And I'm about to get into even more.'

I yanked my hand back. 'What's the hurry? Are you OK?'

He stopped and looked at me. There was something in his face I couldn't place, some urgency. I was reminded of being shunted away from my dead father's bedside – all of his associates had known what was coming, while I had not. 'Yeah . . . yeah, I'm OK. But I have something to tell you. It can't wait.'

My chest felt constricted, like someone was hugging me far too hard. I nodded. I had something to tell him too, and I wasn't exactly sure how.

I liked him.

I liked him a *lot*.

I followed him to the gate, and out a small door where personnel passed in and out of the compound. Night was deep, now, and the trees had become malevolent, many-armed shapes on the horizon. He took me down a dirt path to an open area studded with trucks and tanks and other equipment.

'What are we doing here?' I asked.

'Privacy,' he said, as he kept walking.

We stepped around a heavy transport unit, and all of the vast speeches I'd been composing in my head petered out when I saw the airship.

'Oh!' I moved toward it. 'I've never seen one of these in person!'

'Never?' Bram sounded like he didn't believe me.

'Never! We use zeppelins, but not things like this. The piratey kind. The actual *ships.*'

He laughed, although the sound lacked the richness it'd had before. This subtle little thing bothered me. 'Not all air sailors are pirates.'

'I know, it's just . . .' I turned to look at him, and held out my hand. He hesitated a moment before taking it, and he didn't grip it as fervently as he had earlier. I had the sudden idea that he was going to reject me, or run away from me, and without even thinking about it I tightened my hold on his fingers and pulled him up the plank. I took a breath. 'We need to talk.'

'Yes, we do.' He was starting to sound frightened, and that made *me* nervous in turn. 'Nora . . .'

'I'm sorry.' I stepped onto the deck and turned around to look at him, while he was still low enough on the plank to look me directly in the eye.

He stared at me for a moment. 'For what?'

'I'm sorry,' I sighed. 'For the whole . . . head thing . . . back there. I'm sorry I put my head on your chest. I don't know why I did that.'

Bram didn't move, his other hand resting on the plank's railing. 'Oh,' he said at last, and my stomach lurched. I felt like I'd ripped his heart out and shown it to him. That wasn't what I meant!

'I mean . . .' *Here goes.* 'I think you're . . . amazing. Where I come from, the boys just sort of want you to sit there and look nice. They figure they know what you want, or just don't care what you want. But you don't act like that . . . you respect me. You *acknowledge* me. And I've been under so much stress, and your chest was just there, and it suddenly looked like the nicest pillow in the entire world.'

'Nora . . .'

'I know we've only known each other a week, and there are other things to worry about just now, big things. But what I'm trying to say is that I *shouldn't* have done that whole head thing, but . . . but I *wanted* to do it, and . . .' I buried my hands in my skirt. 'I'm sorry. You're going to think I'm creepy. I'll shut up, now.'

I heard Bram climbing up the plank and approaching me. I lifted my head, though it felt like I was balancing an anvil atop it. He stopped in front of me. He didn't seem to know what to do with his hands, either. 'Creepy?' He laughed, shortly. 'Nora, you're making my decade, here.'

I felt a flutter of hope in my breast. 'I just never thought I'd actually want to *be* around a boy, before. It's kind of weird.'

Bram regarded me with soft eyes. He took a deep, chest-expanding breath, and when the air came out he said, 'I'm dead, Nora.'

I'd known this was going to come up, either from him or someone else. 'It's hard to think of you as dead when you laugh with me, walk with me, smile at me . . .'

He shook his head, some of his hair coming to rest before his eyes. He didn't brush it away. It shadowed his face, made him look sad. 'I'm dangerous.'

'Oh, and other people aren't?' I heard the growing temper in my own voice. 'You've spent the last week convincing me that you're not a monster, and now you're going to make like you are? Don't try to pull that. Men turn on their wives of twenty years with hatchets, men . . . men go insane and murder their children. Everyone is capable of becoming dangerous, going mad. What makes you so different?'

'*Different?*' He took a step closer, and grabbed my wrists before I could back away. 'Do living men have dreams about people dying? Do they occasionally get the urge to chase you? Do they, no matter how well they repress it, no matter how well-behaved they are, always have in the back of their mind the idea that your *flesh* would be the best thing they ever tasted?'

I held my ground. 'Probably not,' I replied. 'But *I* have

dreams about people dying. I've been so angry that I couldn't think straight. I know what it's like.'

He let go of me, his expression folding into confusion. I slowly reached up and touched his bottom lip. He flinched away, but I persisted. 'Go ahead. If you're so out of control, go ahead. This isn't my shooting hand.'

Bram folded his arms over his chest. He didn't fight it as I traced his lips, his chin, the top half of his throat. He did catch my hand before it ventured any lower, though. My tongue flattened against the roof of my mouth as I kept my eyes on his, letting him do what he wanted.

He kissed my satin-robed wrist, over the glove's buttoned opening, and dropped my hand.

In that moment, I found him fully, absolutely beautiful. The way he kissed me was so honest; the way he stood there, calmly embodying his own space, was attractive in that it simply *was*. He just *was*, when he shouldn't be.

'I dream of my father's death all the time,' I told him, breathless from what he'd just done. 'I watched it. It would have been cruel not to watch it, when he had seen my birth, and so much of my pain. And I know what it's like to have thoughts you can't control. Just before I came here my Aunt Gene showed me how badly she's managed my family's money . . . she's ruined me. I was so, *so* angry that I didn't know what to do. But I didn't do anything horrible. And I won't. That's the difference. But *you* must do the same thing countless times every day. You're so strong, Bram, and I really admire you for that.'

His hand came for me again, and I welcomed it. He touched my cheek. His fingers were cold and dry, as always, and I found the sensation strangely enticing. 'I wouldn't even be around very long. I would rot to pieces in front of you.'

I cringed. How could his touch be so tender, and his focus still be on denying me this? 'How long does anybody ever have *anyone*? I had my mother for nine years, my father fifteen. There are no guarantees in life.'

Bram turned his back on me and approached the wheel of the ship, draping himself over it with a sigh. He turned his attention to the sky. I looked up, in turn, for guidance. This whole situation was exasperating.

I almost fell backwards where I was standing.

'Oh, look at all the stars!' I had never seen so many in my life. The sky was festooned with them, like the spangles on my borrowed black fingerless gloves.

Bram's voice was full again, and low. 'That's one thing they always tell us about you Victorians – that your cities are so bright at night that you can't see the stars. That the Vics deny their children such a simple thing.'

I argued, 'You can see *some* – not all, but some. The brightest. And where I live, they reflect them on the screens above, so that even those deep underground don't have to be without.'

'They aren't real, though.' He straightened up and came closer to me. 'That freaked me out, when we came to get you. All those trees, that sky, and none of it was *real*.'

I felt my blood rising, and opened my mouth to lash out with something like, '*So, how many human sacrifices have you attended?*' . . . when I realized the humor of the whole situation. It was one of those moments where things in your atom-sized corner of the universe make sense, where you are utterly at peace and somewhat smug.

'You're right,' I laughed. 'I've been trained, all my life, to expect natural things to appear in unnatural forms.'

Bram looked at me as if I had lost my mind. I suppose it was payback for how I must have looked at *him*, the first time we met. 'What are you laughing at?'

'This!' I spun around before him, on a lark. 'All of this! You know . . .' I stopped, my skirt moving still, and leaned closer to him. 'We never would have met if you hadn't become a zombie. You're a Punk, I'm a Victorian . . . but here we are, united in death.'

Bram laid his hands on my shoulders and looked at me. I wanted him to try and kiss me. No way was I going to slip him the tongue, but I wanted him to do it, just to show me that he wanted it too. I wanted just *that* much validation that I was not babbling on like a complete loser, here.

He pushed me back. 'Nora . . .'

I would have thought I had more pride, but I pressed it. 'Bram, please . . .'

He shook his head. 'I have to tell you something, *now*.'

'I know you want something like this. In time. Bram, you said you were waiting for the right girl . . . couldn't I be her? I mean, not right now, but *maybe*. We shouldn't even be talking about this, but we are, so let's just finish . . .'

'*You are!*' he suddenly roared. I backed up of my own volition, startled by the outburst. His voice had sounded almost primal. 'You are, in ten thousand ways! I've never done anything like this before, I don't know . . .' He pushed his hair back, and took to pacing. 'But Wolfe is right. I'm not the right guy for you. I know that I could never be everything . . . *anything* you need.'

My corset suddenly felt oppressively tight, the fabric-covered steel digging into my ribs. Bram opened his jacket. His waistcoat flashed red beneath, like he'd been stabbed and bled. 'But . . . I've had the time of my life, pretending. Thank you for even letting me.'

'Bram, no, it wasn't—'

'*Will you just let me get it out, already?*' He stopped in his tracks, facing away from me.

I held my breath. I didn't want to hear it. I wanted to run away and hide myself in my father's bedroom and cry my lungs and eyes empty. But I stayed.

'Nora,' he began. His tone had utterly changed. Within the space of thirty seconds, he'd become a defeated man. 'You were right. There are things we haven't told you – things *I* haven't told you. Wolfe ordered me not to tell you. He said that if I did he'd send me away, and I didn't want to leave you alone here. Hell, I didn't want to leave *you*. The moment I saw you on the street, I fell for you; I would have done anything to stay with you. He told me they were taking care of it . . . but they've failed.'

He did like me. But now, I didn't feel like crowing. 'What?' I asked.

'Please,' he said, closing his eyes. 'Please, *please* don't hate me. I didn't mean to keep you in the dark. This is all my fault. I'm so sorry . . .'

Now I was honestly terrified. *Had* they found my father? Was he dead? 'What is it, Bram?'

He moved his fingers, slightly, as if counting to five. 'The undead have taken over the EF.'

I had absolutely no basis from which to comprehend this statement. 'What?'

He looked at me, and I saw how serious he was. 'It was the Grays. I mean, it had to be. They locked down the Fields, sent live men in to fight them . . . but they've won.'

I still wasn't on board, yet. 'The undead are in New London?' I could barely hear my own voice.

Bram punched the railing. 'I don't know how bad it is,' he growled. 'Wolfe didn't tell me.'

The sound of that punch rocketed my body through space and time to the present. It took my brain two seconds to see the entire thing play out. I fell to my knees on the deck. 'Oh my God,' I whispered, unable to think of anything else to say.

Bram came closer and reached out for me, but I clawed my way back from him. 'Don't touch me!' I heard myself shriek, before the tears started, and there was nothing but my chest shaking, my eyes burning, splinters of wood catching on my gloves as I pounded on the deck of the ship. I'd been thinking of Pamela constantly since my abduction, knowing that she must be going through hell – but now I had visions of her and her family being hunted, being eaten, and it was enough to nearly kill me.

He didn't listen to me. I came to when I felt Bram clutching me against his solid chest, restricting my spasming body. I writhed against him, but he was far stronger than I was, and soon I was weeping on his shoulder, my arms around him.

'I'm so sorry, Nora, I'm so sorry,' he kept saying, his lips near my ear, his hand in my hair.

'Pam,' I gasped. 'My friend, Pam. She's up there. I have to help her. I have to go, now.'

He shook his head, his nose brushing my earlobe. 'We can't, Nora. It's suicide.'

'I have to go *now*!' I sobbed.

'The army won't go with us, and they won't come after us!' Bram sounded so helpless, and I hated it. If *he* was helpless, we were lost. 'What about your father? What if your friend is already gone?'

I tried to fight my way back to control. Bram slid his hands over the sides of my neck and tipped my face up as I took cleansing breaths. What about my father? There was no trace of him. But Pam – Pam, I knew, had been alive and well when I'd been taken. There was a better chance of her being safe, now, than him. 'She has a mobile phone. We can call her. Just let me *call* her, like I've been saying!'

I swallowed my own tears. Bram was already standing up and helping me to my feet.

This time I didn't mind that he pulled me along, because I didn't think I could walk on my own. He took me not to the med facilities or Wolfe's quarters, where I would have guessed we'd find communications equipment, but to one of the barracks. I didn't question this. He finally stopped at a door and knocked on it.

Renfield opened it.

And immediately shut it again.

'Ren, this is not a drill! *This is important!*' Bram shouted.

The door opened once more, and Renfield stepped back shakily. He was still dressed in the brown sack suit he'd worn to the party, although now he was wearing black leather gloves. He hadn't had those on before. 'What is it?'

'We need to get on the AetherNet,' Bram said, slamming the door shut as we stepped in. 'Go to the lab, ask Doc Sam where Wolfe put your equipment, and get it set up. Bring Sam with you. It's urgent.'

Renfield glanced at his desk. 'I . . . already have.'

Bram looked surprised. 'You mean you've been breaking the rules all this time?'

'Yes.' Ren sounded worried.

'Good.' Bram guided me to the bed.

Renfield's room looked like it had been built out of antique non-digital books. Hundreds of them. They were neatly stacked, floor to ceiling, on every available surface. They even made a little fortress around the bed. Bram pushed a pile over to clear the way for me.

Renfield slid his hand over his face. 'Don't ruin the Sanctum *Sanctorum!*'

'It's your *bed*, and her knees are going to give out,' Bram argued. He was right. I sat down weakly. My heart was going a million miles a minute, and my vision was blurry. Not so blurry that I couldn't see Ren's desk, though.

The guy's bedroom *was* a communications center.

There were several computers there, open-work models with their wires and drives exposed. A few parts were made up with scrap from old machines. Most interesting of all, though, was the steam holographic projector. If I'd been in better emotional condition I'd have jumped up to coo over it, but for now I stayed where I was.

The Punks didn't want our holographic technology, but they'd achieved something like it through the use of steam. Ren's was a tabletop model, a brass column with a space between the top and bottom plates. Showers of steam jetted down from the top one, and the bottom one responded with concentrated jets of air. Between the two, misty, semi-solid images could be projected. Sensors allowed one to interact with them, as well.

I could see vaporous images in it, even now. A young woman's hand, wearing several rings, including the traditional bow-shaped ring sported by Victorian girls whose parents would choose their future mates for them, hovered over a chess board. He was playing AetherNet chess with someone.

'I know, I know,' Ren was saying, as he punched rapidly at the old typewriter keyboard he'd modified to fit into his system. 'I know I'm not supposed to be on. But there's no voice chat with this one, I swear, and I'm using about nine thousand proxies so they can't tell where I'm coming from. It's just chess.'

'Renfield, I really, *really* did not come here to yell at you, but I'm starting to feel like I should,' Bram said, out of patience.

The girl in the steam moved her bishop, and the move sprung up on Ren's screen. He sat down and typed back, 'Have to go now, my apologies. Save game?'

A second later he got his response. 'Of course. Have a good night. Stay safe.'

He shut off the program, and the cloudy chess board evaporated. Renfield peeled off his wet gloves. 'Now, what can I do for you?' He looked at me, and that's when he got it, I think, his eyes widening a bit. 'What's wrong?'

'You know about the Grays in the EF?'

'Of course.' He looked at me penitentially. 'Salvez told me.'

'Wolfe says they've taken over.'

Renfield's hands slowly migrated to his lap. 'My word.'

'We need to see if we can get in touch with Nora's friend in New London. If she's still alive . . .' Bram looked to me. 'What do you want to do?'

I pressed my palms together. Now was not the moment to

break down. I'd had plenty of chances to do that over the last week – why should now be the time? I had to keep going. 'Go after her.'

Bram nodded slowly, and turned his eyes back to Ren. 'If she's still alive, we're going to go in the *Black Alice* to get her.'

Renfield gaped at Bram. 'You do realize that that might be the death of you.' He looked at me, and said, tone again apologetic, 'I mean no offense, nor is it my intention to make light of the situation. But it's the truth.'

'Yeah, it is,' Bram said. 'Guess we'll just have to deal with it.'

Renfield thought about this for a moment, before reaching for the bowler hat he'd hung over a nearby oil lamp. He put it on at an angle. 'All right. I'm in.'

Bram held up a hand. 'Whoa, you don't go on missions.'

Ren spun his chair about. 'You don't usually take my airship on missions.'

'*Your* airship?'

Renfield started tapping on the keyboard again, ignoring Bram. 'I set this system up for voice chat a few months ago, before I was barred from getting on the 'Net at all,' he explained, for my benefit. 'Wolfe was afraid that I'd get online and find a sympathetic ear and tell them my life story. Maybe mail them some coordinates?' He rolled his eyes. 'He knew a password wouldn't keep me out, so he confiscated everything. I just picked the lock and got my equipment back the next night.'

'I should have asked *you* about calling out,' I said, regretfully.

'Trust me, Wolfe spoke to me about that. If I'd let you, and I'd gotten caught, my head would currently be decorating a tree somewhere, done up like an extremely morbid bird feeder . . . here we go. And here's the moment where the rules fly out the window for all of us. Have you got a number?'

I found my legs and walked over, resting my hand on the back of Ren's chair. I recited the information, a bit slowly. Ren keyed it, then flipped a few switches and brought out a set of old brass headphones, which he handed to me. I put them on.

'Here goes,' he said, clicking a button on the screen that said, '*Initiate wireless contact.*'

I held my breath. I heard the phone ringing through the headset. No one picked up. The ringing stopped after half a minute or so, and a message popped up on the screen. '*Wireless tele/phone/graph out of range of service.*'

I felt like screaming. Bram sat on the edge of the desk and said, 'Again.'

Renfield looked at me and I nodded, cupping my hands over the headphones. 'Again.'

And there we stood, dialing. C'mon, phone. Work.

Please, Pam.

Pick up.

Chapter Twenty-seven

Pamela

I let them have Christmas Day.

I'd already gotten my gift (and ruined it), and had succeeded in alienating my family, so I didn't join in the festivities. I wasn't hungry, or thirsty, or even tired. I wondered if it would last, this sensation. I felt like a nun must feel after coming out of a particularly intense session of prayer. I was high on purpose.

I waited until after supper, when I could hear that they were gathered together in the parlor, before taking one last good look at my archery awards and heading for Issy's room.

My brother's bedroom was decorated in more masculine colors, all of his things put exactingly away. I tore the place apart looking for what I wanted, tossing the contents of his dresser drawers on the floor and ripping things out of his closet. I'd clean it up later, if I lived to care.

I dressed in a pair of linen trousers and a wing-tipped shirt and one of his older, smaller waistcoats. I tied my hair up in a bun. It took a few seconds to get used to the sensation of walking in pants, rather than a skirt, but I reminded myself that now was not the time to be embarrassed. I strapped my archery harness and braces on, and took a deep breath.

I made my way to the parlor.

'You'd think they'd have the power on by now,' Isambard was complaining. 'Or at least have brought out the town criers.'

'Might be dangerous for the criers on the streets,' Dad responded.

'How else are we supposed to get any news?'

'They would find some way to tell us, if there was anything to know,' Mom said.

With this statement as my introduction, I entered the parlor. 'Let's talk about that, Mother.'

Mom looked up from her library book. 'What on earth?' My father was lighting the candles on the tree. He put down the lighter and made as if to approach me, but then apparently thought better of it and stayed where he was.

Issy boggled at me. 'Are those my clothes?'

'Listen to me, all of you,' I said. My body was engulfed by a raw, nervous energy. I was taking my first baby steps as a leader. The entire situation felt more theatrical than I knew it to be – I was deadly serious.

'Pamela, what's going on?'

'A lot.' I looked at my family members, each in turn, holding their eyes with my own until they looked away. 'Because you seem to be incapable of seeing it, I'm going to presume that I've been given some sort of gift. They thought Joan of Arc was crazy too.'

'Pamela,' my dad tried to interrupt.

I pointed right through him, to the window. 'Our streets are filled with the ill and the dying. The disease responsible for this apparently makes some of its victims attack people and attempt to *eat* them.' I pointed to the side of my head. 'Is this sinking in, at all? Do you just not see it? Or are you waiting for the screens to come on and for some disembodied head to give you *permission* to panic?'

'Pamela,' my father tried again, 'calm down. There's no use panicking.'

'There are cannibals in the streets, Father!'

'Your father is right!' my mother interjected. 'Besides, where would we go? Who knows if those who did leave are even safe? Maybe there are more ill people out there in the countryside! We'd be told what to do if there was anything we *could* do!'

'I've thought of something for us to do.' I looked at my hands. They were shaking, moving in small, wild ways.

'We need to get into hiding. And I think I know of a place.'

Dad stepped closer. 'Now, wait just a minute . . .'

'You have a better idea, sir?' I raised my voice, just a tad. 'I would love to hear it.'

'Yes!' His hands balled into fists, and he took to gesturing at the window, himself. 'My idea, as *crazy* as it sounds, is to leave the handling of this situation to those who are actually equipped to handle it! If everyone turns into a vigilante, the city will fall apart! What has gotten *into* you?'

'This isn't about being a vigilante.' My voice faltered. 'This is about surviving.'

'Right now, we're fine! We're safer than most people!'

I didn't want to have to do this. I was frightened and desperate, but I didn't want to have to do this.

But it didn't seem like I had a choice.

'You are my *family*. I love you. But let me remind you that I have a weapon on my back. I will march you out of here if I have to, because I *love* you.' I reached back, as if to unhook my bow.

That was the moment when my family fully perceived, in *their* minds, that I had broken from reality. I could see it settling over them as they stared at me. I had prepared for this possibility. I didn't care if they thought I was insane.

I didn't care if they hated or mourned me, so long as they remained alive to do so.

'Pamela,' my mother said, her voice trembling. At the sound of it, I almost relented. I almost threw myself at her feet and begged for forgiveness. You never want to hear your own mother sound like a bewildered child.

I almost did, but I didn't.

Before I could say anything else, the power came back on. I started a little. The screen on the wall fizzed angrily with static, before it found a signal.

The man on the screen was a well-known reporter, his dark hair sweaty and matted. He was broadcasting from outside the

Elysian Fields. The cameraman was having trouble holding the camera steady, and it was hard to get a read on what was happening. All of us seemed to momentarily forget where we were and what we were arguing about, universally compelled to watch the frightened face on the screen.

'They're out! The infected are everywhere! What the devil? Man, get back! *We need to fall back!* This is Marcus Maripose, broadcasting from the Elysian Fields, where . . .'

The sound cut out at that point, and all we had was the image – the ill shuffling, crawling, sometimes running out of the gatehouse. The cameraman managed to focus in on the broken gates, and my entire body felt like it wanted to vomit itself up through my skin.

There were so *many* of them, a literal *wall* of them pressing themselves against the gates, snapping them apart. It was like watching a ball of ants floating on the waters of a flood, a tangle of limbs and bodies.

'Good God,' my father whispered.

'I don't think He's listening right now,' I replied, still staring at the screen. 'We need to go. *Now.*'

'Where?' my mother asked helplessly. *Finally.*

'To the Cathedral,' I said, divulging the idea I'd been working on since the night before. 'It used to be a bank. There are still two vaults in it – the one behind the altar, and another in the basement, where they hold Sunday school. I remember, a priest told us once that the vaults are made of two feet of solid metal.'

'There's no way they'd let us hide in there,' Isambard argued.

Mom stood up. 'There's got to be another way. Maybe they'll tell us . . .'

I pointed to the screen. 'Look how many of them there are! Look what's been *hidden* from us! Are you going to sit there and wait for the government to make an emergency broadcast? Or are you going to get up, get some supplies, and come with me?'

'If we lock ourselves in the vault, we won't know when to come out,' my father said. He was finally turning, mentally, in my direction.

'There's nowhere else to go,' I said. 'There's no better option that I can think of. But even if we have to hide somewhere else – we can't outrun them, now.'

Dad ran his hand over his mouth, and nodded. 'Malati, get up. Get some food and water, come on. As much as we can all carry. It will take the infected a while to get here, they're not in the streets yet. Get up. Isambard, go down into the bakery and get some empty flour sacks.'

Satisfied that they were starting to move, I headed in the direction of the back door.

My father called out, 'Pamela, where are you going?'

I opened the door. The lights were on in the buildings around us, but not in the building across the way, where the Delgados lived. Perhaps the power wasn't on on Halperin Street yet.

'You know where, Father!' I said, as I stepped out and shut the door behind me. He'd been there when I made my promise.

I ran across the courtyard. I let the striking of my body on the Delgados' back door announce my arrival, and followed it up with frantic pounding. Thankfully, Mr Delgado opened it quickly, candle in hand. He appeared even more haggard than he had before, the circles around his eyes quite black. 'Miss Roe?'

No time to mince words. 'Do you have power?'

He shook his head, his eyes widening. 'No. Is there news?'

'It's on. It's on, and the EF is filled with the infected, and they've just broken out.' I tried to think. 'Lock yourself inside. If you go anywhere you'll probably be attacked or killed, I'd imagine. If you need to move somewhere else, come to our house. My family is leaving.'

Emanuel nodded swiftly. 'Is your family healthy?'

'Yes.'

'Good luck, then.' He held back a moment, and then said, 'We're all ill. We're . . . not in good shape. But we're not like the ones they were telling stories about. I heard, in the market, these stories . . . I would never harm anyone, I swear. I *never* would.'

I stepped back. 'Hold on to that, and hide.' I took a breath. 'Good luck, Mr Delgado.'

When I got back to my house, the broadcast's sound was back on. There was screaming, crying, the correspondents yelling as they tried to keep reporting. Mother was packing supplies into a flour sack, her cheeks wet. I felt a pang of remorse. I hadn't meant to make her cry. But then again, no part of this situation had been my doing. I had to keep telling myself that.

I couldn't stop it. I could only try to make it better.

With everyone's help, we were ready to go in perhaps five minutes. Just as we were strapping the last bag on Issy, who was quiet for once in his life, the broadcast changed. The seal of the Territories flashed upon the screen, and there was a very quick, 'We now introduce the Prime Minister of New Victoria, Aloysius Ayles.'

'Wait, wait,' my father said, adjusting his own load so he could slip through the parlor door.

'Father, we don't have *time*!'

'Just wait!'

I sighed. We all followed.

The PM looked frightened out of his wits. His eyes kept darting off-camera, and he couldn't find it in him to speak. 'Ladies and gentlemen,' he eventually tried, although his voice lacked its usual bombastic flair. 'I . . .'

'Just let me get *up* there! It's out of the bag, now, you fools!' said a voice from off-camera. It sounded vaguely familiar, but I couldn't place it. My family and I exchanged looks. What was this?

There was a lot of arguing, bumping and crashing, and it was clear that the PM was watching someone come nearer. Still, he tried to continue. 'I have . . . ah . . . gotten on here to . . .'

'Aloysius, tell the nice people why you're leaving.' The voice was very close, now.

Mr Ayles swallowed and stammered, 'I . . . I will address the people of New London in short order, but . . . my father would like to speak, now.'

'Good man. Get up.'

'Father?' Dad asked. Even now, he was dissecting political shows. 'Lord Ayles? He hasn't been seen in public in years.'

The PM rose shakily from his chair, and stepped out of the way. Lord Ayles didn't take his place immediately, but said, 'Ladies and gentlemen, my son likes big, fancy speeches. Now is not the time for such things. It's been a while since I've spoken to you, myself, for reasons that will become abundantly clear once I actually take my seat. I ask you not to react in fear, although I am bloody ugly, it's true. Just listen to what I have to say, because time is running out.'

'What's going on?' Issy asked. I had absolutely no idea.

Another interminable beat passed, and then Lord Ayles sat down. I almost fell to the ground. Mom cried out.

He was ill.

I mean, really, *really* ill.

The man had no nose or lips or hair, his head horrifyingly streamlined. His rotten brown skin was stretched taut over the bones of his skull, and his recessed eyes glittered, dark points in the caves of his eye sockets. His entire chest cavity was hollowed out, and there was some sort of machinery mounted within, screwed to his spine. The back of his clothing was visible *through* him. He wore only trousers and an open silk shirt with blousy sleeves, and I could see his ribs and the bones in his neck hidden beneath a thin, mossy layer of blackened skin.

He looked like a monster from a fairy tale.

'Pretty, eh?' he said, gesturing to his frame. 'I've been this way for nearly a decade, now. Ever since Dr Victor Dearly saved my life, and in the process, infected me with his blood. This disease we're currently facing has been around a while, my good people. It is not a weapon of war. And it was wrong of us to keep it a secret from the public – but we honestly thought we could battle it, contain it, and not have to trouble your sleep with the knowledge that the dead can come back to life. Yes, I'm dead. No heartbeat, rotting away, dead, dead, dead. Any of the infected you see are probably dead too, or will be shortly.'

My chest was wracked by a dry sob. The Delgados – little Jenny Delgado – they were *dead*?

'Look, there's no time to explain everything. I'm going to arm you with some basic facts. The reanimated dead are known as zombies. Not all the zombies you will encounter are, as you can see from exhibit A here, evil or insane, but there is no time to sort them out now. If you have infected loved ones who are acting as well as they can be expected to, given their circumstances, keep them inside. But if they turn on you, kill them. Kill any you see on the streets. Aim for the head. Destruction of the brain is the only way to get them to drop. If you don't think you can fight, hide. We're recalling more troops for the sole purpose of battling the dead, but it's going to take a while.

'And if you see any zombies on the streets with guns, wearing flashing red badges, *don't* target them. Those are our boys and girls. It's . . . I'll explain that one later.' He nodded at the camera. 'Good luck.'

The seal of the Territories went back up for a moment, before the station returned to the news broadcast. My family and I stood there, the rapid-fire light from the screen playing over our faces.

'Our former Prime Minister is a . . . zombie,' I said.

'Indeed,' my father said. Mom nodded.

We all processed this, each in his or her own way. I gave myself thirty seconds or so to silently scream and furiously pray, and they passed like lightning.

They didn't make me any safer, though.

I curled my hands around the straps of my pack. 'Let's go.'

The streets were a mess. Everyone was fleeing in the direction we were going, and we had to struggle to keep up. This, combined with the fear that someone, *anyone* in the crowd might be running after you, not *with* you, made for an exhilarating and terrifying experience. We did our best to cling onto one another, our hands sweaty and cold. Several times I had to let go of Dad, or Issy, and then spend a frantic few moments searching for them, begging God above that I would find them. Luckily, I did.

Some citizens had decided to try and drive to the other end of town, but their carriages were going nowhere. One, pastel pink, was caught on the curb against a fire hydrant. A woman and her child were crying within as a top-hatted gentleman equipped with a pearly cell phone pushed at the carriage with one arm. I saw another carriage tipped over, its dazed occupants standing on the side of the road.

Some of the advertisement boards were working again, and they were all showing the same thing – the rotting form of the former PM. Bullet points flashed beneath him. *Aim for the head. Disease is transmitted via body fluids.*

About four blocks away from our house I finally registered a constant beeping in the background. I looked over my shoulder, and saw Michael Allister's enameled blue carriage crawling through the crowd. Without even thinking about it, I stopped.

'Come on, Pamela!' my mother called back.

'It's Mr Allister!'

She pulled on my hand. 'Let him catch up!'

I knew that this was wise advice. I even took a few steps more with my family, craned back though my head was. But then I realized that Michael's carriage wasn't moving. He was caught in the torrent of people.

I couldn't just abandon him.

'He doesn't know where we're going! I'm going to go get him!' I said, tearing my hands free. 'Go to the church! Get in the vault!'

'There is *no way* I am leaving you behind!' my mother said, crying anew.

'Just go! If I don't come, get in!' I shrugged off one of my packs, and handed it to my father. I hugged both my parents, or as much of them as I could reach. 'I'll come. I swear, I'll make it! Just go!'

I heard them shouting my name as I dove into the crowd. I ignored it, and fought my way through the ocean of people as I had before. When I got near the carriage, I caught the fancy eagle-shaped hood ornament in my hands and used it to pull my way through. The driver's door opened, and I ducked underneath, pushing myself along the ground for a moment.

'Miss Roe!' Michael said as I stood up. He looked relieved. He was dressed in only his trousers and a shirt and jacket. He honestly looked like a dashing explorer. He swept his eyes over me and asked, shocked, 'What on earth are you wearing?'

Despite the horrific situation we were in, I flushed. Michael Allister was looking at my legs. 'Where're Lord and Lady Allister? And Mrs Ortega?' I asked, trying to keep my cool.

He indicated that I should get in, drawing his legs out to make room for me to scoot by. 'They started for the north. I didn't go with them. I came to find you, but you weren't at home. Here, get in, we'll drive to the other side of town. Are your mother and father coming?'

I shook my head. 'They're on foot, and still moving. You're not going to get anywhere in this thing, Mr Allister.'

He shut off the engine, and took a moment to compose his thoughts. 'Do you think we can get to the other side of the city on foot?' he asked. He sounded doubtful.

'Possibly,' I said. 'But we weren't aiming for the other side of the city. What's there, anyway, the port? We were going to the Cathedral of Our Mother.' He gave me a dubious look. 'The bank vaults. Kind of hard for the infected to chew through solid metal.'

Michael grabbed the bag he'd brought with him. 'All right, I guess it's worth a try.'

It was a stupid thing to feel giddy about – especially now. But I extended my hand towards him. 'The crowd will try to pull us apart. We have to stay together.'

Michael nodded, and wrapped his fingers around mine. His skin was hot.

If I was going to die, I might as well die happy.

He shut the carriage door, and we let the tide carry us forward. I tried to find my family in the crowd, but they were too far ahead of us. 'Why didn't you go with your parents?' I shouted at Michael.

'Because I knew they were all right!' he shouted back, fixing his eyes on me. 'I wasn't so sure about you! I couldn't call on you after your arrest. All I could do was vouch for you.'

I blinked. 'You vouched for me?' New Victorians charged with crimes could get out of paying bail or remaining imprisoned if they had someone powerful and aristocratic enough to speak on their behalf.

'Yes! Didn't your parents tell you? I met them at the courthouse the day your council summoned them.'

I shook my head, and committed a note to memory: if parents survive, kill them.

There was a mob outside the cathedral. Apparently, my idea wasn't as original as I'd hoped. The priests were outside, yelling at the crowd, trying to get everyone to calm down, or line up, or some combination of the two. I shook my hand free of Michael's and ran up to Father Rodriguez, the priest I knew best. 'Father! Have you seen my family?'

He looked at me, his eyes alight with a terrible energy, and pointed to the doors. I repeated this for Michael, and he and I moved to get inside. As we attempted to squeeze through the line people screamed at us and tried to physically shove us out again. Michael actually elbowed one particularly frantic man in the face after he grabbed my waist, yelling at him, 'Be still, man! The young lady has family already within!' The man let go, and Michael pushed me inside.

'I don't know which vault they're in, though,' I told him. 'As long as they're in one or the other, that's all I care about.'

'Right. There's one in the basement, yes? You go check that one, I'll check the one behind the altar.'

Plan arranged, I ran as fast as I could down into the basement. There was already a crowd gathered on the stairs, and I had to fight my way through them. 'Roe!' I screamed. 'Roe!' No one replied, although many people were doing the same thing. Some were weighed down with supplies; others were empty-handed.

'Roe!' I finally reached the bottom floor. The basement was a damp, water-stained place, with a low ceiling and a singular smell that decades of industrial cleaner use had never been able to eradicate – a combination of stale coffee, acrid ink, and cheap air freshener. The smell of Sunday school. Large pieces of furniture ate up useable space and crippled the flow of traffic. There was no room for anyone to do more than stand.

It was then that I heard my father's voice. *'Pamela!'*

I turned in a circle, trying to hear the direction it was coming from. It took me a few moments to realize that it was coming from the open vault, just a few yards off. My joy was so deep, at seeing him safely within, that I indulged in a little cry.

My father started pushing his way through the crowd towards me. I shook my head. 'Stay there! We'll come to you!' I called out. But before I could think about fighting through the mob, or going to find Michael, my cell phone rang – its familiar little, '*Princess Kitten, what adventures will you have today?*' jingle.

Yes, I still like *Princess Kitten*.

I fumbled through my belongings and found my phone – a pay-as-you-go model designed to look like a curled-up cat, made of molded pink plastic. I flicked it open. Missed call, unknown number. Missed call? I hadn't even had a chance to answer it. There were no bars down here; maybe it'd come in while I was on the stairs.

Ordinarily I would have brushed this off, but given the catastrophe at hand I wondered if someone was trying to get in contact with me because they were in trouble. Only a few friends and family members had my number. Maybe one of them was on someone else's phone.

I studied the plastic kitten in my hand again, my stomach in knots. It was a long shot. It was stupid. I wasn't a heroine. I was a baker's daughter.

My father still yelling for me, I turned and ran back up the stairs.

Sure enough, before I even reached the top my phone started to serenade me again. Bracing myself against the wall, the frightened horde still pressing by me, I answered it. 'Hello?'

'Hlll?' someone said. The signal was weak, the voice garbled. 'Akkt eeo mmmrrt?'

'What?' I shouted. 'I can't hear you! Who is this? Are you in danger?'

'Pakkmma?' the voice tried again.

Suddenly, I felt as if my entire body had dropped a foot or so and rubber-band rebounded into itself, my skin crackling. It was her. I could tell. How could I not recognize her voice?

Beyond the fuzz was Nora.

I screamed her name, only to hear the call drop with a click. Before I could cry or slap the wall or even try and redial, I felt a hand on my shoulder. I pointed to the phone before I knew who it was, blind with terror and ecstasy. 'It's her! It's her!'

'Who?' Michael was standing beside me, shielding me with his body.

'Nora!'

Michael regarded me steadily for a few moments, before saying, 'I really think you need to get into the vault, Miss Roe. I'd feel better if I knew you were safe. Give me the phone.' He extended his hand.

I almost did it. I looked into Michael's beautiful eyes and saw there someone willing to take up my burden for me. I could be with my family, I could help them weather through . . .

'No, no, no!' someone shrieked from below. Another familiar, distant voice.

Dad.

I ran back down the stairs, Michael falling in behind me. They were closing the vault door. I bullied my way through the crowd, kicking and crushing toes, trying to get into a position where I could see within. 'Dad!' I yelled. 'Nora needs me!' I held up the phone, hoping that he'd see it, and understand.

'Pamela, get *in* here!' he shouted back. I saw him, then, fighting to stay at the front of the people in the vault and beyond the reach of the grasping, many-armed, octopus-like crowd trying to get inside. Isambard was beside him, pale and wide-eyed.

'Miss Roe, *go!*' Michael argued.

'I love you!' I replied, shaking my head.

Dad realized that I wasn't coming, and his hands slowly fell to his sides. He watched me as I stepped backwards, away from him, his eyes stormy with emotion. I turned my back, then, because I didn't have the heart to watch the vault door shutting out the sight of him – especially because he'd called for me, waited for me.

He still loved me. He still wanted me with him. He still thought I was worth saving.

But out there, somewhere, Nora might need me. I might be her only hope.

Somebody smacked into me. As the roar around us grew deafening, people crying out for the door to stay open, begging to be squeezed in, I turned around and saw Isambard hanging onto my waistcoat. 'I'm coming with you!'

'You *idiot*! Why didn't you stay in there?!' I screamed.

He didn't answer, but fixed his frightened eyes on mine. I gripped his hand as painfully as I could manage, and pulled him with me through the crowd. Michael's jaw dropped when he saw Issy, and he reached out and grabbed his collar. 'You *moron*. Were you inside?'

'Yeah,' Isambard said. 'But you guys can't be the only brave ones.'

'Boy, I am going to feed you to the infected myself,' Michael growled. I think he almost made my brother cry. But for the first time in a long time, I actually admired my brother.

I turned and began fighting my way up the stairs again, phone held out in front of me. It kept singing the *Princess Kitten* song, but every time I tried to answer the call, the signal cut out.

'Head for the roof!' Michael shouted, when we reached the main hall of the church. I sprinted up the grand staircase, to-wards the second floor. The church was still packed, and on our way through we heard the death cry of the denied as they shut the other vault.

Fighting for air, my leg muscles burning, I climbed. The boys lost steam behind me and fell a ways behind, but I kept going. The calls were relentless, and I held the phone up in the air, as if I could physically catch one with it, like a falling snowflake. I chased the signal through the second-floor offices of the clergy, up onto the third floor, and out the topmost exit.

When I finally got out onto the roof of the cathedral, the phone rang again.

I hit the button and held it up to my ear. 'Hello?'

'Pamela?'

The sound of her voice stopped me cold. I clutched the phone to my ear with both hands, as if to drag her closer. 'Nora?' I whispered.

'Bloody hell,' I heard Michael say. He and Isambard had joined me, and were catching their breath near the edge of the roof. 'Miss Roe, come look at this.'

'Pamela, are you all right? Have you been bitten, or anything? Are you still alive? Pamma, please say something, oh, thank you, thank you . . .'

As Nora spoke, I slowly dragged myself closer to the side of the building. Michael and Issy were staring at the street. The part of the city we were in was built in a large circle, with a monument in the middle.

The dead were spilling in, a gray and roaring wave. All the way down George Street I could see them massed, a never-ending river of hungering corpses.

'I'm alive, Nora,' I said, my voice very tiny. 'But probably not for long.'

Chapter Twenty-eight

Bram

'Pam? Pam, what's wrong?'

Nora was scrubbing at her face with the heel of her hand, erasing the latest batch of tears. I wanted to help, but I knew that I was in the doghouse, big time. Or, I should be. I wasn't sure.

Renfield looked at me. 'Is Miss Pamela the friend?'

'Yeah.' I hooked my fingers into the useless little pockets on the front of my waistcoat.

'What?' Nora's eyes widened. She gestured for our attention. 'Renfield, is there a way to rig this so that we can all hear her?'

'Ah, yes, of course.' Ren seemed relieved to have been given a task, and he tapped away at his keyboard. 'Take off the headset.' He pulled the wire.

'Hello?' A girl's voice echoed through the speakers mounted on the sides of the computer. It was a little deeper than Nora's, more mature.

'Can you hear me?' Nora asked.

'Yes. Oh, Nora . . . I'm going to save all the gushing and "Ithoughtyoumightbedeads" for later, all right? Because . . .' There were other voices in the background, male voices.

'Tell us what's going on.' Nora set her lips together in concentration.

'All right.' The girl on the other end inhaled, and then let it out. 'I'm on top of the Cathedral of Our Mother with Michael Allister and my brother. My parents are in one of the vaults inside. They told us that the people who attacked the EF the night you disappeared released some kind of biological weapon or something, so it was quarantined, and they sent in troops, but . . . I think some of the troops are *down* there, in fact. The disease spread, and . . . and Lord Ayles has it too, he's like a *skeleton* . . .'

'What about the EF?' Nora asked, trying to get Pam back on track.

'They broke out. Everyone inside must have gotten sick, and they broke out. They're all in the streets down there. I mean, we are *watching* them come into the city. There're hundreds of them! How many people lived in the EF?'

'Three hundred families or so?' Nora looked to me, then, as if she couldn't believe what she was about to say next. 'So . . . with the troops . . . could be almost a thousand.'

'A thousand,' I echoed, just because it needed to be said a few times.

A thousand. Bloody hell.

'And I killed one, Nora.' Pam's voice was growing a bit shrill. 'I killed one! I stabbed it in the head with a parasol.'

Even Nora couldn't find words for this revelation. Renfield was the first to comment. 'I can't tell if that's the most inspiring thing I've ever heard, or the most horrifying.'

'Yeah, I'm with you,' I agreed. Chalk one up to ingenuity.

'Who are *you*? Nora, who are you with?'

Nora's eyes found mine again. She said, 'We'll be right back, Pam. Stay on the line.'

'*What?* Don't you dare!'

'Miss Roe? Again, give me the phone,' a male voice said. Whoever he was, he didn't sound happy.

Nora gestured to Ren, who got the idea and paused the call. 'OK, what do I tell her?'

I stood up and untwisted my fingers from my pockets. 'What do you mean? Tell her whatever you need to.'

Nora seemed uncertain. 'But . . . your secret . . .'

Wait, she was concerned about giving away our secret? My brain followed this demonstration of loyalty to the cause to its illogical conclusion.

'You don't hate me?' I blurted out. *Classy*.

Nora shook her head. 'No. Far from it. You did what you thought was right.' She stabbed a finger at my chest, reaching over Ren to do so. 'I'm going to beat you within an inch of your unlife, later, but I don't hate you.'

Dancing would have been inappropriate. I bore my weight onto the balls of my feet to keep them from moving, and snapped an arm out. 'Turn it back on, Ren.'

'Yes, sir,' he said, tone sarcastic, as he clicked the button.

'Hello? Hello?' Pam was asking.

'We're here,' I told her.

'OK. So, *you* . . . who are you with? How did you know about the biting? Are you watching this? Because the former PM, whatever the heck's happened to him, he got on and told us about the . . . zombies? Is that what he called them? He said they were *dead*!'

Nora leaned against the desk. 'Well, I'm with people who . . . fight the evil dead. They saved me.'

'*What?!*'

Nora looked at us. 'Here, want to talk? Say hi.'

The voice on the other end was slow in doing so, so I spoke up. 'Hi.'

Renfield followed suit. 'Good evening, Miss.'

'You . . . you fight these things? Where are you, then?'

'Who are you talking to?' the male voice asked again. He was growing angrier, I could hear it.

'We're south of you,' I said. I snuck a glance at Ren. Despite the seriousness of the situation, I could tell that both he and I were finding the same shard of humor in it. 'But right now we're going to concentrate on moving north and getting you out.'

'You are? Mr Allister, Issy . . . seriously, you are?'

Nora stood up taller. 'Yes. We are.' She reached out and laid a hand on one of the speakers, as if she could feel her friend's warmth through it. 'Oh, Pam, I'm so glad you're safe.

We're coming, OK? Just stay on the roof until we can get to you.'

'They're going to come get us! Yes! OK, yes, we'll be here. Oh, trust us, we're not going anywhere.'

'We'll be there as soon as we can. Keep your phone on.'

'All right! Oh, Nora, it was worth leaving my parents behind just to hear your voice.'

I motioned for Renfield to cut the call, keeping a careful eye on Nora. She gripped her hands into her skirt and settled her shoulders back. Having already failed her spectacularly two times, I was determined not to do it again.

'I'm sorry I didn't tell you.' I pulled my dress uniform jacket off. 'I'm going to make it up to you.'

'How?' Nora asked. I was relieved to hear no hint of defeat in her voice, only honest curiosity.

I tossed the jacket over my shoulder. 'By telling a whole hell of a lot of other people.'

Just then a clarion call seemed to well up from the very floor. Nora stood up straight, looking about instinctively for the source of it, before realizing that it was some sort of siren.

Renfield's head shot in my direction. 'Muster?'

I almost snarled.

'What is it?' Nora asked.

'They're telling the troops to get suited up and meet in the courtyard. Bet you five gold pieces they're sending us back to New London after all. If they'd done this to begin with we wouldn't be in this situation.'

'Wait. You said they keep you around to send you after the evil dead . . .'

'And Wolfe didn't send us to the EF again,' I completed for her, 'because he didn't think he could trust us. He didn't think he could trust me.'

'*Idiot*,' she breathed.

'Tell me about it.' Time to move. 'Go get suited up, Ren.'

'But I've never—'

'Just *do* it. If you see the others, tell them to do the same thing. The minute they release us to the vehicles, head for the *Black Alice*.'

The siren dogged my every move as I tore through the base in search of my friends. I found Coalhouse in the armory, and pulled him bodily away from his big boy toys to a corner, where I told him, 'After they dismiss us, don't enter the usual transport. There's a real old airship out there. Board it.'

'Why?'

'Because we have a special secret mission to complete cooked up by yours truly?' I tried. 'Because that'll be five fewer zombies on Wolfe's side? Anything I can do to nudge his odds in the direction of being taken down I consider to be done in the national interest at this point.'

He seemed to accept this, and made an index finger salute. 'Got it.'

I helped myself to a rifle on my way out. I couldn't find Chas, but I did grab Tom when he passed me in the hall. He leaned close and said, before I could get a word out, 'Airship.'

I nodded smartly, and continued to my room. I got suited up, as usual, and pulled my black mask down over my face. Before I joined the others outside, however, I took a side trip to the med bay.

The sirens had also woken up the living staff, and most of them were gathered there. Some were preparing to accompany the troops. Uniformed and masked, I was paid little mind. It didn't take me long to find Samedi, who, even at this hour, had a white lab coat thrown on over his blue striped pajamas.

I crooked my finger, indicating that he should follow me into one of the empty labs. He did so, recognizing who I was after looking into my eyes. He shut the door.

'What's happening, Bram?'

'There are hundreds of zombies loose in New London because Wolfe is a *tool*, that's what's happening.'

Samedi cursed colorfully, and sank down onto one of the rotating stools.

'The crew and I are going to take an . . . alternative route north. We'll get there before the others do. We've got someone waiting on a ride.'

Samedi lifted his brows. 'And Nora?'

'She's coming along.'

The doctor pushed at the skin on his forehead with two fingers. 'I don't suppose you've got a few minutes to listen to me spout off the many, many reasons why taking her is a bad idea.'

'No, not really. But . . .' OK, I couldn't help but gloat a little. 'She likes me.'

Samedi didn't even look at me. 'Well of *course*, you've had that bloody uniform on all day. *I* was half ready to tell you how much I liked you.'

'Never mind,' I sighed. 'Anyway, I need you to grab a com unit and stay in touch with us.'

Samedi glanced up at this, his eyes deep with confusion. 'Why?'

'Because we're sort of at zero hour, here, and we're taking Ren with us. We might need you for intel.'

Samedi stood up again and nodded. 'All right. Channel sixty-eight?'

'Sounds good.'

With that done, I headed for the courtyard and fell into one of the lines of black-clad undead already massed there. Wolfe was in his full regalia, barking over our heads. I let the sound roll into the background and cast my eyes about. I saw Tom's unmistakable shape, and then, next to him, a very skinny soldier – Ren. I couldn't see any of the others, and whispered a few choice swear words to myself.

'Your primary mission is to destroy all undead that you

visually identify. There's no time to sort out the good ones from the bad ones,' Wolfe said, as I searched. 'Intelligence reports that most are abandoning the Elysian Fields, so we're going to land on the eastern side of the city and mow our way west. The port provides a natural firebreak, but be sure to scour the water for any, as well. Don't want 'em washing back up after a few days. Do not enter private buildings; search and rescue will be performed by the living. And remember: I want each of you to function as an individual killing machine. Anyone has trouble, leave him. Now, fall out!'

The lines turned and began to file, one at a time, out of the gates. I knew that the large ground transport units would be waiting for the soldiers at the far end of the vehicle holding area; I'd been through this before. Once my line got outside the gates, I broke away and hotfooted it to the *Alice*.

Nora was already there. She was back in her practice gear, and she grabbed my hand when she saw it was me. I gripped hers tightly this time. 'Did you find the others? Ren and I found Chas.'

It made me feel better to hear that. 'I got the other two, then, yeah.'

Nora let go of my hand. She looked up at me for a second, as if contemplating saying something else, but then dropped her eyes. I wanted, more than anything, to take her in my arms and hold her. But I didn't dare. It was neither the time nor the place.

The others were with us in a few minutes. Renfield pulled off his mask and ruffled up his hair, complaining, 'Argh, it itches. How on earth do you people tolerate this thing?'

'Less complaining, more airborning,' I said as I pulled up the gangplank.

'That's not even a word,' he groused. 'Come on, everyone below deck.'

Nora looked around. 'But don't you ride on this deck?'

Ren dug his glasses out of his pocket and put them on. 'Not

when the airship is outfitted with an engine like the angry fist of Zeus.'

'Not yet,' Coalhouse said, glancing out across the field. 'Wait for their transport to take off. Then we can do it right.'

We all ducked down to wait. Within ten minutes or so, the other soldiers were loaded up and on their way. They'd meet up with the ships and head north again, same as before. The ships were no slouches. With luck, they'd be landing in New London in a little under two hours.

We'd be there in about an hour, though – if we survived the flight.

As soon as the transporters were out of sight, Ren hopped to his feet and said, 'In, in.' We followed him down into the hold. Ren hurried over to the engine and started tinkering with it – pressing this in, pulling that out. He danced about it, almost, as if he were the male of the species and it the female, and he was attempting to court it.

'All right,' he said, as he flicked a switch. 'Tom, you're shoveling coal. There should be a button to ignite the furnace.'

Tom looked around and found the boiler, and several open crates of coal waiting to be fed into it. He groaned. 'Why do *I* always have to do this crap?'

Ren ignored him. 'Coalhouse, you go release the balloon. It's self-filling, you just need to pull a lever. Think you can handle that?'

Coalhouse pointed to himself, and said, 'Ah, I *am* a Punk, remember?'

'And Bram, you steady the secondary wheel.' He pointed to the front of the hold. There was another steering wheel, there, standing beneath a shuttered window.

'What do I do?' Nora asked.

'Ditto,' said Chas.

Renfield pointed to another wooden crate. 'You two sit there, and try not to touch anything.'

Chas considered this, and informed him, 'You know, when

you say that, it just makes me want to touch things *more*.'

Nora took her by the arm. 'Come on. Normally I'd be with you, but not right now. Let's just get her up in the air.'

While I knew that Renfield had a point – the airship wasn't completely archaic, and wasn't meant to require a full crew, with a full crew's worth of jobs – I hated to think that Nora was at the point where she wasn't going to fight, anymore. I beckoned to her. 'Come help me hold the wheel. You, Chas, you try not to touch anything. OK, let's fly, here!'

Nora came over and took hold of two of the wheel's spokes, but asked me, 'Do you *really* need help, or are you just patronizing me?'

I opened the shutters. 'Oh, trust me, Nora . . . I *really* need help.'

She eyed me disdainfully for a moment, before smirking.

It was as close to a smile as I'd had from her in a while, and I was willing to take it.

CHAPTER TWENTY-NINE

Pamela

The plastic kitten lay curled up in my palm once more. I cradled it as if it were real, for it was now very precious to me.

The tide of undead hadn't slowed. I wondered if it was as bad as it looked. It didn't seem like many of them were making intelligent choices down there – they weren't trying doors, or even filtering off into the side avenues unless some sound or movement happened to catch their attention. Most were shuffling forward as space was made for them, like liquid following a groove. George Street might simply have become a giant funnel for them.

To the east, I could hear shouting. I swallowed, and tried not to think about the living people still in retreat. The zombies at the head of the column were moving faster than the ones behind, spurred on by the hunt.

I tried to think instead of Nora – who was *alive*.

'Miss Dearly's all right?' Michael asked me. There was an edge to his voice. 'She's alive?'

'Yes!'

'Thank goodness.' He looked as happy to hear it as I was, and the sharpness in his voice vanished. His attention soon returned to the street, though. 'What's happened to them?' he asked, uncomprehending.

'Didn't you see the news?'

'No. I heard the emergency warning on the wireless. It said that the city was under siege. The adults evacuated, then – we've had a carriage on standby for a few days, now, and my father sent servants ahead to the house near Morristown.' He paused, and then asked, 'Ah, what's this about the former Prime Minister?'

Issy was seated near the roof's edge, his chin resting on his knees. He gave me a hound dog look, moving nothing but his eyes. I sat down next to him. It took about ten minutes to get Michael up to speed, and I found myself surprised by that – it felt like I had a lot more story to tell. It felt like I was *wearing* more than ten minutes' worth of angst.

Michael remained standing, watching the dead. 'So, we're pretty much all doomed.'

'Don't say that,' I said fiercely. 'All we have to do is sit here.'

'Not just us. I mean . . . everyone. Humanity.'

I didn't know how to respond to this – mostly because I didn't want to acknowledge that it might be true. How many had already died? How many more were going to?

'Are you sure Miss Dearly will come? You should have let me talk to her, Miss Roe.'

I reached over and stroked Issy's hair. He scooted closer to me, while obviously trying to look as if he was just shifting to the side. 'Yes. She said she was going to come with people who could help. I—'

'Wait.'

I shut up and watched Michael watching. He moved a few feet along the roof, and then crouched down low. The electricity was still on, and the rooftop was a garden of shadows brought out by the old-fashioned filament bulbs arranged around the statue.

'There's someone in the shop over there,' Michael said.

I stood up and moved to join him. Isambard rolled onto his hands and knees, but remained where he was. Michael pointed. The building he was looking at was the Mink String Emporium, a narrow shop with a fanciful pistachio green facade, a storey shorter than the buildings around it. There were several dead people standing by the front entrance, fiddling with its handle and hinges, as if it was a very large and confounding puzzle box.

They knew something was inside.

'Do you have binoculars, or anything?' Michael asked.

'No, just a little food, and a bottle of water, and my bow and arrows. I gave the rest of the things to my father.' I cupped my hands around my eyes to block out some of the light, trying vainly to see further across the street. It looked like there was possibly some movement behind the windows, but I couldn't be sure.

Michael paced behind me, about a foot in each direction. 'What do we do?'

'It could be anything,' I pointed out. 'An animal? Maybe there's nothing in there at all, maybe one just started messing about and the others started copying him. Who knows how they think?'

Michael unbuttoned his jacket. 'But if there's someone there . . .'

'We have to help them, if we can,' I finished.

Michael ran his hands over his eyes. '*If* we can.'

'No, we don't,' Isambard said, like the brat he was.

I turned to him. 'Issy, nobody invited you along. You don't get a vote. Mostly because you're an idiot.'

'A total idiot,' he said. 'Look, right now, I am completely in agreement with you. I am an idiot of epic proportions. But I'm an idiot who wants to *live*, thank you. Besides, you told Nora we'd wait right here! What if she can't find us?'

'The idiot has a point,' Michael allowed.

I pressed my palm to my forehead. 'Issy, you suddenly decided that you wanted to be a hero, and now you are seriously telling me you wouldn't do everything you could to try and save someone's life?'

Isambard climbed to his feet. 'That's before you decided that we had to go rescue some John Doe trapped on the other side of a river of *walking dead*! Sometimes you are so frustrating!'

'Calm down,' Michael said. 'We don't know that there's anyone over there. Hell, there could be people in all of these buildings. We can't help all of them. We might not be able to help *any* of them.'

I bit my bottom lip. Maybe he was right.

'*HELP!*'

At the sudden cry, I rushed to the side of the roof again. Michael was at my side in a heartbeat. There was someone on the roof of the Mink Emporium – a girl. She was holding an electric lantern in either hand, waving them up and down. The streetlights were still on, and I squinted. 'Wait.' Realization thudded into me. 'Is that . . . Vespertine Mink?'

Michael leaned far off the roof. 'She's blonde . . . yes, I think it is.'

'See?' my brother said from the sidelines. 'You got all excited and gung-ho, when it's someone you hate. Now we can settle in and wait for Nora.'

I counted to ten. 'Issy, I don't hate anyone. Just because I dislike her doesn't mean we let her die.'

Michael looked confused. 'Wait, why do you dislike her?'

'Because she's a pompous priss with a mean streak. She and Nora have always snipped at one another.' I glared at Isambard. 'But she's still a human being.' And with that, I jumped onto the roof's stone railing.

Michael reached out and put his hands on my waist. 'Careful!'

I forced myself not to respond to his touch – instead I called out across the street, 'Vespertine Mink? Is that you?'

The girl on the roof opposite lowered her lanterns, and called back, 'Pamela Roe?'

'Yeah, let's both let that sink in for a minute, it's a doozy!' I yelled in return. 'Are they inside?'

'No!' she said instantly. Apparently, she was on board. She really had no choice. 'But they're going to get in! They're beating at the doors and windows!'

'Can you get to the roof next to you?'

'It's too high!' The buildings were very close together, no

more than a few feet apart in places, making a neat little shopping plaza around the church.

'What about on the street behind you? Are there dead there?'

'What do you mean, *dead*?!'

She hadn't heard, then. 'Ill! Are there *ill* there? Just look!'

Vespertine held up a hand, and went to look. She came back a few seconds later. 'A few, but not as many! But there's no way I'm leaving on my own!'

'There's no one else with you?'

'No, I'm alone!'

'OK,' I said, to my posse on the church. I leaned back against Michael's hands, and he helped me step down. 'What are we going to do?'

'We could tell her to hold on, and when Nora comes, pick her up too,' Michael offered.

'She might not have that much time.'

'We could get her and bring her back here.'

'Except we'd all have to climb back *up* some pretty big roof height differences. Going down is no big deal. And we don't exactly have climbing equipment with us. If we go over there . . .' I swept my eyes over all the buildings. 'We can't get back.'

Isambard pushed his cheeks back towards his jaw joints. 'This is such a bad idea, this is such a bad idea . . .'

'I would say we can go over there if we need to,' Michael said, ignoring him. 'But tell her to sit tight for now.'

'*GUYS!*' Vespertine shrieked.

I turned around. The zombie that'd been trying the door-knob was now halfway up one of the metal spouts that ran down the side of the building. Others were trying the same technique, with less success.

My heart started to race. 'My word. They heard she was up there, and up they started.' OK, it was as bad as it looked.

'They're not going to stop,' Michael said, watching the

scene. Once more, Isambard looked completely terrified. Twice in one night! This was going to be a diary entry for the ages.

'We're coming, Miss Mink!' I shouted. 'Go back inside!'

'We're going?' Michael asked.

I didn't respond until I saw Vespertine retreat down through a door set in the rooftop. 'Yes. We have to.'

'OK.'

I grabbed my brother's hand, pulling him with me to the eastern side of the cathedral. 'We need to cross the rooftops. Just try to roll when you have to make a big jump down.' Luckily, the building next to us was just a little lower than the church, to start with, and the biggest fall we'd have was the final one that would end with us on the roof of the Mink Emporium. 'Just like those old holo games, right? With the little man leaping about all the platforms?'

'I guess,' he said, voice a bit shaky.

'Are you all right with this?' I asked Michael.

He tightened his bag around his body, and nodded.

I turned Isambard around and made him look at me. 'I'm scared too, all right? But we have to do this. We'd want someone to do it for us.'

It took him a moment, but my brother nodded his head. Once.

'OK. Here we go.' And with that, I jumped. I ended up tumbling onto my side on the next building over, but it really wasn't all that bad. Michael joined me, landing cat-like on his feet. He helped me to catch Isambard, who jumped like his life depended on it, and like the cavern he was crossing was ten feet wide.

One down, ten to go.

By the time we got to the building next to the Emporium, I felt like one giant adrenaline-filled bruise – but we'd done it. That was the hardest jump, the equivalent of jumping off of a shed. I landed right on my rump, and I knew sitting was going to be painful for a month afterwards. But at least I hadn't landed on my back.

There were no zombies on the roof, at least not yet. Michael and Issy helped me up, and we hurried to the flat door set in the roof. The door led us into a crawlspace containing a set of hinged wooden stairs that we had to push out ahead of us until they finally cleared the ledge, and fell with a clatter into the room below.

I heard a shout from beneath, and knew we must have startled Vespertine. 'It's us!' I called out.

'Oh, thank goodness,' she said, appearing at the bottom of the retractable steps as we climbed down.

The upper floor of the Emporium was a workshop, home to long tables full of rough wooden shapes that would one day be carved and molded into instruments. Tools lined the walls, and a thin veil of sawdust covered the floor. 'How on earth did you get here?' I asked Vespertine, as Michael folded the stairs back up. 'Where's your family?'

Her eyes cut to my lower half. 'I've no idea. I might as well ask you where your *sanity* is. I have officially seen all of you that I ever wish to, now, Roe.'

Shame pricked at my cheeks again. 'Don't evade the question, Miss Mink.'

Vespertine stepped back and smoothed her gown down in front. It was finely made – everything about her was finely made. Her dress was of thick cobalt blue silk trimmed with subtle gold lace, and about her throat was a golden chain choker set with an enormous peacock-colored pearl. White pearl combs held her blonde hair back, and she wore several golden rings. She'd had bangs cut since the PM's public address. 'My mother and Miss Perez fled to the country a few days ago,' she said simply. 'I decided to remain here.'

I gaped at her. She was wearing thrice my father's yearly income, and she had not a brain in her head. 'Why?'

Her gray eyes narrowed. 'I don't really think it's any of your business.'

'Oh, I think it is,' I said, feeling myself growing uppity. 'Seeing as we're going to the trouble of saving you, when we were perfectly fine on the roof of the church. Nora's coming for us.'

That got her. 'Miss Dearly is alive? You've spoken to her?'

'That she is.'

Vespertine looked at Michael and Isambard, her lips pursing. 'All right. I'll buy that. Now, enlighten me. *What* is going on? Because that *thing* out there was crawling up the side of the building towards me . . .'

Michael gave her the five-sentence rundown. 'A fluid-borne disease made the dead come back to life. They like to attack the living. There are hundreds of them out there. The only way to kill them is to get them in the head with a weapon. There's a good chance we're all going to die.'

Vespertine was quiet for a moment, before saying, with her usual coolness, 'That will be engraved on a plaque someday, sir. I vote you Poet Laureate of the Undebuted Set.'

'It's a long story. We'll explain later.' I glanced around. 'I guess we're going out the back door. We should find another rooftop to wait on.'

'Where?' Michael asked.

Vespertine looked to the bow I had strapped between my shoulders, and asked, 'Can you still use that thing? You beat me at the last competition.'

'Absolutely, I can use it.'

'How many arrows do you have?'

'Five.'

Vespertine folded her arms. 'Sounds to me like we're heading for the sporting goods store, then. They should have guns there, too . . . hunting rifles.'

'Anything here we can use as a weapon?' I asked.

She nodded, and pointed at one of the walls. There, arranged by size, were strings – everything from synthetic catgut to piano wire. She walked over and took a pair of plastic handles from one of the shelves. She then removed a piece of piano wire from a hook, threading each end through one of the handles. She pushed a button on each handle, causing the piano wire to wind up within them. When she was done, she had a sort of wire jump rope. She tugged on the ends to test it.

'Garrote,' she said, when she caught me looking.

'I don't think you can strangle the dead.'

Vespertine lifted one perfectly groomed eyebrow, and said, 'Perhaps not. But, with a bit of effort, I might be able to cut their heads off.' She turned and grabbed two hammers off of the wall, tossing one to Michael and the other to my brother. 'Here.'

Isambard was staring at her, and almost caught the hammer with his face.

'Nice,' I admitted. 'Now, let's go.'

We headed downstairs. The ground floor of the Emporium was done in the Belle Époque style, with fifteen-foot ceilings, intricate tile floors, and vast pastoral murals on the walls. Pianos, violins, cellos, and other stringed instruments were displayed on rotating plinths. Gas fed the enormous crystal chandelier overhead, providing the room with warm, flickering light.

'For the record,' Vespertine said, voice distant, 'this building is my family. It is the only thing I'm loyal to. My adoptive father, Lord Mink, is the only person who has ever loved me, and he's made it abundantly clear that in his continued absence, I am the acting head of his business.'

I was honestly shocked by this. 'You're adopted? I never knew that.'

Vespertine continued on, as if I hadn't spoken. 'So, I have devoted myself to this store and to our family's legacy. My mother loves me no more than a statue could, and that hussy she flits about with can burn in hell.' She turned, and waved to the back door. 'But enough about me. This way, ladies and gentlemen.'

'Alrighty, then,' Isambard said, ducking down beneath one of the leaded glass windows.

We listened at the back door, but heard nothing. Michael slowly opened it, just a crack, to peek out. He shut it after about two seconds. 'I don't see anything. Which way are we headed?'

'Up that side street out there,' Vespertine told him. 'It's just a few blocks straight in that direction.'

'Yeah, it seems like they're only now starting to wander,' I said. 'They were pretty much staying in a crowd, before. They're attracted by signs of life.' I tapped Michael's shoulder. 'Maybe we should just stay here until they definitely breech the shop.'

'No,' Vespertine said sharply. 'First of all, who can say that the back streets will be empty, then? And secondly, the sooner we leave, the sooner those disgusting things will go elsewhere, and leave the shop in peace.'

'Miss Mink, your *shop* can burn in hell, for all I care.' Her feline eyes wanted to roast me, but I turned away. 'However, your first point is valid. Come on, out we go.'

'You first,' Vespertine said. Isambard stepped behind her.

Michael nodded, and said, 'On three, then. One, two . . . three!'

He opened the door, and we ran for it. It was dark, the streetlights fewer and further between off the main avenue. My body ached as I pounded after Michael, second in line. Vespertine and Isambard were content to bring up the rear.

For once in my life, I was somewhere near the top of the pecking order. So long as I could avoid being eaten, I was OK with this.

CHAPTER THIRTY

Wolfe

'Yes, Major. Yes . . .'

We'd only been on the water a few minutes. The dead-meats were still forming themselves up into their usual squadrons, and the techs were still setting up the med bay, crashing their crash carts into one another and tripping over wires.

But I could sense that something was wrong.

I marched along the first level, peering into the rooms I passed. In my ear, the voice of my commander hummed like an angry wasp from a steel-plated miniature com unit.

'Bloody hell.' Major Sweeney's voice trailed off. I could hear people talking behind him. He must be in a war room somewhere.

'What is it?' I inquired, as I opened another metal door and looked behind it.

'The dead are starting to stray away from the main drag,' he relayed. 'It's going to be messier than we thought.' He had a deep voice, and the sigh that followed sounded like a muted foghorn. 'Damn the Ayles. Damn them.'

'I always told you that their pro-zombie agenda would come back to bite them.'

'It ends tonight.'

Finally, people were smartening up.

Where the hell was Griswold?

'Any updates to our mission, Major?' I asked, as I paused and ran a hand through my hair. 'Our communications room should be up and running in a few moments.'

'No. I'll be in touch if there's anything to update. Major Sweeney, out.'

I pulled the chip out of my ear and caught a passing zom by the shoulder. 'Where's Griswold?'

The dead man shrugged. I cursed, and picked up the pace.

'Griswold?' I asked of every dead person I passed. 'Where's Griswold?'

None of them knew. It wasn't long before I realized that I hadn't seen any of his little friends, either. It took me a while to dredge their names from my memory. My mind was currently a tornado of information.

'Todd?'

'I'm looking for Private Gates. No?'

'Look, has *anyone* seen Sweet?'

Ben gave me a confused look. 'Sweet? I'm not familiar with him, Captain.'

'Her. You know, Sweet.' He shook his head at me. I slapped the side of the hallway with my hand and roared, 'Chastity Sweet! Girl! Dead! Sweet!'

Ben's expression jerked a bit. 'Her last name is *Sweet*? Chastity Sweet?' Behind him, one of the men on his squad snickered.

They weren't on the ship.

I left before I could decide to rip Ben's head off. I made my way to the communications room in a fog. At first, it was profound, temple-pounding anger that blinded me to my surroundings.

Then, it was fear.

What was Griswold doing? What did he know? Did he know *anything*? What had he told the girl?

When I got to the room, I found that a map of the Territories had been thrown up on the big screen. Our boat was a little red blip on the sea, headed for Nicaragua. The wave of undead in New London was indicated by green arrows. On either side of the screen, dead techs were busy setting up more equipment.

I sat down in the chair that'd been dragged out of storage

for me, and forced myself to breathe. It wasn't coming undone. Not yet. Griswold had probably made his squad sit this one out as some form of protest. I'd worry about them later.

I'd kill them later.

The chip in my hand buzzed to life again. 'Captain Wolfe?'

I slipped it back into my ear and looked at the screen. 'We're up in the com room, Major,' I muttered.

'This is for your ears only,' he said.

'Dead, out.'

The technicians saluted and departed. I waited until I was alone before informing Major Sweeney, 'Done.'

'Update,' he said. 'The Punk commanders we've been working with are no longer playing ball. They're going after the zombies on their side of the border with extreme prejudice. Fires are already going strong in Brunswick.'

I congratulated myself. 'Great.'

'There's more. In response, Parliament has given the military leave to wage war against the zombie plague as we deem fit and proper. Come oh-six hundred hours, we're to exterminate all infected, including red-light troops. You have until then to do as much mopping up as you can.'

I stood up, slowly. My entire torso felt numb. 'Care to repeat that, Major?'

'All undead are to be exterminated, by order of General Patmore.'

'And who is he getting this order from?'

The silence that followed this question told me that Sweeney knew exactly what I was asking. 'The Prime Minister has nothing to do with this. And he doesn't need to. It's become clear that he has a major conflict of interest, embodied in the continued existence of his father. This is about the common good, here.'

I picked the chip out of my ear, my hand shaking.

'Are you there? Captain, respond!'

They were finally doing it. After all these years. They were finally going to kill them all. Dearly wasn't here to plead their case any longer.

It *was* all coming undone.

I crushed the chip beneath the heel of my boot, and stumbled from the room. 'Ready an escape boat,' I croaked to one of the corpses waiting outside.

The zombie stood up and eyed me with surprise. She was a narrow woman with a hole where her nose should be and a sleek, neat bob. 'Sir?'

'You heard me. I need to return to Z Base. Get me a boat. Do it now, woman!'

My heart felt stretched tight and thin. I gripped one of the metal railings to steady myself.

I needed a bargaining chip.

I had to figure out where Dearly's brat was.

CHAPTER THIRTY-ONE

Nora

'Plan A?' Bram asked.

Behind us, Renfield was delivering orders, his voice grown newly bossy. It was a good thing Tom'd been assigned hard labor – the work kept him quiet. I could see him cutting his eyes at Renfield occasionally and waggling his head in a mocking fashion, his skin alive with pumpkin orange firelight.

I looked out of the window. We were rising quickly, the ground sinking away from us like a stone from the surface of a pond. A few moments before I'd heard the rush of compressed gas from the storage units, and the stretching of the air bag. The gas was fed into the bag through plastic piping embedded in the nanofiber ropes that attached it to the ship – at least, that's how it'd been explained to me. Bram seemed to be making a special effort to feed me terms and definitions. I suppose he felt he had a lot to make up for.

But I didn't hate him. I wasn't even angry at him, not anymore. The situation was too big to feel anger about – for really, even if he had told me, what could either of us have done?

'Plan A is to simply fly in over the church and pick them up,' I replied, coming back to myself.

'OK.' He then gave a general call for, 'Contingencies?'

'You and your contingencies.' Okay, maybe I was annoyed, still.

'It's just good sense, Nora.'

I sighed. 'I know. I'd just . . . I'd just like, once, for everything to go smoothly.'

'Chances of that happening?' Bram said, training his eyes on mine. 'Slim to none.'

I felt my head nodding so minutely, it might've been the motion of the ship. He was right. He was telling me like it was, too, and I appreciated that. 'We should call before we land, to make sure they're there. If they're not . . . well, I know the city fairly well. We should be able to direct them to a landmark, at least.'

'What if they can't get to it?' Bram challenged me.

I looked to the window again, as if I could see the city out there already. 'We can't get the ship close to the ground in the city, unless we aim for a park. We'd have to land in a park, or on a really big rooftop.'

'OK, so our potential points of entry are parks and roofs.' Bram turned his attention to Renfield. 'Rooftops are probably best. Less chance of contact.'

'I can work with that.'

And thus, it began. Bram quizzed us all. What would we do if the dead were *on* the rooftops? What about a huge crowd of them in the streets? What if one of the people we were headed for happened to be injured? I didn't see the point of it, and observed more than I participated, but the others shot answers right back at him. I'd grown used to viewing my new-found companions as rather jovial sorts, but this was apparently their way of shifting into a military mindset. Bram was excellent at it, calling them out on inconsistencies, challenging their ideas, but somehow managing to never belittle them.

Tom's ideas aside ('We can land the airship *on* them! Ten points for each!'), we settled on our plan: keep in contact with Pam, meet them at the church or a convenient high point somewhere close to the edge of the city, and take right off again.

'And Ren . . .' Bram turned to him again. 'What do we do if the military has men in the air? We're not exactly cleared to fly.'

Renfield grinned brightly, and pushed a lever down. 'We let them eat our dust.'

The only reason I remained near the window was because my fists were already curled around the steering wheel. Bram had let go in order to pace around and play Socratic Method with his team, and he and Chas were flung to the back of the hold. Tom caught himself on the side of the furnace, just in time. I couldn't hear anything at first over the roaring wind and screaming engine parts, but I swear Renfield was cackling.

'Holy hell!' I shrieked.

'Throttle it down!' Bram yelled from the back of the ship.

'Never!' Renfield called back. 'Time is of the essence, yes? We've got a nice tail wind, here!'

'Yes, but we need to be able to *steer*!' Chas shouted.

The steering wheel was vibrating in my hands, and my body shook in sympathy, my teeth knocking together. 'Needs to be slower, *needs to be slower*!'

'It's a straight shot northwest, how hard can it be?'

'Slow it down, Renfield!' Bram bellowed. He put that little extra something into his voice that gave me the chills.

Renfield raised the lever a touch and grumbled, 'Killjoys.'

We slowed down, just a bit – enough for the others to find their feet and grope their way along the belly of the ship. Bram was soon at my side again, and he took the wheel from me. When I let go, my body was still quivering.

'What the hell was that?!' Tom asked, fighting his way to his feet.

'That . . . was not normal,' Bram said, gripping the wheel like he was afraid to let go.

'I modified the engine, somewhat,' Renfield confessed. That grin started sneaking back onto his face.

'Modifications?' Bram asked. He slowly released his death grip on the steering wheel, and turned around to look at Ren. 'What modifications?'

'Modifi*ca*tion.' Ren really stressed the 'shun' at the end of the word. 'I just removed the governor. I told you some parts needed to come out. You were there when I did it!'

'The what?' I asked.

Bram stared at Renfield, his expression going completely slack. 'You did what? I didn't see you . . . you did what?'

'What's a governor?'

'You didn't,' Tom said, voice filled with awe. 'You are not telling me that you left a piece of the engine behind on the ground.'

Renfield sighed, and turned to address me, waving a hand casually. 'The governor, on an airship engine, caps the maximum pressure the engine can achieve. If too much pressure is created, the governor vents it off. It's that pressure that makes us go. So, by taking the governor off, I've allowed us to go much faster.'

'And then we'll blow up!' Bram yelled. 'Because you took the safety valve off!'

'You've turned the ship into a freaking death trap!' Tom shouted.

'It isn't *critical*. We just have to be mindful of the engine pressure ourselves, that's all! Trust me, she can take it!'

'Please, please don't blow us up,' I pleaded as I sank onto a crate near the steering wheel.

'I will not blow you up!' Renfield sighed. He turned his back on me, adjusting a few of the pressure gauges so as to be better able to watch them. 'Just trust me.'

Chas went to see if Tom was all right. I looked up at Bram. 'Is this bad?'

He nodded slowly. His hair was a wreck. He looked at me, his eyes widening suddenly. 'Ah, Nora . . .'

'What?'

He coughed, and gestured at me. I gave him a blank look. He pointed more emphatically to my skirt, and I glanced down. It was up about my waist, the petticoats having caught it. Beneath I had white bloomers on, which were now on display for the world to see. I forced my skirt down and blushed. Bram laughed, though there was no cruelty in the sound – that had disappeared.

'You're laughing,' I pointed out.

Bram searched for the right words before replying. 'It's bad,' he said. 'But not that bad. We just have to watch the engine, like he said, and . . . beat him, once we land. Beat him into a spectacularly bloody pulp. Get really inventive.'

'I heard that,' Ren muttered.

'What's with that whole question and answer thing?' I asked, in order to distract both of us from the fact that we might die in mid-air. And from the fact that I'd just flashed him. 'You were so serious, so . . . professional.'

He shrugged and smoothed back his hair, keeping one hand on the steering wheel. 'Kind of pumps you up, gets you thinking. No room to be stupid, out there.'

'You're good at it.'

He chuckled. 'I figure it's the same thing any poor Punk's raised to do. The "OK, But" game. "What happens if the crops don't come in? OK, but what if we can't get a loan? Okay, but what if Uncle Bert won't give us work or take us in?"'

'Was your life really so hard, down there?'

'Sometimes, yeah,' Bram said, as he opened up a panel next to the window. Within sat a variety of navigational equipment, none of it digital. There were little brass globes with moving parts that spun on bolted-down axes, astrolabes, compasses. It was the compass he checked.

My fingertips were cold, as I pressed them together in my lap. Talking to Bram seemed to make me feel better, no matter the situation. But now I had Pam to worry about, and I was starting to feel guilty for being otherwise preoccupied.

I focused on her. I willed her to be safe, waiting there right where she said she'd be. I wondered what she was seeing, what she was feeling, how she was handling it.

I wondered, on a side note, how in blazes she'd ended up in a church with Michael Allister.

Renfield was prattling on about the ship's specs to anyone who'd listen. Chas'd taken a break from helping Tom, and her eyes were practically glazed over.

'Ren, you're acting like a fanboy,' Coalhouse said.

'Hush,' Renfield said, stroking the side of the engine. 'Do *you* have three-foot intakes? I think not.'

'No, you are, Ren,' Bram said, looking up from the cabinet. He was aligning the compass's readings with points on one of the little globes inside. Must be some sort of positioning device. 'I thought northerners were all about the horses.'

Renfield pushed his rolled-up jacket sleeves back again. They kept slipping down his scrawny arms. 'Horses don't fly. I mean, that's obvious, but . . . they're not as *romantic*, let's say. When I was a boy, I wanted to be an airship captain, you know.' The others groaned. 'It's true! I wanted the tricorn hat, the whole nine yards.'

'What does your family do?'

He smiled slightly. 'They work for the mayor of our city, Gladsbury. My mother works in the teleautomata registration department, and my father works in the parks department. He's an expert on insects. Now insects, I like. They're very interesting.'

''Cause they fly?' Coalhouse snarked.

Renfield sniffed. A moment later he adjusted his flak vest, and asked, in a small and hopeful voice, 'I take it that the situation is far too serious to warrant singing a pirate shanty.'

'Oh my God,' Chas mouthed, looking at me. 'Shoot me.'

Bram was still trying to master the positioning globe. His brow was wrinkled, and he appeared to be having trouble with it. 'You would be correct.'

Renfield held up his hands in a posture of surrender, although he looked a bit pouty. 'Just making sure.'

Bram couldn't get the globe to work. 'Tiny . . . little . . . freaking . . . parts! If a real pirate tried to use this thing, he'd starve to death!'

So I kept watch at the mullioned window. Within half an hour, I could recognize certain sites from our maps in geography class; within forty-five minutes, I could tell definitely where we were. 'A bit further north of here,' I said, bouncing on my toes a little in my excitement. 'We're almost there!'

Bram tossed down the little gold stylus that he'd been attempting to adjust the globe's sections with, and took out his communications device for me. 'Call. I'm gonna go toss this thing off the side of the ship.'

'You do and you go after it,' Renfield snapped.

I punched Pam's number into the device and held it up to my ear, plugging my other ear with my finger. Like before, it dialed and dialed, and eventually hung up on me. My stomach dropped. I dialed again. The same thing happened.

'Oh, not again,' I groaned, dialing a third time.

Bram stepped closer, peering at the screen with me. 'She's not picking up?'

'No! She should, if she's sitting right there.'

Third call was a no-go. Through the window, I could see the city just floating into view beneath us. 'We're there. The cathedral is on the western side, on the same main street that runs from the EF.'

'Lovely,' said Tom. 'Let me guess – zombie central.'

'Let's get closer and look,' Bram said.

While they concentrated on that, I kept calling. After the tenth or eleventh try I gave up, my teeth on edge.

'Is it that big one, there?' Bram asked. I looked. Ren had lowered our position, and the rooftops were now individually visible.

'I think so,' I said, pointing to a wide, white one. 'But it doesn't look like there's anyone there.'

'Can you get her any lower?' Bram asked Renfield, who went to work on the controls. 'Here, we're slow enough now – you can go up on the top deck if you want, Nora.'

I raced up the little staircase, using my arms as well as my legs. I ran to the prow of the ship and hung over the railing where the black wooden Alice was mounted.

'Do you see anyone?' Bram shouted up.

'No!' I had to reply.

Where the hell had she gone?

CHAPTER THIRTY-TWO

Pamela

Every shadow embodied the possibility of being torn in half.

Funny thing was, I was starting to get used to it. Just another day in the neighborhood.

Being the person in our group with the most hands-on zombie experience – only one zombie, but still – I was impressed by how Michael seemed willing to be the one to lead us through the streets. All right, so he wasn't terribly witty, but he was certainly a gentleman. Nora could keep her opinion to herself.

The only one whimpering was Isambard. He flinched away from every shift in the light, jumped at every noise. Vespertine, who'd just learned what we were up against not ten minutes ago, was more composed than he was. It must have gotten to her, for at one point she turned around and took him by the back of his shirt, much as Michael had done in the church, and whispered to me, 'This is yours?'

'My brother, Isambard,' I told her.

She waggled him by his collar. 'Make it shut up. It's going to get us killed.'

Isambard struggled. 'Hey!'

'Issy.' I gave him the hairy eyeball. 'Hush. Miss Mink, please let him go.'

Vespertine nodded graciously, and released him. He scurried over to walk near me.

'We're coming upon an intersection,' Michael said.

I slowly pulled my bow out and threaded an arrow onto it, though I didn't pull it taut. 'Let me go ahead.'

Michael glanced back, and nodded when he saw what I was doing. He flattened himself against the wall on our left-hand side, and I took his place at the front of the line.

I stopped when we got to the corner, and took a look around. Nothing. I could see the sports store directly across the street from us.

'We need to run across the street. On three again, OK, guys?' I asked.

'OK,' Michael said.

'One, two . . .'

Michael gripped my shoulder, and I almost dropped my bow. 'Wait!'

I took a few steps back, and felt Michael's breath on my ear as he whispered, 'One o' clock.'

I looked. There, in the shadows across the street, was a zombie shuffling past a pile of tin garbage cans. It was a young man in a highwayman's coat, his hair held in a ponytail by a soiled ribbon.

'What do we do?' I asked softly.

'Go back,' Michael said, his hand tightening on my shoulder. 'Come on.'

I felt him tugging gently at me, but I stayed rooted to the spot, watching the zombie. I didn't dare call out to it – that idea had flitted to mind, momentarily, but I'd dismissed it. Even if this was a 'civilized' zombie, caution said to treat it as if it weren't. But we needed to get to the store. It was a two-storey building, even – we could wait on the rooftop. What could be safer than a sports store? It was the pot of weapons at the end of the rainbow.

I wasn't about to let one zombie stand in the way.

I pulled my bow tight, and sighted down the arrow.

'Miss Roe, what are you doing?' Michael asked.

'We need to get to the shop,' I told him, as I took aim.

'Are you mad?'

His incredulous voice was just loud enough to attract the zombie's attention. It looked at us, and proved it wasn't tame by rushing at me, coat cuffs flapping, voice rising in the howl of the hunt.

'Thanks a lot, Mr Allister,' I said, teeth gritted, as I let off the shot.

I got the zombie through its open mouth, a feat that I would probably never be able to recreate, no matter how hard I tried. It went down right where I capped it. There was no blood, no gore. It twitched a few times, and was still.

Two for two. I am the zombie hunting queen! Engrave that *on a plaque.*

I fell back into our little group, my heart pounding. Michael whirled me around and shook me. 'You little fool! You could have been hurt! We could have found another way to get there!'

I shouldered him off, even as my heart celebrated the fact that he cared. 'It's taken care of now! Come on!'

Vespertine shoved my cowering brother forward. 'She's right. Let's go.'

We took a few steps clear of the corner.

That's when we saw that the undead highwayman hadn't been alone.

There were five or six of them, a street off, visible through the alleyway on the side of the shop. They immediately caught sight of us and started bobbing and ducking, like wolves scenting the air. They raised a communal screech of their own, and I wondered if they were attracting more zombies, alerting their brothers and sisters to the presence of prey.

Seeing as I *was* that prey, I wasn't really all that eager to find out.

'Come on!' Michael yelled. He didn't need to. I was right with him.

We raced further away from George Street, into the city's warren of side avenues and alleyways. I could hear the zombies running behind us, their hellish cries. I tried to think of where we were in relation to the big landmarks, where our next hiding place could be, my brain a tangle of images and sensations – the latter mostly fear. Fear that burned like acid, fear that made my muscles feel like lead.

We thundered out onto another arterial road, Wesker Street. There, I caught sight of the holographic columns of The New Victorian Museum of Natural History.

It was only a few blocks away from us. It was big. It was stone.

It would work.

'This way!' I shouted.

I could hear the others pounding the asphalt with me, but I felt the need to look back. I almost didn't dare, fearing that any break in my stride would result in teeth in my flesh, but I had to. Turning my head just a bit, I saw that Michael was a few steps behind me. Vespertine had picked up her gown and bunched it about her waist, revealing her embroidered heeled slippers. They weren't the best shoes for running in, but even she was far ahead of Isambard. He wasn't doing well. He'd never been terribly athletic.

I groaned, and stopped where I was, my feet skidding a bit.

'What are you doing?!' Michael asked, as he came upon me.

'Keep going! The museum! See if you can find a way inside!' I launched myself back the way I'd come, towards the howling pack of zombies. They'd made it out onto Wesker Street and were maybe five yards behind my little brother, and closing in fast.

'Pam!' Isambard wailed. He was flagging.

'Come on!' I yelled, catching his arm and pulling him forward. 'Come on, you can do it!'

'I can't!'

'You have to, or they're going to *eat you!*' I screamed. That should give anyone incentive.

I ran like I've never run before, dragging Isambard along. He managed to pick up some steam under my urging, but there still lay only a few yards between us and certain death.

We made it to the museum steps with the zombies still hot on our trail. '*Climb!*' I bellowed at him, pushing him up the stone stairs. He did, on hands and knees, as fast as he could.

The hammer Vespertine'd equipped him with slipped out of his pocket, but he didn't stop to pick it up. I fought my way up alongside him, and surpassed him near the summit.

At the top I could see Vespertine and Michael. Michael was trying to beat his way through one of the smaller access doors set into the huge show doors of the museum's facade.

'They're almost here!' Vespertine cried, still clutching her skirts.

'Just give me . . . a minute . . .' Michael huffed, as he took several steps back. He hurled himself at the door again, and it burst inward. Michael ran out and grabbed Vespertine by the shoulder, pushing her inside. He then turned to help me. My entire body felt like it was on fire; I barely felt his hands on me.

Just as I was clearing the threshold, I heard my brother screaming. I tried to turn around and fight my way back, but Michael shoved me within.

'Issy!' I yelled.

'Stay here and figure out how to barricade the door!' he shouted, pulling his hammer out of his belt loop. He turned and left me, rushing back out to the marble steps.

No.

I took a step to follow.

Vespertine pushed the door shut with a massive bang, almost hitting me with it. 'Come on, listen to him! No one will be safe unless we figure out how to keep them out!'

I couldn't move. What had happened? I could hear my brother and Michael, their voices muffled behind the door, so far away . . .

'*Move*, Roe!'

I didn't respond. I had no idea what was going on. Were the boys all right? What if they weren't?

Vespertine struck the loosened lock with her hand in frustration. 'Blast him, he broke it!'

For some reason, this statement jolted me back to reality.

I looked around. The foyer of the museum was vast, its sandstone walls engraved with important moments from New Victorian history. There were images of the First Families on the wall above the doors, people clad in denim trousers and T-shirts crossing the Rio Grande. The long wall opposite the entrance was decorated with a mural of the Genesis Flood, with more carvings arranged about it in octagonal panels – the founding of the Byron Institute, the Reed Massacre, scenes of Nicaro life. There were several artifacts on display, vases and suits of armor and large marble statues rescued from cities in the Wastelands, the museum's finest treasures. In the middle of the hall, a stone fountain babbled.

'Those,' I got out, pointing at one of the statues. Vespertine turned, her back to the door. 'We need to try and move them.'

'There's no way we can move anything that big,' she argued.

'Do you have a better idea?'

Before Vespertine could reply, she was bumped forward by the door. Her scream reverberated in the hall.

'It's Michael!' I cried, watching as he and Issy pushed the door open and stumbled inward. The writhing arms of the un-dead followed them. Michael turned and forced the door back at them, and Vespertine quickly moved to help. Still, they couldn't close it entirely. The dead were clogging the gap.

'Don't stop pushing!' Michael grunted. 'Shoot them, Miss Roe!'

I only had four arrows left, and shooting them in the arms wasn't going to do any good. Thinking fast, I ran to one of the suits of armor – one that happened to be holding a smallish double-headed battleaxe. I slid it out of its bearer's metal fist. 'Everyone get out of the way!'

Michael's eyes widened when he saw what I meant to do. He echoed my cry. 'Everyone over here, behind the door! Get your weight on it!' Isambard slowly joined the others in their efforts.

And with that, I ran to the door and started swinging.

The sound the axe made as it bit into the limbs of the zombies was sickening, wet, and savage. It wasn't a neat chopping sound like you might hear at the butcher's – it was violent and mean. The zombies screamed in rage. I closed my eyes, clamped my mouth shut, didn't even *breathe* as I wailed away on them. I didn't stop until I heard the door shut, and felt the axe land on wood.

'Go get that table! Everyone move!' Michael shouted.

I slowly opened my eyes, and looked down. My clothes were covered in blackened blood, and there was a pile of slimy severed flesh on the floor in front of me.

Oh, God.

I dropped the axe and rushed over to the fountain, splashing myself, scrubbing at my skin. Everything around me ceased to exist. I heard nothing, I saw nothing. It was like the world was contained within a boiling tea kettle – kettles go quiet just before they start to whistle loudest. Wasn't this how Lord Ayles had gotten sick? When Dearly's blood had gotten on him? Is that what he'd said on the screen? I couldn't remember. Oh, God, what had I done? Why wouldn't it come off?

I didn't even notice that I'd ducked my head completely underwater until Michael pulled it out by my bun. I gasped for breath.

'Miss Roe? Miss Roe?'

'I'm all right,' I coughed out.

Michael's hands slid over my face. I opened my eyes to look at him. 'Are you sure?' he asked. He looked terrified.

I could feel the frigid water dripping down my neck. 'I had to get the blood off.'

He nodded, and I could see that he was worrying about the same thing I was. I reached out to him, my hands going to his chest, his arms. 'Are *you* all right? Were you bitten?'

Michael shook his head, and said, 'I'm . . . fine.'

The way he said it, I knew Issy wasn't.

I turned. Isambard was helping Vespertine to pile things in front of the door. Neither one of them was very strong, and they had to roll and scoot the items along the floor rather than lift them, even as a team.

Isambard's shirt had a bloom of blood on the left sleeve.

I ran over to him. Vespertine stopped moving, brushing her bangs out of her face.

'Issy!'

He looked at me, his eyes somehow lifeless. 'One bit me, Pam.'

I captured him in my arms, and he didn't fight it. He started to cry. I stroked his hair and whispered, 'It's all right.' I knew it wasn't, but it was all I had to give him. 'It's all right. Nora will come soon . . . we'll try to call her, OK? We'll get up on the roof. We're not far from the church. Nora will know what to do, she'll find us.'

'It hurts, it hurts,' he sobbed.

'How do you know she's coming?' Vespertine asked, dropping her hands. Her voice had taken on a dull tone.

'She told me she would come,' I said, not willing to let go of my little brother. I could hear the zombies – the things that'd tried to *eat him* – beating on the door.

'But how do you *know*?' Vespertine prodded. 'I mean, it's not as if Miss Dearly has her own personal air force. Or is she coming by ground? Did she tell you anything? How do you know?'

I almost crushed Issy, my arms contracting as I screamed over his head, 'Because she told me she would! Maybe *you* don't have anyone you can count on, maybe you don't have anyone you love, but I do! Nora said she was coming, and she'll come if she arrives here to die, I know she will!'

'Ladies, calm down!' Michael said. I took a breath, and concentrated on comforting my brother. 'We can't stay here. They're still trying to get in. We need to make our way to the roof. And we can probably arm ourselves while we're here, as well.'

Vespertine gave him her attention. 'Would any antique weapons on display still be functional? The guns, I mean?'

Michael shrugged. 'It's worth a look, right?'

Vespertine glanced down the hall. 'Right, then. I know they keep maps at the visitors' desk.' She started in that direction, without another word.

Isambard had gotten his tears under control, but I held onto him regardless. I looked up at Michael. 'Thank you for going out to get him. Thank you for everything.'

Michael reached into his jacket, pulling out another hand-kerchief. 'This one is for your brother,' he said as he offered it. I took it, in understanding.

'Here, Issy, show me your arm. Let me wrap it up.'

'I found it,' Vespertine called out. '"Weaponry Through the Ages," third floor.'

I took the battleaxe with me, though not for defense. Rather, I used it to smash open museum cases along the way. In case of emergency, break glass. Each time I did so an alarm would ring for about a minute or so and then stop, possibly switching into silent mode. I wondered if anyone was even monitoring the alarms. I decided not to bet on it.

On the second floor we passed a gallery of costumes, and I broke in to help myself to clean clothes – nothing fancy, simply bits and pieces from the historic military garb on display there. Striped trousers, another man's shirt, a leather waistcoat. I grabbed another shirt for Issy too.

I changed in the public restroom and scrubbed myself again, this time with the rose-scented soap from the dispensers. I hadn't tasted any blood, and I hadn't breathed any in. I checked my skin for cuts, but found none. Hopefully I'd be

OK. I didn't feel ill. Isambard looked sickly and sweaty, but that was to be expected given what he'd just gone through, so I ignored it.

We eventually made it to the third floor. At the head of the stairs, there, was mounted the five-hundred-year-old Corpus Clock, or Chronophage. It was one of the few things the people known as the Britons had managed to get off their island before it disappeared forever. The seconds scrolled rapidly past on it, measured in blips of blue light. A giant grasshopper on the top of it opened its jaw widely as each second progressed, and then swallowed it down.

Eating time. Fitting.

'This is what I'm talking about,' Vespertine said, as we entered the weaponry hall and started our search. She pointed at a case. Within sat a weapon with a barrel a little wider than a large gun's, fitted with leather straps to attach it to one's arm. It was displayed, conveniently enough, right next to a wooden box full of gunpowder and the round lead balls it was meant to fire.

'"Personal Arm-Mounted Cannon",' she recited from the card. '"Proto-rift offensive weaponry with a decidedly Punk flair. Good example of the fading influence of Victorian aesthetics on Punk style in the Later Period, as demonstrated by the minimal engraving on the barrel," blah blah blah, give me the axe.'

I handed it over, and she hurled it through the glass. Michael borrowed it next, having found some blunderbusses and ammunition in the case next door.

'Pam,' Isambard said. He pointed to another case. Within sat a contraption of tooled brass and gold. It was openwork, pieces of coggy clockwork exposed – Punk, definitely.

'It's an automatic crossbow,' he said, reading the card. 'Fires up to five bolts at once.'

I didn't need to hear anything more. I pulled him back and picked up the axe from the floor where Michael'd left it. I broke the glass, helping myself to it and its quiver full of arrows.

'I'm going to test this,' Michael said, aiming for the staircase. We all got behind him, and I couldn't help but admire the figure he cut just then – his shirt loosened invitingly at the collar, his jacket casually open, his sandy hair in disarray as he pointed his weapon bravely at an invisible foe.

Unfortunately, the gun didn't work.

'Blast!' He looked at it, brow furrowed. 'Go ahead, Miss Mink. I'm going to try some of the others in the case.'

'Sure,' Vespertine said, as he retreated. Isambard helped her to strap the cannon on her arm, and she messed with it for a moment, figuring out that she'd have to feed one ball in at a time from behind. She got it all set up – but it didn't fire. She clicked the thumb trigger again and again in irritation.

Michael wasn't having any luck, either. He tossed another useless blunderbuss back into the case. 'What, do they make a habit of *ruining* perfectly good guns before they go on display? Why would they do that?'

'Maybe it's a safety concern.' I loaded one of my old arrows into the crossbow, after figuring out how to open it. I aimed for the stairwell. It went off without a hitch, the arrow disappearing into the darkness. 'This works. Here, Miss Mink. I've got my other bow. Take this one.'

As I passed the crossbow over to her, Isambard said, 'I hear something.'

I turned to look at him, and saw that his attention was fixed upon the stairwell. I listened. At first I couldn't hear or see anything unusual, but then I noticed that the dim light spilling up from the second floor was wavering slightly, as if something was passing through it.

'They got in,' I whispered. Issy made a little sound of fear.

'Quiet,' Michael said, lowering his voice. 'We have to go.'

Vespertine glanced at the ceiling. 'Take a right. The map downstairs said the building is symmetrical. We can get to the staircase on the other side, and head up from there.'

We moved cautiously towards the opposite end of the hall, bunching together.

Of course the sweet strains of the Princess Kitten theme song had to regale us, then.

The others cringed; Vespertine aimed her crossbow at me, but thankfully didn't shoot. I'd tucked my phone into my canvas gauntlet, and I couldn't fish it out in time to catch the call. 'Come on, come on, come on!' I squealed. The ringtone seemed to go on forever, only to stop as soon as my anxious fingers touched the phone.

Beside me, Isambard gasped. 'Pam! They're coming!'

I looked up. The shadows of our dead stalkers were playing over the wall in front of us.

'Go!' Vespertine yelled.

Once more, we ran. The phone kept going off, but I couldn't get to it. I knew it had to be Nora. Once we got to the other stairwell, I paused for a few moments to dig it out.

'Miss Roe, come on!' Michael said.

'One second!' I opened the phone and looked at the screen. I re-dialed the origin number, and then started clambering up after him.

It picked up on the first ring. 'Pam?'

I clung onto the banister. 'Nora! We had to leave the church!'

'I can *see* that! We're right above it! Where the hell are you?!'

CHAPTER THIRTY-THREE

Victor

I expected to be killed at any moment. The fact that Henry and I made it a few long, groddy days longer seemed to me infinitely miraculous.

Then again, it was the season for miracles, was it not?

We were kept in the longhouse. We were given water only on the second day. I managed to administer our injections without attracting any attention – a full syringe for both of us. *Merry Christmas, medication for all!*

But we had no time to talk, no time to formulate a plan. We had only ceaseless, empty hours, which Averne filled with ranting and violent threats. It grew tedious. It also gave me hope. My guesswork and teasing had obviously filled him with real paranoia. He could be manipulated. This was promising.

I kept a close eye on Averne. He took his meat cooked, every time, eating with his back to us. He drank from bottles he removed from a nearby crate – alcohol, I could smell it. Without a working circulatory system, unless he had a pump inside his body capable of washing that alcohol up to his brain, he certainly couldn't enjoy the effects of it. I suppose he could have been using it as a poor man's preservative.

But I was more willing to bet on the fact that he was alive.

It seemed that Averne swung daily between fits of manic activity and periods during which one could be forgiven for thinking that he was truly deceased. With his scarf in the way, sitting in the shadows, I couldn't tell these quiet moments from sleep. That's probably why he wore it. He probably wanted to throw his undead troops off. It certainly threw me off.

We didn't dare attack him. I might be a zombie, but I was

also an old man with one leg. Henry was freshly dead and had already lost an arm. Averne could probably take us, unless we used the explosives – and we both knew where that brilliant idea had gotten us before.

When Averne was not threatening us, he devoted himself to his maps. I could hear him muttering to himself as he poured over them, his fingers pushing out the crumpled edges of the paper. It sounded like he was making grossly over-zealous plans, or deciding just how he would place his troops during the mass vaccinations he assumed would come. Occasionally he would work some zombification multiplication on scratch paper in order to figure out how long it would take to convert a village, a town, a city. I wasn't sure if he was computing this in order to make plans to contain an outbreak, or to create one.

The evening of Christmas Eve, he decided to speak to me again.

'Is your daughter infected?' he asked, out of the blue. He was lit from behind by oil lamps, his silhouette hidden by the back of his chair.

'Not that I know of,' I said, honestly.

He laughed harshly. 'All the better.' Averne took a deep glug from his bottle. 'Mine was. And my son. And my wife.'

'I'm sorry.'

'No, you're not.' He set the bottle down. 'You meant for this to happen. But you have to understand, it doesn't feel like honest warfare – the thing you've made feels like a personal *curse*. When I took my men and left the front lines, and got home, to find that I had to kill my family, it felt as if you had personally reached out and turned my life into a living hell.'

I didn't know what to say to this. 'I don't think that's a very rational way of looking at things, Major.'

'I gave up being rational long ago.' He slid his hands within his cloak. 'Now, my only wish is to get out alive. You've seen what's happened to my men.'

'You did that to your men.'

Averne coughed. 'It happened so fast. Yes, in the beginning, we acted like foolhardy schoolboys . . . myself, especially.
It was a way of confronting the thing, of poking a stick at it
like one might at some strange ooze in the jungle, of becoming unafraid. But I never meant for all of this to happen. For all
of my men to die . . . and here I am, not dead, vulnerable and
yet, not . . .' He tugged on his scarf. 'Who was it that said, "Give
a man a mask, and he will tell you the truth?" Do you feel you
wear a mask, now, Doctor? Do you accept your new face? Your
death mask?'

I exchanged glances with Henry. 'I accept it,' I said. 'And I
have told you the truth.'

'No, you haven't.' Averne picked up his bottle again. 'But
that doesn't matter. When I have the vaccine, I'll have the
proof I need. Just like Wolfe said. I can return to my people
with honor. Perhaps the anti-Victorian spirit will be rekindled.'
He shrugged. 'At the very least, I get to kill you and your
daughter. I think I'll kill her, first. Then you'll get to watch your
child die, just like I did.'

I did my best not to think of my daughter and my friends
back on base. I knew if I let my mind wander too far in that
direction, despair would kill any resolve I had remaining.

Averne went on drinking.

On Christmas morning, Henry took a chance. And in the end
it was his simple, straightforward action that made the
difference.

We were awoken in the wee hours of the morning by a
massive crash. I opened my eyes to see that Averne had sent his
desk toppling, scattering his maps and blueprints on the salt. I
reached out and touched Henry to wake him, sensing that we'd
best prepare ourselves for more than the usual madness.

Averne advanced over to his radio equipment. As I realized that he was going to use it, I swear I saw a nimbus of light glowing around him. This was it. Out of the corner of my eye I saw Henry curling his legs to the side, preparing to sit up.

Averne reached into his scarf and pulled out a narrow, folded piece of paper. He nearly tore it in his urgency to get it open. Once he had it unfolded, he pulled an oil lamp over to read it by, and began adjusting controls on the ancient radio set in front of him.

'Wolfe,' Averne said sharply, as he twirled the dial. He didn't bother with the headset. 'Wolfe, you'd better be there. I need to know what's going on. Wolfe? Listen, you bag of pus! Listen to me!'

Henry rose to his feet, and helped me to mine. Averne didn't notice. 'I'll take c-care of him.' There was a fire in his eyes that hadn't been there before. I watched as he flicked my folded coat open with his single hand, and carefully drew one of the vials out. He then slowly made his way towards Averne, approaching from the back and side.

'Wolfe!' Averne grabbed the headset and put it on, having finished with the dials. 'Wolfe, come in! You'd better be doing your job! I need to know where we are!'

With that, Henry grabbed Averne's scarf, and tore it free.

Behind it was a worm-skinned, sickly-looking man with a scraggly beard and mustache. He might've been hale, at one point, but his flesh was now toneless, his teeth yellow, the skin around his nose inflamed. He opened his mouth to scream and curse at us, and Henry leveled his arm back and let him have it. Averne fell from his chair to the salt and clawed at it, attempting to push himself up.

'Monsters!' he bellowed, blood dripping from the corner of his mouth. 'Demons from *hell*!'

Before he could get up, Henry sat on his chest and jammed the test tube halfway into his open mouth. 'Break that glass, you're d-dead. Like me.' Henry held onto the other end of the tube, keeping it firmly in place. Averne's eyes widened, and he stayed where he was. It was a rather unconventional ring through the nose, but it worked.

I wasted no time in hobbling over and sitting down at the controls. I put the headset on and brought the microphone to my lips.

'This is Dr Victor Dearly, broadcasting from unknown co-ordinates. Do you copy, over?' I paused, to make sure my voice was fully under my control, before adding, 'Captain Wolfe, you sorry piece of flesh, are you there?'

I forced my hand to lift off the transmission button, my fingers shaking. I'd practically been punching it down through the table.

Averne was struggling, but Henry had him pinned. He kept thrusting the tube down a little farther than it needed to go, until Averne coughed for air; then he would let up.

There was no answer on the radio, so I tried again. 'This is Dr Victor Dearly, broadcasting from unknown coordinates. Do you copy, over? Wolfe?'

After a few more moments of static, I gave up. I pushed my glasses up on my nose and leaned closer to the radio, dialing in one of our usual radio frequencies.

'This is Dr Victor Dearly, broadcasting from unknown coordinates. Do you copy, over?'

Please, someone be there.

'Dearly, your voice sounds unto my ear as air must taste to a drowning man.'

I laughed uproariously and thrust my arms into the air, before hitting the button. 'Baldwin, you old fiend, I could say much the same!'

'I'd been half ready to write you off! It's a lucky thing I was here . . . Salvez, get over here!'

I now understood what the phrase 'giddy as a schoolgirl' meant. 'Horatio!'

'Victor! You're all right!' Salvez sounded like he was ready to faint.

'Relatively, yes. Can you trace this signal? I'm somewhere in Bolivia.'

'I'm on it. Once the computers do their magic, we'll be golden,' Samedi said, from a bit in the distance.

Steadying myself, I inquired, 'Is Wolfe there?'

'No, why?'

It took me a moment to formulate my reply. 'I do not know conclusively, but from what I've gathered . . . Wolfe has sold us out. He sent me here. He's been working with the Punks.'

'What?' Salvez asked.

'Bloody hell.' Samedi sighed, and said, 'Look – this is where we stand. The dead are loose in New London. Are you telling me that Wolfe had some hand in that?'

'Lord.' I sat back in the chair. 'The commander here kept ranting about that very thing. He was right.'

'Commander?'

'There're several hundred undead here, being commanded by a man known as Major Dorian Averne. He's alive, he's a Punk, and . . .' I glanced over. Henry was still toying with him. 'He's not been having a good time of it, of late.'

'How're you managing to broadcast? Is he there? Are you safe?' Salvez asked.

'Oh, he's here. A new associate of mine, Mr. Macumba, is making him play tonsil hockey with a test tube full of home-brewed explosive compound.'

'It's such a shame?' Samedi called out. 'I never get invited to the fun parties anymore!'

'But what are you *doing* there? This doesn't make any sense,' Salvez fretted.

'It has something to do with revenge,' I told him. 'It has something to do with the vaccine. They wanted me to work on it here, so they could have sole control of it.' I shut my eyes. 'I didn't tell them that I think it might be finished.'

At this news, Averne thrashed furiously against Henry, and got another sucker punch for his troubles.

'Finished?' Samedi asked. His voice was distant again. 'Are you serious?'

'Yes. The last batch of models I ran – number 77-A, I think. If you just subject it to a few more mathematical tweaks . . . try C-series . . . I think that's the one. At least, it should have a very low mortality rate. I'd start subjecting it to the virtual rats now. Even if it's not entirely effective, it should help restore some order, if things are truly as bad as my vivid imagination is leading me to believe.'

'Are you serious? Oh, thank heavens.' Salvez sounded suddenly exhausted. 'I'll go fetch Elpinoy and do that right now. We'll . . . what is it, Dr Samedi?'

'Got it!' Samedi shouted. 'He is in Bolivia. How did you end up *there*?'

'We'll have to ask our friend Wolfe later.' But first, I had to ask after someone else. Steadying myself, I inquired, 'And . . . my daughter? Is Nora all right?'

There was a pause, during which I entertained a thousand ways of doing myself in. Without her, with my work potentially completed, I had no reason to continue to exist.

'She's in good hands,' Samedi said. 'Bram's been taking care of her. She's fine with him. Hell, she's taken right after you. She's fine with all of us.'

I breathed a sigh of relief. 'That's the best news I've had in days.'

'She's quite angry at you, though, old man,' Salvez added.

'I expected nothing else.' I opened my eyes. 'At any rate, I'm afraid I must be going.' I didn't want to, but now Henry and I had to deal with a very angry Averne. 'We'll be waiting.'

'We're coming,' Samedi said. 'Just hang on.'

I let go of the controls.

Averne chose that moment to try and fight his way out from underneath Henry again. Henry managed to get the vial to clink against his teeth, and pushed him back. 'Calm down, or b-boom,' he said.

'Sounds like you're coming back into your own,' I said, as I stood up and made my way over. Henry shot me a sideways grin. 'Good to see.'

I pulled up in front of Averne, and, balancing on one leg for a moment, thwacked him in the ribs as hard as I could with my crutch. He made a sound of pain, his shoulder sinking on that side.

'That's for my leg,' I growled, as I got my footing again. 'Heaven knows you deserve more, but it's going to have to wait.'

Henry left the vial in Averne's mouth and put his arm against his throat. 'We're not going to k-kill him?' He sounded relieved.

'No. We're going to save him for the proper authorities.' I leaned in close to Averne and snapped my teeth together. He went still. He *was* afraid of contracting it. I smiled slowly. 'Not so crazy that you're fearless, I see. Either one of us can bestow upon you a short, brutish second life, if you so desire, Major.' I stepped back. 'Knock him out. We'll tie him up.'

Henry grabbed the vial from Averne's mouth and tossed it lightly onto the salt. He then elbowed Averne in the chin to disorient him, before taking him by the front of his face and hammering and hammering him back against the salt until he became unresponsive.

'That's for my a-arm,' Henry said, retrieving the vial. He wiped it off on his trousers and handed it to me. 'Your half of the weapons c-cache.'

'Thank you, Mr Macumba.'

We unwrapped Henry's bandages and twined them to- gether in pairs to make ropes, which we used to bind Averne's hands and feet. Henry studied his injuries, as they were revealed. He asked, as he fingered the leathery burned skin still clinging to his raw muscles, 'Is there a w-way to fix t-this?'

I nodded. 'It will never heal, but we can patch you up easily enough once we get back to base. Please don't worry, Mr Macumba. The worst is over. It's just survival, from here on out.'

He nodded, and glanced to the door. 'Is that what we t-tell the t-troops too?'

Oh. Them. Bother.

'We . . .' My eyes landed upon Averne's scarf. It'd fallen on the salt, a patterned patch on the white ground. 'We adhere to the principle, "what they don't know won't hurt them".'

CHAPTER THIRTY-FOUR

Bram

Nora jumped back into the hold and fell in a heap at the bottom of the stairs. I ran over and helped her up. 'I got Pam,' she said, holding out the com unit. 'How do I put this on speaker?'

I took it from her and punched a few buttons. 'Nora!' Pam said, on the other end of the line. She sounded out of breath.

'We're here,' I told her. 'Where are you?'

'We're in the Museum of Natural History!' she got out. 'We rescued someone, and the dead followed us! They're right behind us!'

Nora grabbed the com back from me. 'Pam, can you get to the roof of the museum?'

'Maybe! It's confusing in here, and we're trying to avoid the zombies.'

'Just keep going up,' Nora instructed. 'Go up, no matter what. We're on our way. It's just north of the cathedral, right?'

'Yeah! Should be! They're coming, keep going up! No, Issy, you idiot, *up*!'

'Keep the phone handy!' Nora ran to the window and set the com unit down on a nearby crate. 'Museum. Go north. There's a huge lion on the top, you can't miss it.'

'Right.' I pointed to the others. 'Everyone who's not controlling the ship, weapons on.'

I noticed that Nora's hands were shaking as she slipped her shotgun's strap over her shoulder. She'd gotten a thigh holster for the pistol. When she saw that I was watching, she straightened up and put her hands on her hips. 'Ready to meet my best friend, then?'

I clipped my vest together in front, and smiled tightly.

'Should I bring a bottle of wine? Any taboo topics? Politics, life after death?'

'Yeah, just stay away from that one entirely.'

Coalhouse'd taken over by the window. 'There's a big lion rearing up on that building down there. It looks almost . . . shimmery. Aw, man, don't tell me this eye is going too.'

'Shimmery?' Tom asked him.

'Holographic,' Nora said.

I slapped the beacon on my shoulder, and the light started flashing red. 'Find a place to dock her.'

Leaving the others to command the *Alice*, I accompanied Nora back up the stairs to the main deck. We picked up a bit of speed again as we started to descend, the ropes creaking within their mountings, and Nora's hair flapped about her face. 'That's it,' she said as she rushed to the prow. The lion appeared to be crafted of speckled gray stone, but Coalhouse was right – it had a slightly transparent, almost magical look to it. I found myself blinking several times. Combined with my cloudy vision, it looked more like a drug-induced hallucination than a real statue.

'I don't see anyone on the roof,' she said, leaning over the railing to scan it. I reached out and hooked a finger into the belt of her skirt. She decided to go with it, and leaned even farther out.

'They might still be inside,' I said. 'We'll go in if we have to.'

'I just hope something hasn't happened to them,' she said, falling back again against my hand. I slipped it free and let it rest between her shoulder blades, instead. She didn't buck it off. 'She's like my sister.' Her voice told me, '*You know what it means, to have a sister.*'

I remained quiet, because I did.

'Prepare for impact!' Renfield called up from the hold.

I curled my arm around Nora's shoulders and urged her to kneel down beside me. She did, her face close to mine in the darkness. I could feel the heat of her breath on my skin, and marveled at it. My senses were amazingly attuned to her, even now. She reached out and gripped my knee as we bumped against the side of the building, and I took blatant advantage of the opportunity to pull her closer, if only for a moment.

'Are you sure you want to go down there?' I asked.

Nora nodded. 'I have to. She's always come for me – maybe not like this, with guns and armor and all, but she's been there for me in ways I couldn't be there for myself. I don't care what happens to me, as long as she's safe.'

I knew the feeling, exactly. Whatever happened to me, I'd get Nora out. I had to. There was no way I could die peacefully, knowing she had been hurt. 'You don't need to worry. I've got you.'

Nora laughed a little. 'Yeah, you do.' She looked into my eyes, her expression quieting, although a funny smile still haunted her lips.

As soon as the rocking of the ship calmed down, I stood up. Nora took my hand and pulled herself to her feet. The rest of the crew, minus Renfield, climbed up the stairs to join us.

'Ren's going to stay with the ship,' Tom said, as he activated his beacon.

I pulled my mask out of my pocket and rolled it on. 'OK. Let's go.'

Just as Tom and Coalhouse kicked out the gangplank, the stone lion in front of us vanished. The glow from the city lights that had surrounded us, weak as it had been, dissipated. I pulled out my rifle, although I kept it pointed at the sky.

'The electricity's gone out,' Nora said. 'That's all. Maybe they had to abandon the stations.'

Chas hit the electric lantern on her belt, and the others followed suit. The yellow light did little to chase back the yawning darkness. 'We'd better hurry, then. 'Cause if they're still inside in the dark . . .'

Nora sprinted down the plank. The rest followed her,

drawing their own weapons out. I stayed where I was, though, looking at the city below in horror. All down the street holograms were going out, their halos of light melting away. What had been, from the air, an impressive-looking city with grand columned buildings and intricately-painted storefronts was reduced to rows of ugly concrete shells, endless aisles of blank rectangles, like pre-planted and uncarved tombstones. It was a shudder-inducing vision, and it enthralled me longer than it should have.

'Bram?' Tom called.

I pushed what I'd just witnessed to the back of my mind, and rejoined the team. Nora was watching me with concern in her eyes, but I didn't stop walking until I reached the service door that'd let us into the museum. A few bullets took care of the lock. 'Nora, back of the line. No buts.'

'I'm not arguing with you, this time.' She let Chas go ahead of her and pulled out her shotgun.

Once our lineup was established, we started in, weapons at the ready. We took the stairs slowly, almost in unison, remaining close together.

We hadn't gone ten steps before we heard screaming.

'Hey!' I heard Chas exclaim, and I figured Nora'd gone racing forward and been caught. 'You'll get yourself killed!'

'I can hear them!' Nora cried.

'Calm down. They've gotta be nearby.' I raised my voice. 'This is Captain Abraham Griswold of Company Z! We're here with Nora Dearly! Can you hear me?'

My voice echoed so loudly in the stone corridor that I was afraid it'd all come back to me. I was about to try again, cupping my hands around my mouth to project it, when I heard a little, 'Nora! It's Nora!'

'Pamma?' Nora shouted.

'Where are you?' Pam rejoined.

'Near the roof!' I yelled back. 'We're coming down! Keep making noise!' Returning my voice to a conversational level, I called back, 'Nora, I'm not attempting to embarrass you, or single you out. I know you're capable. But *stay behind Chas*, OK? You die, you die *permanently*, and for various reasons that we've already gotten angsty about together, I don't want that to happen.'

'OK, OK,' she sighed.

'Angsty?' Chas asked. 'Ooh! Later, details!'

'Yes, *later*.' With that, I waved the team forward.

We pounded down the staircase a little more quickly than before. Pam and her crew either took direction well, or had good reason to shout, because they made plenty of noise. Soon we'd run out of stairs, and found ourselves in a darkened attic storeroom with rows of muslin-draped shelving. I could hear Pam's group on the other side of the room from where we'd come in, behind yet another door. It was thumping slightly, like a beating wooden heart. They were trying to break it in.

'Stand back!' I yelled, taking aim. 'I'm going to shoot the lock!'

I waited until their voices had retreated, then I pulled the trigger. I kicked the door open, and found four people waiting on the other side. They lost no time in joining us. A dark-haired girl in trousers panted out, 'You might want to start running.' I recognized her voice from the com unit.

As if on cue, I heard the unmistakable sounds of the dead coming from the hall outside.

'Grand idea,' I said, waiting until the newcomers had passed me before pressing everyone forward. 'OK, back to the ship! First one who gets there, jump down into the hold and tell Renfield to go nuts!'

No one needed me to ask twice. Behind us the evil dead started crashing through the storeroom, tall shelves and cases full of priceless artifacts falling down like dominoes in their wake. When he could, though, Tom fell back to run beside me. Like me, he understood that the last line of defense had better be undead.

Once we got outside and got those in front of us started up the gangplank, Tom and I turned around and shouldered our guns. We blew away the first comers, their fallen bodies becoming an obstacle course for the second wave. Neither of us relented until we heard the others shouting at us and saw that they were ready to go. We ran like hell to catch up with them, Tom putting up his gun and starting to direct everyone into the hold. I turned and pulled up the gangplank as Renfield got us airborne again.

Below us, on the rooftop, the mad zombies screamed and made futile attempts to leap for the ship. One fell to his final death in doing so, landing with a sick splat on the asphalt below.

'Inside.' I felt Nora's hands on me, and turned to look at her. She was tugging on my jacket. 'C'mon, we're going to floor it. Better blown up than eaten.'

Inside the hold, Renfield was preoccupied with his buttons and levers again, his back to the newcomers. Coalhouse took my place near the window to steer. Pamela's group was still trying to recover from the race to the airship, all of them seized over and breathing hard.

Nora pushed her way past Tom and Chas and took Pam into her arms. Pamela clung tightly to her in turn, as if Nora embodied every form of salvation imaginable, at the moment. 'Everything's okay now.'

Pam's shoulders began to shake. 'No, no, it's not,' she whispered. 'My family is locked up, with no idea when to come out. And Isambard was bitten.'

I looked sharply at Pam. 'What?'

Pamela untangled herself from Nora and wiped at her eyes. She kneeled down beside the youngest boy, who was seated on the floor. Her voice was thick. 'Show them, Issy.'

The boy didn't look well, I could see that much. He was

green around the gills, and his eyes were bloodshot. He obligingly, but limply, offered his forearm, which was wrapped up in a blood-stained cloth.

'I couldn't run . . . fast enough,' he got out. He was still breathing heavily. 'Mr Allister . . . saved me.'

The other young man was staring at Nora as he caught his breath. 'Not just him. Miss Roe, as well.'

'Were *you* hurt, Mr Allister?' I asked.

'No. By sheer luck, I managed to avoid them. They pressed in all around, and so quickly, it's a wonder I did. I beat them off, gave up when the hammer got stuck in one.' Michael finally turned to look at me, and that's when he started. He asked, tone slightly suspicious, 'Excuse me, but . . . whom am I addressing? I've never known our servicemen to hide their faces, before.'

'Yeah, who the hell are you?' asked the blonde living girl, more bluntly. 'Not that we're not grateful, and all.' Nora looked at her in shock, before casting a worried glance my way.

'Fair enough,' I said, mostly for Nora's benefit. Time for the big reveal.

Bracing myself, I pulled off my mask. The newcomers stared at me for a moment, but the gravity of the situation didn't seem to sink in until Coalhouse removed his, revealing the cavernous right side of his face.

The blonde girl was the first to scream. She pressed herself back against the wall of the hold, producing a shriek that would've traumatized an alley cat. Michael rocketed away from me and stood in front of her, watching as Chas and Tom divested themselves of their masks. Renfield finally turned around, as well, to see what the commotion was about.

'They're monsters!' the blonde girl cried.

Pamela pulled Isambard to her side, eyes full of fear.

'What's the meaning of this?' Michael's eyes jumped from zombie to zombie, seemingly growing bigger by the second.

'I can explain,' I said, showing an open hand. 'We're going to take you someplace safe, all right?'

'Shut up, Mink! They're *not* monsters! Are *you* the one they rescued?' Nora glared at Mink for a moment, before returning her attention to Pam. 'I told you, Pamma.' Attempting to appeal to the person who might understand her best, Nora dropped to her knees in front of her friend. 'I told you, I was with the good guys. These *are* the good guys. They got to me before the bad zombies did. It's a long story.'

'Stay away from us!' Michael ordered. He was looking at Nora in horror, as if he couldn't believe what she was saying.

'No one's trying to get near you,' Chas snorted. 'I don't do living guys. Call me prejudiced.'

'They're . . . they're dead, Nora . . .' Pam's voice was shaky. 'Ayles said they were dead . . .'

'Pamela.' Nora reached out to cup her friend's face. 'You have to believe me. Look, I traveled here with them, and they didn't hurt me. I've been with them for days, and they never hurt me. Just think, OK? Am I lying to you?'

'But, but . . .'

Nora held up a hand, and Pam shut her mouth. 'Right now you just need to know that they're not going to harm you. Do you see the red beacon they're wearing? Think of it, like, um . . . "red light, they're all right!"' Everyone, human and zombie alike, stared at her. She grumbled, 'Well, it works.'

Renfield started his beacon up.

For a moment, no one spoke. Allister and Mink remained against the wall, eyeing everyone around them distrustfully. I took a step back from them as a show of good will. Their expressions told me that they weren't buying it.

'Isn't there something that can be done?' Pamela asked. 'For Issy?'

I shook my head. 'No, unfortunately.' She was Nora's friend, so I figured I might as well be straight with her. 'It takes about six hours. He might wake up fine at the end of it, he might wake up . . . not. We won't know 'til then.'

Pam didn't reply immediately. For a minute, I was worried that we'd really blown her mind. When she did finally speak up, her voice was filled with sadness. 'There *are* good ones, aren't there? There's this family near me, and they're dead, but . . . they're not violent, they're just really confused, and I didn't know what to tell them. I mean, how do you phrase something like that?'

Relieved, I told her, 'That's who we're out to help. That's what we're like. Not all of us go insane.'

Nora ran her hand over Pam's head, and said, 'It's OK. Just because Isambard was bitten doesn't mean he's going to become like the ones that were chasing you.'

'But he'll become like *them*!' Pam said, pointing to us. She hid her face against her brother, and Nora embraced her. Isambard started to weep.

I couldn't watch. I felt like I was intruding on yet another moment of private grief. So I joined Coalhouse by the window, and took over the steering wheel from him. Below us, the city was gone; we were flying over grassy fields dotted with large manor houses. According to the compass, we'd drifted west. I twirled the steering wheel to bring us back south. Renfield throttled our speed down a bit to steady the turn.

As the engine quieted just that much, I heard the com unit go off. 'It's gotta be Doc Sam. Someone get it,' I said.

Chas picked it up. 'Samedi?' she asked.

'No.' Wolfe's voice boomed from the com. 'Turn on the screen, you stupid bitch, and listen up. Where's Griswold? I want to see his face.'

CHAPTER THIRTY-FIVE

Nora

Bram abandoned the steering wheel and took the com unit from Chas.

'What's going on?' Pam asked.

'Shh,' I told her, as I stood up.

'Care to apologize to the lady, scumbag?' Bram asked angrily.

'Shut up, deadmeat. Turn on the screen.'

Bram hit a button, and glow from the screen on the com unit lit his face from beneath, making him look ghoulish. The fact that what he saw made his eyes narrow and his mouth pull back in a growl, revealing his teeth, didn't help any.

Chas's eyes widened. 'Oh my God,' she said, taking a step back. She ended up tripping over the crate behind her and sitting on it.

I ran over. 'What is it?'

Chas put out her arms, stopping me. 'He has Sam.' She sounded scared.

'What's going on?' Bram demanded. 'What the hell are you doing, Wolfe?'

I stepped between Chas's legs, climbed onto the crate beside her, and looked over Bram's shoulder.

My heart stopped.

Wolfe was in Samedi's lab. Sam was seated on a stool in front of him, glowering at us through the camera of the unit they were using to transmit. Off-screen I could hear yelling and banging. Wolfe must have locked everyone else out.

He was holding a gun to Samedi's head.

'Baldwin!' I heard Dr Chase scream.

'Samedi! Wolfe, you monster, let him go!' Salvez was with her.

'What the hell are *you* doing?' Wolfe said. His hair was rumpled, his eyes intense. 'Where are you, Griswold?'

'On a ship,' Bram said. 'Just not the one you wanted. We had to rescue some people.'

'Had to?' Wolfe laughed, brokenly. 'Had to? Why? Because that spawn of Dearly's wanted you to? You think she'll love you for this? You think she'll give a damn about you, if you do what she wants? You're *dead*, Griswold!'

'We did it because it was the right thing to do,' Bram told him, stiffly.

'Is she with you? She *better* be with you.'

I leaned over Bram's shoulder, so that he could see me. 'I'm here.'

Wolfe's furious expression relaxed for a second. 'Good. Good.' He repositioned his finger on the trigger. 'Now, Griswold, you bring her back to base, or I'll blow this meat-sack's brains all over this room. Do I make myself perfectly clear?'

'Don't do it, Bram,' Samedi said. 'Dr Dearly is fine, he's . . .'

Wolfe hit him in the head with the butt of the gun. 'Shut up!' Samedi snarled. Wolfe turned his attention off-camera. 'Anyone out in the hall speaks, I shoot him! You got that?'

'Why do you want her so bad?' Bram asked. As he spoke, he reached back and took my hand. I clung onto it with all my strength.

'Dr Dearly?' Pam asked. 'He's not dead?'

'That doesn't matter!' Wolfe yelled. 'Show some loyalty to your own species, damn it! Even I know that this sorry sack of bones is worth more than Dearly's stupid little louse of a daughter!'

'Then why do you want her so bad?' Bram repeated, his voice low and filled with barely-repressed rage. 'We're heading back to base. We're on our way. Tell me why you want her.'

'Because everything has been ruined!' Wolfe bellowed, his face going red. He jabbed the barrel of his gun into Sam's temple. 'Do you know how long I've waited to eliminate your kind? Do you know how long I've waited to see you all dead – the plague gone? But not before I could prove myself!'

'What are you talking about?' I asked. Bram squeezed my fingers to hush me.

'*Shut up!* Shut the girl up, Griswold!' Wolfe glared into the camera. 'I will not have this taken from me! Do you know how *long* I've had to fight to prove myself? Can you even imagine what that's like?'

'Prove yourself?' Bram asked. 'You're not making any sense. Take the gun off Samedi and talk to us, all right?'

The gun didn't move, but for some reason, Wolfe talked. 'I remember that day so well – the day the PM was attacked. My company went with him, to guard him. We'd never seen the dead before. So can you blame us for being curious?'

Bram and I shared a quick look of mutual confusion.

'We were supposed to be guarding the front gate,' Wolfe said, voice quieting somewhat. 'But we were distracted by a zombie. Girl. Fresh. We just wanted to talk to her, but she was scared of us. She tried to run, but some of the boys were intent on cornering her . . .' He took a breath. 'I knew chasing after her like that was stupid. But before I could call them off, we heard the commotion, everyone yelling and running. The Punks'd gotten in. They'd shot at the PM.'

'So the Punks attacked the Prime Minister on *your* watch . . . and an infected man was the one to save him,' Bram realized aloud.

This statement set Wolfe off again. 'A plague-bearing *rat* gets lauded . . . meanwhile, the only reason I ain't court-martialed is because I've seen the living dead and can never return to civilian life!' Wolfe tossed back his head, but he didn't laugh. 'Forty-three years old, and I just barely make captain again. Barely.'

'So what, this is all over a freaking promotion?' Bram asked, appalled.

'No!' Wolfe yelled again. 'This is about justice!' He swept his free arm behind him. 'I did hard time after messing up that bad. I was made to fight the zombies on the ground, made to work with the Punks. You wouldn't believe the things I saw, the things I had to go through. I knew the only way to stop the dead was to wage total war on them, hunt them down mercilessly. I told my superiors this, again and again . . . and you know what? Every single one of them agreed with me. But they kept listening to Dearly and Ayles, trusting them, hoping they'd come up with a vaccine.' He returned his hand to Samedi's shoulder. 'I tried to bite my tongue. I tried to be a good soldier. I even tried to help. After they let me have my stripes again, I maneuvered myself into command of Dearly's little research project. Hell, I'll be honest – I figured, "Hey, at least I can be in charge when the cure is produced." And I paraded Company Z around for years, cleaning up the messes the dead were making, containing the outbreaks, so that Dearly could spend his time in the lab. And still there was no vaccine! Fool spent all his time patching up the walking dead, instead of worrying about the living!'

'You want the vaccine?' Bram asked, not understanding. 'We all want the vaccine!'

It clicked. 'He wants credit. He wants to redeem himself.'

Wolfe carried on, ignoring us. 'Then, Dearly died. I knew he couldn't be trusted after that. I couldn't wait any longer.' He took a hot breath. 'When I was on the ground, we heard about this Punk named Averne. He went AWOL, and soon there were rumors that he was marching around out there with his own little undead army. So, last February, I tracked him down. Bugger's completely crazy. He bought every lie that I fed him, and soon he wanted *personal* revenge against the man he thought had started the plague.'

'The Grays,' Bram whispered.

'Exactly. Back then I was afraid that radio might be too risky. We'd meet somewhere quiet, and plan, while our "kids" ran around in the dark and shot at one another.' Wolfe actually laughed. 'It was quite beautiful, the way it worked out. I told him that I wanted to put the fear of God into Dearly, to make him work faster on the damn vaccine. Averne said he wanted to kill Dearly's entire family, not just him. So, Averne figured, why not kidnap Dearly's daughter? You know, sometimes the craziest guys are the most brilliant. What could possibly scare Dearly more than the idea that his living girl was in the hands of a madman? So, I made it happen.'

'But . . . Dearly got on a plane . . .'

'Of course he did.' Wolfe smiled. 'One I pulled a few wires out of. I'd worked with the man for years. I knew he had a habit of doing things without thinking them through. He took those bullets for the PM, he would head off to rescue dead men at a moment's notice . . . I figured he'd run off into the fray. Which was good . . . he'd be too distracted at base, worried over the fate of his daughter. I never intended that he'd stick around and moon over her – I wanted him to work. Alone, isolated, afraid. Nora was meant to be my insurance against getting double-crossed, to keep Averne from getting too cocky. I told him I'd hand her over in exchange for the vaccine. Never meant to, of course – too risky. I figured I'd just kill her after he delivered.'

I sank onto the crate. I'd stood not two feet away from the man, and all the while, he'd been planning – coldly, calmly – to kill me.

Bram looked like he wanted to eat Wolfe inch by inch. 'But . . . why were Averne's troops in New London, then? If this was all your idea, your big plot, why didn't you just send us to get Nora instead of putting the whole city at risk?'

I couldn't see the screen from my position. I could only hear Wolfe's voice, suddenly smug. 'You would have questioned me every step of the way, Griswold, unless you thought there was a real threat to deal with. You would have challenged me. And you would have blabbed to Dearly – you never can keep your mouth shut.'

Bram's face went slack, and Wolfe started laughing. 'Besides, you had the chance to kill them all! I never denied you that! You're useless, Griswold, to a man! Of course, I figured that if a few nippy dead survived, if our people got a taste of the plague they're facing, the plague the government's kept hidden, they'd be even more grateful for the vaccine when I brought it home.' He sighed. 'It did get a little out of hand, though.'

'A little out of hand?!' Bram shouted. 'People are dying down there! You did this!'

'What did you do with my father?' I asked. I felt a tear sliding down my cheek.

'Never you mind!' Wolfe cocked the gun. Beryl screamed. 'I can't wait any longer. The military's finally smartened up. They've put out the order to exterminate every last zombie, and that means that a vaccine is now meaningless!'

'Exterminate?' I heard Renfield ask.

Pam hugged Isambard even harder.

'You're my only chance, now, Nora. You're the prettiest scapegoat there ever was. I'm going to let the whole world know that your love affair with a dead boy brought this unholy hell upon your people. I'll tell them that he came for you in the night, like some rotting Romeo. And I won't hand you over to be torn apart 'til I'm in the clear.'

'Over my dead body,' Bram snarled.

Wolfe started laughing fully, insanely, at that.

'Nora,' Chas said, reaching out for me. I let her take my other hand.

I saw nothing. I felt nothing. I stared at the wall as Wolfe continued to laugh, knowing that my only option was to hand myself over to him. It would be a small price to pay. I didn't care what happened to me, as long as Bram and Samedi and Chastity and the others were bought some time. They could run away. They could hide. As long as they were alive, I'd be fine. There'd be hope.

But then another idea entered my head.

I stumbled over Chas. I fell to the floor of the ship, and she helped me up.

'What's going on?' Pam asked again, a bit more hysterically.

I held up a hand to hush her, and made my way behind the com unit, where Wolfe couldn't see me. Bram watched me, his eyes filled with questions.

'Bite me,' I mouthed at him.

'What?' he barked.

Wolfe went off on a tangent, thinking that Bram was speaking to him. 'You know perfectly well what. I've explained it all. You're about the stupidest thing on two legs. Haven't you learned to listen to me yet? Haven't you learned to just do what you're told?'

'Bite me,' I mouthed again. Bram was staring at me in disbelief, as if I were trying to persuade him that his entire existence as a dead man was simply an incredibly realistic dream.

'Of course not. You think you're intelligent, still. You think you're human, still. Why do I bother?'

'Take me hostage. Bite me.'

'Idiot!'

It seemed like an eternity before Bram started moving.

I saw him shake the com unit. I heard him yell at Wolfe, 'Idiot, am I?' It sounded so fake. He handed the unit to Chas and told her, 'Make sure he gets a good look!'

'Griswold? Griswold, what are you doing?'

The others watched as Bram stepped closer to me and took me in his arms. He whirled me around, so that I was facing the com unit. Chas was all eyes, her mouth open, as Bram wrenched my borrowed blouse aside and revealed my shoulder. His left hand, huge and powerful, splayed scandalously across my waist.

'You want her so bad?' Bram said, looking to the com. 'You forget, she's currently up in the air with a whole hell of a lot of hungry people, Wolfe. I think we have the upper hand, here.'

'*Griswold!*'

He bit me.

I didn't even feel it at first. I felt his hair against my cheek, his cold breath and skin against my neck, his big fingers sliding into my curls, but not the bite.

I slowly shut my eyes.

I knew it was a stupid, stupid thing to do. I knew there was the risk that he wouldn't be able to control himself, and that pretty soon it could spiral toward chaos. I waited for that. I waited to feel my flesh stretching, tearing. I waited.

I felt Bram's mouth moving.

He was kissing me.

Pain rushed in, and with it, the world.

I opened my eyes. On the screen, Wolfe was screaming. He took the gun off Samedi for an instant, just an instant.

Samedi took his chance.

The stool went flying across the room as Sam stood up and grabbed Wolfe by his uniform jacket. The gun went off, and Salvez and Beryl started shouting again. Sam went in with fast, snake-like strikes, biting Wolfe repeatedly, ripping off chunks of his skin. Wolfe fell, and Samedi kicked him as he went down, roaring like a lion.

Wolfe tried to crawl across the floor to get away, his fingers slippery with his own blood. He was making high-pitched, animalistic sounds of fear and panic.

'No! No! Get away from me! Get away!'

Samedi, his white coat streaked with gore, stalked after him. He picked up the stool.

'*Get away from me!*'

Bram turned me around. He was licking my blood from his lips. When he saw that my eyes were open, he pulled my head to his chest so I didn't have to watch. My shoulder throbbed. He'd given me what I wanted, but not in a way I'd ever expected.

I could hear Wolfe's scream as Sam started to beat him.

'Oh my God, oh my God!' Isambard started shrieking.

'Is he killing him?' Tom asked. 'Is he dead? Sam! Sam, back to reality, here, smart guy! C'mon!'

The undead in the airship tried desperately to catch Sam's attention. They cried his name, clapped their hands. Eventually, it must have worked, for I heard something drop, heard Wolfe's voice cease. As the zombies around me fell silent, I could hear that someone was still screaming Sam's name on the other end. Dr Chase.

'Open the door! Baldwin, open the door! Let me in!'

'Let me see,' I whispered to Bram. He slowly released his hold on me, and I turned around to watch with the rest.

Samedi stood perfectly still before the body of Captain Wolfe, absently sliding his hands over his face, his coat. Eventually he said, voice strained, 'I can't, Beryl.'

'Just do it! Baldwin, please!'

'I don't want to hurt you. Please don't ask me to do this.'

'Maybe this isn't such a good idea, Dr Chase . . .'

'Baldwin Anthony Samedi, you let me in there this instant!' Dr Chase yelled, ignoring Salvez.

Samedi tore off his lab coat angrily, like Wolfe's blood had contaminated it somehow. He clutched his stomach. 'All right, all right! Give me a moment. Just give me a moment!'

Everyone, on both sides of the broadcast, remained quiet. Samedi waited for five endless minutes, still as a statue, before walking to the door. It took him an interminable second to unlock it.

When he opened it, Dr Chase rushed into the lab and threw herself into his arms.

'Oh!' I blurted out, suddenly afraid for her.

But he didn't hurt her. He clutched her to his chest and burrowed his face into her hair. 'I'm so sorry, Beryl. I'm so sorry.'

'It's OK.' She seemed half-afraid, herself, but she held him nonetheless. She was wearing a long nightgown, and her hair was a mess. 'I'm sorry . . . *I'm* sorry. Calm down. It's OK. You're not a beast, you're not a killer. You had to do it. It's OK. Just calm down.'

'What happened?' Bram managed to ask. He was still shaken. 'What's going on, down there?'

Salvez appeared in front of the camera. '*Wolfe* is going on. He returned to base a bit ago, but we'd learned that he was a double agent. He turned on us when we confronted him. Samedi tried to restrain him, and . . . you saw what happened.'

'How'd you know?' I asked.

'Because your father got in contact with us a few minutes ago.' Salvez rested his hands on his chest. His heart must have been going a mile a minute. 'He's alive, Miss Dearly. He's at a Punk compound in Bolivia, being held by a man named Averne. He's alive . . . and we have his coordinates. You can go get him.'

'We have to get the other members of Z Comp,' Bram realized. 'If the order's gone out to kill them . . .'

'Not 'til oh-six-hundred hours,' Salvez said. 'Go. Get them. I'll tell them to return to the docks. And . . . he's done it.' He actually smiled. 'We have a vaccine. We don't know if it will *work* . . . no vaccine is one hundred percent effective. But at least it should be safe. We can start to test it here. I'll get in contact with the army. We might be able to pull out of this.'

A whoop went up in the airship. I turned and hugged Bram, and he squeezed me back, more tightly than he ever had before. I couldn't breathe, he was so strong, but I liked it.

Behind Salvez, on the screen, Beryl stepped back from Baldwin and went to check on Wolfe. She felt for a pulse at his neck. She must have found one, for she announced, 'He's alive! We need to get him somewhere secure, before he reanimates!'

'I do believe we should call *that* justice, eh?' Salvez asked of Samedi. He sounded relieved.

Samedi laughed, before sinking down onto the bloody tile

floor. Beryl rushed to his side again and wrapped her arms about his neck. He let his head fall against her shoulder.

'I'm so sorry you had to see that,' he said regretfully. 'You can disconnect me if you want.'

'Baldwin . . .' She lifted a hand to his missing ear and traced the hole. Her fingers were trembling. 'When he had you . . . do you think I would have done any less to him if I'd gotten my hands on him? After all we've been through?'

Samedi laughed again. 'I knew there was a reason I've always loved you. Aside from your figure, that is.'

Beryl slapped him gently upside the head, before rolling her forehead against his cheek.

Bram pulled my sleeve up. I looked to my shoulder. The wound he was covering was deceptively small compared to the amount of pain I felt. It was still bleeding, but not enough to worry about.

'I'm sorry,' he whispered.

'I asked you to.' I slid my fingers over his, taking up his hold on my shirt. 'And I'm asking one last thing . . .'

'You don't need to,' he told me, before raising his voice. 'OK, guys. Let's head for the docks.'

Chapter Thirty-six

Pamela

I rose to my feet. 'Nora,' I fought out. The ship swayed, causing me to rock where I stood.

She turned to look at me. There was no fear in her eyes.

She was just bitten by a zombie. *Why is there no fear in her eyes?*

'You were bitten!' I screamed. 'You were just bitten by that . . . that . . .' I looked at Bram. I looked at all of them in turn. It was like I was caught up in a carnival freakshow, or one of the lowest levels of hell. In my panic, I felt like they were looming over me – creatures full of holes, their flesh missing, their skin stitched together like horrifying rag dolls, watching me with eyes like mirrors reflecting a sickly moon.

The big zombie lifted a hand, but before he could speak, I tore myself from away from Isambard and approached Nora. Tears were starting to burn my eyes. I couldn't lose them both, there was no way I could lose them both and remain sane . . .

Nora clutched my shoulders. 'Pam. Pamma, calm down. I'm immune. It's a long story, but I'm not going to become one of them. That's why I asked him to bite me. I knew the idea of me being *eaten* would scare Wolfe. *Calm down.*'

'Immune?' I knew I sounded like an idiot. I felt like an idiot. I didn't understand. 'Immune? To all this? To . . .' Wait. 'They said they had a vaccine.' I ducked out of Nora's grip and ran back to Isambard, pulling his head against my side. 'Then we can cure Issy!'

Nora was starting to tear up. 'No. It's too late for him. I'm so sorry. I should have just left the base and come for you. I should have just run away and *walked* back home. They wouldn't let me call anyone, or . . .'

'I should have fought Wolfe harder,' Bram said. The one-eyed zombie tilted his head in Bram's direction. Bram went silent.

'It's my fault,' Nora got out. Her voice was choked. 'Please forgive me.'

Forgive her?

Nora started to make her way closer. I shut my eyes and sobbed, 'I killed a woman. I killed her . . .'

'Miss Roe,' I heard Michael saying. 'There's no time for this.'

'They put me in jail for it, with whores and drunks! And then I killed a man with an arrow . . . and others . . . I chopped them up with an *axe*. I . . . I was covered in blood. My family is locked up. I started drinking to sleep, I . . . I was trying so hard to be you! I was trying to be *you!*'

I felt Nora's arms around my neck. 'Pam, I'm so sorry.'

'But then Issy was bitten, and I couldn't do anything for . . . I can't *do* anything for that. No one would listen to me! No one would listen to me!'

Nora was crying, now. 'Please, Pam . . .'

I collapsed against her. *'And I'm wearing pants!'* I keened, before fully breaking down.

She held me. I don't know how long I cried, but she didn't leave my side. I felt Isambard's fingers in mine, after a time, and distantly realized that it was him who ought to be breaking down, him who ought to be comforted. But he didn't make a peep.

The zombies concentrated on flying the ship. They talked amongst themselves, but I couldn't hear anything they said. Bram kept looking at Nora. I couldn't read anything in his expression. His eyes weren't clear.

Zombies. There were zombies here, not five feet away from us. I had to pull myself together. No matter what Nora said, they were different from us. They were dead. They were cannibalistic. Surely, we shouldn't trust them. Maybe they'd done something to her, brainwashed her, to make her think they were safe.

But my little brother was becoming one, now.

I turned my head to look at him. He didn't look well. There were dark spots on his skin, like black veins. I reached out and stroked a hand through his hair. He looked at me with tired red eyes.

'Are you OK?' I whispered.

Isambard shook his head. 'I don't feel good,' he admitted.

Nora wiped at her eyes. 'We need to get him help,' I said, as I lifted a hand to my own.

'You're right.' Michael straightened up. He and Vespertine were still leaning against the wall, unwilling to step any closer to the zombies.

'You'll do it, then?' Vespertine asked. She seemed to be sharing some sort of understanding with him that I didn't. Her expression was dark.

Michael's hand disappeared behind Vespertine for a moment, as if he were touching her in a most uncouth way. Before I could question this strange occurrence, or even blush, he stepped closer to me. He was holding the crossbow. 'Are you sure you're not infected?' he asked Nora.

'Yes,' she said. She sounded as confused as I felt.

'OK,' he said. He turned to me. 'Miss Roe, stand up.'

'Why?'

'No!' Bram was with us in two beats. He took Nora's hand and hauled her up to her feet. 'Give me the bow, Allister.'

I realized what he meant to do.

'No!' I screamed.

'Pamela?' Issy asked me, panic creeping into his voice. I pulled him closer to me, shielding him with my body.

Michael leveled the bow at us. 'I'm sorry, Miss Roe,' he said. His voice was hollow. 'Let go of him. Move behind me.'

'He's going to become one of them, Roe!' Vespertine said. 'You can't let him live! He might turn on us!'

'He's my brother!' I cried. 'He's still alive! He's not evil!'

'Allister, you moron!' Nora screamed. 'Stop aiming it at them!'

Bram grabbed Michael by the back of his jacket and spun him around. He delivered a blow with his fist right to Michael's face, breaking his nose and rendering him unconscious. He tossed him aside, and he landed limply on the floor of the ship, the crossbow skittering out of his hands.

Vespertine leapt upon the opportunity. She abandoned the wall and ran for the bow, but Bram's long legs got him there first. His boot landed atop the crossbow just as she bent down to retrieve it. 'I don't hit girls, unless they try to hit me first,' he warned her.

Vespertine went white as new milk. She slowly retreated, her eyes on the big dead boy. She stumbled a bit, and Renfield, the nearest zombie, thrust an arm out to steady her. She shrieked and backed away from him.

'My lady, be still,' he told her. He looked injured by the slight.

'Get away from me!' Vespertine curled her dainty little hands into fists and held them before her face.

Renfield opened his mouth to say something else, but then went still. He seemed to be captivated by something he saw on her hand.

'Get back here, Ren,' Bram said, breaking the spell.

Renfield looked curiously into Vespertine's face. 'Harpist one-two-three?'

Vespertine backed against the wall again and pressed her fists to her throat. After a few moments, during which her eyes roved madly over the body of the zombie in front of her, she ventured a very small, 'Zboy sixty-nine?'

'I knew it!' He pointed triumphantly at Bram. 'I recognize her rings!'

'What?' Vespertine asked breathlessly.

Renfield grinned, and said, adjusting his glasses, 'You see?

Death really isn't that bad – just a minor inconvenience. I would never have had such a lovely chess partner while alive. Miss Mink, it is an honor to meet you. You know, that bishop strategy you often use is incredibly devious, and I was just about to try a new way to block it before we were so rudely interrupted by the end of the world.'

Vespertine stared incredulously at him as he blathered on. 'Mother was right. Only weirdoes hang out on the AetherNet.'

'Pam.' Nora was speaking again. 'Look. We're going to meet up with the other zombies on the docks. Did they come on one of the big boats, do you think, Bram?'

'Sure of it,' he told her, as he picked up the crossbow and snapped it in two.

'We can take Isambard there. We'll figure out what to do. Maybe they can take him back to Z Base.'

'OK,' I said, relieved. 'OK. There'll be a boat there, Issy. It's going be OK.'

He nodded, but he didn't let go of me.

Renfield slowed the *Alice* down as we reached the eastern side of the city. Bram passed control of the steering wheel along to Coalhouse, and I felt the ship lowering.

Nora climbed the steps to take a look outside. 'Come look at this, Pam!' she called down.

'Stay here,' I said to Isambard. He was starting to surrender to his own weariness, and he didn't argue.

I joined Nora up top, and leaned over the railing of the ship, marveling at what I saw. There was now a full-fledged war going on in the streets below us – zombies throwing themselves at our troops, only to encounter a hailstorm of bullets. Citizens who, like us, had taken shelter on the rooftops of the city, waved to our airship as it passed; we were close enough that I could see a few of them recording the fighting with their high-end mobile phones. Further east, a column of soldiers in black was assembling on one of the docks. A massive wave of soldiers in New Victorian red was marching the other way, into the city – the living relieving the dead. There were more ships in the water than I'd ever seen before – freighters, ironclads, galleons.

'Wow,' I whispered.

'I think we're going to be all right,' Nora said, with a grin. Her expression faltered, and she reached out to slide her hand over my shoulder. 'I am truly sorry, Pamela. For everything.'

I tore my eyes from the scene below and looked at my best friend. 'It's all right,' I decided. 'I just . . . did what I had to. Just like you did.'

Bram joined us a moment later. What caught his attention was not the action or the soldiers, but the ships in the bay. 'That's the *Christine*. That's the ship we brought you back to base on, Nora.'

'You'll have to tell me more about that night, some day,' she said. 'I mean, it was an important event in my life, and I don't remember a thing.'

Bram chuckled. 'The *Christine*'s outfitted with a med bay. We can take Isambard there, Miss Roe. There's got to be a doctor on board. We never go far without our docs.'

'Can I go on the boat with him?' I asked.

'I don't see why not.' Bram continued to look out across the water, his attention distantly focused. 'Might be the safest place for you.'

Nora reached out to take Bram's hand. I found myself surprised by this. Had that horrible man on the com spoken true?

The airship eventually came to rest on one of the wide stone docks designed to accept big shipments from overseas freighters. A living mustachioed officer in red came to greet us, driving a little open-topped electric coach and accompanied by two soldiers. All three stepped out, reaching for their rifles as they did so. 'Captain Griswold?' the officer called.

Bram kicked out the plank and moved down, saluting once he got to the bottom. 'That's me.'

The officer stared at Bram in wonderment for only a second, before cocking and lifting his gun, aiming it at Bram's head. The soldiers, fear far more evident on their faces, did similarly. Bram stopped where he was and showed the men the palms of his hands. Nora gasped and started for the gang-plank, and I reached out and snagged her sleeve. The last thing I needed was for her to be caught in the crossfire.

Despite the fact that he was clearly threatening Bram, a well-bred veneer of politeness settled over the officer's face. 'A precaution only, I assure you. Colonel Edmund Lopez, New Victorian Army. My men and I are here to make sure that the red lights don't get into trouble.'

'By all means.' Bram sized Lopez up. 'Did our men get in touch with the army, by chance?'

'Yes. We know about the situation with Captain Wolfe, and the main army medical facilities are currently downloading information about the potential vaccine from your base.'

'Thank goodness,' Nora sighed, as she pulled her sleeve out of my grasp and ran down the plank. I followed her.

Bram nodded. 'And the order's still out to kill us, I take it?'

The colonel didn't hesitate. 'Yes. The violent dead can be targeted at any time, as they are clearly enemy combatants, but your people are in the clear until oh-six-hundred hours. Honestly? We're here to make sure that the living soldiers follow that order and don't try to take you out sooner. Consider us your guards.'

'I see.' If Bram was disappointed or scared, he didn't show it. Instead, he pointed to the *Christine*. I stepped up behind him. 'She still a Z ship, then, or did your guys take her back?'

Lopez looked in the direction he indicated. 'She is. She's

been ordered to stay in the port, to be used as a hospital. The *Erika* is on route for the same purpose.'

'Fantastic.' Bram gestured to me. 'We've got a boy who was recently bit. Non-hostile and doing well, but he needs a doctor. This is his sister. Their family is locked up in the basement of a church, and they'd prefer to stay near the city.'

Lopez crooked a black brow, and looked at me. 'He's not a red light?'

'No. But hopefully he's going to be.'

Lopez thought it over, before addressing me directly. 'The order stands. At oh-six-hundred, unless the order is rescinded, your brother will be exterminated.' His stern expression cracked, and for a moment, his eyes were filled with regret. 'I'm sorry to put it so forcefully, Miss, but you have to understand that.'

'It's not oh-six-hundred yet.' Bram looked back at me. 'Do you want to risk it, or do you want to stay with us? The only medical attention we're equipped to give him is a bullet if he doesn't wake up right.'

No matter the location, it seemed that our only choice was a bullet. But I still had ammunition of my own left. I shrugged my shoulders forcefully, causing the bow strapped to my full quiver to knock about. 'I'll risk it, if Issy will.'

Lopez hit a button on the dashboard of his coach, and a bucket seat flipped open. By the time it was down, he had once more donned a prim, professional demeanor. 'I can escort you, then.'

I heaved out a massive sigh. 'Let me ask him. It should be his choice.'

I climbed back onto the ship. Isambard had made his way out of the hold, and was watching the scene unfolding across the docks. He turned to face me when he heard me approaching. He looked like he didn't expect good news.

'It's up to you, Issy,' I said. 'They can take us out to that ship over there to get you looked at, if you want.'

'We can stay there?' he asked. He looked like he was going to throw up.

'Yes.' I decided to be honest with him. 'They might try to kill you, at some point, depending on how things go. They've not retracted the order to exterminate the zombies, yet. But I figure, we have a few hours, and I can still fight. I won't let them take you without a fight. This is the best chance we have, right now. We could run, but then I don't know what will happen to you.'

Issy looked away again. 'I don't deserve that much thought, you know,' he said miserably. 'After all the things I've done to you, after all the times I've run my mouth off . . .'

'Yes you do,' I told him firmly. 'You're my brother.'

The one-eyed zombie climbed out of the hold. He shifted the gun on his back, and bowed. 'Name's Coalhouse. I'll go with you, if you want. I can fight too.'

For some reason, this offer caused my eyes to start stinging again. 'OK. Thank you. We'd like that.'

Isambard tugged on his vest, rolling it between his fingers. 'If we ran, I don't think I could get very far.' He bent his head and wiped at his sweaty brow with the hem of his shirt. His movements were palsied, like his muscles wouldn't completely obey him. 'So I guess we get on the boat, then.'

I nodded. I reached out and stroked his damp hair, before moving to take his hand and guide him down the gangplank.

When we got off the ship Nora nearly tackled me to the ground, wrapping her arms around me and pressing her face into my neck. 'Good luck,' she whispered.

I hugged her tightly back. 'Same to you.'

Coalhouse shook Bram's hand. 'Mind if I go with 'em, Cap?'

Bram smiled thinly. 'No. Not at all.' He suddenly seemed to remember something, and added, 'Take the other two living people with you.'

'No.' Michael appeared at the top of the gangplank. He was holding a woman's lacy handkerchief over his nose, and

Vespertine was helping him to stay upright. They walked down the plank gingerly. 'No, I'll say goodbye to you here, if you don't mind. I don't care to be attacked again.'

'Oh, shut up, Allister,' Nora said, glaring at him. 'You were a danger to yourself and everyone else. Bram did the right thing.'

'Bram?' Michael paused at the end of the plank, shrugging off Vespertine's arm. He took a few shaky steps towards Nora. 'On a first-name basis, are you?'

'Yes, we are.'

'Huh.' Michael looked contemptuously up at Bram, who eyed him right back. He returned his eyes to Nora, and bowed. 'I look forward to seeing you again, dear Miss Dearly. Perhaps we can discuss the lengths I went to to preserve your good name, then.'

'*What* did you call me?' Nora demanded. 'What lengths?'

Michael didn't respond. Instead, he found me in the crowd, and bowed. 'Thank you for the . . . interesting time, Miss Roe.'

I watched him with suspicion, as I slid my arm across my brother's shoulders. He'd tried to shoot him. He'd tried to *kill* him. 'Don't you dare speak to me. You are nothing to me now, do you understand? If I never see you again, I shall die happy.'

Michael rubbed the hanky at the dried blood crusted on his top lip. His nose was a horrible shade of purple. 'Likewise, Miss Roe.' He laughed shortly. '*Now* I am nothing to you? Don't tell me that you thought I was *something*.'

'Huh?' Nora asked of the crowd at large.

'I have no idea,' Vespertine replied. 'But . . . ah . . . not that I'm on your side now, or anything, but you haven't exactly got a lot of time for drama of this quality.'

I began to realize that something was terribly wrong. 'What?' I asked, numbly.

'Surely you must know that I've had my sights set on Miss Dearly for years, now,' Michael said. 'You didn't honestly think I'd have anything to do with you, did you?'

Isambard squirmed like a cornered rat. 'Pam, you're hurting me.'

I gripped him tighter still, anger starting to replace all my fear and stress. The winter air around me started to feel incredibly warm. 'But . . . but you've been helping me! My family! You vouched for me to get me out of jail!'

Michael shrugged. 'You're Miss Dearly's friend. Of course I would be kind to you, to please her . . . well, it started out as kindness. Then I was trying to clean up the mess you made to preserve Miss Dearly's reputation. I always figured that once she was mine, I could convince her to drop her less suitable friends . . . that would be you, of course. But until then, I didn't mind slumming.'

I felt my jaw working, but no words came out. My entire body felt hot, flushed with humiliation. I'd seen something that wasn't there. I'd deluded myself. My family had bought it. My mother had *entertained* him. She'd made me sick with her predictions and seriousness, when there'd been nothing there to be serious about! I was a moron – a complete moron. A loser of the highest caliber.

Then I remembered that I'd not slept for twenty-four hours, and had spent all that time running and hiding and killing zombies. I stopped being a loser, at least for a moment. I became Pamela Roe, Disenfranchised and Cheated and Embarrassed Zombie Hunting Queen with a Potentially Undead Brother and Parents Who Thought She Was Insane Who Deserved a *Little* Happiness for the Love of All That is Right and Just.

I stepped free of Isambard and shoved Michael in the chest. I caught him off guard. He tumbled to the dock, and then rolled into the water with a splash.

'*I hope there are zombie sharks in there and they bite you and you die!*' I screamed.

'What in blazes?' Lopez asked, craning his head back. He lowered his rifle and took his finger off the trigger. The other members of Bram's zombie crew appeared on the deck of the ship above us, peering overboard at the man thrashing in the water.

Nora and Vespertine just stared at me.

I turned around and pushed Isambard up into the little coach. '*Get in and drive!*' I bellowed at Lopez as I climbed up beside him. Coalhouse hurried through the crowd and hopped in after me, squeezing me to the side with his bulk.

The colonel's eyes widened, and he shared a look of confusion with the two soldiers – but all three got into the coach. We left Michael attempting to pull himself out of the icy water, staining the stone dock gray with it.

'Pam,' Issy attempted, voice high with fear. 'I can tell you, from this side of the fence . . . you really need to calm down.'

'I will shoot you in the face if you say one more word to me,' I fumed.

'So noted.'

'I am so glad that I am an only child,' Coalhouse remarked quietly.

Chapter Thirty-seven

Bram

I hauled Allister out of the drink and got him and Mink walking towards the living soldiers. After a few uncertain steps, both started running.

Then I got back to business.

I was scared out of my wits, but I knew I had to keep my cool. Lopez had given me no sign that he'd regret carrying out the extermination order. Then again, he'd been a very proper, crisp sort of New Victorian gentleman. Probably kept his emotions to himself. I found myself glad that Nora wasn't like that.

God, Nora.

I didn't know where to turn for help, which meant that I could only turn inward. Right now, I was in charge, and I had to do what was best for everyone involved. We had to get to Dr Dearly. We had to help get New London under control. We just had to keep going and hope that whoever was in charge up top got his act together or started receiving pro-zombie messages from a higher power – living or divine. It really didn't matter, at this point.

'What's our next move?' Nora asked.

I looked over the six score zombies amassed on the other dock, and realized that there was no way the *Black Alice* could carry all of them.

'How many additional men can we get on this thing?' I asked Renfield, as he climbed down to join us.

Ren glanced over the crowd, and did some quick calculations involving his fingers. 'Forty, perhaps.' He shook his head. 'Wait . . . no. With the governor gone, on that long a trip, I wouldn't risk more than . . . thirty. The weight will increase the . . . oh, cripes, I'm sorry . . .'

'Apologize later,' I said. 'It's probably my fault. Apparently I'm destined to *never* have enough men.'

Nora looked unsure. 'Only thirty?'

'Let's go with it. We're running out of time. Tom, Chas, go talk to the nice red-coated people. Tell them that we need another load of coal. If the *Christine*'s staying here, we could empty her bunkers. Try not to scare them too badly.' Both saluted and started off. 'Renfield, prepare the ship. Nora, stay with him. I'm gonna go ask for recruits.'

'What about the others?' Ren turned in my direction. 'We can't leave them here to—'

'Die. I know.' With that, I began to make my way over to the other members of Company Z.

When they caught sight of me, the men straightened their rows and saluted. I found myself disheartened by this. I didn't exactly have good news to share.

'Captain Griswold!' Ben said, lowering his hand. 'Sir, word is that an order has gone out to kill us!'

'You've heard right,' I said. I walked between the rows, getting into the midst of my fellow zombies, so that everyone could hear me. 'We've got 'til oh-six-hundred. I'm stupid enough to hold out hope that perhaps the order will be cancelled, but those of you who are less trusting than I am had better come to your own conclusions.'

Around me, I heard muffled cursing, threats against anyone who might try it – a few sounds of fear. I let the men have their fear, for a moment, before continuing. 'There's still work to be done, though. I need thirty men for a mission to Bolivia. Dr Dearly's been found, and he needs a ride home.'

This news got a cheer out of them at least. I had no trouble getting my recruits. Ben was the first one to raise his hand. Along with him, I picked zombies that I knew to be strong and relatively healthy.

'And what will the rest of us do?' a woman named Hagens asked, as I chose my last man. She was tall and angular, her cheekbones poking out through the skin of her face.

'I would take every last one of you, if I could,' I said. 'Unfortunately, that's just not possible.'

'So what – we stay here? We stay here and twiddle our thumbs and wait to get shot?' she countered. 'Are you seriously telling us that?'

'I been watching the red coats. We could take 'em,' another zombie pointed out.

'They're here to protect you, Franco,' I said. 'They're here to protect you from their own.'

'C'mon, you don't buy that, Gris – you're smart.'

If I was so smart, why didn't I have the answer? As I looked at my fellow zombies, I understood what Wolfe had meant when he'd raved about 'loyalty to my species'. I felt it. The idea that they would be singled out, hunted down, with no chance to fight back, made what little blood I had left in my body boil.

'Captain Griswold?'

I turned around. Lopez was pulling his little carriage to a stop at the edge of the crowd, right next to the men I'd selected to accompany the crew on the ship. This time, he was alone. He hopped out and folded his hands behind his back, his posture so perfectly aligned that if someone had told me he'd swallowed his rifle, I might've been tempted to believe it. My men, to their credit, did nothing to threaten him.

'Yes, Colonel?' I asked.

Lopez stepped forward, his hazel eyes serious. 'I just wanted to let you know, Captain Griswold, that I have been ordered not to let any more of your men get onto the boats. The *Erika* will be with us shortly.'

'All right,' I said, for lack of anything better to say.

Lopez continued to stand there. 'I just thought you should know,' he pointed out, slowly. 'Seeing as no other restrictions have been placed on your movements, I thought I had best make things absolutely clear for you.'

Franco finally growled. 'Are you sayin' our cap is stupid?'

Confused, I looked into Lopez's eyes. *So?*

It took me a second to realize what he was *really* telling me, and why he hadn't brought anyone with him.

I approached the colonel swiftly, the men stepping aside to make way for me. 'What if my men wanted to go back into the city?' I asked.

This question elicited a few grumblings from the zombies around me. Lopez ignored them. 'Well, seeing as I have been instructed to protect the red lights, but not to unduly hinder their movements . . . aside from preventing them from boarding the boats . . . I suppose we'd be going into the city together.'

The muttering around us died down. Hagens spoke up again. 'And why would we want to do that, Captain? Seeing as the living want us put down, like a bunch of rabid dogs?'

'Because you've not been put down yet,' I said, without taking my eyes from Lopez. 'Because you still have time. Because you might be dead, but you're still human.'

'Because anything has to be better than waiting here, watching the clock tick down,' Lopez said, his deep voice infused with purpose. 'Now, let me be abundantly clear – it will be our duty to find you if you try to hide, to stop you if you try to get away. I stress this because . . . rumor has it you're a clever lot.'

I laughed lightly. Lopez smiled beneath his dark mustache. He then bowed from the waist with a flourish, a movement I'd never seen carried out with such aplomb, even by Renfield. The man had to have come from a high-bred background. 'Ladies and gentlemen. Shall I ready my men?'

I looked to the crowd. It was up to them.

'I've got family in there,' another woman said. Her speech was slow and slurred from a mouth injury. 'I should make sure they're OK. They ain't seen me like this, but . . . I owe it to them.'

'The whole area's country 'round the city. We get through

413

the city . . . take out a few baddies along the way . . . hunker down,' Franco said, reevaluating the situation.

'This is our only choice,' Hagens verified with me, her expression cold and distant.

'Pretty much,' I told her.

Hagens unslung her rifle. 'Then let's do it.'

The zombies around her roared in agreement.

I looked to Lopez. 'Thank you,' I said.

Lopez nodded smoothly. 'As far as I understand, you are technically part of the army. Therefore, despite our differences, I have an obligation to treat you and your men with as much dignity and respect as I possibly can. If your men attempt to escape, mine will attempt to stop them.' He looked out across the water. 'But at least you will die on your feet.'

I understood this code perfectly. 'I don't know why you're helping us, but a chance is all we ask for.' I extended my hand. Lopez hesitated for a moment, but shook it. 'If we survive all this, I'll owe you.'

'Port,' he said, with a nervous laugh. 'I can always be paid in port. I'll need it, after tonight.'

When the soldiers were packed below deck and we'd taken in a new load of coal, brought to us from the *Christine* by a battered little tugboat, we flew off again.

My men crowded around me for information. It wasn't long before we were talking shop, and I'd lost track of Nora. They brought me a bit more intel, but not much. As far as we could figure, we were headed into a shooting gallery situation – lots of Grays, lots of targets. Potentially, not all of them were as well-maintained as the ones that'd been sent after Nora, and *that* was saying something. None of us wanted to get our hopes up, especially with only a handful of us going into battle, but it was kind of hard not to.

Of course, hanging over our heads was the prospect of extermination. The men who'd made up the first flank reported that they'd been able to clear a handful of city blocks before being recalled for the current mission, which I found heartening. Maybe the army would take that into consideration when it came time to cap us all.

A few hours into the trip I located Nora by the sound of her voice. She was seated next to Chas, a com unit to her ear. From what I could hear, she was talking to her friend again. 'No, no, I'm not the least bit interested in him! Ew!'

Was she talking about me? Had I done something to upset her? I'd tried to include her, tried not to talk down to her, tried to . . .

'I mean, I don't even *like* guys with light hair, for one thing! Never mind the fact that he'd knock me into a coma every time he opened his mouth. Oh, and that he's a hateful, violent half-wit. Yeah, that's prime courtship material, right there.'

It wasn't me. Yes.

Wait. Was this that Allister fellow?

I drifted over and sat next to her. She looked at me and offered the com unit. 'Bram, tell Pamma that there's no way I would want Michael Allister, ever.'

I ran this through my 'girl talk' translator, and boiled it down to, 'I could eat him, if either of you'd like. Seems like it might be the easiest thing to do.'

'Yes, please,' I heard Pam respond.

Nora rolled her eyes and took the unit back. 'Forget him. How's Issy? Still alive? Oh, no, don't freak out, the valve thing is normal, I guess.' She winced, and pulled the unit away from her ear. I could hear Pam's voice buzzing on the other end. 'Look, you need to start working on redefining your entire concept of "normal". Things'll seem a lot brighter then, I promise.'

I shut my eyes and leaned back against the wall of the ship. A few yards away, I could hear Renfield complaining to Tom about the fact that Mink hadn't said goodbye to him, and wondering what the meaning behind this might be.

'The hidden, secret meaning of that,' Tom said, voice tight, 'is that she *didn't say goodbye*. For the love of all that is holy, most girls do not speak in code. Most girls are what we like to term "sane".'

'He speaks from experience,' Chas noted. She was sitting on a crate with her legs akimbo, fiddling with her gun.

'Look, Pam, I'm serious. It's OK. Issy has a few hours yet. I'll call you again once we're done with the sick freak who has Dad. Ah . . .'

I didn't open my eyes, but I could sense she was looking at me. 'Oh, no, he's definitely a freak. You can call him that.'

'I love you too. OK, bye.' I heard her press the button. 'How much longer?'

'Few hours,' I informed her. She didn't say anything. I opened my eyes, and found her pushing down the sleeve of her blouse to scrutinize the bite I'd given her. Suddenly embarrassed, I sat up. 'Nora, I'm really—'

'It looks fine,' she interrupted. 'I should bandage it up when this is all over, but it's fine. I figure if what Dr Chase said is right, you've got a cleaner mouth than most living people.'

Sighing, I said, 'I mean it. I've never bitten anyone. You're kind of . . . my first. So I'm really, *really* sorry. At least let me keep that much of my humanity . . . let me apologize to the only person I'll ever bite. Hopefully. And accept it. OK?'

Nora smiled. 'OK. I accept your apology.'

It hit me, then, that she wasn't half as disgusted as she should be. 'Are you . . . *sure* you're OK with it?'

She pulled her sleeve up, and shrugged. She was quiet for a minute, before asking, 'Did you enjoy it?'

I decided to tell the truth. 'Yes. You wouldn't believe how good you taste. I don't think I could even describe it.'

She laughed. 'Good? Like filet mignon, good? Or like . . . candy, good?'

I loved her.

'You should catch a nap, if you can,' I told her. I was worried that fatigue might be responsible for her calm acceptance of my human taste test. I hoped not, but it was likely.

She took this advice, and settled her head on my shoulder. I sent my hand in search of hers, and found her doing similarly. This time, I let myself fully enjoy it – the fact that I had already come to care for her, and that she obviously cared for me. The fact that I could touch her, and she wouldn't rebuff it. The fact that she sought me out. It was the simplest, purest thing I've ever experienced.

If I'd come by nothing else easily in my life, I *had* been given that. I really couldn't ask for anything more.

It was the slowing of the ship that woke me. Nora was asleep, bundled against my side. Renfield had his glasses low on his nose, and was keeping a close eye on the engine equipment. 'All right . . . yes.' He flipped open his pocket watch. 'ETA fifteen minutes.'

I cleared my throat, and reached out to lift Nora's chin with a fingertip. She came to, slowly, her eyelids heavy. 'We're almost there,' I whispered. She sat back, rubbing at her cheek with her knuckles, and I stood up. 'OK, men, listen up,' I said, for the room at large.

What little noise there had been faded away. Eyes turned to me. I took a moment to savor the sensation of impending disaster, before telling it to get lost.

'Things are pretty messed up right about now,' I began. 'What started as a weird phenomenon, something rare, is quickly building into what we might affectionately call "The Apocalypse." But there's hope. For those of you who've not been told, as of a few hours ago a possible vaccine has been found. We all owe a debt to the man who made *that* happen, and that's why we're going in to get him.' The men hooted in agreement. I waited for everyone to quiet down again before driving the point home. 'He's the one who grabbed us all at a *really* bad moment in our lives and made it seem like it was going to be OK. I can't speak for any of you, but I'm willing to go down permanently for him for that, if I have to.' There were nods all around, and I could see Nora's eyes starting to shine.

'So, let's do it. Shoot anything that isn't Dearly. Get him back on this ship. That's it. As soon as he's out, it's cleanup time. You know the drill. And after that, if we haven't heard that the extermination order's been cancelled – we run like hell. We hide. We don't go down easy. Because we're good people, and we deserve to live.' This statement occasioned a shout of triumph. Renfield smiled at me from across the hold.

I could have gone on for hours, but they didn't need that. I threw my jacket on again and belted down. Around me, my troops did the same. Nora threaded her way through them to my side. She didn't say anything, although I'm sure we were both thinking it. If, by some wild toss of the dice, we actually tried to make a go at it, we'd always be thinking it. Her dark eyes were glistening, but clear.

'I'm going to start bringing her down,' Renfield said. 'This is going to be a little tricky. Please expect mild turbulence.'

'Can we go up top?' Nora asked him.

'Uh, I wouldn't recommend it.'

Nora started up the steps anyway. I followed her. The sudden contrast between the darkened interior of the ship and the morning sunlight reflecting off of the desert of salt below took a few moments to get used to.

'Look,' I heard Nora say.

My vision cleared, and I saw it – the ramshackle base, the undead legions, like plates of lichen on the white bark of a birch tree. 'There's hundreds of them,' I said, astonished. We might not make it out of this one, after all.

'I take it I'm staying on the ship.' Nora's voice was hard. She gripped the railing as the ship swayed.

'Hell yes, you're staying on the ship.' I unbuckled the holsters over my pistols. 'If necessary, just take off. I'll leave behind another man to help if you have to.'

She nodded, and reached out to take my hand again. I turned to look at her fully. I didn't want to say it, but I felt like I should. I'd never had a chance to say it to my sisters, to my mother, and I'd always regretted it. 'Just in case,' I said, leaning down.

For once, the Laz remained respectful. It didn't want her. *I* wanted her.

Knitting my fingers into her curls, I kissed her forehead. I limited myself to one word, this time. 'Goodbye.'

Her hands slid up to my shoulders, and she turned her head to press her mouth against my cheek. Her lips felt like a branding iron – I wished they were. 'No,' she said, stubborn as ever, though her voice wavered. 'Good luck. And thank you.'

I drew back and smiled at her. She smiled in return, although two tears had trailed their way down her cheeks, meeting in a point in the hollow of her throat.

And with that, I turned and left her, her form silhouetted by the sunlight, made even smaller.

Renfield slammed the ship down hard, rutting her into the salt. Nora fell onto her knees. I gripped the railing to keep myself steady, but it was exactly the opening that we needed. The zombies were pumped, and they exploded out of the ship like angry red ants, the blaring light of the sun only irritating them *more*. Still half-blinded by it, they kicked down the plank and stormed out before I could even tell them to. I caught Ben by the sleeve and yelled, 'Stay with Miss Dearly, in case she has to leave before the rest of us!'

A look of deep disappointment wrinkled his features, but he saluted and said, 'Sir!'

That done, I threw myself into the fray.

By now, the enemy soldiers knew we were there. There were perhaps ten times as many of them as there were of us, and the first wave that came our way appeared strong and healthy enough. Only a few were equipped with weapons, though. The majority seemed ready to rely upon their teeth and nails, and beyond them lay a sea of the weak and the crawling.

Tom and Chas found me. Over the beat of gunfire and the screams of the enraged double-dying, I shouted, 'Focus on finding Dearly! He's probably in one of the buildings!'

'Right!' Chas said.

As we fought our way into the middle of the action, two things struck me as very odd. First of all, I could see strong enemy zombies fleeing towards the eastern horizon – defecting from the cause. Secondly, some of the zombies in front of us were running *away* from us, towards the big building in the center of the compound. Were they going to arm themselves? I pulled up short and picked a few off; Tom did the same.

'Might be weapons inside! We should find a way to take the whole thing down!' I called to my team members.

'Wait.' Chas had just lifted her gun when she spotted something through her sights. 'Wait, they're running at Dearly!'

I stopped shooting and zeroed in, my muscles tightening in fear. She was right. At the door of the big building stood Dearly with a man in a gray uniform and patterned scarf. Must be Averne.

'I got him,' I said, my finger stroking the trigger.

Dearly reached out for Averne, shouting at him. Averne turned and headed back into his hut, running like the coward he was – Dearly wasn't strong enough to stop him. I noticed then that he was missing a leg.

A zombie shambled into my line of fire before I could pull off a round. I swore loudly, and began running towards the building. No way was Averne going to have another moment alone with Dearly. No *way* was he going to have another chance to hurt him.

Tom's position let him take the shot. I heard the retort of the rifle, heard his cry of success. The bullet entered Averne's head right at the place where his skull joined his neck, and he went down mid-step, like an automaton suddenly and completely devoid of power. Dearly yelled something, and hobbled into the building.

Tom and Chas ran after me. We downed the dead that were still in pursuit of Dearly, clotting in the doorway. I could hear Dearly screaming as I got closer, but I didn't understand what he was saying until I was in the actual building with him, Tom and Chas filling the doorway with their bodies, keeping the way clear outside. It was all done in a rush, and yet, we seemed to be moving in slow motion.

'That wasn't Averne!' Dearly was yelling, jabbing his crutch at the ground. 'That wasn't Averne! That was Henry! *Henry!*'

'What?' I asked, uncomprehending.

Dearly pointed to a living man bound in the corner. 'We captured Averne! Henry put on his clothes so that his soldiers wouldn't suspect anything!'

I looked to the uniformed man who lay, dead, on the salt. I slowly approached him and removed his scarf. Beneath it was a zombie with burned flesh, his eyes unseeing.

'Damn it all,' I breathed.

Tom glanced back, and I saw a number of reactions play out on his face – sudden understanding, and guilt, and grim acceptance. 'Bram, take over!' He stepped out of the doorway, and I filled it before I could think of what he meant to do. 'Come on, Doc. I'm taking you to your daughter.'

'Nora? Nora's *here*?' Dearly asked. His limbs were trembling, his eyes wild with grief.

'Yep, pretty as a rose and waiting to see you,' Tom grunted. Without stopping to ask for permission, he scooped Dearly up over his shoulders. He took a few moments to steady his passenger, before looking at us from beneath his heavy brows. 'Got me covered?'

'Yeah,' I said. My eyes fell on the fallen, innocent man known as Henry again, as I stepped out of the doorway. What had we done?

'OK, then.' Tom paused at the entrance, and kissed Chas. 'See you when you get home.'

'Don't wait up,' she said, voice filled with forced cheerfulness, as she clicked in another clip.

When he saw an opening, Tom left the cover of the building. The fighting was still going strong, our men being rushed from multiple directions. Tom ran as fast as his size and burden would allow, keeping his head down. Chas and I resumed our positions, taking out those who had the bright idea of targeting him.

He couldn't outrun bullets, though.

I don't know who hit him. Our side, accidentally? Those of Averne's men who still had guns, and the ability to fire them? When he was within fifty feet of the ship I saw his legs buckle, saw him teeter and collapse with Dearly still atop him. Chas screamed his name, and I had to catch her and hold her back. She was prepared to drop her gun and run for him.

'*Tom! Tom!*' she cried out.

'You run out there, they'll get you, too!' I yelled. '*Think!* Help me shoot!' But she was in hysterics, and I couldn't let go of her. I could only watch as Renfield and Ben leaped off the ship and helped Dearly aboard. Nora was waiting for him on the top deck, and I swear, it was all I could do not to go running out there myself. She needed to get *down*, she needed to get out of here . . .

Ben jumped off the ship again once Dearly was on board, and helped Tom to his feet. Tom shuffled with him up the gangplank. Some feeling returned to my arms, and I shook Chastity to get her attention.

'Tom's fine! They didn't get him in the head! Look, Chas, he's fine!'

She looked, and went limp in my arms. 'Oh, thank God, thank God . . .'

We watched together as the ship took off. I could have burst into song. Chas regained some strength and looked up into my face, laughing a little, relieved. 'That's one for . . .' Her expression crumpled, and she shouted, 'Behind you!'

I turned just as Averne landed his first blow on me, sending my rifle skipping across the ground. He'd freed himself from his restraints and stood before us, body twisted and terrible with anger, as if his skin might snap with the mass of it welling up from his soul.

With a barbaric cry, he launched himself at me. I couldn't pull my pistols out in time, and we ended up going hand-to-hand. I landed several punches, and he got one on me that was good enough to split my lip.

'*Monster!*' he screamed, spittle flying from his lips. 'I'll kill you! I'll kill every last one of you! You'll all burn in the hell the earth has become!'

'I'm a Punk!' I yelled at him. 'I'm a Punk! Listen to me. The royals didn't do this to us!'

'Wolfe told me they did!' Averne advanced on me again. 'They made you what you are now!'

'They have the vaccine!' I said, as I ducked back and forth, like a boxer preparing for a blow. 'Wolfe lied to you – he just wanted it for his own glory! But they have it now, and it's going to be all right!' I looked to the door. 'Chas! I could use some help, here!'

She was staring out the door. 'I hear planes.'

Averne went for my throat, and I struggled to get him off. 'Transport!'

'Transport?' She stepped through the door, out into the sunlight.

'Chas!' I yelled.

An explosion outside drowned out my voice.

Chas stumbled back in, her hands catching the doorway. 'They're firebombing us! They're not here to get us, they're here to kill us! The order's gone out!'

Averne lashed out at me again. 'You're a fool!'

I took a page from Tom's book and rushed at his lower body, catching him in the chest and sending him flying back across the room. He landed upon a pile of clothing and rags in the corner. I heard him screaming more obscenities; heard a faint tinkle of broken glass. Part of what looked like a test tube rolled towards my foot.

The world became fire, just as Averne'd predicted.

Chapter Thirty-eight

Nora

Despite Renfield's warnings, once I'd gotten my father set up comfortably upon the floor of the hold, I returned to the top deck.

I wasn't up to the task of speaking to him. Not yet.

I could barely see, at first, for the brightness of the sun and what the wind was doing to my hair. The fighting was still going on below, but I couldn't make out Bram amongst the others. We were rising fast and everything on the ground was becoming microscopic.

I could hear something, though.

Turning in the direction of the noise, shielding my eyes with one hand and tightening my hold on the railing with the other, I made out several specks on the horizon – planes. They must be coming to pick up Company Z after they were done – at least that's what I hoped they were there to do. I prayed that that's what they were there to do.

When they got closer, I saw that they were far too small for that.

They were bombers.

'No!' I screamed at them. 'Stop it! Stop it!'

'What's going on?' Tom hollered up through the door.

Fireballs started blooming up from the desert below. I pounded the railing and screamed incoherently.

The zombie known as Ben was soon at my side. When he saw what was going on, he pulled me into the belly of the ship by my skirt. I struggled against him, but I was no match for his strength.

'They're killing them!' I cried. Renfield stopped working on the engine.

'No,' my father said, sitting up. 'No.'

Ben went for a com unit. 'Ben Maza, to Z Comp. Someone, *please* come in!'

'No,' my father repeated, staring at the wall of the ship as if he could see through it.

'Someone come in *now*!' Ben shouted into the com.

'Mr Maza!' Salvez answered. He was absolutely panicked.

I ran over to Ben to look at the screen with him. Behind Salvez, I could see techs packing up. 'Who's with you?' Salvez asked.

'Dr Salvez, they're bombing them! They're firebombing them!' I punched Ben's arm for emphasis. He didn't seem to feel it.

Salvez rocked on his feet, but his expression didn't shift. 'The order went out at oh-six-hundred,' he said. 'We got in touch with General Patmore himself, an hour ago, pleaded with him, but . . . they put out the order anyway. There were planes sent to the coordinates your father provided, to eliminate Averne's army.'

'But the others are still down there!'

Salvez stared helplessly at me. 'They know.'

'What's going on?' Tom wasn't accepting it. 'What's going on?'

I didn't understand, at first. I mean, I literally *didn't understand*. I stood there, watching the com unit's screen, expectant and patient, even after Ben turned it off. I knew that if I only stood there long enough, someone would tell me differently. Ben took me by the arm and guided me away, and I went with him without protest – for surely, he would tell me differently?

But he couldn't.

I started to shake, deep in my bones. Ben got me to my father's side. My father reached out for me, but I ignored him. My mind now viewed him as somehow incomplete, incorrect. This was absurd, for he'd been all I wanted, all I'd dreamed of. But now, something else was missing. The picture was still not whole.

My knees gave out.

'Nora!' my father cried.

'Captain Griswold . . . Chastity . . . they're lost,' Renfield said, attempting to explain my actions. He sounded as if he didn't believe it, himself, and for an eternal second I let myself feel better. See? None of us accepted it, so it couldn't be true.

I felt my nose pressing to the wooden floor of the ship as I broke down.

We hid the airship in the jungle.

We didn't know what else to do.

When we'd gotten to Z Beta, the others had been waiting for us. They'd boarded the ship quickly, half of the base's equipment in tow. When we took off again, Samedi went to see to my father, and Beryl came over to see to me.

I didn't feel her arms around me. I didn't hear a word she said. That evening, after we'd touched down, I barely even remembered that she'd been there beside me.

There was a lot of arguing over the next few days. Constant arguing about where to go, how to get news without being spotted, how to get messages out that couldn't be traced back to us.

I didn't care.

I thought of him, and I thought of Pamela and her brother. I wondered if they were safe.

I wondered if I would ever know.

It was three days before I finally took my father to task.

In full view of Samedi, Isley, Chas's mom, and the rest of the surviving undead, I screamed my case at him. He bowed his head and took it.

'You killed my mother!' I said, as I slammed his wooden crutch into the wall. 'You lied to me! You didn't tell me *anything*. You let me think you were dead, that you were gone, that I was an *orphan*. And now, because of everything you were involved in, I will spend the rest of my life hiding in the outback, mourning the death of a man who was dead when I met him!'

'I'm sorry.' His voice sounded so small.

I said it. '*I hate you!*'

'I don't deserve any less.' He looked to Samedi, who couldn't meet his eyes. 'I don't. I'm sorry. I've done what I needed to carry on to accomplish . . . and now, if you want to leave me . . . Nora, if you want to *kill* me . . . it's your right. It's your right, and I wouldn't take it away from you for the world.'

'I don't want to kill you!' I sat down, my knees up, my arms around my head. 'You're all I have left!'

'I love you, Nora,' he said, voice cracking. 'I love you. I didn't want you to be touched by this horror. Why else do you think we kept mum . . . all of us? Why else do you think it became the enormous secret it did? Why should anyone be touched by this horror?'

I'd been physically touched by it. The bite Bram'd given me ached every time I thought of him.

'I love you too,' I sobbed into my skirt. 'I can't lose anyone else. I can't lose anyone else.'

My father stayed with me almost every second of the day, after that. He stroked my hair, kissed me, pledged the world to me. It didn't affect me. It didn't register. I didn't care about the reappearance of his love – not fully.

I'd missed him so much, and here I'd had him given back to me, only to be ignored – a toy a child had begged for, only to abandon in the corner of her closet.

'We need to get some news,' Samedi decided on the fifth day. 'We need to know what's going on, or we're all going to go mad.'

'Let's just pirate a signal,' Beryl said. 'Let's just do it. If they trace the signal all the way out here, they care entirely too much about us. If they *find* us, maybe they deserve to kill us.'

And so we finally learned that all was not lost.

Aloysius Ayles had been impeached from the position of Prime Minister. It seemed that after it'd become apparent that our soldiers were exterminating all the undead they could find, he'd been caught attempting to smuggle his decrepit father out of the city. They had escaped, and both men were still missing. The deputy Prime Minister was dead.

According to law, the man who had to take over was the Lord Speaker of the Houses of Parliament. The Lord Speaker was an elegant, silver-haired man named Esteban Alba. When we saw him appear on the news in order to address the public, it was with his dead wife seated next to him. She was a beautiful woman with high cheekbones and no visible wounds. The wrinkles on her face were deep and dry, though.

'While we are still working out the details,' I watched him say, 'and while it's clear there was a massive coverup involved, some facts have emerged that are very encouraging. One of them is seated right here. Some of the dead are still . . . alive.'

He wasn't an eloquent speaker. It was clear he hadn't memorized anything to say. He waved his hands as he tried to come up with words that would adequately convey his meaning. 'They're still . . . themselves. They have new challenges ahead of them, certainly, but . . . all people do. Why should we punish the infected if they have shown no signs of violence? And so, I am asking Parliament to decree that all zombies who can be shown to be sane and capable people be permitted to continue to exist. I know for a fact that many are in hiding. Until this moment, my wife was in hiding, and my son still is.' He stroked his wife's yellowed hand. 'And I would kill an entire living army for one more moment with her. I admit this plainly. If this means that the people wish to impeach me, as well, so be it.'

I wasn't alone.

Samedi was seated beside me. He patted my shoulder.

'We can get in touch with him,' Dad said. 'Even if he's impeached, he's an ally.'

'Yes,' said Chas's mother. She was a petite, plump, nutmeg-colored lady named Silvia. Death had lent her dark eyes a forbidding hunger, but she seemed good-natured enough. She used a wheelchair, rarely spoke, and seemed mostly content to keep company with her own thoughts.

Later that day, I watched the bodies of the zombies that had already been killed in New London burning in massive pyres that seemed to blot out the sun with their smoke. There would be no funerals for them. No wakes.

'I want to go to Z Base,' I said, without taking my eyes from the screen. 'Just for a moment. I want to see it again.'

'I'll take her,' Beryl volunteered.

This time, no one argued.

We went the next day. We took a small motorized cart that the techs had used to haul equipment to the transport yard, before. Both of us were armed.

The base was quiet. It didn't appear as if it'd been sacked or searched, and it certainly hadn't been bombed. We left the cart by the gate and strolled slowly, almost reverently, through the med halls, the cafeteria, and the armory.

But Beryl and I both knew where I wanted to go.

'I'm going to get some things from my room,' Beryl said, finally breaking the silence. 'I'll meet you at the cart in a few minutes, all right?'

I nodded, and proceeded to float through the hallways towards Bram's room.

At first I didn't want to touch anything, as if his room were a crime scene, or a tomb filled with offerings. After a few minutes, I had to, or I was going to go insane. I curled up in his closet, as I had in my dollhouse, inhaling the scent of him. I trailed my palms over his books, the cool leather so much like his skin. I packed up his diary and his watch, to take with me.

He'd changed in a hurry for his last mission, and his dress uniform was on the bed. I found one of his cufflinks on the floor. The insignia – the Z with the two interlinked rings on top – was, turned sideways, something like *NB*. I stared at it for a good two minutes before deciding to pick it up.

Later that evening, back at the airship, I cut a hole in a ribbon Beryl had given me and attached the cufflink, before tying it around my neck.

Symbols are powerful.

When he saw this, my father finally decided to ask after the extent of my loss. 'I feel,' he said, glancing across the rain-speckled deck of the ship, 'like I have lost a son.' His hand was trembling slightly, as it'd always done whenever he had to admit great emotion. 'I take it that you'd grown fond of him, as well? He was such a noble young man.'

'Something like that,' I confessed brokenly.

Papa was at my side in an instant, drawing my head to his shoulder. He didn't judge me. He didn't question it. He let me cry.

He'd had to confirm it, but the others didn't. They gave me space. Even Samedi managed to hold his tongue. He busied himself with his latest assignments – designing Tom a leg brace and my father a whole new leg. Occasionally I would go and sit outside the ship with him as he worked, neither of us saying a word. I tried to hypnotize myself by watching the machinery slip back and forth, the sparks that erupted from his spot welder. Anything to make a few minutes go by.

Renfield and Tom mourned, as well – though their lack of real action told me that they both thought the worst. Still, they talked a good game. 'If there's any chance at all,' Tom pledged, 'I will go out there and find them myself. Bram's a friend.' His voice grew loud. 'Chas is my girl. I don't care if I have to pull myself across the ground to get to them, if I need to.'

'Not without me,' Renfield said. He reached out and laid his thin hand atop mine. 'Don't give up.'

I remembered the disk my father had recorded for me, and nodded. 'They're not gone.' These two three-letter phrases became our password, our mantra. Even if none of us probably believed it. We'd seen the fires. We'd seen the explosions.

Don't give up. They're not gone.

A few days later, I finally guessed the password to Bram's digital diary. 'Adelaide-Emily.'

I stayed up reading by its own light, tears flowing cease-lessly down my cheeks. He'd begun keeping it when he'd joined the army, and I learned how he'd had to mature and adapt – for he'd quickly had to learn how to fight, how to strategize, how to be a soldier instead of a boy trying to support his family. I learned how much he missed his mother, how much attention he paid to how brightly the sun shone and how healthy the trees around him were and how fragrant the soil. How much he'd grown to care for and respect my father. How sometimes he still thought of giving up and going beyond the gate and putting a bullet in his head, but knew he couldn't do it – that he had to hang on.

On the last page, he'd written simply, 'She's so beautiful.'

I shut the diary and kissed it. I took to carrying it about, like a blanket. I slept with it beneath my cheek every night, pretending that it was the inside of his arm.

After three weeks in exile, we learned that we could go home.

Any talk of impeaching Alba was shouted down by friends and family of the functioning dead, and the army was charged with safely escorting the undead to the *Christine* and the *Erika* for quarantine and treatment. A few went mad there, and were put down. One was euthanized as a television personality stood in front of a cloth screen, reporting on conditions in the ship; she jumped when she heard the popping of gunfire, and nearly fainted. I watched the same scene blandly, unfeelingly.

When we were sure it was safe, I called Pamela. I sobbed like a child when I heard her voice. She was OK. I only cried harder when I heard Coalhouse and Isambard shouting my name from somewhere else in the room she was in.

As Pam told it, Charles Evola had been one of the meds on the *Christine* that night, and had ended up taking care of Issy. When the order to kill the zombies had gone out, he'd hidden Pam, her brother, and Coalhouse in the newly empty coal bunker, and smuggled them off the ship after nightfall. They'd been hiding out in the bakery cellar for the last few weeks. Pam's family had come through all right, and they were back home. There was no more talk of sending her to stay with relatives.

'I think they still don't know what to make of me, yet,' she said. 'But then again, they're fixated on Isambard. Mom keeps trying to cook for him. Oh! Those people I mentioned, the Delgados? They're fine. Mr Delgado came over to tell us that they were going to the ships, and asked us to keep an eye on their house. Isambard keeps talking about babysitting for Jenny, when they come back. He never would have thought about doing something like that, before.'

I had to laugh a tad. 'He's got some perspective?'

'Yes! That's it exactly. As he puts it, he was re-born in a coal chute, so he can't look down on anyone now.'

I slid my hand along the edge of Bram's digidiary, watching it. 'I think the people who reanimate and then really make good on it? I mean, don't just survive, but do well at it?' I felt my eyes burning again. 'I think they are the strongest people on the face of the planet. I think they're far stronger than us. Far better than us, really.'

Pamela was quiet for a minute, before saying softly, 'I agree.'

'I'm trying to be as strong as that. I am. I'm going to ask Dad to send me up there soon. We'll probably all be up there soon.' I sighed, and said, 'I should go.'

'Are you sure? I just don't want you to think you're alone, Nora. I'm always here. I'll always love you, and I'll always be here. No matter what.'

I smiled mistily. 'I know, Pam.'

I heard the hold door slamming above me. Samedi's head appeared. 'Nora? Nora, come with me!'

I looked up at him. 'What is it?'

'Is that that doctor guy again?' Pam asked on the other end of the line.

Samedi jumped down into the hold, and took the com unit from my hand. 'Nora needs to be somewhere right now. She'll call you back in a bit.' He hung it up, and I stood up angrily. I was just about to open my mouth and give him what-for, when he grabbed my hand and started pulling me along.

'What's the meaning of this?' I asked.

'You need to see something.' His voice was all urgency, its usual undertone of anticipatory sarcasm gone.

He yanked me onto the deck of the ship, and I blinked in the midday sun. 'Right, like I can see anything . . .'

'Nora, shut up and look.' He took me by the shoulders and turned me around. I squinted.

There was a line of people walking through the forest towards us. From the slowness and difficulty with which they moved, I could tell they were zombies.

'Zombie survivors?' I asked excitedly. 'From around here?'

Samedi didn't say anything, but held onto my shoulders. I held up a hand to block out the sunlight. There were about twenty zombies, faces I'd never seen before, save for . . .

Samedi's fingers dug into me, to keep me steady.

At the front of the line was Bram. Behind him was

Chas. She had a half-starved Doberman with her, on a chain.

I broke away from Samedi and sprinted down the gang-plank, screaming out Bram's name. Bram's head turned, and he started limping towards me.

I tilted so far forward that I thought I was going to fall onto the hard-packed earth; my fingertips brushed it at one point. I fought my way past nests of tangled young tree trunks, hoping that I wouldn't hit my head before I could get to him.

'Nora!' I heard someone yell.

Bram met me halfway. He scooped me up with one arm and pulled my head towards his. I didn't fight it in the least. He kissed me harshly, and I returned it, leaping up on my toes, seeking out his chapped, broken lips with my own inexpertly, needfully. And then he just held me as I cried, soaking his dirty T-shirt with my tears, his cheek on my head.

'I thought you were gone,' I managed to get out. 'I thought you were really gone . . .'

'I thought I was too,' he said, laughing weakly. 'But I'd never leave you, if I had the choice. I was going to get back to you, or grind to dust trying.'

There was shouting all around us. Someone'd found Tom, and he was barreling across the jungle floor, his newly-installed leg brace squeaking. Chas tackled him when he got close enough, clinging to him. The dog, meanwhile, had spotted my father and gone for him with a joyous bark.

'Old boy?' my father asked as he tried to pet the leaping animal. 'My word! What have you been up to, eh?'

'What?' Samedi asked. 'You know this dog?'

'This fellow was assigned to guard me,' my dad laughed, scratching it between the ears. 'It got away the night of the ex-plosion. Oh, I'm very glad you're all right, chap! I . . .' I heard my father trail off, my face hidden in Bram's chest.

'Ah . . . I should have told you about that,' Samedi said, sounding a trifle embarrassed, as Bram urged me back again and bent down to give me another peck on the lips, a calmer one. I melted into it.

'You do realize that this is wrong?' Bram joked, as I opened my eyes and found him looking at me as if he wanted to re-memorize my face.

'So, so wrong,' I agreed, as I reached up to finger another new cut he'd acquired on his hairline. The skin along his right cheek was lightly singed. He was still the most beautiful thing I'd ever seen.

'No, it's all right, Samedi,' I heard Dad chuckling. 'It's all right.'

Although the general consensus was that we should celebrate, now, it had to wait. Chas's throat had been crushed by a falling beam in the explosion, and she'd lost her voice. Bram'd gotten the worst of the actual fire, and some of his skin was blackened and ready to come off. The meds determined that they could patch them both up easily enough, but they'd have to make another trip to Z Base. We started off that afternoon.

I stayed with Bram through as much of it as they'd let me. They replaced the skin they had to remove with a synthetic compound doctors had developed for living burn victims a few years ago, using a strong adhesive to get it to stay in place. They kicked me out when they opened him up to repair some internal injuries, though. He waved at me as I was escorted to the door. There was no need to put him under.

Samedi was going to have to whip up an artificial voice box for Chas. Until then, she communicated via a screen and a quill stylus. She told us about the explosion, and how they had both come to, only to find that they were alone. They'd spent half a day digging through the rubble, to find Averne and make sure he was really dead. Then they'd hotwired one of Averne's tanks and headed eastward, in the direction they'd seen some of his men fleeing.

'Bram sad he wasnt gona make teh same mistaek twice,' Chas wrote slowly. Apparently, part of spoiling her had included not demanding much of her academically, smart as she obviously was. 'That he was gona get evry last one of em. So we spnt a few days hunting em in the jungl, once we got out of the desert and fond water an patched ourslves up. We fond sume other zombys whod made it. Then we walkd til we fond anothr base, and told em that we are good guys so they woldn't cap us. That was hard.'

'What about the dog?' my father asked her. We'd taken to calling him Fido – original, right? – and he was currently wolfing down a huge helping of tofu. There was no meat on base to give him, but he didn't seem to be too picky.

'We fond him with his chain caght in sume tree rootes,' she wrote, looking at me to make sure I was following along before lowering her eyes to the screen again. 'We thout he was dead at first, but Bram let im go and with sume water, he was fine.'

I leaned forward, hands on the desk, and kissed her temple. She gurgled, which I took as laughter. 'I'm so glad you're here, Chas. As soon as you have your voice back, we'll have a massive party. Desert rag, the works.'

'They've got you listening to that awful stuff?' Dad sniffed.

'Nooooo,' she wrote out, with a pout. 'Party *now*! Dont nead to talk to party!'

'First,' Dad said, giving me a stern look. 'Captain Griswold and you and I must have a little chat.'

I batted my lashes at him, even as my cheeks heated. Chas choked, and scrawled out, 'You stil ow me detales! *Detales!!!*'

We waited until Bram was done with his various surgeries and tune-ups. He dressed in a black shirt with rolled-up sleeves and herringbone trousers, borrowed from Sam. We sat on the deck of the *Black Alice*, waiting for my father's arrival. That morning Samedi'd greeted him with the news that his leg was ready to be hooked up, and he'd been in surgery in the hold all day.

I liked the casual look on Bram, and told him so. His upper lip flattened as if a weight had been pressed to it, and he confessed, 'I really don't feel like playing soldier anymore.'

'You're preaching to the choir, here.'

He smiled, and reached over to twist one of my curls. I turned my head slightly, but his lips were on my cheek before I could look at him. He slid his thumb over my chin and pressed his forehead to mine. I adored it. I wanted him this close to me, always.

'I kept having moments out there,' he whispered to me, 'where I'd look at you and realize, "Wait, she's not afraid. She wants this as much as I do. Maybe this could work." And then something else would happen to knock the truth back into my head – that there were just too many horrible things that could happen, to either one of us.'

I kissed his stitched-up lower lip and replied, 'Me too. But I still think that can happen to anyone. And when I thought you were gone . . . I don't even want to remember what that felt like.'

'There will still be obstacles,' he said.

'I don't want to talk about them right now.'

'We have to. We have to talk about them every day. No matter what we might feel, this isn't normal.'

I sighed. 'Fine. Like the fact that I'm a walking meal?'

He laughed. 'Or the fact that I'm a walking corpse?'

'No, no points for that one, it's too unoriginal. Oh, I know, I know. Social stigma!'

'The fact that we can never, ever imagine . . . forever?'

I lightly touched his cheek. 'I don't want forever. I want *now*.'

He smiled. 'You take after your father.'

'Pardon me,' my father said. We rocketed apart, and I put my hands in my lap and assumed my very best 'unassailable, innocent princess' pose. Bram stood up and bowed, but my father just waved him down again. 'Oh, stop it, Bram.'

'Hey, the leg looks good,' Bram said.

I stood up to get a look, and Dad pulled up his trouser leg a little, showing it off. The machinery that controlled the cybernetic leg was half-hidden behind a brass casing. Very pretty. Samedi was a wizard.

'What do you think?' he asked of me.

I mulled over my response, before going with the truth. 'You're a zombie cyborg, Dad.' I started to giggle and had to sit down, because I couldn't get myself to stop.

He shrugged. 'I've been called worse things in my life.' He took a seat on the ship railing. Bram reached over to thump me between the shoulders. 'Now. Bram, you are a good friend and an upstanding young man, but I'm afraid that tradition dictates that I now attempt to scare you within an inch of your unlife.'

'Understood,' Bram said, taking his arm back as I got myself under control.

My father is a gentle-looking man. Thus, why I started laughing again as he attempted to look stern. 'What are your intentions concerning my daughter?'

Bram cast a look my way, laughing himself, before clearing his throat and doing his best to look scared. 'Why, to care for and protect her until I rot away, sir.'

I coughed, and spoke up. 'I mean, we've only really just met each other. Granted, we've killed and battled and laughed and survived together, which makes it all seem rather accelerated, but . . .' I let the sentence fade. I didn't know what else to say.

Dad nodded. 'I'm glad you can see that.' He looked off into the trees. 'You're both intelligent young people, so I'm sure you've already imagined all the colorful ways such a courtship could go wrong.'

We both nodded. Had we.

'And you're willing to accept that nothing will ever change that?'

'Yes,' I said.

'Absolutely,' Bram agreed.

My father eyed Bram and chuckled, tipping his head back. 'I'm not about to say a thing, either way. If there's one thing I know about my daughter, it's that she likes to work things out for herself.' He smiled softly at me. 'I trust you.'

I loved the sound of those words. 'Thank you.'

Dad sat forward again. 'So, where do we go from here?'

Bram looked at me. 'I'd like to arrange for my discharge, if possible. I've had my fill. I mean, the fact that they set out to destroy us . . . and the innocent man that we killed at Averne's base . . .' I reached out and found his hand. Dad had told me what had happened.

My father frowned. 'I'd only known him a few days, but Henry Macumba was a good man. I don't think I can ever forgive myself for that. There's so much for which I can never forgive myself. Perhaps they should have killed all the zombies years ago. Perhaps they were right. I can look at you, and my daughter, and see they were wrong, but . . . perhaps they were right.' He sighed, and returned his attention to Bram. 'What do you intend to do, then?'

'Well, I'd like to continue to study under you,' he admitted. 'But I realize that might be impossible if I leave the army. I can't go home. Maybe there's something for me in New London. From what Samedi's told me, they're allowing the healthy dead to return to their families, there.' He laughed. 'I never would have thought, a few weeks ago, that the living and the dead'd be co-existing.'

'I just want to stay with Bram,' I said, realizing . . . that's mainly what I *did* want. One of the top ten things, at least.

Dad looked at me pointedly and said, 'You're still in school, young lady, and you will finish up there. You haven't got a choice.' He fixed his eyes on the canopy of leaves above. 'But I might have an idea of my own.'

'What?' I asked.

His mouth curled into a smile. 'Oh, let me keep it a surprise.'

I glared at him. 'No. No more surprises. No more secrets. Or so help me, I will rip off your own leg and beat you with it.'

Bram's chest started shaking with laughter. 'I think we're back to normal.'

'As normal as we're ever going to get,' I said, crossing my arms over my chest and staring at my father. He started laughing, as well.

Hmph.

EPILOGUE

Nora

Old habits die hard.

Back in our sylvan hiding place, where the ancient trees had dwarfed us all, I'd dared to imagine that we were on the cusp of something great. I had my father again; I had Bram back. We were a newly-fashioned crew of soldiers and inventors and cheeky teenagers, armed with an airship and plenty of guns. We could, in theory, pack it all in if we wanted to, and strike out for parts unknown. Colonize some little forgotten island, somewhere, and continue our adventures. Live generously; die gloriously.

I knew we wouldn't. Still, I dreamed about it.

In reality, we cautiously returned to New London in late February, shortly after the government decided that the vaccine was safe enough to be deployed. Papa, Salvez, and Elpinoy were all nerves. While the government's best scientists had subjected countless generations of computer-model mammals to the vaccine – the days of actual animal testing were long gone – there was still enough room for doubt. The world itself would be the drug's proving ground. To those in the know, that idea was downright scary.

Still, given what was going on in New London, there was no choice.

The city was disorganized. New London had been facing an unceasing tide of undead immigrants since the end of the quarantine, as zombies sought medical help and strength in numbers. The military was a constant presence, as well. Debate still raged over the existence of the walking dead. The infected and their allies argued that they posed no threat so long as they still had their wits about them; their opponents argued that they ought to be killed, imprisoned, or moved somewhere else.

Just like the Punks.

It was dangerous for a dead man to walk alone at night. It was nothing like what the undead were facing in the Punk territories, though. We heard stories about the fires still burning down south, the lynch mobs, the public executions.

Everyone hoped that once the living were rendered immune to the Laz, or at least thought they were immune, they'd calm down.

But I began to doubt my own judgment.

It was miraculous that our house even survived. The houses to either side of ours were totaled; workers had yet to haul the burned-out carriages off our street. And yet, in the midst of the devastation, my home was nearly untouched. When we'd arrived there I'd raced through the halls, laughing, amazed to find everything almost exactly as I'd left it – including Alencar and Matilda. They'd locked themselves in the basement, subsisting off of canned vegetables and Papa's wine collection for the duration of the lockdown and the Siege. Matilda vowed that she would never drink, or date, again.

From them, we learned that Aunt Gene was missing.

While my father concentrated on making inquiries into her whereabouts, I took over the management of the house. We fitted everyone in. Medical and scientific equipment filled the celestial parlor; men bunked on cots in my father's study. Chas and her mother got Aunt Gene's room, and its luxury, I think, reminded them of their roots; they couldn't have been happier.

In an effort to tread carefully until the vaccine had been proven beyond a doubt to work, we implemented Protocol D and kept the belongings of the living and the dead separate.

Beryl, it turned out, enjoyed calligraphy, and spent her free time creating fancy signs that spelled out the house rules. *Dead folks use plastic! When in doubt, throw it out! Please use the bathroom appointed for your gender and mortality!*

I loved those signs, silly as they were. They told me that I had a family again. A huge, weird, twisted, incredible family.

I no longer wanted to be on my own.

The twenty-ninth of March was a dreary, rainy day, but that didn't discourage the crowd gathering to witness the execution of Captain James Wolfe.

Of our entire social circle, the Roes were the only ones who'd declined to come. I'd spoken to Pamela on the phone that morning, and when Dr Evola joined us on the green slopes of Dahlia Park, he confirmed that they were all at home. He'd been rooming with the Roes since the Siege, helping the zombies in their neighbourhood and enduring long shifts on the hospital ships.

'Said they would wait for the news on television, but they'd rather not see it,' Charles said, as he took his place beneath Sam's umbrella. 'When I left they were recapping the trial.'

'I don't really blame them,' I said. I wrapped my arms around myself. I was wearing a new dress of dark red and green plaid satin, and it wasn't all that warm, even beneath my black coat and Bram's umbrella. Bram, seeing this, took off his scarf and looped it around my neck. He smiled at me encouragingly, and leaned forward to brush my forehead briefly with his chin. I loved his touch, and hated the fact that it didn't make me feel any better.

Several yards off sat a collapsible gallows of ribbed steel. Normally, it'd be set up for a hanging – the accepted form of execution in the Territories – but, given that zombies didn't need to breathe, they'd erected three walls of bulletproof glass around it to outfit it for a firing squad. Police barricades had been set up on all sides of us, and protestors of different stripes were marching behind them. There had been protests every day since our return to the city. Generally it was the living protesting against the dead or against the government for covering everything up for so long, although occasionally a group of zombies would get together and march for equal treatment when it came to housing or medical care, or against some act of anti-zombie violence. Chas'd gone to one of them, and come home disappointed that she hadn't been able to chant along with the catchy protest slogans. Sam was still working on her new voice box.

I didn't want to be there.

And yet, I had to see it. I had to see this through to the end, had to see him fall. I didn't *want* to see another person die – far from it. Life was not a holo documentary.

But the man who would meet his end today had harmed my father, threatened to kill Bram and me, and put an entire city in danger. He had started all of this.

So far, the vaccine appeared to be working, which gave the living some confidence. There'd been no further zombie attacks. The Punks, despite the madness of their methods, had killed off many of the dangerous wild packs. And the army had given up Wolfe, tried and condemned him, as a gesture of atonement for everything they had hidden.

And so, I told myself that *this* was the end. When this man was dead, my life could resume *something* like a normal flow.

I looked back. My father was leaning upon his cane, watching the scene dispassionately – though his eyes were active. I wondered what he was thinking. Bram, I knew, felt much as I did. He was still touching me, his hand on my shoulder, and I sent my fingers up in search of his. I wanted to be there for him. He'd known the man far longer than I had, and had endured far more of his evil.

'Are you OK?' I asked him.

'Yeah.'

People were giving us disgusted looks. I couldn't immediately label them mortalists – in truth, even if Bram were alive, he shouldn't be touching me in public. Still, I felt myself shrink against him, ever so slightly. 'Do you think it's sick that after all that's happened, I'm *choosing* to watch yet another man die?' I asked softly.

'No. Given what he did to you and your father? I'd be more worried if you didn't want to watch it.' Bram stroked my hair. 'Besides, if you're sick, I'm on life support. As wrong as that joke is.'

When the appointed hour rang out from the Cathedral of Our Mother, the crowd hushed. The protests went on, a few voices rising – zombies calling for Wolfe to be let go, for mercy to be shown to the dead. An announcer in front yelled something that I couldn't hear, through the mutterings of those around us and the endless *tip-tap* of fat raindrops on the umbrella above me.

Four soldiers, wearing black masks, marched Wolfe through the crowd. He was stripped of his army regalia, clad in a plain pair of trousers and a white shirt. His beard and hair were unkempt, and it looked like a wildfire was raging around his face. He was dead, now. He'd not had recourse to regular post-mortem medical treatment, and his flesh was rotting upon his bones. When he passed by the very front of the crowd, several bonneted women cried out at the sight of him. I couldn't see him well, from where I was standing, but it must have been bad.

He was led to the scaffold, and forced to back up against the glass. His hands and feet were already chained, and those chains were locked to the floor of the gallows. The four soldiers then took their places in front of him, each equipped with a rifle.

I heard another statement from the announcer, and knew that he was asking Wolfe if he had any last words.

'No,' Wolfe said, his voice thundering over the crowd.

Bram's fingers gripped into my shoulder at the sound of it. I held my breath, so that I couldn't say anything. Everything that man had done, and he couldn't even be bothered to make a last statement? Apologize? Indulge in another big villainous speech?

'Just get it over with,' I heard Samedi say. Beryl shushed him.

The executioners raised their guns and took aim. The protestors grew louder. 'Mercy!' one dead woman shouted. 'Mercy! He's suffered enough!'

The soldiers fired. Wolfe's body crumpled to the ground.

It was over.

The bonneted women began to wail, huddling together before the scaffold. Their cries mingled with the shouts of the zombie protestors. Through the sudden accumulation of sound I could make out someone screaming, 'Daddy! Daddy!'

I realized, with a start, that the women in front were Wolfe's wife and daughters, the ones he'd spoken of in his office.

Pity for them welled up from within me, nearly choking me. That single, tearful word told me that they were in the very position that I now counted as my greatest fear, the nightmare that, if ever realized in the flesh, would utterly undo me – *had* almost undone me once before.

They were living women forced to watch the dead man they still loved die.

I felt sick. 'It's done,' I whispered to Bram. 'I want to leave. Now.'

Before he could say anything, gunshots rang out from the direction of the protesting crowd.

Bram pulled me to his body, sheltering me; screams went up around us. 'We have to get out of here!' Charles yelled. 'The protestors are fighting!'

Behind the police lines the living and the dead were facing

off, both sides brandishing signs, one side brandishing teeth. Reporters were attempting to escape, contributing to the bottlenecks swiftly forming at the gates of the park. I'd never known any of the protests to turn into a riot, but here it was, happening before my eyes.

'Have we got everyone?' Bram shouted over my head. 'Come on, head for the western gate!'

I let myself be led along, so I didn't get to see much of the fight. I saw a living man beating a zombie with his sign, which read, 'No Special Rights for the Rotten!' I saw a New Victorian soldier firing into the air, attempting to get everyone to disperse. I prayed that that was the original source of the gunfire.

We were parked on a nearby street, which was choked with bodies as protestors and bystanders ran away from the clash. By the time we got there, I'd recovered, and, alongside Bram, I helped everyone into the carriages. I saw Dad hobbling towards one of them, Salvez and Evola with him. I knew that they'd be heading for the hospital ships, in case they were needed.

'Chas, squeeze into the front seat with me,' I said, grabbing her arm. She nodded, her face creased with worry.

'What *was* that?' Coalhouse demanded from the back seat.

'Anger,' Bram said, as he got behind the steering wheel. He flashed me a frightened glance, before starting up the carriage. 'Misguided anger.'

'Wolfe was up for the death penalty not because of what he is,' I argued. My voice was shaking. 'It was what he did. But they don't see that, and . . . oh, God. His family was there. I didn't even think that his family would be there.'

'It's all right.' Bram sounded as if he was attempting to convince himself. 'It's all right. We were overdue for something like this, really. Let's just get home.'

I knew what he was thinking. I knew what he was scared of. It was the same thing I was scared of.

A backlash against the dead.

Maybe Wolfe had gotten his way, after all.

I didn't sleep that night.

I cuddled against my pillow, my fingers stroking the cool cotton, as Beryl snored beside me. I couldn't get the day's events out of my mind, or be rid of the gnawing anxiety, so potent that it seemed I was wishing the very thing I dreaded into existence, that the riot would lead to further anti-zombie sentiment. The idea of the living deciding to take out the dead once and for all made my entire body cramp with fear.

I understood, now, what Bram had been trying to tell me on the deck of the ship. We would never be normal. We would always live with this. It would never change.

It wasn't over yet.

We'd watched the riot on the news. It had been short-lived. The protestors had been separated, the guilty parties arrested in record time. Only a few people had been bitten. The zombies hadn't attacked, at least not en masse. Still, I knew some would view it as if they had.

I wondered how it would come. A knock on the door at midnight? A letter, telling Bram to show up somewhere and submit to a bullet? I shivered.

My door opened, slowly. Matilda was outside, holding a candle. 'Nora?' she asked quietly.

I sat up. 'Matilda?' Beryl stirred. 'What is it?'

'Your father wants you – he wants everyone living. Downstairs, in the kitchen.' She sounded scared.

At this announcement, Beryl got up and put on her dressing gown. When she saw that I was still sitting in bed, motionless, I think she understood how frightened I was. I was sure this was it.

'It's all right, Miss Dearly. Here, put on your robe . . . there's a good girl. Come on, let's go see what your father wants.' Her voice was artificially cheerful.

I obeyed her, and we journeyed to the kitchen in silence. There we found my father, Salvez, and Evola waiting. My father looked mournfully at me, before turning to whisper something to Elpinoy as he staggered into the kitchen, sleep-drunk. Whatever he said made the man suddenly alert.

'What is it?' I asked.

'Nora . . .'

'*What is it?*' Without pausing another beat, I started pleading. 'Please, *please* don't tell me that they're attacking zombies, that they're punishing them for the riot. Because if they are, I have to take Bram somewhere and hide. Tonight! I can't live without him, I can't . . .'

'No. No, it's not the zombies.' My father came to me and wrapped me in his arms. He was trembling. 'It's not the zombies. It's the living.'

'What do you mean?'

My father tightened his hold on me. 'I'm so sorry, Nora. I'm so sorry.'

I stiffened. '*What do you mean, you're sorry?* What are you sorry *for?*'

Evola took over. He looked exhausted. 'Three people were bitten during the riot.' He leaned against the sink and removed his monocle, shakily. 'Two of the bitten reanimated.'

I felt my entire body go cold. 'Were they vaccinated?'

My father started crying. He was incapable of making tears, and still, he cried.

'We don't know if it's the vaccine, yet, Victor. Calm down.' Salvez came near and tried to gently pull my father off of me. 'Come, sit down.'

'The prion might be mutating,' Elpinoy whispered. 'Prions themselves can evolve, even though they're not alive. It works so fast . . . perhaps it's fast in this regard too.'

'It's all conjecture, at this point.'

'It wants to live.' Elpinoy tugged at his tight pajama top and laughed, slightly manically. 'It's not even alive, and it wants to *live*. It wants to *survive*.'

I bucked my father's arms off and stared at him in horror. He fell against Salvez, and let the man guide him to a chair. 'But then . . . we're not safe. The living. And if no one feels safe, they'll take it out on the dead!'

'I'm sorry,' my father said again. He sounded like a two-year-old gazing across a broken toyland – like he had built his own empire, and destroyed it, and could not now fathom why he'd done so. 'I'm sorry for giving everyone false hope. I'm sorry for letting all of this go on so long. It should have been me they shot today, it should have been *me*.'

'Don't say that!' I'd never heard Salvez sound angry, before. 'We'll get to work in the morning. We'll figure out what's behind the apparent failures. We don't know anything, yet, so everyone just calm down.'

I bolted from the kitchen. I flew up the stairs to the guest room, where Bram was staying with the other boys. I knew the way, even in the dark. My father's voice followed me, rising in volume, a dark siren.

I found Bram on his cot, slumbering peacefully. He didn't breathe, he didn't move. His body was laid out for my viewing, as legitimately dead as any body I'd ever seen on display at a funeral. And every funeral, no matter how hard one might wish otherwise, eventually came to an end. There was no way I could stop him from slipping through my fingers, now. Absolutely no way.

But Bram wasn't dead. He was alive in ways, before I'd met him, I'd have been incapable of describing. My heart, my very body cried out for him.

I couldn't let him go. Not yet.

Like him – with him – I had to keep going.

ACKNOWLEDGEMENTS

This book is pretty much *the* accomplishment of my life. I never expected that a story that started as a joke would get me this far.

First of all, I would like to thank my mother, who has always believed in me – even when I've refused to believe in myself. I'd also like to thank my father for always helping me out, and raising me to be a proper carnivore.

Thank you to my best friend Josh, for all of his support. Shout-outs to Desmond and Iason, for always being there for me. You know I mean every word I sing.

Enormous thanks go out to my fantastic agent, Christopher Lotts, who has the patience of a saint. I am willing to forgive him for the bad things he's said about my Mountain Dew habit, as he's proven himself invaluable and dedicated in every other way. I sincerely cannot thank him enough for all of his help.

Likewise, thank you to my American editor, Christopher Schluep, whose belief in me has been completely humbling and overwhelming. I still occasionally have to remind myself, 'He's not lying to you. He really thinks you're good.' Same to my British editor, Lauren Buckland.

A big thank you to all of the professors who inspired me and helped me to hone my craft through the years – David Schmid, James Holstun, and Howard Wolf foremost amongst them. And a shout-out to the managers of my local movie theater is due – Steve and Jim, you rock. Seriously. Thanks for all the free 'research' passes.

And finally, thanks are due to everyone who ever made me love zombies or seriously think about the lessons that the dead and the weird have to teach us – Halperin, Romero, Raimi, Fulci, Lynch, Hill, even Russo and O'Bannon. When it seemed like everyone else in the world was addicted to the concept of beauty frozen in time, these people taught me about the greater beauty to be found in tragic decay. (<3 you, Bub.)